DANGER!
PASSION!

Rommany!

EUSTACIA

The first mistress of Rommany, her love for Duncan Blackmore was not to be denied. Yet in their surging desire, an agony began—a sinister evil that would spread its stain across three generations!

AMELIA

The only child of Eustacia and Duncan, she could not escape the tangled legacy of horror that they had begun in the dark halls of Rommany . . . and in its shadows, where witches met.

CONSTANCE

Granddaughter of Eustacia, she blindly loved Leonard—a man cruelly linked to the past. It was for her alone to pierce the veil that enshrouded her hopeless passion—for only then would Rommany's curse be broken!

FLORENCE HURD
ROMMANY

FLORENCE HURD
ROMMANY

AVON
PUBLISHERS OF BARD, CAMELOT, DISCUS, EQUINOX AND FLARE BOOKS

ROMMANY is an original publication of AVON Books.
It has never before appeared in book form.

AVON BOOKS
A division of
The Hearst Corporation
959 Eighth Avenue
New York, New York 10019

First Avon Printing, June, 1976

AVON TRADEMARK REG. U.S. PAT. OFF. AND
FOREIGN COUNTRIES, REGISTERED TRADEMARK—
MARCA REGISTRADA, HECHO EN CHICAGO, U.S.A.

Printed in the U.S.A.

Part I

EUSTACIA

(1868)

Chapter 1

"Mama," I whispered excitedly, "there is a most attractive man sitting behind us. I . . . I believe he's been staring at me."

Mama, without changing expression, casually turned her head as if to adjust her shawl.

"It is Duncan Blackmore," she said a moment later in a disapproving low monotone. "I don't think he would be of much interest to you."

Duncan Blackmore, not of interest?

Oh—but he was! Even I, so short a time in London, had heard of him; handsome, rich, unmarried, he had recently returned from South Africa, bringing an aura of mystery with him. Spoken of openly or behind fluttering fans, Duncan Blackmore had been the topic of many a speculative conversation at teas, in anterooms, in the mirrored lamplight of boudoirs, in all the random corners where girls such as myself, coming out into society that season, might gather for a few moments to gossip and assess their prospects. Arriving as he had on the fringe of our narrow, protected lives, this tall, dark-eyed man had provided an excitement which the other young bachelors of our acquaintance found hard to compete with.

Duncan Blackmore.

And he was here—at Lady Bolton's musicale. Who would think it!

All through Mozart and Haydn, while the interminable violins scraped and the pianoforte thumped, I could feel his eyes upon me. When the performance was finally over and before Mama and I could follow the crowd into the dining room for refreshments, our hostess came up to us on the arm of Duncan Blackmore.

"This man insists on meeting you, Eustacia, dear," she said.

And so we were introduced.

Strange—if I had been asked to describe Duncan Blackmore later that evening, I would have been at a loss. Dark eyes, I would have said, magnetic eyes, but the exact color of his hair, the shape of his face would have eluded me. What I could have described vividly, however, was the odd feeling in the pit of my stomach when he smiled, the manner in which my pulses jumped as he bent over my hand, the peculiar racing of my heart when he spoke.

Though I knew I was reacting in exactly the same besotted manner as a dozen females before me, it did not matter. He was everything and more that gossip had made him—handsome, charming, electrifying. How could I remain immune? How could I help but fall madly in love with him?

That night, as I lay in my bed in the tiny bedroom of the house my parents had rented for the season, my thoughts were all of Duncan; and the more I pondered, the more convinced I became that he, and no other, would do as my husband.

It was a conviction held against formidable odds. For one, Duncan was twelve years my senior. Second, though sought after by many beautiful, richly dowered girls, he was reputedly a confirmed bachelor. Third, my parents, straitlaced, the very epitome of propriety, found Duncan eminently unsuitable. It was not so much the disparity in our ages that Papa frowned upon as his occupation. Duncan had been—still was—in trade. To my father, an Ulster country squire whose sole contact with earning a comfortable living was to hire a competent bailiff, "trade" smacked of grubby shop owners and brash-voiced innkeepers.

"No gentleman would stoop to soil his hands with commerce," Papa remarked after hearing that Duncan had been present at Lady Bolton's musicale.

And what commerce! Duncan and a partner, John Hempstead, were in import-export, a rather nebulous trade which Papa dismissed as an euphemism to cover a "multitude of nefarious dealings."

Mama, even more of a snob and a stickler than Papa, had reasons of her own to distrust Duncan. After his first formal call, she had his background thoroughly checked and found to her horror that he had sojourned in Africa, Brazil, and India longer than was decent for an educated traveling Englishman. "White men, who live in the tropics, even briefly, are inevitably led to native women and other dissipations." Never mind that Uncle George had served the Queen for twenty years in Rangoon. Uncle George was *family*, and therefore above reproach.

Poor darling Mama. How was she—or Papa, for that matter—to know that every point they made against Duncan only enhanced his charm, his mystery, his desirability in my eyes?

That he contrived to see me again and again—though we were rarely alone for more than a moment or two—was a great source of encouragement. I knew that I had been singled out and that in time he would propose. But how to get around Mama and Papa? The thought of elopement never entered my mind; I had been too strictly brought up to contemplate it even fleetingly.

I am sure Papa had no inkling of how desperately, hopelessly, his one and only child had fallen in love until almost the last; else he would have whisked the three of us back to Ulster without delay. As it was, he continued to trudge dutifully to dinner parties, soirees and teas, eschewing the comforts of home, having been convinced by Mama that his daughter would make a much better marriage in London than in man-shy Ulster. I believe Mama guessed my infatuation, but she chose to ignore it, hoping, I suppose, that I would meet someone superior to Duncan, a younger version of Papa, perhaps.

Those weeks of champagne suppers and parties and balls come back to me dimly now, for after I had met Duncan, nothing but his face, his voice, the accidental touch of his fingers was real. Being of good family, and a bachelor, he was welcomed by society's hostesses, and Mama, though she might want to avoid him, found it impossible. But she did watch us with an eagle eye. Duncan said it was a challenge, and I sometimes wondered as we danced or snatched a few stolen moments of conversation if it was my inaccessibility, the provocative dare which attracted him to me. Perhaps, I thought ruefully on those occasions, he is just passing the time and does not love me at all.

But one Sunday afternoon at a thronged reception given by the Peabodys for some diplomat whose name I have long since forgotten, Duncan and I managed to sneak into the humid, but blessedly quiet and secluded conservatory. He did not waste any words, for at any moment Mama might appear and hurry me away. "I love you," he said, taking both my hands in his and drowning me in his dark, intense eyes. "I've loved you from the moment I caught you staring at me so boldly."

"Duncan . . ." I began in protest, but before I could utter another word, he drew me roughly into his arms and kissed me. I could feel his hand cupping the back of my head, pressing me closer and closer until I thought my very bones should melt like wax under flame.

"Will you marry me?" he asked, when he released me at last.

Stunned, half out of my head, I could only nod yes. He took hold of my wrist and pulled me to him again.

At that very moment, Mama found us.

She did not make a scene, not there; Mama was too proper, too well bred, for public scenes. But later when we had returned to our lodgings, she berated me roundly.

"I love him!" I pleaded, close to tears.

"Love him? What do you know about love? You—why, you are just a child."

"I'm eighteen!" I replied hotly. "And you do not seem to think I am too young to marry off—to someone else."

"Don't you dare speak to me in that manner," she commanded, eyes snapping. "Do you realize how tongues would be clacking if Lady Bolton or Mrs. Peabody had come upon you instead of me? Kissing that man! And he—he could not hold you very highly, behaving as he did. Inexcusable!"

"He wants to marry me," I sobbed.

"Marry you? How presumptuous! I shall say nothing of this to your father. Best to forget it, to pretend it never happened. But in the future, Eustacia, you are not—I repeat, *not*—to speak to him, or I will have to inform your father. It goes without saying he shall order us home."

"No!" I cried. Not to see Duncan again? "No ... I promise to behave. Please don't tell Papa."

However, unknown to both of us, Duncan had already made an appointment with Papa to ask for my hand.

The first I knew of it was when I looked through my bedroom window and saw Duncan, tall and broad-shouldered, alighting from a chaise. As I watched him open the iron gate and disappear under the portico, I experienced a series of descending emotions from wild delight to black despair. I knew why Duncan had come, and I knew what Papa would say. I was right on both counts.

"I told him," Papa said later at the dinner table, "I would not contemplate such a match and advised him to look elsewhere."

"Papa! You didn't!"

"Indeed, I did. Furthermore, I think we have tarried in London long enough."

"No—Papa. You must listen to me. What have you got against Mr. Blackmore? He comes of good family, you said so yourself. The Blackmores have a baronet among them ..."

"I am not one easily swayed by titles."

". . . and he's well off, some say rich, and he's—"

"He's a dark horse, Eustacia. You will get over him."

"I won't! Ever! I won't!" And with that I flung down my napkin and fled to my room.

I suppose one could say here that I was behaving in typical schoolgirl fashion—thwarted over a hearts-and-flowers romance with the first man who had held my hand. But it wasn't so. My anguish was real, and I knew in my innermost being, as I had from the start, that if I could not marry Duncan, I would never marry at all.

Three days later we were back at Newberry, our home. By that time I had cried myself out, and I no longer argued with Papa, no longer pleaded with Mama. A terrible lassitude had settled upon me. Night and day became the same, empty voids to be filled somehow, vacuums echoing with the sound of a hundred clocks tickling away in endless monotony. Waking and dressing bored me; food bored me. Mama's personal maid, Chalmers, took charge

7

of my toilette, fussing and rearranging my hair. Curls, chignons, ribboned coronets—all were the same.

I tried to take up the old routine, riding in the mornings, music in the afternoons, reading before dinner, but the effort was more than I could tolerate, so I gave it up. Unable to bear strong light, I spent most of the time in a darkened room, with a bit of embroidery lying limply on my lap, staring blankly out the window.

I grew thin; my cheeks lost their roundness, clothes hung on my frame. Dull headaches became my constant companion. Alarmed, Mama called the doctor. He prescribed rest, a soft diet, and headache tablets, none of which helped.

My parents were worried, I could see that, but I could not help how I felt. Finally Papa came to me one evening as I sat listlessly at the dressing table, too tired to lift the brush to my hair.

"Do you love him that much?" he asked, taking my hand.

A lump rose in my throat. "Yes, Papa," I whispered.

"I had meant to prevent this marriage for your own good. You do realize that, Eustacia?"

"Yes, Papa."

"You are my darling, my child. I would do anything in the world for your happiness, and if you sincerely believe. . . ."

"Oh, Papa, I do!" I exclaimed, flinging my arms about his neck. "I do, I do! I love him so much!"

Six months later Duncan and I were married at All Saints near Newberry. It was a large wedding, the church filled to capacity with relatives, friends, and neighbors, my father's tenants and their families. I can look back now and see myself as I must have been on that day—long white veil thrown back from a radiant brow, clinging to Duncan's arm and laughing up into his face. To say that I was happy barely describes my almost hysterical joy. Not even Mama's embarrassing "little talk" of the night before in which she had outlined the duties of a wife could dampen my spirits. I knew, too, that she had not meant to be unkind when she had said, "You are to make the best of your marriage, even though things may not turn out as you wish." It was her way of telling me that my marriage vows were to be taken seriously, and though my choice of a husband was not the wisest (in her eyes), I was to accept my lot with fortitude.

It had been a grim little lecture, completely forgotten in the excitement and gaiety of my wedding celebration. Papa, outdoing himself, had hired extra servants to help Cook prepare a feast of baronial proportions. Trestle tables, set up in the forecourt, literally groaned under platters of cold roast beef, hams, pork pies, fowl, and game, while kegs of ale and quantities of Irish whisky stood by to assist in washing the good food down.

Papa had also seen to it that I was well dowered and Duncan, as if trying to match Papa's generosity, showered me with gifts, from the almost trivial—a charming little ivory fan, delicately painted in Japanese fashion—to a perfectly matched rope of pearls.

Everyone smiled upon us, kind, benevolent, wishing us well. And I went from my father's house amidst the cheers and pelting rice, thinking now that I had Duncan, we should live like a fairy prince and princess in tales of old, happily ever after. We didn't, of course; no one really does, as Mama had pointed out. But I don't think even she could have guessed that my marriage would be so soon tested, that before November was out I was to face a horror which would bring me to the very edge of madness.

Chapter 2

We honeymooned in Venice, an experience that still remains like an enchanted dream in my memory. I adored the city, and Duncan was every bit the husband I expected and more—amusing, companionable, kind, a passionate and tender lover. We spent our days wandering about narrow streets, leaning over bridges, eating at little cafés, and at night we would float down the myriad star-mirrored canals under the shadows of leaning houses. For three weeks we were locked in our own world—as only honeymooners can be—so that when we returned to England and the shocking news of John Hempstead's murder, our awakening was doubly rude.

Duncan's partner had been shot through the head while sitting at his desk in the library of his house. Apparently robbery had been the motive, since the house had been ransacked, but curiously, according to John's brother, nothing had been taken.

I had not known John Hempstead well, but I had liked what I had seen of him. A tall, quiet man in his mid-forties, he had been widowed years earlier and had never remarried. John had attended our wedding, of course, and I remember how he had stood a little back from the others while they pressed about us, guests shaking Duncan's hand and kissing me. When the crowd finally thinned, he came forward and touched my cheek shyly with his lips, wishing me well, and then, grasping Duncan's hand, stood for a moment fighting what looked suspiciously like tears. "I am happy for you, Duncan. Happy and envious." And, with a sigh, "I shall miss you, my good friend."

"Here, here," Duncan had interrupted, laughing. "You speak as if this were the end. Nothing can be farther from the truth. When I've returned from our honeymoon, you and I shall get together for an evening at the club, just as we have in the past."

Now John, the good friend of so many years, was dead. And no clues as to who had murdered him.

John had been childless. His estate was divided between a ward, a young girl attending a convent school somewhere in France; and his favorite nephew, Harold Hempstead. Harold, a serious young man, had dropped his studies at Cambridge to take over his late uncle's business affairs. Duncan liked Harold and thought he would do well, but he himself confessed to having lost his taste for the import-export trade and persuaded Harold to buy his share of the company. "I don't need the money," Duncan told me. "And besides, if I retire, it will make your Papa happy."

As a new bride, anxious to succeed in marriage, I was not as concerned with Papa's happiness as I was with Duncan's. He had taken John's death very hard, and I saw where the firm of Blackmore and Hempstead might have served as a diversion. I tried to persuade him to reconsider, but it was useless. He simply did not care.

The firm was not the only aspect of Duncan's life in which he had lost interest. He seemed indifferent to everything—our need for a suitable house, for instance. We were presently staying at his former lodgings, a cramped suite of rooms barely large enough for the two of us to turn around in, and we had decided long before our return to London that we must have other quarters. Now Duncan left the house hunting to me—a novice whose acquaintance with London was limited to my one season, and who knew less about sound flooring and snug chimneys than a Laplander living in a tent.

The hiring of a cook and a maid and how or where to lodge them, the acceptance of dinner invitations, the ordering of wines, a hundred and one other decisions, it seemed, were all left to me. "Suit yourself," Duncan would say whenever I asked for his opinion, his advice. Meanwhile I floundered about, trying to cope.

I confess that I grew secretly impatient with Duncan

and had all sorts of unwifely thoughts—thoughts which would have caused poor Mama to shudder. But my husband's obvious indifference did hurt, and I sometimes felt that John Hempstead's death meant more to him than the well-being of the bride he once professed to love so passionately. Where, I would ask myself as my smile became more painfully fixed, have all the kisses, the sweet endearments gone?

Thus it went for several weeks, Duncan spending more and more time at his club, and I looking at houses, struggling with accounts, wondering how I could bridge the growing gap between us. Then one morning Duncan received a letter which brought a smile to his face.

"Look here," Duncan said, handing me a sheet of crested, cream-laid note paper as we sat at the breakfast table. "We've an invitation."

The handwriting, in black ink, was slapdash, almost illegible, but I managed to decipher it:

Dear Cousin, I have only recently learned of your marriage. Congratulations. My wife and I would like to extend an invitation to you and your charming spouse to spend a fortnight with us at Rommany. Will the eighth of November be convenient? Please, say yes—I think it's time we became friends. Yours, Ian.

I looked up from the letter. Duncan was smiling at me, the old smile with pinpoints of merriment in his dark eyes. "You're wondering, aren't you?" he asked.

"Yes . . . yes, I am. You have never mentioned this Ian Blackmore." I had found Duncan to be rather close-mouthed about his past, and I was beginning to suspect there were a good many things he had not mentioned to me. "At least, I don't recall him at the wedding."

"Ian wasn't there. Quite honestly, I had forgotten to ask him. You see, years ago, before I was born, in fact, his father and mine had a bitter quarrel and since then, with one or two minor exceptions, there has been no communication between the two branches of our family."

"Was it such a terrible quarrel, then?"

"It was," Duncan said, settling back and reaching for

12

his pipe. "My uncle and father fought over a woman." He smiled again, his eyes watching for my reaction.

"A woman!" I said, properly shocked.

He went on, "Edward, Ian's father, and my father were courting the same girl. Her name was Caroline, and she was the most beautiful, the most personable, and the most sought-after young lady in the district. Now, the brothers were almost equally matched as to looks, rather handsome, both were gentlemen of education and refinement, and Caroline, I don't doubt, was having some difficulty in making up her mind between the two. Edward, the elder, did have an edge, since he came with the title and Rommany. However, my father was very much in love with Caroline, and as you have seen, my darling, both he and I are nonplused by obstacles when it comes to love." He reached across and squeezed my hand, and I secretly thanked this unknown cousin for that touch and the tender smile which went with it.

"But," Duncan continued, "Father did a very unscrupulous and, I suppose, unforgivable thing. It was known by quite a few in the neighborhood—though not by Caroline—that Edward had sired a bastard son by a farm tenant's daughter, Alice Woodhill. Father told Caroline, and the rest is simple history. Caroline spurned Edward and later became my mother."

"It *was* somewhat underhanded," I said, after a pause. "But perhaps Caroline—your mother—would have learned of the affair after she had married Edward and then it would have been too late for her to change her mind."

"Perhaps. On the other hand, Edward might have denied it, or persuaded Caroline that it did not matter that much. After all, he would not have been the first to father a bastard. As it was, my mother—from what I'm told—did not give Uncle Edward a chance to speak one word on his own behalf."

"Then I can't really blame the poor man for being angry. But he must have gotten over the affair and married someone else, since there's Ian."

"Yes, he did marry—Margaret Fowles, a meek little thing who died shortly after Ian was born. But Edward never forgot. Toward the end of his life he became quite eccentric. Among other things, he published a tract at his own expense in which he maintained that he had been slandered by my father and that he had every intention of suing him. My father, of course, had died years earlier, so the man was raving."

"Mad, you mean?"

"No—I wouldn't say mad. Off his head a bit, maybe." He grinned. "No, seriously, he was not insane. I won't have you wondering now about the Blackmores and whether our children will have tainted blood."

"I should hope not," I said. And we both laughed. Children! And I had thought we had grown apart.

"What is Rommany like?" I asked.

"I don't know," he answered, tapping the ashes from his pipe. "The place has been in the family for centuries— male-entailed, always going to the eldest son—but since Uncle Edward never got over the quarrel, never invited us, I can't tell you anything about it."

"Have you ever met this cousin?"

"Yes. I met him at Cambridge, quite by accident, when we were both students there. Still, we did not become friends. Different interests, I suppose, that sort of thing. I hadn't heard of or from Ian until about three years ago, when I read in the *Times* that old Uncle Edward had died and Ian had inherited Rommany. I sent him a letter of condolence and congratulation which he did not acknowledge. Then a few months ago—I think it was shortly before we were married, my darling—I ran into him at the club." Duncan paused and smiled reminiscently. "I'm afraid we had an awful lot to drink and got to talking and boasting."

"Boasting about what?"

"Oh—about the money we had made. I, in India hemp, he, in Scottish wool. Where we had been—that sort of thing. Well, at any rate, he has invited us to Rommany. Frankly, I am curious about the place. Would you like to go?"

"I should love it!" I cried happily. Duncan had come out of his depressing, restless mood; he was his old self again. A fortnight in the country seemed like a heaven-sent boon. And we would be together, lovers once more, just as we had been in Italy.

So Duncan wrote his cousin, accepting the invitation,

and the following Friday we set out for Rommany. Fortunately, Ian had mailed us a map, since no one in Colchester, where we left the train, had heard of Rommany. Moreover, we had difficulty hiring a conveyance. None of the drivers seemed willing to make the fourteen-mile journey, until Duncan finally managed to persuade a surly, hawk-nosed fellow with the jingle of extra coin.

By the time our shabby chaise rumbled past the last house in Colhester, dark towers of purple-black clouds had obscured a dying sun, and gray dusk, heavy with the threat of storm, had begun to close in. We were on the road less than ten minutes when the first few drops spattered against the glazed windows and thunder growled in the distance. Darkness came swiftly then. Lightning flickered and thunder grew louder, crackling and booming overhead. A moment later, the sky opened with a torrential downpour.

Our wheels rattled over a bridge and past an isolated hamlet, the twinkling lights dimly visible through the wind-driven sheets of rain. Those hazy lights seemed friendly, and I pictured a warm, cozy inn, which surely must be among them—a small, cozy inn with a leaping fire on the hearth and the homely aroma of roasting fowl and dark, strong ale. I thought of asking Duncan if we might stop for a while before going on, but I knew he was impatient to reach Rommany. He was the sort of man, I was beginning to discover, who, once having set his mind on a goal, grew annoyed at an unnecessary delay.

"Has Sir Ian any children?" I asked.

"Not that I know of. Are you cold, darling?"

"A little."

He fixed the rug more firmly about my legs. A small leak had sprung in the roof of the chaise and I could feel the slow drip-drip of water falling on my hat. I shifted my head and the drops splashed on my gloved hands. I tucked them under the rug.

"If we had timed our arrival earlier," Duncan said, "then we might have missed this rain and perhaps have seen something of the countryside."

"It doesn't matter," I said, smiling up at him in the dark, though I still felt cold and uncomfortable.

"That's my darling," he said, patting my shoulder.

We lapsed into silence. The thunder and lightning had passed on, but the rain continued to drum steadily on the carriage top as the road beneath us wound round and round, climbing to some invisible height, then slowly unwinding as we descended. At one point the driver took the wrong turn, neither he nor Duncan realizing his mistake until we drew up in a muddy farmyard ringed by a pack of snarling, baying dogs.

A door opened and the householder's lantern threw a beam of yellow light across the slanting rain.

"We are looking for Rommany," the driver said.

"Rommany?" The man had a wrinkled, weatherbeaten face. "Rommany, did you say?" He spat into the rain. "I doan know. This be Green Oaks. Mind the dogs, there now." And with that he went back into the house, slamming the door behind.

"Pleasant fellow," Duncan murmured. And then to the driver. "We'd best get back to the main highway."

We found the road again, and the horse went doggedly on through the night. It seemed the longest fourteen miles I had ever traveled. I grew more tired, more cold and hungry with every passing minute. Duncan must have felt me shiver. "Another few miles, sweetheart," he said, drawing me close to him, "and we shall be there. Put your head on my shoulder. There. Nap if you like, I'll wake you in time."

I closed my eyes, but I could not sleep. It was more than the cold and damp which kept me awake. My nerves were curiously on edge. I had the strange feeling that we were leaving the world we knew behind and at each trit-trot of the horse, each rumble of the wheels, we were traveling deeper and deeper into the unknown. It was absurd, of course. Sir Ian's invitation and the letter which had come in response to our acceptance boded a most hospitable reception. We were not journeying into the wilds of Africa, the jungles of Brazil, but to a house in Essex; a little remote, perhaps, but still on English, not alien, soil.

Suddenly the chaise jerked to a halt, throwing us forward.

Duncan got out and consulted with the driver. I could hear the murmur of their voices through the window and pressing my nose to it I saw by the coachman's light a marker at the side of the road: ROMMANY LANE.

The chaise tipped at an angle as Duncan got in beside me again, bringing with him the damp odor of earth and fallen leaves. "Just a few more minutes now," he assured me.

The carriage turned and we jolted into the narrow, hedge-bordered lane, bouncing and swaying as the wheels ground over the water-filled ruts. Again I pressed my face to the window. All that I could see was blackness, occasionally broken by the distant glimmer of lightning. The rain continued to fall, heavy, unremitting.

The few minutes Duncan had spoken of seemed to drag into hours as we rocked and bumped along. At last the way became smoother and once more I peered out into the driving rain.

I saw it then. Rommany, a great, looming hulk with a single light in a bottom-story window, a vast, dim edifice, blotting out the darker, rain-swollen horizon. And I huddled closer to Duncan, wondering with a sudden sharp stab of disquiet why I had been so eager to come to this lonely, godforsaken place.

Chapter 3

Duncan lifted the great bronze knocker and clapped it smartly against the heavy oaken door. A moment later lights sprang up in the other rooms, and a seamy-faced servant in livery opened the door.

"Please to enter, Mr. Blackmore. You are expected," he said when Duncan had introduced himself.

We were ushered into the hall, a large, dimly lit chamber, empty of furniture except for a beautifully carved chest beneath the stairs and a magnificent rich carpet spread before a cavernous fireplace. Duncan had just given instructions to have our trunk brought in when a door on the far side of the hall burst open and a sandy-haired man came striding toward us, arms outstretched.

"So it's you," he said, pumping Duncan's hand. "I'd almost given you up."

"We got lost once, and the rain—" Duncan began.

"Never mind. You're here. You can't know how happy I am to see you. And this"—turning to me with a smile—"this must be your wife."

"Eustacia, darling," Duncan said, "meet your cousin, Sir Ian Blackmore."

"None of that stuffy formality," laughed Ian, a large man, handsome, in a dissolute, rather seedy way. Though younger than Duncan, he was already running to fat, his neck bulging over his collar, his thinning hair carefully combed to conceal a receding hairline. "My, my Duncan, you old devil," he chided, "you never told me what a beautiful child you had married."

The "child" grated, but I knew Sir Ian meant it to be a compliment, so I smiled and murmured a thanks.

"Welcome to Rommany, my dear," he said, taking my hand.

His fingers were hot and damp, and I wondered if beneath the hearty manner and affable smile he was nervous and ill at ease. I could not imagine why, since he was the host, secure in his own home, while we were practically strangers, far from ours.

"It was good of you to ask us," I said.

"My pleasure, entirely my pleasure." He turned aside and speaking to the man in livery instructed him to pay the driver and then to have our trunk taken upstairs. "Do come and meet Violet," he urged. "She is in the drawing room with the other guests."

At our entrance a fashionably dressed woman rose from her chair and came toward us. "Here we are!" said Ian in his cheerful baritone.

There were too few lamps and as a consequence the lighting was poor but on the whole my first impression of the drawing room was one of simple elegance: polished satinwood, tapestry-covered chairs and rich ruby-red curtains drawn against the night.

"Violet, these are the cousins I have talked about for so long."

"I am so glad you could come," Violet said, lips drawn into a smile, her eyes assessing me from head to toe in one quick glance.

"And this is Maurice Peale, a dear friend." Ian indicated a hollow-eyed youngish man who advanced to shake Duncan's hand. He had a prominent Adam's apple and a sober, diffident air.

"And Daphne Peale, his wife," Sir Ian said.

Daphne, plump, pink-cheeked and blonde was "absolutely delighted" to meet us at last.

"Well, now," said Ian, rubbing his hands together, "I expect you haven't had dinner. We've held it back, and if either of you should like to have a wash...."

"I would, thank you," I said. My coat had been taken by the servant, but I still wore my hat and my face felt grimy from the long train ride.

"Of course," Violet said. She went to the bell pull. "I'll have Carla show you to your room."

"A glass of sherry?" Ian inquired of Duncan. "Or something stronger?"

Duncan moved from my side and laughed. "Something stronger, by all means, please." A well-seasoned traveler, Duncan was already at home while I stood uncomfortable, uncertain, trying to think of something to say as we waited for Carla to answer the bell's summons.

"Such a pretty dress," Daphne remarked. Her husband Maurice had gone over to join the men for a drink. "May I ask who your dressmaker is?"

I told her.

"Oooh, expensive, that one," she remarked. There was a faint trace of cockney in her speech. "So I've heard."

Violet shot her a look of distaste which I felt sure I was not meant to see. "It seems as if no one is answering my ring," Violet said impatiently. "Domestic help is of such poor quality when one lives in the country. Come along, Eustacia, I'll show you up." Her eyes were very blue, but cold, like frozen forget-me-nots.

We went out into the dim hall and ascended a broad staircase. The light was so faint I could scarcely see my way. Violet said; "We are making some repairs, and part of the house has been closed off. But I don't think it will inconvenience you."

The guest room set aside for Duncan and me, though small, was airy and pleasant. It held a large bed, clawed chests of polished mahogany, and a lovely dressing table with a cheval glass. I was glad I had said nothing to Duncan about turning back as I had been tempted to do in the lane. Whatever had come over me? The house was charming, and had it not been for Lady Violet's unfriendly eyes, I would have been perfectly happy.

"I hope you will be comfortable," she said in a cool, formal voice.

"I think I shall."

I thought she would leave me then, but she did not. I brought the lamp—the only one in the room—over to the dressing table and sitting down before the mirror removed my hat.

"You are very pretty," Lady Violet said, watching me.

"I hope you won't think me impertinent, but—how old are you?"

"I shall be nineteen in a month."

She seemed about to say something, but apparently changed her mind.

After a short, awkward silence, I turned from the mirror. "Your invitation came at an opportune time." I explained about John Hempstead and how I hoped a week in the country was just what Duncan needed.

"Yes, to be sure," she said, her eyes fastened to my face.

Now that I had a closer look at her, I noticed Lady Violet used powder and color for her cheeks. Even so, she could not disguise the faint lines on her forehead and the deep groove above the bridge of her nose. She was older than Ian by five years at the least, I guessed, and I understood now why she seemed to resent me. It was my youth. Or was it the loss of her own she found so intolerable? Perhaps the dim lighting was hers by choice, a way of visually forestalling the appearance of age.

"How long have you been at Rommany?" I asked, groping for conversation. The silent scrutiny of those chilly blue eyes was becoming more and more uncomfortable.

"Three years," she said, after a moment's hesitation.

I got up and went to the washstand behind a laquered screen. The water in the pitcher was tepid, but I splashed some into the basin and with the aid of a cloth managed to remove the soot from my face. I was drying my hands when Lady Violet suddenly asked, "Do you love your husband?"

The question rapped out so abruptly startled me. I came out from behind the screen. She turned from inspecting herself in the mirror. "Yes," I said. "I love him very much."

"I thought you might." The faintest of smiles. She seemed relieved, friendlier.

Perhaps she had wanted reassurance, wanted to feel that if I were happy enough with my own husband I would not be casting eyes at hers. As if I could. What an extraordinary woman!

We joined the others a few minutes later and went into dinner. The meal, a delicious repast, was served impeccably by two men in livery. Sir Ian's appearance might have been unimpressive, but the complements of his table and the furnishings I had seen were all of high quality and in excellent taste.

Earlier I had wondered what Lady Violet's feelings were toward pretty young Daphne. It did not take long, however, to realize that Daphne was the sort one would find hard to envy. She was far too silly. Another girl with the same empty-headed, pink and blonde bonbon beauty might at least have been wise enough to follow the old maxim, "Silence is golden," but not Daphne. Addicted to sudden bouts of irrelevant chatter, she would burst out from time to time with foolish remarks about anything that popped into her head. At one point, turning to me, she asked if I knew that Rommany had a ghost.

"I'm afraid I didn't," I answered.

Sir Ian, smiling tolerantly, explained, "Every old house of decent age has a ghost. And Rommany, having been built in sixteen hundred and nine, should qualify, I suppose."

"What sort of ghost?" I said.

"Oh, the usual," he replied. "Some thwarted lover grumbling or sighing through the corridors each night after the stroke of twelve."

"You aren't serious?" I asked, suddenly thinking of Ian's father, Edward, and his blighted love affair.

"Very," he answered and laughed, while Duncan watched me with amused eyes.

As the meal progressed, I observed that Sir Ian, far from being interested in Daphne, seemed visibly annoyed at her, so much so that he finally asked her not to interrupt. "My dear," he said with a tight smile, "why don't we *listen* for a while? Duncan's had a most fascinating sojourn in South Africa, and I would like to hear what he has to say."

"South Africa!" Daphne exclaimed. "Yes, well it's such a vast place, isn't it? Why I was saying only yesterday to Maurice—"

Her husband stanched the flow. "Please, do be quiet, love."

Sir Ian said, "Thank you." Then, turning back to Duncan, "You were telling me at the club that you had

22

stumbled upon a site which you believe indicated the presence of diamonds."

Diamonds? Until that moment I had been listening to the conversation half-attentively. Now, I sat up all ears. Duncan had only briefly talked about his time in Africa. He had never mentioned a word about diamonds.

Duncan leaned back in his chair. "As I told you at the club, Ian, I don't really *know* if diamonds can be found there or not. It was simply a guess."

"But you described the terrain."

"Well, yes, the terrain was similar to that of a site on the banks of the Orange River where, as you may remember, a child picked up a pebble, later identified as a twenty-one-carat diamond."

Daphne gasped audibly. "Oooooh, I say!"

". . . the circular patches of yellow clay," Duncan went on with a faint smile in her direction, "are called, 'yellow ground.' Beneath this, I am given to understand, is a hard bluish rock and the tops of so-called 'pipes.' Sometimes these pipes contain diamonds."

"And you did not stop to make sure?" Sir Ian asked, his eyes reflecting amusement.

"I saw no reason to. We were hunting game at the time, and I was more interested in meat for our table than grubbing about in the ground."

There was a small silence while the manservant removed our plates. Daphne started to speak, but was quelled by a look from Sir Ian.

When the servant had retired, Sir Ian said, "Do you think you might find that place again?"

"Oh, I daresay," Duncan replied, sipping from his wine-glass.

"Suppose"—Sir Ian leaned forward, chin in hand—"suppose we go treasure hunting, then. I have plenty of money and can finance an expedition."

Duncan shook his head. "No, thank you." Then, smiling across the table at me, he added, "I'm afraid my treasure hunting days are over."

"All right," Ian said. "Draw up a map and I will buy it from you."

"You would be buying a pig in a poke," Duncan laughed, and a moment later Sir Ian joined in.

"Ah, well," Ian gave a mock sigh, "it would have been an amusing change."

I looked quickly at Lady Violet, but she sat expressionless, staring into space. Were things going so poorly between them that Ian must look for a change? I thought of my own recent situation and wondered how close Duncan had come to wanting to go off on his travels again. Perhaps I had exaggerated the rift between us, though, for hadn't he said only a moment ago that his treasure-hunting days were over?

Then Sir Ian began to speak of Rommany with such genuine fondness that I realized how oversensitive I had become. Here was a man not the least bit bored with his existence. "My father had no real interest in Rommany," he was saying, "but I do. At present we are renovating some of the rooms in the house, and I've also taken it upon myself to repair the tenants' cottages. I make it a point to let our tenants know we care about crops, the price a good steer will fetch at market, how they are getting on. It helps them, as well as myself, you know, to give personal attention to matters."

"Very true," Duncan said. "By the way, how is the hunting at Rommany?"

"Poor, I regret to say. Else I would have asked you to bring your gun. Because of my father's neglect, the park has been cleaned out by poachers. Not a partridge or a pheasant in the whole place. In time I hope to build up a preserve again. Fortunately, I have the means to underwrite all my schemes."

"Scottish wool?" Duncan said, smiling.

"Indeed. Shall we drink to the good Scottish sheep?"

After dinner, the men went to a small room just off the drawing room with their port and cigars to play cards, while we three women sat before the drawing-room fire. Had Lady Violet and I been alone I would have been hard put for conversation for she seemed to be lost in thought as she stared into the flames. As it was, Daphne took up the slack, chattering on and on, flitting from one subject to another; the latest Mayfair scandal, the effect of rain on the complexion, the new shorter length of skirts. "Imagine, boot tops showing as you walk!"

It was all very tiresome, and my head soon began to

ache. I was trying to think of some graceful way to excuse myself when Lady Violet came to my rescue. "You must be weary after your journey. If you wish to retire, you have only to say so."

"Thank you," I said gratefully. "I believe I will go to bed. It's been a long day."

"Let me call the maid and have her fix you a hot drink. It will relax you."

"No . . . no, really."

"It's no trouble for *me*." Her lips twitched into a ghost of a smile.

Instead of ringing, she went out. Perhaps the bell was not functioning, or the maids responded only to Lady Violet's personal summons.

During her absence, I looked in on the men playing cards, thinking to say good night. But they were so intent on their game; shirt-sleeved, puffing away at cigars, I decided not to disturb them.

A few minutes later Violet returned. "Carla is waiting," she said.

A slim figure in a maid's uniform bearing a tray with a mug stood in the shadows beyond the door.

I bade my hostess and Daphne goodnight and followed the maid up the long staircase. I noticed she walked with a graceful, straight-backed poise rare in serving maids. She opened a door and I preceded her into the room. A fire danced on the hearth, its leaping flames bathing the walls in a rosy glow.

"Do you wish further assistance, madam?" the maid inquired. She spoke with a foreign accent, in a low, cultured voice.

I turned from the fire to look at her. She was a pretty creature, young, the skin a dusky peach velvet, the nose pert, the mouth a little too wide, perhaps, but the eyes—thickly black-fringed, sloe eyes—were ravishingly beautiful.

"You are not English?" I asked, curious. I could not place the accent. Having once had a French governess, I knew it could not be a French. Spanish, perhaps.

"My father was English," she said.

"And your mother?"

She hesitated. "She was a native of Bombay."

The girl was a half-caste, then. "You have lived in Bombay?"

"Yes, madam."

"My husband resided there for a time," I said. I looked at her more closely, and suddenly a dozen questions surged through my mind—one uppermost. I knew I ought not to ask it, but I did. "Perhaps you knew him? Duncan Blackmore?"

She did not speak for a moment. "Yes—I knew him." The answer came with slow reluctance, a reluctance which seemed to have a hidden, erotic meaning, And Mama's doomlike words flashed across my mind. *Men who live in the tropics are inevitably led to native women.*

Not Duncan, I thought silently. Mama had been prejudiced against him when she had said that. It couldn't be. Dozens of natives in Bombay must have known Duncan. Besides, the girl was too young. She couldn't have been more than fifteen or sixteen. I burned to ask her when she had known Duncan. How?

"If you will, madam," she said in her liquid voice, "please do not mention me to him—or what I have said to the others."

"Why such secrecy?" I asked, more sharply than I had intended.

"It is—" she bit her lip. "It is a long story, madam, and I do not feel I am at liberty to tell it."

A sick knot formed under my ribs. "Your real name—is it Carla?" I hazarded.

"No. But I cannot say more. You will not give me away?"

I stared at her, trying to control the trembling inside. Indian girls matured early, most of them married to men of their parents' choice by the time they were fourteen. And this one, though young, was not a child, but a lovely woman. She had known Duncan, and now she wanted me to keep her presence at Rommany a secret. There could only be one reason for that. I wanted to shout at her, to scream, "Were you his mistress?"

But I couldn't. The bonds of propriety, the rules of how a gentlewoman must act, no matter what vixens gnawed at her entrails, were too strong. But more than that, I was afraid of her answer.

"I promise not to give you away," I said, suddenly wanting to cry.

Chapter 4

After the maid had gone, I sat for a long time staring at my image in the glass. Ever since I was a little girl, I had been told that I was pretty, and were I a stranger looking at the face in the mirror now, I would say unequivocally that the little girl had grown into a most attractive woman. The hair had darkened a trifle, but was still a honey-gold, the blue eyes were well spaced, the skin was of porcelain delicacy, the mouth a fashionably shaped bow. Yes, a pretty face. Why should I concern myself with this half-caste, then?

I was not so naïve as to think that Duncan had come to me an innocent. He was too virile a man for that. But while the faces of the women who had shared his bed remained unknown, his past did not disturb me. But now, having seen Carla, those dark fathomless eyes, that wide, sensuous mouth, and thinking of Duncan embracing, kissing her, his ardent gaze wandering over her slim waist, her full, young bosom. . . .

I got up abruptly and parted the heavy curtains on the window. Nothing could be seen but darkness and the black, streaming rain running in rivulets down the pane. I suddenly thought of our place in Kensington—those cramped rooms I had found so irritating—with a pang of homesickness. Why had I been so anxious to leave? I recalled Duncan's eagerness, his fresh interest in life the morning we received the invitation from Sir Ian. Had Duncan been aware that the half-caste girl was at Rommany? If so, he certainly gave no hint of it.

I went back to the mirror and began to draw the pins

from my hair. My eyes looked tired and strained; the ache behind them had grown worse.

Carla knew Duncan in Bombay. Had the girl's English father been a friend of Duncan's, or had he met the girl casually on the street? No, she seemed too well-bred for a woman of that sort. One could tell—even in a maid's uniform—if a girl was free with her favors: a whiff of cheap perfume, the glint of an earring, the flash of a red petticoat. But this one wore an air of refinement; she was neat and trim, from the tip of her polished boots to the demurely coiled hair beneath her cap. And jealousy-prone Lady Violet would have never employed a flirt. No, Carla, as she called herself, was something apart from the ordinary mistress. Which made it all the worse.

Had she followed Duncan from India? Or had he sent for her?

I closed my eyes unable to bear the thought. Why, I asked myself, must I go on with this torment. Hadn't he married *me*?

I got undressed and drank the hot chocolate and crept into bed.

I must have fallen asleep the moment my head touched the pillow for the next thing I knew it was morning. I lay on my side, my sleep-heavy eyes traveling the curtained room. My tongue felt thick, my throat parched. It seemed that an ax lay buried in my skull, so sharp was the pain. I saw my little hat with its single feather on the dressing table beside an empty mug. I puzzled over the two objects for a few moments longer and then it came to me. I was at Rommany.

With an effort I pushed myself up, my heart missing a beat as I looked down on the pillow next to mine. Duncan had not come to bed.

Everything that I had thought about the sloe-eyed girl and Duncan rose in my mind and hit me with a renewed, sickening force. I got out of bed and stumbled across to the washbasin, hanging over the rim a long moment before I tipped the pitcher and let the water pour. There wasn't much water, but I could not bring myself to ring for the maid. If she did not answer, then I should know for certain where Duncan had spent the night.

My movements were slow and awkward, my mind in a

fog, but somehow I managed to get into my clothes. Once dressed I sat on the edge of the bed, too heartsick to wonder why I should feel so heavy-limbed, so dazed. I had to go downstairs, of course. I could not sit there all day. But I kept hoping from one moment to the next that Duncan would come in the door.

The curtains were still drawn, but I could hear the rain tapping at the windows. I wondered what the time was, and rising slowly so as not to jar my head, I went to the dressing table where I had left my watch. It was a small timepiece, gold-cased, ornamented with seed pearls and amethysts, a pretty thing which I wore as a brooch rather than a pendant, but I had forgotten to wind it. The hands had stopped, curiously, at midnight.

I looked about the room for a clock, but there was none. And thinking of it, I recalled that I had not seen a timepiece of any kind in either the drawing room or dining room downstairs. Strange. A house without clocks? Was this lack another idiosyncrasy of Lady Violet's? Perhaps she had some notion that she could cheat the passage of time by not having to take note of it.

I reckoned it must be mid-morning, and winding my watch I set the hands at ten and then pinned it to my waist. I waited another five minutes and then, no longer able to endure my own company, descended the stairs to the great hall below. As I stood there indecisively, a door opened at the far end and Lady Violet appeared.

"There you are, Eustacia," she said. "I was just about to send someone to fetch you. We're in here, having breakfast."

As I came to her from across the hall, she went on. "You must excuse the poor service here at Rommany. Generally, I have the maid bring my guests their morning tea, but we are shorthanded at the moment."

"That's quite all right," I said, resisting the impulse to ask her about the half-caste girl.

I entered the dining room and threw a quick, hopeful glance at the table. Duncan was not there.

"Good morning," Sir Ian said cheerfully, rising to his feet.

I felt my cheeks go hot with embarrassment. And anger. Surely Duncan would not leave me in this predicament, having to answer for his absence? Should I lie to them, say that he was sleeping late?

"I'm . . . I'm sorry, but Duncan. . . ." I began haltingly.

"I'm afraid it is all my fault," Sir Ian said.

"Your fault?" I asked, puzzled.

"Yes, my dear," he said sheepishly. "We spent the night drinking and playing cards. Forgot completely about the time until Daphne came down this morning. Your husband, a little worse for wear, went out for a stroll about an hour ago."

"In this rain?" I asked, resisting the impulse to laugh as a marvelous relief swept over me. Duncan had been playing cards! While my vivid imagination had pictured him (my dearest, my love!) in Carla's arms, he had been playing *cards!* What a fool I had been.

"He said he wanted air," Sir Ian explained. "I am sure he will return shortly."

"Yes, of course," I said smiling, feeling as if a thousand years had been lifted from my aching head.

Breakfast consisted of eggs, bacon, a large ham, sausages, fish, fruit, and a great urn of tea. I had never seen food look so tempting, never felt so ravenously hungry. So much worry over nothing, I thought, heaping my plate, smiling at Daphne who was chattering on about gypsies and fortunes and whatnot. I did not mind her talk. Nor did I mind Lady Violet's silent eyes upon me, nor the booming heartiness of Sir Ian's laugh, nor Maurice Peale's nasal twang. For the moment each of them seemed like a lifelong friend and Rommany a delightful place; all because Duncan had been playing cards.

After breakfast we went into the drawing room. The curtains had not been opened, and when I went to the window, Lady Violet said; "I hope you don't mind, but the light bothers me." Then she picked up a sewing basket. "I've been trying to embroider a tablecloth for a niece, but I'm not much of a hand with a needle. Can you give me some advice on this, Eustacia?"

Embroidery had once been a hobby of mine, and I still enjoyed working with intricate stitches and colorful threads. Lady Violet had made a botch of her tablecloth, so together we cut and picked out her mistakes. Then I gave a demonstration of the cross stitch and the French knot. She had a book of floral designs and asked my advice on a sampler she was also planning to do. By the time we had chosen a design, I was shocked to see by the watch at my waist that it was already noon.

And Duncan had not returned.

"Perhaps he walked to the village," Sir Ian said, "and has decided to have a late breakfast at the White Boar."

"The village? I . . . I don't remember," I said, confused.

"Tenwyck. Small. You must have missed it in the dark."

"How far would Tenwyck be?"

"Oh." Sir Ian pursed his lips. "Five or six miles, I'd say. Eh, Maurice?"

"Six miles," Maurice answered.

"But that's such a long way to go, especially on a wet day," I protested.

"For most people, yes. But your husband is an outdoor man, isn't he? Very athletic. So he's told me. He's done mountain climbing and all that walking on the African veldt."

It was true. Duncan was an indefatigable hiker, as I remembered from our honeymoon in Italy. Yet Ian's assurances did nothing to ease my growing anxiety. Supposing he had slipped in the mud and hurt himself and even now was lying helpless in a ditch? No, I argued with myself, it wasn't like Duncan, a man who had come through so many dangerous ventures unscathed, to slip clumsily.

And thinking that, I went from anxiety to annoyance. Anger, really. How dare he go off as he had without leaving word, without any concern for my feelings?

Two o'clock came and went, and then it was three. No word, no sign of Duncan. I laid aside all pretense of reading, of calm patience, and began to wander aimlessly about the drawing room.

"You will wear that rug out with pacing," Daphne said.

"I cannot sit still," I said, surprised at the quaver, the threat of tears in my voice. "Perhaps I am fretting unnecessarily, but I . . . I think I will go out to look for him."

Sir Ian, who had been talking in low tones with Maurice Peale at the other end of the drawing room, spoke up then. "That won't be necessary." He got to his feet. "Maurice and I have decided to search for Duncan. We'll get the servants to help us."

He crossed the room to me, and lifting my chin with his hand, admonished, "Now, now, no tears." And I caught a fleeting odd glint in his eyes. Or had I imagined it?

"I'm willing to wager we shall find Duncan peacefully dozing before the fire at the White Boar," Sir Ian asserted. "What do you say, Maurice?"

"I agree," came the reply.

When the men left I felt better in spirit, though my head had begun to ache again. Lady Violet, pressing one of her own headache powders upon me, urged that I go upstairs for a nap.

I had meant only to lie down for a bit, but I must have been more exhausted than I had thought and I fell into a restless sleep. Sometime later I was awakened by the sound of men's voices in the hall below. The room was pitch dark; night had come again. I got up, felt my way to the door, and ran out on the landing.

Maurice Peale, Sir Ian and the butler with the seamed face were standing in the hall talking quietly together. I clung to the railing, my hands damp with apprehension. Something had happened to Duncan! He was mortally injured, dying in some cottager's parlor, and the men below were discussing how best to break the news to me. I went through the whole thing as I stood here. I could see the crowd of relatives clustering around the churchyard at the funeral, and myself leaning on Papa's arm. It was so real to me I did not realize Lady Violet was at my side until she spoke. "You must try not to be upset," she said.

"What has happened?" I cried, feeling frightened and sick.

"They have not found him."

"Not found him?" I echoed her words. "Then there is hope—a chance?"

"Of course," Lady Violet said. "Come downstairs and have a glass of brandy. Your face is so white."

She took my arm and led me down the stairs and into the dining room. I wanted to lean on her and weep, but Lady Violet was not the sort one leaned on, though I knew she was being as kind as her stiff character would permit.

I had a sip of brandy and then, on Lady Violet's insistence, another. It warmed my cold hands, but not the icy dread inside me.

Sir Ian came in, looking very grave.

"You have not found him?" I asked, knowing the answer, but wanting to hear it from him.

"I am sorry, my dear. Maurice and I went directly to the White Boar while the servants remained to search the grounds. The tavernkeeper has not seen anyone of Duncan's description. Nor has he appeared at the baker's or the chemist's, our only two shops in Tenwyck."

"And the servants?"

"Found no clue."

I clasped my hands together, holding them so tightly it seemed I could feel the knuckles turn white. "What are we to do?"

"What we *cannot* do is give up," Sir Ian said. "We shall comb the entire countryside. Of course, we shall need more help. After dinner—Violet has ordered it early—I propose to return to Tenwyck and ask Constable Meacham to assist us. He's an obliging soul, and I'm sure he won't mind."

After dinner? How could he speak of dinner when even now Duncan might be injured, helpless, groaning in pain somewhere out there in the dark and the pouring rain? But I could not expect them to share my frantic impatience. They were concerned; they were doing everything they could. It was not their fault Duncan had wandered off, had spoiled their prospects of a pleasant fortnight as well as my own.

I sat between Maurice and Daphne at dinner, my heart like a stone, heavy, numb. I could not taste food. I drank a little wine and, despite my earlier more charitable thoughts, wondered how the others could eat. Perhaps when Duncan was found (he *must* be) unharmed, I would look back on this episode and laugh.

"What do you think might have happened to him?" I asked, cutting across Daphne's account of a partridge shoot.

"Oh, a dozen things," Sir Ian said. "He might have slipped and knocked his head against a stone. Or inadvertently got caught in a poacher's trap—"

"Oh no!" I exclaimed.

"Better than finding him dead," Daphne pointed out.

A sick nausea overcame me and I got up from the table at once, clumsily upsetting the wine. It made a puddle, like a dark pool of blood. The serving man came forward with a napkin. "I'm sorry," I apologized. Then, biting my lip, I hurried from the room.

Sir Ian called to me as I was crossing the hall.

"This is a terrible ordeal for you, my dear. Forgive me for being so dense. Of course, I have more faith in Duncan's ability to survive—the man has nine lives, really . . . but I forgot you are so young. And newly married. We shall go at once to Tenwyck, Maurice and I."

"But your dinner. . . ?"

"We've finished."

"May I go with you?" I asked.

He looked at me speculatively.

"Please," I urged. "I don't think I can bear the waiting a minute longer. If only I could *do* something."

"All right. I don't see any harm in it."

The others came out and joined us. "I have a better idea, Eustacia," Sir Ian said. "Why don't you go into Tenwyck with one of the servants and enlist Constable Meacham's aid, while Maurice and I start making the rounds of the cottages?"

"Yes, yes," I agreed, readily. "Anything."

"Dress warmly," Lady Violet spoke up. "It is still raining."

I ran up to the room and threw on a hooded cloak. Our trunk had been unpacked by the maid and our clothes neatly hung in the wardrobe, Duncan's as well as my own. I touched the hem of his riding jacket with my finger. It was a new one, delivered from his tailor's prior to our leaving for Rommany. He had looked very handsome, very elegant in it. I couldn't believe that he would never wear it again. *God, please bring him back safely*, I whispered, burying my face in the rough sleeve.

The seamy faced butler had brought the trap around, and he now sat hunched against the wind in the driver's seat, waiting. The night was dark, black as an abyss, filled with the sounds of water: steady rain beating on the stone steps, rain running and gurgling in the gutters, rain gushing from the spouts.

Sir Ian hurried me toward and into the trap. "I hate to think of you out in this," I said.

"Never mind about me. Your job is to get the constable. Good luck." He grasped my hand.

We started off with a jerk, splashing through the wet darkness, leaving the lights of Rommany behind.

If I had thought our ride of the night before (had only one day gone by?) was interminable, lasting hours, the one on this night took an eternity. The roads were deep in mud, and the horse plodded along at a snails' pace, the wheels of the trap squeaking and whining in protest as we ploughed through great swaths of brown swirling flood. At one point, the water reached the axles and the horse stopped. I could hear him snorting in the darkness. The butler got down, cursing under his breath, wading forward in muck up to his knees. I heard him coaxing the reluctant beast, and gradually we moved to drier land.

The rain never let up; it kept pouring down in hard, driving sheets. There were no houses that I could see, not a single sign of human habitation.

It was nearly midnight when we finally reached the cobbled streets of Tenwyck. All was dark; not a single crack of light shone from the shuttered windows. Somewhere a dog bayed halfheartedly, his forelorn wail dying to a whimper as the sound of falling rain closed over it. A few minutes later, the trap halted before a shadowed house, the lone chimney rising like a black finger above a thatched roof. The butler helped me down.

"This is Constable Meacham's house," he said. "I've instructions to return immediately to Rommany, as I am needed there."

"But supposing—supposing the constable is not at home?" I said, a little dismayed. Sir Ian had not told me that I would be literally dumped on the doorstep.

"I shall wait, of course, until someone appears," he said grudgingly.

I went through a low wooden gate and up a garden walk. I knocked on the door and waited, drawing my hood tighter against the cold. In the distance the dog commenced to howl once more. I knocked harder, insistently, and suddenly a light went on. Presently the door was opened by a short, stout red-faced man wearing a nightcap over a shock of white hair. He held a candle in his hand.

"Constable Meacham?" I inquired.

"Yes, that is me," he said, holding the candle higher, peering at me with some surprise.

"I am Mrs. Duncan Blackmore," I said. "I am here to ask for your assistance. May I come in?"

"Yes, yes, by all means. Please do."

I turned to wave at the butler but the trap was already disappearing down the street. As the constable closed the door behind me, I could hear the distant wheels rumbling over the stones.

The constable led me into a small untidy room crammed with overstuffed chairs, a ponderous desk and several squat tables, all littered with books and papers. Setting the candle down on the desk, he cleared a space for me on one of the chairs.

"Now," he said, seating himself behind the desk, "what brings you here on this miserable night?"

Quickly, as concisely as I could, I told him. As I spoke, a frown appeared between his eyes, and when I had finished he was silent for a few moments, staring at his hands clasped across his prominent belly.

"You say you have been staying at Rommany?"

"Yes," I answered, "with cousins of my husband, Sir Ian and Lady Violet Blackmore."

His frown deepened. "You are certain it is *Rommany?*"

The tone of his voice made me uneasy. "Of course. Why do you ask?"

"My dear," he shook his head, "forgive me if I sound doubtful. But, you see, Rommany"—his eyes resting on me were puzzled and my skin grew colder yet—"Rommany is not now inhabited. It is an empty house—has been for the last twelve years."

Chapter 5

An ornate brass clock on the mantle ticked away fussily in the ensuing silence. Outside a sudden flurry of rain dashed against the window, rattling the panes.

"You ... you must be mistaken," I said, finding my voice at last. "I have just come from Rommany and it is inhabited—very much inhabited."

The constable unhooked his hands from his belly. "I do not mean to be contrary, Mrs. Blackmore, but...." He paused as if searching for words.

The clock struck the half hour, one single bell-like tone, and at the same moment a woman appeared in the doorway. She was as round as the constable, a fresh-faced little person, wearing a fringed woolen shawl over a long nightdress. "I heard voices, Clem," she said. "Oh—I see you have a visitor."

"Yes, my dear." The constable introduced me to his wife and explained the purpose of my visit.

"Rommany?" Mrs. Meacham asked. She had several chins and they quivered when she spoke, "But . . . ?" she flashed a doubtful look at her husband. He nodded his head.

"You are new here in Tenwyck?" I ventured with a dry mouth, hoping perhaps that Rommany was unknown to them.

They both laughed. "Lordy, no," said Mrs. Meacham. "Born and bred in Tenwyck. Been here all our lives and plan to stay until our time comes."

"Then you must know Sir Ian."

"Not Sir Ian," the constable said. "We knew his father, Sir Edward, and then not hardly to speak to. After Sir Edward's son was born and his wife died, he rarely stayed at Rommany. Twelve years ago he moved out altogether. A man—his solicitor, I believe—would come down from London once a twelvemonth to collect the rents. Still does, far as I know."

"We did hear that Sir Edward died, and his son had inherited the house," Mrs. Meacham said, "but we've not seen him."

I wished now that the butler had waited before returning to Rommany. "I . . . I don't know what to say." It was all so confusing. "I remember distinctly Lady Violet telling me they had been at Rommany for these past three years."

The constable and his wife exchanged another glance. My face felt suddenly hot and the beginnings of a headache began to throb behind my eyes. I put my hand to my forehead. "I . . . I don't understand."

"Perhaps there's been a mix-up of sorts," Mrs. Meacham said kindly. "You know, Clem, Rommany *is* out of the way. There's the new road goes the other side of Tenwyck and Sir Ian and Lady Violet *could* have moved in without us knowing. And," she dimpled at me, "Mrs. Blackmore here might have misunderstood her ladyship. Perhaps she meant three *months*."

"Yes, yes," Clem Meacham agreed eagerly, his frown disappearing. "That might explain it. Now, Mrs. Blackmore, you say your husband is missing?"

I went through the whole story again. At the conclusion the constable said, "Of course. I shall be most happy to give what assistance I can." He studied the clock on the mantel for a long moment. "I doubt if I can round up a search party at this hour."

My heart sank. I thought of Duncan lying helpless through the night, in the cold, wet to the skin with rain.

"Please don't look so downcast," the constable coaxed. "If I thought I could find your husband without having to call on others, I would go at once. But don't you see how futile it would be, alone and in the dark, too?"

"Yes. You are quite right," I said, consoling myself with the hope that perhaps Duncan had already been found and even now was sitting in front of the fire drinking brandy with Sir Ian and Maurice.

Mrs. Meacham, sympathetic and kindly, put me in her

spare room. It was tiny, hardly more than a closet, an old-fashioned bed taking up most of the space. On the wall was a sampler. TRUST IN GOD, it said, a plain homily which my desperate mind grasped as a good omen. I had been lax in church attendance since my wedding, but I promised myself and God that I would never miss a Sunday again as long as I lived. *Please, dear God, please bring him back to me,* I murmured as I removed my dress and hung it on a peg. Then climbing into the high bed I sank deep into the goose-feather pillows, fragrant with lavender and camphor.

When I awoke it was morning, and the gray light was seeping through the curtains. To my dismay, I saw it was past ten o'clock. Dressing quickly, I went out into a small, narrow passage.

"Ah, there you are," Mrs. Meacham said, her round, rosy face peeping out through an open door. "Come and have some breakfast. Clem has gone out to fetch the men."

There were fresh-baked muffins and new butter, red raspberry jam and thick cream for the porridge, all the simple but delicious country edibles someone like Bess Meacham would set out for a guest. But I had a pain in the pit of my stomach and could not eat. I sat crumbling a muffin between my fingers, my thoughts going round and round. If Duncan had been found, then someone from Rommany would have brought the news. Surely Sir Ian would not keep me in such anxious suspense. Where was Duncan, then? And why wasn't the constable ready to go? I had wanted to start at daybreak; in fact, understood from Mr. Meacham that he had planned to do so.

"Poor Clem's been trudging about since early morning," Mrs. Meacham said, as if guessing my thoughts. "He's not had much success persuading someone to go with him. They are all such superstitious folk here in Tenwyck."

"Superstitious?" I inquired, wiping my fingers on a napkin. "I don't get your meaning. Has that something to do with the search for my husband?"

"Why, it's Rommany, my dear," she said, offering me the plate of muffins again. "The house has a reputation for being haunted."

"No, thank you. Haunted?"

"It's all foolishness, of course. But they say Sir Edward's ghost is to be heard there on dark nights, muttering and sighing. The poor man was supposed to have been thwarted in love."

"Every old house has a ghost," I said, repeating Sir Ian's words. "But I saw none there, nor did I hear any ghostly mutterings."

Mrs. Meacham looked away.

"At any rate, I have other things to think of." I bit my lip.

"Yes, of course, my dear." She reached across the table and pressed my hand. "The constable is doing everything he can."

"I do appreciate your kindness," I said. But behind my words, there was an aching awareness of the passage of time, the minutes going by, one by one, inexorably inching past, and Duncan in an unknown void—lost. It has been little more than thirty-six hours since I had last seen him; it seemed forever.

"The rain has stopped," Mrs. Meacham said.

I looked out through the window at the gray scud of swollen clouds. In the east they were beginning to thin, moving swiftly like smoke over a pale, watery sun.

After breakfast we adjourned to the parlor and I sat where I could watch the street. At eleven, the constable's stout figure came through the garden gate—alone. I watched as he carefully scraped the mud from his boots on the fender near the door. A moment later he entered the parlor.

"My horse has gone lame," he explained in an exasperated voice. "I shall have to borrow one from James." Then, turning to me, "I stopped by to urge you not to lose heart, Mrs. Blackmore. I've two good strong men waiting, and as soon as we can harness another horse to the wagon, we shall be off."

It was lunchtime before the horse was procured. But there was another delay, since the men must have a "bite to eat" to sustain them on the way. A half hour passed, while I sat wrapped in my cloak, tapping my foot, in a sweat of anxiety. I could not understand why there was no word from Rommany. And again my fancy took flight, my mind seesawing between hope and despair, despair and hope. We would be too late—no, Duncan had been found. He was mortally injured—no, he was unharmed. By the time the wagon drew up to the door, my nerves were close to breaking.

I gave hurried thanks to Mrs. Meacham and went out to meet the constable. He helped me on to the high seat beside him and then introduced me to the two men, ruddy-faced farmers who tipped their caps politely. I thought I caught the name "Woodhill," but I was too perturbed to take much notice.

The weather, instead of clearing, had grown threatening again. Above us the clouds had regathered, blotting out the sickly sun and casting a dismal light over the village. We clattered down the wet cobblestoned street past the draper's, the chemist's, the dirty, rusty sign of the White Boar, past a lumberyard and a row of cottages with sagging, thatched roofs, and then turning a sharp corner came out onto the highway.

The sodden countryside lay on either side, a flat olive-green broken by an occasional stark, skeletal tree. The ditches were running high with brown muddy water, twigs and dead leaves and debris bobbing and swirling in the current. It was a forlorn landscape, the few cold and desolate dwellings we passed huddled together with their outbuildings and damp haystacks.

The men, sitting in the bed of the wagon, spoke in low tones. "The wettest year yet," I heard one say.

"Aye," the other replied. "Spoiled the harvest, and wheat bringing less than sixty-one shillings the quarter."

"At least yer not workin' for wages, like me. Wi' prices so high, I can scarcely put bread in the mouths of my family."

" 'Tis not much different, John. My rent is fixed from London, come good harvest or bad."

"Hard times—hard times," the other muttered.

Their talk made me feel somewhat pampered and useless, since I never had to think of the price of bread, let alone "hard times." I wondered if they thought me frivolous, if in their minds they found the search for a missing aristocrat a pointless venture. But perhaps they were kinder, more compassionate than I gave them credit for. I must see that they are well rewarded for their trouble, I told myself, and perhaps Duncan and I can find an unobtrusive way to ease their hardship.

The men had fallen silent and I turned my attention to the road. Though I had traversed it twice before, my journey on both occasions had been at night and through driving rain, so there were no familiar landmarks by which I could judge our progress. The scene had become more dreary and solitary. Smoke from a distant chimney half-hidden by the trees seemed to accentuate the loneliness. The sudden appearance of a rabbit, the first living thing I had seen in the entire, vast landscape, startled me. Leaping out from a hedge, he paused for a split moment to sniff at the wind, then darted across the road and disappeared.

"Are we almost there?" I asked Constable Meacham anxiously. The horse was a plodding, worn plug, and it seemed that he should die of old age before we reached Rommany.

"Not too far," he replied cheerfully.

We passed through a stand of bare-limbed birches, and the constable brought the wagon to a halt. To our left a narrow, hedge-bordered lane branched out from the road. It looked very much like Rommany Lane, but the marker was missing. Perhaps it had been dislodged by the rain.

"This leads to the house, I believe," the constable said.

A few minutes later we came in sight of a stone-arched gate. Across it in weathered, raised letters the name ROM-MANY was just barely visible. My heart suddenly began to beat apprehensively.

"My guess was right," Mr. Meacham said.

The men grunted in reply.

The ruts in the lane were deeply puddled, slowing the horse still more as he pulled his weight against the sticky clay clinging to the wheels. The wagon swayed and bounced, jarring my spine, rattling every tooth in my head. In front of us the drive went on and on, disappearing between thick-needled cypress and into the dark unknown.

Suddenly I was filled with a strange reluctance, a desire to hold back instead of going on, a feeling so at odds with my previous impatience I was at a loss to understand it. Perhaps I should have remained in Mrs. Meacham's parlor—better to sit in the warm, to speculate, to hope, than to be here now with this weird uneasiness.

The wagon creaked past a gnarled oak, and my feeling of reluctance deepened into the same terrible foreboding of disaster and doom which I had experienced the night Duncan and I had first approached the house. Something had happened, something terrible.

I closed my eyes and murmured: "Trust in God. Trust in God."

"What was that?" the constable asked.

"A small prayer," I said, giving him a wan smile.

"Ah, yes. Prayer always helps, so the good wife tells me."

We rounded the last curve in the drive and I saw Rommany then for the first time in the clear light of day.

It stood amidst a tangled sea of dead weeds and encroaching wild shrubbery, a silent place, untenanted, deserted, a house of sagging shutters and broken, smokeless chimneys. A house that certainly had not been lived in for many, many years.

Chapter 6

I sat gazing at the scene before me in utter disbelief. Silence, heavy with imminent rain and foreboding, hung over desolation and ruin, pressing at the shuttered windows, laying siege to the rain-streaked walls.

Somewhere in the muddied, overgrown gardens a frog began its mournful complaint: brrUP–brrUP–brrUP. He was joined by another and then another until the throaty chorus became as one voice beating like a pulse in my brain.

"I'm not going to say I was right until we make sure." Constable Meacham's voice startled me.

With a groan, he heaved himself out of the seat and then reached up to help me down.

"There—there must be some explanation," I murmured through dry lips. I clung to his arm for a moment, my head swimming. "Are you certain this is Rommany?" I asked, thinking that perhaps I had misread the weathered legend over the stone arch.

"Indeed it is. When I was a lad, I came here to Rommany several times with my father. He was a carpenter and was hired to do odd jobs now and again when Sir Edard was still at the house."

The two men waited in the wagon as the constable and I went up to the door. The bronze knocker seemed vaguely familiar, though now with the light I could see where the bronze was turning to green.

The constable lifted the knocker and it fell with a hollow clatter, silencing the frogs.

"Sir Ian said he was renovating some of the rooms," I offered in a small voice.

The constable smiled indulgently. "That may be so." He did not add, "What rooms? Where?" There was no sign of a work party, a ladder, a bucket of paint, no sign of recent human activity anywhere.

The constable struck the door again, the echo reverberating like the knock of doom in my ears. A cold little breeze sprang up as we waited, and the tall winter grasses whispered among themselves: NO-ONE'S-HERE, NO-ONE'S-HERE, NO-ONE'S HERE.

Ivy scraped against wood, and glancing to my right, I saw where a window had been boarded up. "It's quite possible that the exterior of the house is in disrepair," I said, grasping for some explanation. "Naturally, Sir Ian would say nothing."

"You did not notice that when you first came?"

"No, it was night and raining."

"And yesterday?"

"Yesterday was the same. And in any case, I was too concerned with Duncan to notice anything."

Mr. Meacham turned and surveyed the muddy drive clumped with ragged nettle and dock. "I'll go round to the kitchen and see if I can find someone there."

"Perhaps they've all gone out to look for my husband," I suggested hopefully, though I doubted Lady Violet and Daphne would bestir themselves.

"Perhaps," he said without conviction.

One of the men stood up in the wagon. "Mr. Meacham, may I have a word with you?"

"Certainly, John," he replied, waddling over to him.

John leaned down and spoke to Mr. Meacham in low tones. I heard the words "haunted . . . best leave . . . don't you think?"

They can't leave, I thought in dismay. Not now. But evidently Mr. Meacham succeeded in reasuring John, for the farmer seated himself again with a stoical look on his ruddy face.

"Be patient, Mrs. Blackmore," the constable said cheerfully. "We'll soon get to the bottom of this."

I watched as he disappeared around the corner of the house. Presently the frogs took up their disharmonious song again. The men, tired of sitting in the wagon, got down and leaned against the wheel, not speaking, but staring into space. The horse commenced to crop the weeds beneath his feet, yellow teeth chomping methodically as he moved his large head.

The deserted appearance of the house baffled and frightened me, but I would not let my mind dwell on it. Too dangerous. Yet was it any safer to think of Duncan? Wherever I turned in my thoughts, there was dreadful enigma.

A clattering noise inside the house whirled me about. Someone was sliding back the bolt. I held my breath as the door creaked open. Mr. Meacham's high-complexioned face looked out at me. "I forced my way," he said. His eyes were solemn.

"There is no one at home?" I asked, trembling.

He did not answer, but swung the door wide and stepped aside.

I crossed the threshold into the gray dimness of the vast hall. Shock held me speechless. The elegantly carved chest, the rich, glowing carpet were gone. Dust covered the wide planked floor, dust thick and smooth as velvet, except for tracks recently made by Mr. Meacham. No fire leaped in the cavernous fireplace. It gaped at me now from across the room like a huge mouth, smoke-blackened and hung with cobwebs.

For a few moments reality seemed to be slowly slipping through my fingers like grains of sand. With an effort, I managed to gather my wits together and still without speaking turned and walked to the door which I remembered had led to the drawing room. I paused with my hand on the knob, afraid to turn it, afraid of what I might find. Behind me I heard the scraping of feet as the two farmers came into the hall. Mr. Meacham said something I could not catch. Then, holding my breath, I twisted the knob and opened the door.

Even though I had prepared myself for the worst, shock hit me a fresh blow. The room was shuttered, but enough light came through to show it to be as bare and dusty as the hall. A cold dampness smelling of age and neglect pervaded the air. Fragile cobwebs stretching from the cornices to the window shivered in the errant draft. Where were the ruby-red draperies, the carved gilt sofas, the tapestry-covered chairs? Where was the soft lamplight, the ivory-inlaid table, the Turkey carpet in browns and deep blues that I had walked on only yesterday?

Twelve years, Mr. Meacham had said.

In the center of the denuded room was a gray shrouded heap. I went to it, and whipping aside the rotting sheet, found a cracked three-legged chair, a broken mirror, a moth-eaten rug, none of which resembled in the slightest the satinwood furniture I recalled.

Was I dreaming then? Was all that had happened since that first night when I had turned down the lamp and crept into bed part of a continuing nightmare? Duncan gone and the long day of waiting, the rainy night, and sitting in the cramped office of Constable Meacham? All those scenes and people, visionary fancies?

Perhaps in a few moments I would awake to find Duncan leaning over me and smiling. And I would say, "Oh, Duncan, I had such a terrible dream." And he would draw me into his arms, then, those strong protective arms, and I would be safe.

"Mrs. Blackmore."

I turned, startled.

Mr. Meacham was standing in the doorway. "I am terribly sorry. There must be, as my good wife says, some mix-up."

"Yes," I said, "yes,"

Mr. Meacham looked so real, his coat buttons bulging over his stomach, the hat he held in his hand, a dark plum-colored hat with a gray band, rather fanciful for a constable. Was it a dream? I did not realize I was staring at him until he turned away, red-faced, embarrassed.

"I want to have a look upstairs," I said.

The staircase had a carpet of sorts, worn thin to a clouded blue-gray. I did not remember it. There was nothing I had seen that was familiar. Yet I seemed to know instinctively which door led to the drawing room, as I seemed to know now the location of the bedroom where I had spent that first night. Behind me I heard the constable puffing as he followed me up.

I came to the room at the head of the stairs and went in. Shuttered, dark, bare, except for a ponderous wardrobe in the corner. Was it the same wardrobe? The maid, Carla, had unpacked our trunk and hung up our things. The door was slightly ajar. Breathing from the top of my lungs, I walked over to it slowly.

Empty. My clothes, Duncan's new riding jacket—where were they?

It wasn't a dream; in my heart of hearts I knew it wasn't a dream, but I clung to the illusion with a stubbornness born of despair.

"Please forgive me, Mrs. Blackmore," Mr. Meacham said. "I realize I have asked this before, but are you certain you were at Rommany?"

"Yes . . . yes, I . . . I am sure," I replied hesitantly, not at all sure of anything.

"Could you have confused it with Brookside, perhaps? It's the big house three miles south of here. Squire Allenby's house."

I shook my head. "Sir Ian is cousin to my husband. The house was—*is* Rommany."

He stood aside as I went through the door. I paused a moment and then walked quickly down the shadowed corridor, opening door after door. Dust and cobwebs. Mold and decay. Here a four-poster, its draperies in faded tatters, there a broken porcelain lamp, and in this room a clouded mirror reflecting my ghost-white face as I gazed into it. Nothing else; no furniture, no trace of recent human occupancy.

At the end of the corridor I found a long room which ran the length of the house. Its walls were hung with portraits, the faces, the colors dimmed by layers of dust. One picture appeared newer than the others and going up to it, I saw that it was a painting of Sir Ian. I could not mistake that sandy hair, the lidded eyes, the smile.

"Sir Ian," I said to Mr. Meacham who had followed close on my heels. "Would I know him if I had not seen him only yesterday?"

Mr. Meacham cleared his throat in obvious embarrassment.

Turning back to the picture I noticed a brass plaque at the bottom. It read, "Sir Ian Blackmore—1865."

"Shall we go down?" Mr. Meacham asked politely.

The two farmers were standing near the door, throwing nervous glances about them.

"I don't know . . . I can't say what has happened here," I said, choosing my words as carefully as a wayfarer would choose one stone from the other to ford a rushing stream. "But the—the one thing I am certain of is that my husband is missing. Perhaps we ought to go ahead with the search in any case."

Mr. Meacham and the men stared at me without speaking, and in their eyes I saw a pity which chilled me to the bone. Did they think me mad?

"He *is* missing!" I cried, the blood rushing to my face. "Don't you believe me?"

"Mrs. Blackmore," the constable began, "you are tired. Perhaps after you have rested, and on reflection—"

"No!" My voice rang out in the empty hall. My nightmare was no sleeping dream, but real, so horribly real. "I was here yesterday, I tell you. And . . . and he . . . he went out for a walk."

I ran to the fireplace. "There was a fire here—and here a rug—and over here by the staircase, a chest." I wheeled. "And Daphne, all pink and white—she talked so much it fairly made my head ache." I was not making sense, but it seemed my tongue had a will apart from my brain. "Sir Ian," I went on, "Sir Ian said I was to go into Tenwyck and fetch you. 'He's an obliging soul,' that's what he said. Duncan is gone! He's vanished! Don't you believe me?"

Mr. Meacham wet his lips. "Yes, of course, my dear Mrs. Blackmore, of course I do. But how can we search for your—your husband when we don't know how or where to begin?"

Was I mad? Was my memory of Rommany, the people, the conversations, the maid, everything not a dream, but a distorted, impossible fancy?

I tried to say something, but words stuck in my throat. The men's faces began to swim in front of me, three pairs of eyes staring and staring. Why did they stare so? The room began to whirl, slowly at first, then faster and faster. I heard Mr. Meacham exclaim in surprise, from a thousand miles away, as darkness closed over me.

Chapter 7

The room was strange—not my room at Newberry, or the one I had shared with two other girls at school. It was a tiny room, a room I had never seen before, so small that the large old-fashioned bed I was lying in took up most of it. Against one wall stood a washstand and a cracked mirror and hanging next to it a sampler. TRUST IN GOD. There was a peg on the closed door from which hung a dress, its hem splattered with mud.

Through the diamond-paned window I could see a row of hollyhocks, their heads drooping under silver-sheeted rain, a walk, and a low wooden gate. The hollyhocks, the cracked mirror, the dress on the peg; none of these touched a single chord of memory.

Fear pinched my heart. "Mama?" I called tentatively. "Mama . . . ?"

The door opened and a short, stout woman wearing a floral print apron stood framed on the threshold. From behind her came the yeasty fragrance of newly baked bread. Cook? But this woman was much fatter than Cook at Newberry—she had three chins—and she was younger.

"Ah, so you've come round," the woman said in a cheerful voice. "You're quite all right. Not a thing in the world to worry about."

"I don't know where I am," I said, worried nevertheless. "Is this London?"

"No, my dear, Tenwyck. Don't fret—you're bound to be confused. You've had a bad shock."

Tenwyck. We were on our way to London. Mama, Papa, and I. Had Papa decided to lay over in Tenwyck on account of the rain? That must be it. We had taken rooms in some wayside inn.

"Now, you are to stay in bed," the stout woman said. She had clear blue eyes, kind eyes. "Doctor's orders, you know."

"Doctor's orders?" I echoed. Had something happened to me? Perhaps there had been an accident. Cautiously, I moved my legs under the blanket and then my arms. Nothing wrong there. A shock, the woman had said. "Are Papa and Mama all right?" I asked anxiously.

The woman blushed a deep pink, and moving her eyes quickly from mine, she gazed out the window for a moment before turning back to me. "They are fine," she said, "doing quite well."

"They are not here with me?"

"No, Mrs. Blackmore."

Mrs. Blackmore? My name was Eustacia O'Neill, *Miss* O'Neill. Why did she call me Mrs. Blackmore? It frightened me.

"I shall bring you some breakfast," she said. "Good food heals."

"No—wait, Mrs. . . . Mrs—"

"Mrs. Meacham," she supplied.

I wet my lips. "Can you tell me what day—the date, please?"

"November eleventh, eighteen sixty-nine."

She was mistaken; it couldn't be! "But . . . but we left Newberry for London in *March!*"

"Dear—oh, dear! I should not have told you."

"If this is November, then what has happened to the months between?"

"You will soon remember."

"Remember? Mrs. Meacham, you must tell me what has happened," I cried, raising myself, my heart knocking against my ribs.

"Now, now, you are not to excite yourself. Later we will figure it all out." She edged around between the bed and the window and, reaching over, plumped up my pillows. "You'll see," she said in a soothing voice. "In a day or two, you will have your strength back—and your memory."

She was kind, motherly, this Mrs. Meacham, but how

could she expect me to keep calm when I did not know where I was? Or even *who?*

"I promise you all will be well," she said, smoothing back a strand of my hair. "Would you like an egg for your breakfast?"

"I'm not hungry, thank you."

"Tsk, tsk," she clucked. "Dr. Jemson says you are to eat. I shall fix you a tray, in any case."

She went out, closing the door softly behind her. I tried to get out of bed, but found I was so weak that even sitting up was an effort. Tears stung my eyes as I sank back on the pillows. What was I to do? If only Mama were here! I wiped my nose with the sleeve of my nightdress (Mrs. Meacham's?) and stared at the sampler. TRUST IN GOD had been worked in blue and green cross-stitch against a white background. Perhaps I should take the message to heart?

In a few minutes Mrs. Meacham returned with a tray. She rearranged the pillows, then tucked a napkin under my chin. She smelled of wood smoke and new bread.

Comforted, I said, "I feel like a child again."

"Why, my dear," she replied, settling the tray on my lap, "you are hardly more than one now. There, you see, I've brought you an egg. And porridge, and here is fresh cream. Can you manage? Good. I shall be back shortly."

I ate slowly, deep in thought, trying to make sense out of my bizarre situation. Mrs. Blackmore. I pondered the name. Did it have a vaguely familiar ring? Apparently I had acquired a husband. Somewhere in the intervening lost months, I had married a Mr. Blackmore. Where? How? What did he look like? No face came to mind. And though I tried hard to remember, the elusive Mr. Blackmore remained a ghostly figure, faceless, unknown.

I slept on and off all that day. In the evening Mrs. Meacham brought me a supper tray, and her husband came in for a chat. He was a short big-bellied man who ostensibly knew my identity, but whose red face and shock of white hair stirred no recollection in me. He did say he was the constable of Tenwyck, but to all my other questions he replied, "We shall get to that in due time, Mrs. Blackmore. In due time."

I thought of asking him to write Mama and Papa, but

the "Mrs. Blackmore" troubled me. How could I explain? Suppose I had eloped—or done something even more disgraceful? No, I must wait and see.

I cried into my pillow that night, muffling my sobs so that the Meachams would not hear. It was frightening to suddenly find myself among strangers, no matter how kind, and to be told I had lost seven months of my life. Except for a year at Miss Dawson's School, I had never been away from home before, and now suddenly, for some reason, I had come to a place called Tenwyck, a town or village I had never heard of, bearing a name that was not my own.

I remained in bed all the next day, but by the second (or was it the third?) morning I was well enough to get dressed and Mrs. Meacham, who had cleaned the dress on the hook (mine, as it turned out), helped me into it. After breakfast we sat in the parlor, Mrs. Meacham with a basket of mending, I watching the rain; the picture, I hoped, of health and calm composure.

Finally, breaking a long silence, I said; "I think I am well able to endure whatever you have to tell me, Mrs. Meacham. I shall never remember anything unless I know what happened."

"Quite right," Mrs. Meacham agreed. She bit the thread from her needle. "But there isn't too much I know either. Does the name Rommany mean anything to you?"

"No," I shook my head.

She took a deep breath like one about to plunge into a cold bath. "You came to the door three nights ago, saying you were from Rommany, that you and your husband were visiting the Blackmores—Sir Ian and Lady Violet—there."

"The Blackmores? Relatives of my . . . my husband?"

"Apparently."

"Who brought me?"

She sighed. "My husband let you in. He said he saw a trap disappear down the street, but he did not know who was in it."

"So I arrived in a trap and I was let out on the doorstep?"

"Yes. That is what we guessed. You were quite distraught. You said your husband had gone for a walk early

54

that morning and hadn't been seen since. And you wanted the constable to assist in a search."

My eyes went to the window where the rain tapped and ran in haphazard crystal streams down the glass. "Then it would be quite simple," I said. "We could go back to Rommany. They must know me there—if you say I was visiting. And perhaps seeing the Blackmores—Rommany might serve to restore my memory."

Mrs. Meacham's head bent over the sock she was mending. Her chins quivered and her lips moved as though she was struggling for words.

"Don't you think that a reasonable suggestion?" I added, growing uneasy.

"My dear," she said, raising blue eyes full of tenderness, "don't you remember how you went back with the constable and the farm people? No one has lived at Rommany for a long time."

Fear, cold as ice, formed a knot under my heart. "No ... no," I said numbly. "How could I speak of a house where no one lives. Mrs. Meacham, please—what has happened to me?"

"Now there," she soothed. "It's too soon. Dr. Jemson warned us."

"This ... this Dr. Jemson," I said, grasping at his name, "what does he say about me?"

"He says the harder you *try* to remember, the more difficult you will make it for yourself. Someone with a delicate constitution like yours."

Delicate constitution?" I had had a few of the usual childhood diseases and a headache from time to time, but I could not remember our own doctor ever describing me as "delicate." Could Dr. Jemson have used that term to mean something else? Mental instability, for instance?

"Shall I get to see this Dr. Jemson soon?" I asked, terribly worried.

"Yes, my dear. He has promised to look in at the end of the week."

The end of the week came and went. Dr. Jemson sent word that he had been summoned to attend his dying mother in Colchester and would call as soon as he returned I had grown quite fearful of what the doctor might tell me, and now I kept hoping and hoping my lost seven months would come back so that I would not need his medical opinion.

The weather cleared and a wintry sun shone upon the rain-drenched garden. One day passed into another. The Meachams continued to be patient and charitable. They watched over me as if I were their own, and I tried not to distress them. When they objected to my walking out alone, I promised to leave the house only in Mrs. Meacham's company. She was afraid, she explained, that on one of my solitary walks my memory might suddenly descend upon me and the shock prove too much. Inwardly I chafed. I could not stay at the Meachams forever. No matter how kind they were, I knew I must be a burden. I was an extra mouth to feed in a household that was far from affluent. Though I tried to be of some assistance to Mrs. Meacham, I was as ineffectual in the kitchen as I was dusting the parlor—more hindrance than help.

One Saturday, an hour before lunch, I sat down to write to my parents. I got as far as, "Dear Mama and Papa," and then held the pen poised above the blank, staring page. I did not know what to say or even how to begin. The same doubts which had assailed me before when I had thought of writing my parents troubled me now. Had we quarreled? The tenuous uneasy feeling that in some way I had displeased them kept recurring. How had I done so? Had they ordered me to leave Newberry? And why had I supposedly claimed I had been visiting the house called Rommany when it had long been uninhabited? Perhaps, I thought, the best thing was to tell my parents the truth, exactly as it had been told to me, and ask their forgiveness for whatever wrong I had done them.

I had started to write again, when it suddenly occurred to me that perhaps the elusive Blackmores (my phantom husband as well) could throw some light on my predicament. I left my pen and paper in the parlor and went through the short passage and knocked on the door of the room Mr. Meacham called his office.

"It's Eustacia," I said. Earlier I had asked both the Meachams to use my Christian name. It disturbed me to be called Mrs. Blackmore.

"Come in, my dear."

It was the first time I had entered the constable's inner

sanctum, and I apologized. "I hope you will forgive me for interrupting."

"Of course, my dear. Sit down, sit down." He indicated a chair.

The room like all the rooms in the house was small, but this one was exceedingly messy. Crammed with papers and books which overflowed from the shelves on to the floor, it was apparently a room declared out-of-bounds to Mrs. Meacham's tidying broom and dustcloth.

"Well, now, what can I do for you?" Mr. Meacham inquired, leaning back in his chair with his hands clasped across his stomach.

"I was thinking if we could get in touch with the Blackmores, perhaps they could help me to fill in the gap."

He cleared his throat. "Yes, yes. Well—I ... I had hoped you would not ask that."

My fingers tightened on the arms of the chair. "Why—why not?"

"Well, you see, my dear, I did write—oh, it must have been the second day you were here. I wrote to that lawyer chap in London, the one who sees to collecting the Blackmore rents."

"And—what did he say?"

"The Blackmores had gone abroad, so his letter claimed. I have it here, if you wish to see it." He rummaged among the papers, upsetting his inkwell. Fortunately it was nearly dry, and together we managed to blot up the inkstains from a pamphlet on animal husbandry. "It will turn up, I expect," the constable said, mopping his face with a handkerchief. "But I remember pretty much of it. The Blackmores, the lawyer wrote, have been out of England for the last six months."

"And me—did the lawyer know me?"

The constable shook his head. "He had never heard of a Eustacia Blackmore."

I wanted to cry. I could feel hot tears burning against my eyeballs. Lost, lost—some part of me was lost. Eustacia O'Neill was there, sitting in a chair in the constable's house in Tenwyck. But where was Eustacia Blackmore? *Who* was she?

Mr. Meacham did not speak. He sat in his chair, frowning down at his hands. An ornate, brass framed clock on the mantle ticked away in the silence.

"He—he must be mistaken," I said, at last, struggling with my voice.

The constable shook his head sadly. "I hardly think so, my dear."

"But how would I know the Blackmores—Rommany?"

"I don't mean to be contrary, but. . . ."

He was interrupted by Mrs. Meacham's appearance at the door. "I thought I heard voices, Clem."

At that precise moment the clock whirred and struck the half hour, a single brassy note.

And then it happened, what I had longed for in theory and feared in reality—a sudden, sickening sensation of falling, of plummeting through time. *I had been here before, in this very room, had heard the clock strike, seen the cluttered desk, the faces—I knew them!*

I hung on to the arms of the chair as my head spun— Rommany, the Blackmores, the empty, dust-filled drawing room, a kaleidoscope of pictures whirling round and round, and through it all I heard myself exclaim: "Duncan!"

I did not faint dead away as I had the last time, though I wished I could blot it all out again. The horror, the weird unreality of my return to Rommany, the mens' eyes staring at me. And Duncan. If he were alive, surely I should have heard from him by now?

"Duncan," I repeated, begging the constable for an answer, for assurance, for anything.

"My dear, your memory's returned. The shock—"

Mrs. Meacham, who had scuttled off at my first exclamation, returned with a small glass of brandy which she insisted I drink before another word was spoken. I coughed and spluttered as the liquor coursed down my throat, but it steadied me enough so that I could speak in a fairly coherent fashion.

"How—how long have I been here?" I asked.

"There, there, don't trouble yourself," Mrs. Meacham said.

"No, no. I'm quite all right. I *must* know."

"You have been here two weeks," said the constable.

"Two weeks!" I rose to my feet. "I . . . we must leave immediately to search for my husband." Neither of them spoke. I looked from the constable's florid face to his wife's dimpled one. Both reflected a compassion and sympathy which recalled only too painfully my experience in Rommany's great hall.

"He's dead," I said, trembling. "Duncan is dead and you do not want to tell me."

"Eustacia, my dear," the constable's wife said, "you are not to upset yourself. We know nothing of your husband. We have not seen nor heard from him."

I stared at them for a long moment and then burst into tears.

"Oh, you poor darling," Mrs. Meacham comforted, taking me by the arm. "Perhaps you ought to lie down."

Aware of her distress as she led me from the room, I tried to control my sobbing, but could not. She helped me out of my dress and tucked me into bed. I was still weeping when she drew the curtains and quietly let herself out of the room.

Hours later, I awoke on a pillow damp with tears to the sound of voices and the clink of china. Mr. and Mrs. Meacham were taking tea in the parlor, a room which adjoined my own. I tried not to listen, but their conversation could be heard so plainly—and they were discussing me.

"We must make an attempt to get in touch with the parents," I heard Mrs. Meacham say.

"Yes, my dear," her husband agreed. "But I'm at a loss as to where to find them, and once having done so, what am I to say?"

There was a small silence, interrupted by a muffled belch. Mrs. Meacham said; "I find it hard to believe she invented a story. Such a well-bred young lady."

"What other explanation is there?" Again the muffled belch. "A houseful of furniture, people disappearing into thin air, no sign of anyone having lived there in years."

"But why?" Mrs. Meacham asked. "Why should that lovely child do such a thing? She seems mentally sound enough, and Dr. Jemson says"—here she lowered her voice—"she's not in the family way."

I felt my face go hot and shrank into the pillows, not

wanting to hear any more but compelled, it seemed, against my will to listen.

". . . I've given it some thought these past two weeks," Mr. Meacham was saying. "Quite a lot of thought, in fact. My theory is that Mrs. Blackmore has been deserted by a dastardly brute of a husband. She's a sensitive creature—there's no doubt there—and I reckon she was unable to face her friends, her relatives with the truth, so she came to Tenwyck and made up the story we've heard."

"But her loss of memory!"

"Oh, I think *that* was real. As I said, Eustacia is a sensitive creature, and it is my belief that the enormity of what had happened—she's too young to have been married long—combined with the necessity of acting out her falsehood was more than she could bear."

"Ah." A deep sigh from Mrs. Meacham. "The poor dear." The cups rattled. "More tea, Clem?"

Trembling, I turned my face into the pillow and pulled the blanket up over my head. Never in my life had I felt so alone, so miserable, and so afraid. My troubled mind, sifting over the Meachams' conversation, picked out one nugget and latched upon it. Rommany seemed less important for the moment than Clem Meacham's appalling theory that Duncan had deserted me.

Appalling—but was it that remote from possibility?

I remembered all too well how disinterested, how bored Duncan had become prior to Sir Ian's invitation. Of course, I had attributed it to his brooding over John Hempstead's brutal, unsolved murder. But suppose that was only part of the reason? Duncan was a man who had been constantly on the move, living a life of exciting change and adventure for at least ten years before he met me. He had never finished his studies at Cambridge, he once told me, because the academic routine had become too tiresome. Had he felt the same about domestic life, our marriage?

And there was the half-caste—lovely sloe-eyed Carla—her very image evocative of temple incense and fragrant spices, of exotic jungle-fringed rivers, of white beaches on the shores of strange seas. Even as I wept, were they now together? I pictured the girl in Duncan's embrace, his brown head bent to her dark one, her eyes, those eloquent eyes filled with love and desire, and my heart twisted in an agony of pain.

Hadn't Mama warned me? "You are to make the best of your marriage," she had said, "though things may not turn out as you wish."

I could not write to her now. I was too ashamed. Whatever I had to do, I must do alone.

Chapter 8

I slept fitfully that night, waking from confused dreams at frequent intervals. Lying in the dark during one such long spell, my mind went over the weeks and months from the day I first met Duncan until blackness had descended upon me at Rommany. Out of the painful muddle milling about in my head, one thing became clear: I loved Duncan—still—I would always love him. And I believed with all my heart that no matter what he felt now, he had once loved me too.

From that thought I gathered strength and when I rose the following morning I seemed to be a different person from the girl who had wept herself to sleep the night before. I had a definite goal now: I must find Duncan. I would not give him up so easily—to the half-caste girl or to anyone else. As long as there was breath in me, I was determined to fight. I refused to contemplate the possibility of Duncan's death.

The Meachams were at the breakfast table when I made my appearance. "My dear," Mrs. Meacham said, surprised, "should you be out of bed?"

"I'm fully recovered. Truly." I smiled. "I've had my cry and I—I think I've come to grips with myself."

"Splendid!" the constable beamed.

"You *are* looking much better," Mrs. Meacham said. "Your color has improved and I hope your appetite has done as well. There are fresh eggs this morning."

We had nearly finished breakfast when I spoke. "I've been thinking a great deal about my situation. I cannot go on staying here." There were murmurs of protest. "No, really. I feel the first thing I must do is to make an attempt to locate my husband."

Neither of them looked at me. Mr. Meacham had found a spot on his waistcoat and, using his napkin, began to rub at it briskly. Mrs. Meacham sat, lips pursed, studying the bottom of her teacup. They were thinking, I suppose, that I was still clinging to the fantasy of a lost spouse.

I went on. "It seems to me that I should return to Rommany."

Almost simultaneously they both looked up and fixed me with their eyes.

"If—if I could return there I might find some clue, something which might help solve the whole mystery," I concluded in a voice that was far less assertive than the one which had begun my little speech.

"But, my dear," Mrs. Meacham said, shocked. "There is no one *there*. You, yourself, saw that."

"I realize there is no one there," I said, swallowing the threatening break in my voice. They were looking at me with that pitying expression again. "But we only gave the house a cursory examination. And I know that Sir Ian and Lady Violet were at the house. . . ." My voice trailed off.

Mr. Meacham said, "We can't permit you to go through that terrible experience again, my dear. Dr. Jemson would be most unhappy with us."

"Indeed," his wife nodded in agreement.

The constable dabbed at his chin. "Bess and I have been discussing the situation and have come to the conclusion that the best policy is to communicate with your parents. If you find doing so too painful, Eustacia, I shall be happy to write a letter for you."

Of course I had no intention of letting my parents know of my predicament. "You are quite right. I shall start a letter today," I said, blushing because the lie came so easily. But the Meachams seemed unaware of my guilty flush.

"That's a sensible idea," the constable heartily approved. "Best to forget this business of Rommany."

The constable and his wife were honest folk with the kindest intentions for my welfare. I could not blame them if they found me a worry, a bit "mental." Last night's tears had probably confirmed their opinion that I suffered from *hysteria,* an aberrant fixed fantasy of an occupied Rommany and a disappearing husband. And I knew it was futile to try and coax the constable into taking me to Rommany. I must make the effort on my own.

I was faced with several problems. First, since the Meacham's frowned on my walking out alone, I had to find a way to elude them. Second, I hadn't the slightest notion of how to get to Rommany. It was five or six miles from Tenwyck, I remembered Sir Ian saying, and going on foot seemed hardly feasible.

Surprisingly, the first difficulty was overcome that very afternoon. The Guild ladies of the chapel, taking turns, had scheduled their meeting for Mrs. Meacham's parlor. They arrived at two o'clock with their sewing baskets and curiosity written on their faces. Apparently they had all heard of me (gossip being what it is, whether in Tenwyck or London), and I could well imagine how I had been the object of much talk—the girl who was "not quite right in the head." But the bold scrutiny of some and the sidelong glances of others did not disturb me. My main concern was the question—how to get back to Rommany?

I declined Mrs. Meacham's invitation to join them in the parlor, pleading a headache. There was a commiserating murmur, but on the whole I had the impression that my announcement was met with a collective sigh of relief. All to the good. They would be busy discussing me over the altar cloth well after tea time and I had the entire afternoon to myself.

I got into my cloak and slipped out the back door. Luckily, I had a pound note in my purse, and with it I thought to hire a conveyance. Surely there was a livery stable in Tenwyck.

I walked quickly along the street, keeping to the shadows and stopped the first person I met to ask directions—a small boy floating a paper boat in a ditch.

"If it's a horse you want, miss," he said, "me bruvver has one for hire."

"No . . . I. . . ." And then it occurred to me how much simpler it would be to go on horseback. The liveryman might ask embarrassing questions or perhaps he might have heard of me and would go running back to the constable's house with the news that the "crazy Mrs. Blackmore" was on the loose.

"May I see the horse?" I asked.

He led me to a small cottage on the far side of the village green. The horse was a rough-coated, sturdy mare, nothing like my beautiful Sissy at Newberry, but she would do very well. I had only the pound note and the small boy's brother—his name was Teddy, I remember—balked at it. "I got no change, ma'am," he said.

"Never mind. Keep it on credit. I might want the horse again tomorrow."

Together the children helped me mount, a rather awkward procedure since the horse was not equipped with sidesaddle, but I managed to get astride and settled, pulling my skirts decorously about my limbs.

"Can you tell me how to get to Rommany?" I asked.

Both of the boys looked blank.

"Rommany," I repeated, "the large manor house."

"The one that's haunted, miss?"

They looked so solemn, I smiled. "Yes."

"It's beyond Tanner's Pond." Teddy pointed. "Foller the road 'til you come to a wood. The lane is a mile beyond that."

By the time I reached the pond, massive storm clouds had gathered on the western horizon. The landscape was bathed in a livid gray-purple light, the air hushed and oppressive. I thought briefly of turning back, but I had come so far without mishap, and I did not know when I would have another opportunity to slip away.

Except for a farmer in a cart, who looked at me with curiosity, I met no one. Mile merged into mile as the sky overhead grew darker. Just as I was beginning to wonder if I had misunderstood the directions, the wood the boy had described came into sight. After I had passed it my eyes began to search for Rommany Lane. Five minutes later, I recognized the white-barked birches rising above the entrance to the lane.

I turned the horse in and far ahead perceived the familiar long avenue of dark cypress trees. The path was puddled with water, and the horse splashed mud on my skirts. My hands gripped the reins, slowing the mare, not so much because I was fastidious, but because once again I felt a strange reluctance to look upon Rommany.

I rode under the arch, following the curve of the weed-choked drive. And then—once more—I was there, face to face with Rommany. Rearing itself in ruined grandeur, it appeared more abandoned and desolate under the frowning sky than I had remembered it.

For one heart-catching moment, I had the impulse to turn my mount and gallop away, to flee from the ravished, rank garden, the sight of the blackened chimneys, those windows like gaping eyes. But the thought of slinking back to the Meachams, still puzzled, still in the dark, urged me on and I rode to the entrance, slipped from the saddle and tethered the mare to a post.

The front door was locked, Clem Meacham having fastened it, I suppose, when we left. The door at the back, surprisingly, was locked too. Thwarted, I forgot my uneasiness in my determination to enter the house. It annoyed me to think I had come this far only to be balked by a lock. I began to walk slowly around the house, looking for another door, a window, anything by which I might gain entrance.

Overhead the clouds quickened, increasing my sense of urgency.

After circling the house twice, I discovered a gap in a window. The shutter had come loose and the glass had been broken. Gathering my skirts I hoisted myself up and climbed through, the jagged glass tearing at my hood. A moment later, I found myself in the drawing room. There was the gray-sheeted mound in the center, the cobwebbed cornices, the blackened fireplace.

I stood there, looking around, a little disappointed, for in the back of my mind, I suppose, I had foolishly still hoped that this vacant Rommany had been an illusion, that I had only to return and it would be like my first visit when Lady Violet, rising from the gilt-scrolled sofa, had walked across the carpet to greet me. The light slanting through the chinked shutters and broken window was dim, and at each moment growing dimmer, but it was enough to give the room an air of harsh reality. Outside a wind had come up. I could hear a shutter banging upstairs, each hollow thud echoing eerily in the empty house.

I went out into the great hall. The staircase led up into shadows; the dusty floor was crosscrossed with footprints, those left by Constable Meacham and the two men.

I thought the kitchen might be the most logical place to begin my search. Though my knowledge of such utilitarian rooms was minimal, it seemed to me that a place where one prepared food would be the last to lose trace of its inhabitants.

I found it finally, after blundering about and trying several doors, a sooty high-ceilinged room with a greasy black stove, a butcher's block, a table and several broken chairs. A hinged door hung loose from a bare cupboard. Nothing here, I thought.

Nevertheless I began to search through the cupboards and was soon rewarded by two finds; a half-full brandy bottle, dustless, the cork fresh, and a maid's cap similar to the one Carla had worn.

I left the kitchen and began to inspect the other rooms. The long, heavy table in the dining room appeared familiar but I could not tell whether it was the same one we had dined on, since at the time it had been covered with a fine damask cloth. Another immense room (probably used for formal state occasions), the walls covered with faded painted murals, was bare of furniture.

I came out into the great hall again. And running my hand idly over the dusty mantel above the fireplace I made a curious discovery. The cobwebs were false! They were not gossamer spider's webs, but cleverly contrived imitations of coarse thread—sheep's wool, perhaps.

A maid's cap, a half bottle of brandy, and cobwebs that were not cobwebs. What did it mean?

The hall had grown darker as I stood there but I was too heady with success to feel uneasy. More evidence, I thought, and I would have a stronger case to present to Constable Meacham.

Mounting the stairs, I began to go from room to room. In the third room I found a beaded purse and a mug with the dregs of tea leaves not yet turned to mold. In another room I came upon a razor just beginning to show rust. I had gathered these items in my shawl as I went along, and looking at them now, I wondered how the constable could possibly deny Rommany's recent occupancy. Still, my assorted "clues" did not explain what had happened to the Blackmores or to Duncan.

I shivered. How much darker it had suddenly grown!

A sudden clap of thunder overhead startled me. I ran to the window at the end of the corridor, forced the shutter open and looked out. The sky was a boiling mass of moving dark clouds. Lightning flickered like adders' tongues as the thunder rumbled and rolled across the sullen sky, and I was dismayed to see that my horse was no longer tied to the post. She must have broken loose and wandered off. I closed the window, whipped the ends of my shawl together, and went quickly down the stairs.

The front door had several bolts, all stiff and rusted, and when I finally managed to draw them back, the door still refused to open. I twisted the knob, pulling, rattling, tugging at it until my fingers ached and the veins stood out on my forehead. The door was locked, had been locked with a key. But by whom? Mr. Meacham? I did not recall his having used a key. But then there had been so many things I could not recall clearly. My memory had become a tricky thing, and thinking of how I had lost it so completely the last time I stood in the great hall, my apprehension grew. What if I should faint now?

With a fast-beating heart, still clutching my bundled shawl, I hurried back to the kitchen, only to find the door there fastened in the same way. *Both doors had been bolted from the inside!*

Thunder cracked and boomed, shaking the walls as I scurried like a frightened rabbit across the vast hall, heading for the broken window I had used to gain entrance to Rommany. The drawing room was quite dark now; stumbling over the mound in the center of the room, I made my way to the opposite wall and began to search for the broken window. Incredibly, unbelievably, I could not find it!

I made the rounds more slowly this time, feeling each window with my hands. And then I came upon a place where the glass had given way to smooth board. Blindly, my fingers groped across the wood.

No gap, no hole, nothing!

Had I missed the right window in my haste? Again I moved from casement to casement. The windows on the ground floor, unlike those above, were shuttered on the outside. I thought that if I could manage to pull a window open then perhaps I could unhook the shutters. But the windows, locked or stuck, were impossible to budge. And still I could not find the opening through which I had climbed.

How could that be?

Confused, disoriented, I stared about me at the paneled walls pulsating in eerie light, the yawning fireplace, the dusty floor. Had I the wrong room? Outside I heard the first onrush of rain, drumming against the shutters.

Still clutching my shawl-wrapped bundle, I fled into the hall. The windows here were high ones, beyond my reach. I turned and ran through the first door on my left, into the mural-painted room. Guided by occasional flashes of lightning I tried each window. And all, *all* were nailed shut!

Frantic now, I dropped the shawl and dashed into another room. There I met with identical, insane resistance. And the same thing happened in the next room and the next. I cannot remember how many shuttered windows I clawed at, how many times I thought: this one or this one or *surely* this one will open. But none of them did; there was not one narrow chink, not one small hole through which I could hope to squeeze.

My hair had come loose, streaming past my shoulders; my face felt gritty with cobwebs and dust and two of my fingers had begun to bleed. But far worse than physical discomfort was the suffocating sensation of being trapped like some desperate half-mad animal.

Fleeing back to the front door I began to jerk and tug at the stubborn knob. Something, someone had imprisoned me in this terrible house. Or was it the house itself? Diabolical Rommany, mysteriously changing from warm charm to ugly menace in the space of twenty-four hours. And in my desperate mind, the house took on the fairytale horror of a grotesque, soulless ogre bent on devouring me alive.

The last remnants of self control vanished and I began to scream, "Help! Somebody, help! Help!" And then I threw myself against the door.

I think it was my head hitting the panel and the subsequent sharp, jarring pain which brought me to a semblance of sanity. Sinking to the floor, I covered my face with my hands and tried to bring my panic under control.

I had been locked in, by whom I did not know. It was terribly cold and I thought of the half-filled bottle of brandy in my shawl. But I could not bring myself to go back through the empty, night shrouded rooms and search for it. Shivering, I pulled my cloak closer about me and leaned against the wall. The Meachams would miss me, if they had not already done so, and logic would lead them to the conclusion that I had gone to Rommany. Perhaps even now the constable was on his way.

Suddenly, without warning, a piercing, hollow shriek rang through the hall. I sat straight up, rigid with fear. The scream came again, horrible, unearthly, raising the hairs on the nape of my neck. It went on and on. Terrified, I put my hands over my ears to shut the sound out. But it didn't help. I kept hearing it—a demented howl issuing from the very depths of hell. It went on, above and around me, throttling the breath in my lungs, clogging the blood in my veins. Unbearable.

"Stop it! Stop it!" my voice tore at my throat. "Stop it, or I shall go mad!"

And then—as suddenly as it had begun—the sound ceased. I let go of my ears. The silence was absolute. My teetering mind groped for a reasonable interpretation. Had the scream been the cry of an animal, a mouse, perhaps, caught in the talons of a predatory owl? A rabbit in a trap? A stray cat? A cat. Yes, yes, I told myself, that was it.

But even as I huddled there, reassuring myself, I heard a chuckle of amusement close by, a soft, insidious trickle of mocking laughter. It rose, higher and higher, climbing a scale of insanity, wilder and wilder, until the sound of shrieking mirth filled the hall.

Crouching there on the floor, trembling, shaking, quivering, I knew that only a fine, thin thread of sanity held me from dissolving into blithering nothingness. One moment, any moment I should go plunging over into darkness.

And then, through the chaos of my horror, I was suddenly aware that the maniacal laughter had broken off. In its place there now was a weird, uncanny silence, a black, swelling, ominous silence. My senses dimly perceived the sound of falling rain pattering at the windows, a far, far-away growl of thunder. Lightning flicked through the hall, illuminating it briefly.

A sound turned my head. There was a shadow standing near the fireplace, a white shadow. Lightning came again, and the shadow began to flow, diaphanous, wraithlike.

A choked cry came from my throat as the phantom stretched long arms toward me. I found myself shrinking back, back, wanting to disappear, to faint, to die.

"Go away!" Was that strangled whisper my voice? "Go away!"

The phantom continued to move—slowly, deliberately making its way across the hall toward me.

"Go away!" I screamed. "Go away!"

The ghost turned and moved silently in the direction of the staircase. I watched as it began to ascend slowly, watched with unbelieving, distended eyes.

Suddenly, the phantom stumbled. Stumbled!

Lightning fanned the vast hall and in the brief moment before it subsided the "phantom's" hood slipped, revealing a woman's blonde head—blonde hair and a white, pretty face. A face I knew.

Daphne!

Chapter 9

My eyes strained through the darkness at the luminous white figure now poised on the staircase. A curse in unmistakable cockney floated down the stairs. A half second later, lightning flicked at the staircase and I saw a white arm reach up to adjust a hood.

I was on my feet. "Daphne!"

The figure began to move upward. Had I been the butt of a game, a joke, a cruel trick played by a silly girl, a masquerade which had brought me to the edge of madness? Angry, furious, I picked up my skirts and raced across the hall and up the stairs.

"Daphne!"

Ahead of me, the figure stumbled again, then quickly recovered and ran up and up into the shadows, I in hot pursuit. When I reached the landing, I heard Daphne cursing as she ran along the corridor. Except for brief, feeble flashes of light coming through a slatted shutter, the passage was ominously dark. But I did not hesitate. Gathering my skirts more firmly I followed.

I was gaining on her; I could hear her panting and the swish of her garments. Suddenly the corridor made a sharp turn and I would have run pell-mell into a solid wall had not a momentary glimmer of lightning revealed the way. Daphne, I thought, gritting my teeth, knows the twists and turns of Rommany well. Again I would have missed her, if I had not paused for a moment to listen. She was climbing. I could hear footsteps and her breath, heavy and gasping now.

With arms outstretched, like a child playing blindman's

buff, I advanced cautiously, feeling for the staircase and stubbing my toes on the bottom of it.

I grasped the rail to steady myself and began to ascend. The staircase was steep and narrow and as I hurried my footsteps clattered on the uncarpeted boards. Straight up it went without a break and by the time I reached a landing the breath was whistling in my throat. But I dared not stop. I could not lose Daphne. If she escaped me now, I should never really know whether all that I had seen and heard had been planned or had been an illusion of a sick mind.

A round stained-glass window glowed momentarily in blood crimson and deep blue. There was another staircase; I could hear Daphne toiling up it.

"Daphne!" I shouted. "Daphne!"

I moved quickly, guided by my hand slipping along the wall. The flight of stairs, like the last, was steep and narrow. And dark. I felt as if I had been climbing forever; my legs ached cruelly; my labored breath came in sobs; a stitch grew in my side. Finally, when I thought I could go no further, the staircase came to an end.

As I stood there, panting, a door suddenly opened. A square of light—and Daphne, clearly outlined in a white shapeless robe went through, closing the door behind her.

I staggered the few steps to the door, found the knob, and flung the door wide.

Astonished, I gazed at the frozen tableau before me.

Daphne was clinging to the back of a chair on which Maurice Peale sat. Across from him at a crude wooden table were Sir Ian and Lady Violet. They all stared at me—even Daphne—my own shock mirrored on their faces. Nobody spoke. The only sound in the room was Daphne's heavy breathing and mine.

Finally Sir Ian broke the silence. "You are a blundering fool," he said to Daphne.

"'Twasn't my fault," she whined, holding up her trailing garments. "This bloody robe. . . ."

Maurice patted his wife's hand. "It's all right, love."

"It *isn't* all right," Sir Ian said, then sighed heavily as Daphne began to whimper. "No use going on about it, I suppose."

Swept up in an overwhelming sense of relief, I scarcely

heard their conversation. I wanted to laugh, to dance, to cry. *I was sane.* Daphne's ghostly disguise, the strange change in the house, the disappearance of the Blackmores seemed of little consequence at the moment. I only felt happy, light-headed, delivered suddenly, absolutely from the thin edge of disaster. I had not invented Sir Ian and Lady Violet. They were real. *Real!* There was nothing wrong with my mind. I, Eustacia Blackmore, was *sane!*

I brushed back my hair and smiled.

"Eustacia, my dear," Sir Ian said, "your return to Rommany was a grave error."

"Ah, but you don't know how glad I am to see you. I—"

"You should have remained where you were," Sir Ian said sternly. "Now you pose a problem, a very serious one for us all."

Lady Violet's eyes glittered with hate.

"What sort of problem?" I asked, my euphoria dropping from me like a stone. "Why are you here in this room? What has happened? What has become of all the furniture, the servants?" The questions poured from my lips. I could not ask them fast enough. "Why was Daphne dressed as a ghost? And Duncan—where is *he?*"

Maurice Peale cleared his throat. "I think the less you know the better."

"But I must know!" I exclaimed angrily. "I have every right to know! Do you realize what I've been through? Why—"

Maurice started to speak again, but Sir Ian raised a restraining hand. "I think Eustacia is right. Now that she has found us, I can't see what difference it would make. Isn't that so, Maurice?

"Do as you like," Maurice shrugged.

Lady Violet disagreed. "I, for one, think it would be foolish."

"How so," Sir Ian asked, "when our dear cousin already is aware of our presence."

Lady Violet pressed her lips together and said nothing.

Sir Ian got to his feet. "Here, Eustacia, there's no sense in standing. Take my chair."

"Thank you." The room was small and the pitch of the ceiling made me guess it was just under the eaves.

"A real gentleman," Lady Violet remarked dryly.

Daphne, now sitting on her husband's knee, tittered and was quelled by a look from her ladyship.

"Would you care for some brandy, Eustacia?" Sir Ian asked, reaching for a bottle similar to the one I had found in the cupboard.

"No, thank you."

He dashed some liquor into a mug. "Violet?"

She shook her head. "No more for me. And I'd say you've had enough, too."

Sir Ian's flushed face turned a deeper color. "Keeps the chill out," he said in a tight voice. He filled another mug and gave it to Maurice. "You can get out of that silly garment now, Daphne. And Violet—why don't you go along and help her?"

"Whatever for?" Violet asked, eyeing him suspiciously.

Sir Ian laughed, a loud half-tipsy laugh which I found rather unpleasant. "Come now, Violet, I shan't devour Eustacia. Maurice will see to that—eh, Maurice?"

When Daphne and Lady Violet had gone, Sir Ian settled back in his chair. He sipped at his brandy, watching me from under heavy lids.

"Well then," I said, irritated by his continued scrutiny. "What have you to say? Where is Duncan?"

"I shall answer all your questions," he said, "if you answer mine. Where is the map?"

"What map?" I asked, my voice trembling with annoyance. "Why are you talking nonsense?"

Sir Ian twirled the brandy in his mug. "You don't remember our discussion of diamonds at dinner the night you came?"

"That?" I retorted. "You heard my husband. He only *guessed* there were diamonds."

"So he claims, but I thought perhaps he was joking."

"There is no map," I said, growing more exasperated. "What has become of Duncan? Has he had an accident?"

"No, he is quite well."

"Then why can't you tell me where he is? Has he gone back to London?"

"My dear." A heavy sigh. "I will explain the entire situation. But it will make no sense unless I start from the beginning."

"Must you? Very well, then," I said, outwardly resigned, but inwardly disturbed. Why was he putting me off? Was he merely trying to divert me from some horrible truth?

Sir Ian took a long pull at the mug. "When my father died," he began rather pompously, "he left me a title, this house and a fair-sized income. I wasn't a rich man, which was a pity, since I have a rich man's tastes. Good wines, good food, the best of tailors and elegant surroundings. I like to live well—no crime, that. I was trained to be a gentleman, and a gentleman, unfortunately, must have money. I enjoy gambling, and at one time I had quite a flair for it. But somehow my luck changed." He poured himself another mug of brandy. "Lady Luck—elusive Lady Luck." He raised his mug to Maurice who raised his in return. "My debts became so impossible the only thing left for me to do was to marry an heiress. Hence Violet."

I was shocked—not because Sir Ian had been forced to marry an heiress; it was common practice among impoverished nobility—but because he had openly admitted it. No *real* gentleman would have breached the etiquette of silence on such a matter.

"She comes of good family, so I did not marry beneath myself. And she is still an attractive woman." He sighed and drank again. "I thought I would do better by switching from cards to horses. And to make a long story short, I am sorry to say, Violet's money went, too."

"But," I interjected, suddenly remembering, "I was given to understand that you had made quite a bit of money in wool."

"Wool? Oh, that. An invention, my dear. I wish to God I had!"

"And your plans for the estate, for Rommany, was that an invention, too?"

He drained his mug and splashed more brandy into it. "Farming is not my suit."

I studied him, his face red with brandy, his speech beginning to slur; a drinker, a gambler, a contemptible liar. Why would Violet be so possessive of him? Why should she want him at all?

"Violet does not mind," he said, as if reading my thoughts. "She loves me. Good, loyal woman—Violet. Eh, Maurice?"

"Yes, her ladyship is all that," Maurice agreed.

Sir Ian lifted the mug to his lips. "Where was I? Oh, yes. All the money gone. You have no idea what it's like to have empty pockets, credit not worth a farthing, and moneylenders pounding on the door. Maurice, here, was not as vulgar as the others, though I owed him the most, eh, Maurice?"

Maurice smiled.

I understood now why Maurice and Daphne had been invited to Rommany, why they were on such intimate terms with the Blackmores. Maurice was a usurer, and Sir Ian was in his debt.

But Sir Ian was saying, "Things were going from bad to worse. Even Maurice, good friend that he was, couldn't go on extending me credit. And then some of the fools who had lent me a few pounds threatened to have me thrown in gaol. I was nearly at my wit's end when quite by chance I met your dear husband at the club."

"Duncan!" I exclaimed. "You promised to tell me—"

"We shall get to Duncan in due course. Maurice, I believe there is a fresh bottle of brandy under the bed."

Maurice got down on his knees and drew out the bottle.

"Fine, fine," said Sir Ian, rubbing his hands. "Violet gets disturbed if I have more than one bottle at a sitting. Break it open, will you, Maurice? There's a good chap. And hide the empty one."

Maurice did as he was asked. After Sir Ian had poured himself another brandy, he continued. "We were drinking together that night, Duncan and I. And in our ramblings—"

"I remember now," I interrupted. "*That* was when you told Duncan about the Scottish wool."

Sir Ian threw back his head and laughed, that same silly, sickening laugh. "I had to say something," he said, rubbing the tears from his eyes. "Your husband was such a braggart. That's why I didn't believe the story of a diamond site, at first. But later I got to thinking about it. I made several discreet inquiries and discovered that diamonds were indeed being mined close to that area. But by that time you and Duncan had gone on your honeymoon."

"Duncan never claimed he had *seen* diamonds," I reminded him again.

"But he thought they might be there. And that is good enough for me. So I went round to see John Hempstead and offered to buy his map. He said it was not for sale. Foolish man." He put the mug to his lips.

Stunned, I stared at him, his cravat awry, the bottle of brandy at his elbow, his eyes half-glazed with drink—stared at him while a light slowly dawned in my brain. "You killed him," I said, feeling cold and sick. "You killed John Hempstead!"

"I did nothing of the sort."

"You murdered him because he would not sell you the map."

Maurice Peale clucked his tongue. "Now, now, young lady. It's bad politics to go about accusing a man of murder. I shouldn't do that if I were you." There was a subtle hint of threat in his voice, but at the moment it did not frighten me. I was too shocked, too horrified to be frightened.

"You killed John," I repeated, ignoring Maurice. "How can you call yourself a gentleman?"

"He was a fool. No loss, really. He was a dreadful fool. It would have been so easy for him to sell it to me. But he wouldn't." Leaning forward, his bloodshot eyes filled with the memory of past rebuff. "And he had the temerity to order me, *me* out of the house. No one does that. No one ever does that to Sir Ian Blackmore!"

"And Duncan?" I rose to my feet, the full impact of his confession hitting me with another blow to the heart. "What have you done to Duncan?"

Maurice Peale tapped my arm. "Sit down," he said quietly. "Sit down."

"I will not!" I turned on him in a fury.

He grasped me by the arm and brutally shoved me back into the chair.

"You must not do that," Sir Ian scolded, wagging a finger. "You must not. Sh . . . she's a lady. Eustacia is a lady, my good man. All right, she knows. What difference does it make? Eh? What difference?"

"You've done something terrible to Duncan," I cried, rubbing my bruised arm.

"He's all right . . . all right." Sir Ian blinked his eyes. "Don't you care to hear the rest of the story? How all this"—he waved his arm—"vanished? Quite a feat, don't you think?"

"But Duncan . . . !"

"Yes, Duncan." He pulled at the mug, swallowed, took a deep breath, and then went on in a more controlled voice. "I knew I would have to use a more clever approach. You see, overeagerness either sends the price of things up or turns a chap off altogether. So I decided I would play the bored man of means, the liege lord of Rommany, anxious to reestablish family ties. Hence the invitation to both of you. With a loan from my good friend Maurice, here, I hired servants, furniture, linens, crystal—all the accouterments with which to furnish a few rooms and brought them to the house. I told the servants I was playing a practical joke on my cousins, so there was no question there."

"I chose the servants," Maurice interposed. "Discreet. They should be, for double pay."

"Just so," Sir Ian said.

Disgusted at the two of them, I said, "But suppose Duncan and I had discovered your trick, supposing one of us had opened the wrong door?"

"Ah, but you see how clever I was." Sir Ian tapped his forehead. "You came at night: the rain helped. In fact, we gambled on it. The curtains were drawn, the lighting was poor and, if you recall, Violet or a servant accompanied you when you left the drawing room. And to make sure you would not walk about during the night, something was added to the hot chocolate you drank as a nightcap."

The hot chocolate, of course. I recalled now my heavy limbs, my thick tongue, the dull ache in my head when I awoke in the morning to find Duncan had gone. Drugged—they had drugged me.

"Lady Violet?"

"She knew from the start. She's been of great assistance to me, a real helpmate. A good woman, if only she wouldn't press me on certain matters." He winked broadly, and I lowered my eyes, hating him. "She doesn't understand," Ian continued, "that a man . . . a man isn't a man unless he appreciates a well-turned ankle, eh, Maurice?"

"Most certainly."

"There, you can see. Maurice agrees with everything.

He is a find card player, too. We played cards all that night—Maurice, Duncan, and I. And we argued. How we argued, back and forth. Duncan refused to go on our treasure hunt, refused to sell us the map."

"He said you would be buying a pig in a poke and—"

"But he knew it wasn't true. Else why didn't he make the bargain when I first broached the subject? I was willing to take the risk."

"Because Duncan is an honest man," I said. "He wouldn't want to cheat you—or anyone. Can't you understand that?"

"Pshaw! Honest man, my foot. He wants to keep the whole secret to himself."

"Where is he, then? What have you done with him?" It seemed to me that I had been asking those same questions for an eternity, anxious, frustrated, frantic with worry.

But Sir Ian must go on with his tale. ". . . and there was only one thing to do—render him unconscious."

"He's hurt!" I exclaimed. "Where is he? Take me to him at once."

"He is not hurt," Sir Ian said. "What good would he be to us hurt?"

"Then he hadn't gone out for a walk as you told me."

"No. We had him hidden in a little room, sleeping peacefully as a babe."

"Drugged," I corrected, "just as you drugged me."

"Yes. But you suffered no ill effects—isn't that true?"

No ill effects! How could I begin to explain my agony, the horror of finding Rommany deserted, my loss of memory, those two weeks in which I had suffered so? "All lies," I said, bitterly. "All horrible lies."

"Yet we carried it off," Sir Ian said smugly.

His conceit was sickening. But there was no use my demanding an end to the narrative, no use shouting or protesting: Sir Ian was getting a perverse pleasure from dragging out his tale.

"Daphne," he said, "Daphne was not much help, I'm afraid. Silly goose."

Maurice stirred in his chair. "I don't think I appreciate your constant harping on Daphne." His voice though smooth and calm, carried a vague intimidating nuance.

Sir Ian flashed him a look. "My apologies, Maurice.

Now—I've lost my train of thought again. Ah, yes—the day our good Duncan disappeared. How the hours dragged! But we maintained our performances throughout, didn't we? It was planned well, planned from the start. We were prepared for contingencies, you see, and when Duncan refused to cooperate we put our plan in motion. His so-called 'disappearance,' then you, Eustacia, to be taken into Tenwyck at night and left at the constable's house. The minute you left, we hurriedly gathered all the furnishings and the servants trundled them off in wagons previously hired for the occasion. Then—and I think this is the cleverest part—we brought out the linen bags in which we had stored the dust we found when we first arrived at Rommany, and the cobwebs Daphne had fashioned from woolen thread. Very carefully we laid down the dust and hung the false cobwebs, all in the right places."

"You did well," I said in a strangled voice. "You even fooled the constable."

He smiled—a sly, secretive smile. "Just so. We hoped that when you returned and found the empty house you and the others would believe you had fallen prey to hallucinations—or better still, that you had completely lost your mind."

"How cruel—how terribly, unspeakably cruel!" The ghostly laughter, the screaming, Daphne done up as a phantom, and my poor mind slipping, slipping toward the edge. I choked back angry tears. "The devil himself could not have devised a more reprehensible scheme. And you shall pay for it—pay dearly!"

"My dear Eustacia, your loving husband could have prevented it all, if only he had said, 'Yes, cousin, here is the map and good luck.'"

"There is no map."

"Then he keeps it in his head," he said, tipping the bottle to the mug once more.

"Duncan would never have allowed you to do this to me if he were not severely injured—or dead," I said, clasping my hands tightly, wanting to weep with rage.

"Not injured, not dead. Merely shanghaied aboard the *Destiny*. A ship captained by Maurice's friend, Bart Landeville."

"But Duncan must—"

"No doubt you've heard of Landeville. Not a very savory reputation, I believe. He's been cashiered out of the navy—a larcenous scoundrel if there ever was one, but admirably suited for our purpose."

"And Duncan is at this man's mercy? Then why are you not on the *Destiny*, too?"

"A good question, my dear." He brought out a handkerchief and mopped his brow. "Maurice, my friend, I have this raging thirst. Are we out of brandy? Be a good fellow and have another look under the bed."

"That was the last," Maurice said.

"There must be others downstairs."

"I believe you've had enough," Maurice said, and smiled.

"Damn you!" Sir Ian cursed. "I *order* you to go and fetch another bottle."

Maurice shifted in his chair, but made no move to rise. "It's my brandy, if you remember," he said, still smiling, though his eyes were hard.

"I don't give a damn if it is!"

"Let's not have a falling out, Sir Ian." The intimidating hint in his voice became more pronounced. "We shan't ever get to Africa if we start out this way. I, of course, won't mind half as much as you."

"Is that a threat?" Sir Ian's bloodshot eyes narrowed.

"Not at all. Just a reminder of the facts. I shall be out a few thousand pounds—and you—"

"Oh, never mind. Never mind." Ian mopped his brow again.

The door opened and Lady Violet, followed by Daphne, entered the room. Daphne was carrying a large tray covered with a cloth.

"Cold pudding again?" Sir Ian asked.

"We daren't make a fire," Lady Violet said. "It is the best we can do, though we've managed tea with a spirit lamp."

"No brandy?" Sir Ian asked, his eyes going over the tray.

Lady Violet did not answer. She uncovered the tray and handed each of us a bowl. I looked at the pudding—gray, doughlike, and lumpy. The rancid odor rising from it brought a sour taste to my throat.

"I think I'll just have the tea," I said, setting the bowl on the table.

Sir Ian had moved to the bed, giving Lady Violet his chair at the table. She sat there now in that bare dingy room, the walls stained where the rain had come in, and poured me a cup from the blackened kettle, poured with dignity and grace, as if she were sitting in what had briefly been the elegant drawing room downstairs. I think that was the only time I came even remotely close to feeling pity for this woman who had sold herself (or been sold) for a title. Or had she married for love? Lady Violet, as I had first surmised and was to reaffirm again and again, lived with the constant underlying fear of losing her husband to another woman. Perhaps that was what made her so cold, so hard.

The tea tasted of raw alcohol, but it was hot and it warmed me.

"Why are you not on the ship, then?" I asked once more.

"The ship sprung a bad leak," Sir Ian explained. "We had to bring her back to port for repairs."

Daphne, perched on the edge of a chair, said brightly, "We couldn't stay on a *leaky* ship."

"Correct," Ian said. "The repairs, so we were told, would take two or three weeks. And there was the bailiff, and a clutch of hungry creditors hanging about, eyeing me suspiciously."

"So we all came back here," Daphne chimed in, as if the whole horrible venture was a grand lark.

Sir Ian scowled at her. "Yes, we decided that Rommany was the safest place to remain incommunicado, so to speak."

"Then Duncan is here!" I exclaimed.

Silence.

Lady Violet sat with pressed lips, staring at the kettle. Neither Maurice nor Sir Ian met my anxious, inquiring eyes. Daphne started to speak, but her husband must have pinched her, for she suddenly exclaimed, "Ouch!" and began rubbing her arm.

"He's here!" I rose from the chair. "Duncan is here at Rommany!"

"You are mistaken," Maurice said in his quiet voice, giving Ian a significant look. "He is *not* here."

"Yes, yes," Sir Ian nodded. "I'm afraid not. You see, after some persuasion, he decided to give us the map, after all."

"But you said—"

"Please hear me out. In the end, he changed his mind and decided to go along with us."

"He never did. You are lying. Lying!"

"Now, now, young lady!"

"You killed him!" I shouted. "All of you, murderers!" Their blank white faces blurred as tears stung my eyes. "You killed him!"

Chapter 10

"Sit down and pull yourself together," Lady Violet said coldly.

Daphne put her hand to her mouth and giggled.

I turned on her. "Have you no heart?" I cried through my tears. "Or is your head so empty you do not know what is happening?"

"Here, here," she said, coloring. "I'd hold my tongue if I was you."

"Hold my tongue!" I exclaimed, beside myself with grief and rage. "You shall all be brought to justice if it's the very last thing I do!"

It was an empty threat. I could see it on their faces. They would never let me go. If they had not balked at murdering John Hempstead and Duncan, why should they spare me? My life, my brief marriage—over. That I had foolishly thought Duncan had betrayed me with another woman served only to twist the knife in my heart.

"You ... you murderers!" I sobbed.

"Such a vulgar display," Lady Violet's voice was edged with scorn.

I went on crying openly, unashamedly. Sir Ian leaned across the table and placed his handkerchief in my lap. I picked it up and hurled it back at him. Lady Violet stared at me, her eyes cold with contempt. I covered my face with the sleeve of my cloak and went on weeping.

"And what are we going to do with her?" I heard Maurice Peale ask.

"Serves her right," Daphne said petulantly. "She's a snob, a rich snob. Imagine, she—"

"Never mind," Lady Violet cut her off sharply. "We have to decide soon."

Maurice said, "The sooner the better. There's a pond not a quarter of a mile from here."

"No, I don't think that's very clever," Sir Ian said.

"Why not?" Lady Violet wanted to know.

I was chilled to hear them discussing me as if I were invisible, and managed to control myself at last.

"Because," Sir Ian replied, "if the locals find her, they might get suspicious, stir up trouble."

The locals. Of course. How could I have forgotten the Meachams? And even if by some chance they had not guessed I had gone to Rommany, there was the boy from whom I had hired the horse. He would remember my having asked directions to the house. Perhaps he would soon come looking for the mare. And the farmer I had passed on the road. Had he recognized me as the "lost lady" staying at the constable's?

Hope, like a small, newly lit fire, began to warm my despair.

Lady Violet quirked her lips. "We shall be gone by then."

"I know," Sir Ian said, "but it will complicate matters. There's the constable, you know. He might not like having to—well, it might prove embarrassing."

Lady Violet stared at her husband with narrowed eyes. The harsh lamplight brought out the flour whiteness of her face, the bright red spots of color on her cheeks. "Ian, my dear," she said with mock sweetness, "you are not by chance thinking of taking her?"

"Why not?" Sir Ian smiled.

"I shan't permit it."

"Violet, you *can't* be jealous," he laughed. "Come now, my dear," he coaxed, "she's too prim for my taste."

"Your taste," she said with acid sweetness, "goes no farther than a pretty face, *any* pretty face."

"How can you say that?" Sir Ian exclaimed, all innocence. "You know very well I am a faithful husband."

"Do I?"

"A slip here and there, perhaps, but in the main—"

"Oh?" Lady Violet regarded him with stony blue eyes. "Was Dulcie Latimore a slip? Was she? No, I think not.

And you had the effrontery to bring that—that coarse woman into *my* house, *my* bed." She did not raise her voice. Her control never wavered, but her anger was there, a devastating icy fury made all the more telling because of that cold white mask.

Sir Ian's cheeks turned scarlet as he glared back at her. "You forget yourself, Lady Violet."

Maurice recrossed his legs and cleared his throat. "I don't think it serves to stray from the subject at hand. We cannot take the young woman if Lady Violet is against it. Therefore, we are still faced with our problem. If I recall, there is an old well just outside the kitchen door . . ."

My heart turned sick.

". . . and if she is put down with weights, I doubt she will ever be found."

The practical matter-of-fact way in which Maurice discussed me—already dead, a corpse to be anchored at the bottom of a well—was macabre, unreal—so unreal I could hardly believe it. But I supposed I was no more to him than any irritant; a pesky mosquito to be gotten rid of quickly and without fuss.

"Mr. Peale," I said, struggling with fear and outrage and the rebellious quaver in my voice, "you are worse than a beast. Is that how you disposed of my husband?" I turned to Sir Ian. "And you, are you to be a part of this, too? Is it to be you who will throw me down the well? Murdering a woman who did you no harm?"

Ian looked away. "I . . ." He rose from the table, upsetting the empty brandy bottle with a clatter. "I . . . I could use some brandy." And he staggered to the door.

"Coward," Lady Violet sneered.

Sir Ian's back stiffened. He turned, and drawing himself up, said, "Maurice, I speak man-to-man to you. I propose we wait until we hear from Landeville before we come to a decision."

"Why wait for Landeville?" Lady Violet asked.

"Because I'll not be henpecked!" he burst out at her. "I am still head of this expedition, and I have every intention of remaining so." And with that he went out the door. We could hear him stumbling around in the dark, and then the sound of receding footsteps.

"Well!" Daphne said, letting her breath out. "I must say—"

"Please don't," Lady Violet advised witheringly.

Maurice's Adam's apple bobbed. "He'll come to his senses in the morning. May I have another cup of tea, your ladyship?"

As I watched Lady Violet pour Maurice's tea, I thought, Constable Meacham will come here long before morning. I must somehow set a light in a window, a lamp, a bit of candle so that Mr. Meacham will know the house is occupied.

Lady Violet suppressed a yawn with her ringed hand. "I'm ready for bed," she announced. "Come along, Eustacia. I'll find a room for you."

She took a tarnished candlestick with a wax-encrusted candle from the shelf and lit it over the lamp's flame.

"Could I have a candle also?" I asked, eyeing two other candles on the shelf.

"You shan't need one," Lady Violet replied.

"Then I'd rather stay here." I said stubbornly, not trusting her.

She grasped me by the arm. "*You* will do exactly as I say."

Daphne tittered, "Good-night," as we went through the door.

The passage was low-ceilinged and thronged with shadows. I followed Lady Violet obediently, numb with fear. Yellow candlelight threw our moving black images upon the wall—Lady Violet's taller than mine—grotesquely flattened and distorted. Her silhouette suddenly brought to mind a frightening story my old Irish nurse had once told me of a wicked witch who lived in a tower and fed on small naughty children. It was no use telling myself I was no longer a child and didn't believe in such nonsense. At that moment I could have believed in anything.

Lady Violet turned. "Why are you lagging?" Her hollow eyes watched me from a stark white face.

"I do not feel well," I said. "You . . . you put something in that tea."

"Nonsense," she said. "Come along now. I haven't all night."

I trailed behind on legs made of straw. She stopped before a door and opening it, motioned for me to enter.

The flickering candlelight revealed a small room with a dirty, sheet covered mattress on the floor, a humped ironhasped trunk, and two broken chairs. The air was stale with the smell of dust and rot.

"Sleep well," said Lady Violet with a sneer to her voice. And then she went out, banging the door shut, plunging me into utter darkness.

My heart leaping, I wheeled about and began to pound on the door. "Let me out! Let me out!"

I heard a key turn in the lock and Lady Violet's footsteps going away.

Imprisoned, unable to see, I was gripped with panic. "Let me out! Oh, please, let me out!" Clawing at the door, I slid down, down its length to the floor, crying bitterly.

There I must have fallen asleep, for I awoke hours later still on the cold, wooden floor, my legs numb, my neck painfully stiff. Through a broken shutter I could see a gray wash of light.

Slowly, with effort, I got to my feet and made my way to the window. I undid the shutter and putting my face to the dirty glass looked down at the weed choked remnants of a garden, and beyond that to a long, low building which I took to be the stables. Overhead a scud of thick rain clouds ran before the wind across the morning sky.

I had survived the night.

I examined the narrow, cobwebbed window, found the rusty latch and worked at it until it came loose. Swinging the shutter wide I leaned out. There was a dizzying fourstory drop to the ground, and I clung to the ledge for a few moments to steady myself. I had realized, of course, that I was too high to escape through a window, but the actual distance, so remote, so removed from the ground below was still a shock. The witch's tower—tall, impregnable.

I stood for a few minutes longer breathing in the faint odor of rich loam and moss and fallen leaves, wondering sadly why I had never before noticed how sweet the earth smelled after rain.

Suddenly I thought I heard the faint sounds of a horse's hooves. I stood very still and listened. Clip-clop, clippety-clop. The horse was going at a brisk trot, coming closer and closer.

Constable Meacham!

I took hold of the sill again and leaned out, not afraid of the height anymore, not thinking of anything but Clem Meacham's genial ruddy face and how surprised he would be to see me, and how I would soon be back in Bess Meacham's tidy parlor.

The sound of the horse's hooves were louder now, and the next moment a man riding a gray cob rounded the corner of the house and headed toward the stable.

It was not the constable.

The figure in the saddle was tall and lean, no one I could recognize.

A stranger, then, someone out for a morning canter, or someone sent by Mrs. Meacham to look for her husband?

"Help! Help!" I cried, leaning out the window. When he did not stop, I summoned a deep breath and shouted again. "Help!"

The man reined the horse in and looked about. He wore a black wide-brimmed hat and I could not see his face.

"Up here!" I shouted. "I'm up here—in the attic!"

He lifted his head and I saw him clearly then. It was the seamy-faced butler, the one who had driven me through the rain to the constable's house.

He was too far away for me to observe the expression on his face. Surprise or curiosity? I could not tell. He dismounted and I watched as he led the horse to the stable and disappeared inside. A few moments later he came out and without looking at me walked briskly across the yard, disappearing around the corner.

I had only hope to go on then, hope that the butler was not part of the plot, that he had returned for another reason and that he would somehow manage to free me.

I looked about for a mirror, but there was none, nothing but the trunk and the old dirty mattress and the two, legless chairs. I pinned up my hair as best I could and smoothed my rumpled dress into a semblance of neatness. Then I sat down on the mattress to wait. Sometime during the last day—in my terrified scramble from window to window?—I had lost my watch. I wished I had it now. The ticking of its small workings, the methodical movement of its gilded hands would have been a comfort, so far from home, so far from everything I knew.

The silence, cold and heavy, twitched at my nerves. I wished I knew what was happening. Had the butler gained access to the house?

Restless, I got up and put my ear to the door. How odd, I thought—there is no murmur of voices, no sound of a step or a closing door, no sound at all.

Suppose, I thought, seating myself again, suppose they have all departed and left me alone, locked in this room. Left alone to starve slowly day by day, while the small creatures watched with greedy eyes from their hiding places behind the wainscoting, watched while I grew weak and . . .

I shivered and got up and went to the window again. A fine rain was falling now, pattering on the eaves and in the gutters, misting the dark trees. I stared out into the gray dreary morning, my courage failing fast. It was terrible not knowing what fate had in store for me, waiting, waiting. For what? A small pulse had begun to throb in my head.

I looked down again at the yard. And suddenly two small boys emerged through the curtain of mist. They were walking hand in hand in the rain across the neglected gardens—not phantoms but real flesh-and-blood children. Why—they were the two boys from whom I had hired the horse!

Hurriedly I undid the window and with a catch of hysterical laughter in my throat I began to shout. "Boys! Boys! Up here! Help me!"

They stopped and looked up, their heads turning from side to side as if scanning the walls. To make sure of attracting their attention I snatched the sheet from the mattress and began to wave it out the window, shouting all the while. "Help me!"

Through the mist I saw their pale upturned faces. They seemed to be staring directly at me. "Up here!" I shouted.

Then the larger boy grasped his brother's hand, and together they turned and ran, fleeing as if the hounds of hell were at their heels, running, stumbling over hummocks of grass. In another few moments they had disappeared.

I stood for a long time at the window, hoping they

would return. But, of course, they wouldn't. Hadn't one of the boys—Teddy—said Rommany was haunted? It must have taken a great deal of courage (plus a scolding, no doubt, on account of the missing mare) for the two of them to have ventured down the narrow muddy lane to Rommany. And when they had heard a faint voice high up and had seen a ghostly sheet waving, what else could they have believed but that the phantom of Rommany had appeared to them in the foggy morning rain?

I was too dismayed to find anything comic or ironic in the boys' flight. Perhaps I *was* invisible. I even began to wonder if the butler had noticed me at all when he had raised his head in the yard. He *seemed* to, and that was all I knew for certain. Whether he was in the house or had since departed (though I had not heard his horse) I did not know.

I leaned my head against the casement, closing my eyes. Tired, hungry, filthy, beset by fear, I could not even bring myself to weep. It was too much to bear. Why didn't someone come? Why?

Presently I roused myself and went to the door once more to listen. Nothing. The door was fashioned of plain oak, not like the doors below which were heavily carved. The handle was of tarnished brass. I stared at it and the keyhole for a long time. Then, kneeling, I removed one of the pins from my hair and inserted it in the lock.

I juggled and twisted the pin, this way and that, not really expecting success. I was startled to hear a sudden click. Turning the handle, I pushed the door open.

For a stunned moment I stood gaping at the opposite wall. Then my blood began to tingle, to dance through my veins. I was free! Yes, yes, I was *free!*

My first impulse was to run like a hare down the passageway, find a staircase, a door, escape, leaving this house behind—I could almost taste the rain on my tongue, feel the wet wind on my face.

But sober judgment prevailed. Closing the door softly behind me, I took a few cautious steps and then stopped, suddenly remembering the barred windows, the locked doors on the ground floor.

I stood in the gloom, biting my thumbnail, not knowing whether to turn right or left when I heard the murmur of voices coming from a room somewhere down the passage. I shrank into the shadows, momentarily expecting a door to open and someone—Lady Violet, perhaps—to emerge.

But the voices went on, male and female talking in turn. The distance was too great for me to distinguish the words or who was speaking, although I thought I heard a little gurgling laugh that might have been Daphne's.

The babble of conversation continued, rising and falling, rising and falling. Suddenly a man's voice drowned out the others, his voice getting higher and higher in anger. I knew that slurred, half-tipsy baritone. It was Sir Ian's. A woman—Lady Violet?—said something sharply and there was a small silence.

A burning curiosity overcame my fear and with a heart hammering like a smith's anvil I tiptoed up to the door and put my eye to the keyhole.

My vision was extremely limited but I could see the butler, who had removed his large black hat. He was seated facing the door. And I had a partial view of Lady Violet.

She was saying, "So then we shall have to be here another week?"

"I'm afraid so, your ladyship," the butler said.

Unharmed, no rescuer, he was in league with the Blackmores.

"Well," Sir Ian's voice reached me, "You are doing the best you can, I suppose, Landeville."

Landeville! The man I had thought of as the butler was Landeville, captain of the *Destiny*, the unsavory character Sir Ian had described.

"The men are not restive?" Lady Violet asked.

"They are anxious to be off, naturally," Landeville replied. "But I can trust them to keep their mouths shut. They're good men."

"Yes," Lady Violet agreed. "I had no idea they could cook and wait table so beautifully."

So some of the servants were participants in the scheme!

Landeville fingered the rim of his hat. "I'm still a little concerned about that maid."

"Carla?" Lady Violet questioned in surprise. "No need to fear her. She's a foreigner, poorly conversant with English. I doubt she understands much."

That had not been my impression, but perhaps Lady Violet had never spoken to the girl except to give her orders.

I heard the clink of a bottle against crockery. "Another brandy?" Sir Ian's voice asked.

"Too early for that," Landeville said. "But I've brought a package of food."

"How thoughtful," Lady Violet said.

A white arm crossed my vision and I saw a flash of blonde curls, and then Daphne said, "Oooh! Roast fowl and cheese and bread—and there's even glazed pears!"

My mouth, despite fear and anxiety, began to water. I heard the sound of rustling paper and rattling cutlery. I knew my position was dangerous, that I ought to move, ought to be on my way down the stairs, but I wanted desperately to hear what they had to say of me.

A moment later Landeville, chewing on a drumstick, said, "Now, the girl, I am against laying a hand on a woman—just as you are, Sir Ian—but there will not be room for another passenger. The *Destiny* is small, already full, and another young lady would make a rather delicate situation."

"Perhaps if she promised not to say anything, we could let her go?" Sir Ian said.

Landeville grimaced. "That never works. If you are squeamish, I shall do it myself. Easy and quick." He pulled a knife from his pocket, a small, slim one with a rapier blade. Then he reached past my view and a half moment later I saw he had an apple in his hand. Tossing it in the air, he caught it with the knife, slicing it neatly in two.

"She shan't feel a thing," he said. "Easy and quick."

Chapter 11

Horrified, I lifted my head from the keyhole and shrank back into the shadows. I had no time to wring my hands, to weep now. As soon as they finished eating, Landeville would come in search of me.

I hurried back to the attic room and slipped out of my cloak. Then, whisking the dusty sheet from the floor I stuffed it into the cloak, arranging it on the mattress to resemble a sleeping person. I closed the shutter and fastened it. The gray light coming through was dim, and I hoped my ruse would work to deceive Landeville long enough to give me a head start.

I wonder now that I had the presence of mind to devise such a stratagem, for once I had closed the door, I found that I was shaking so violently I could scarcely stand. Confusion muddled my brain. Which way to go? On either side the corridor disappeared into murky gloom. Yet there had to be a staircase. This way? That? My head began to ache.

The sound of Daphne's tittering laughter brought me to an impulsive decision. I turned left and, tiptoeing swiftly as I could, I went along the corridor, keeping to the wall. Presently I came to a narrow staircase. I descended it with apprehension, for I distinctly remembered having passed a stained-glass window on the previous night and there was none here. Nevertheless it went down, and when I reached the bottom, I discovered, to my dismay, that this flight of stairs ended at the landing. Ahead of me the dim passage stretched, broken by one lone window thick with dust.

I began to walk, searching for another staircase. The

95

cold here was intense, bottled up, musty and dank. Without my cloak, I felt it all the more keenly. It nipped at my ankles, running up my limbs, chilling my arms, penetrating to the very marrow of my bones.

I had never imagined the house to be so huge. And all the doors I passed; each opening to a room! Not even Newberry could boast such size.

Soon I came to the end of the passage and a blank wall. No window, no stairs, nothing—simply a blank wall. But there *had* to be a way down. Perhaps I had missed the staircase at the other end.

I was turning to retrace my steps when I heard a sound behind the door to my left. I listened another moment—there it was again! The scraping of a chair. Once more I bent my head and put my eye to the keyhole. I saw nothing but the post of a bed. Yet someone was in that room. I could *feel* it. Someone hiding? Or someone involuntarily confined. The constable?

I turned the knob cautiously and with a hand shaking and clammy with fear, I pushed the door open. The room was empty except for a four-poster bed and a small wooden chair. I stepped inside. Behind me the door creaked shut. A dark blue cloak was lying on the exposed mattress of the bed, but whether it was a man's or a woman's I could not tell.

I stood perfectly still, every muscle rigid, my eyes probing the dark, dusty corners. *There was someone in the room.* I could hear breathing other than my own. Slowly, with a beating heart, I turned.

"Carla!" the name tore from my lips in astonishment.

She was standing next to the door against the wall, holding a heavy brass candlestick in her hand. "Don't scream," she whispered, "don't say a word."

Carla, my mind flashed—one of the enemy, one of the villainous staff of so-called servants. Had Landeville discovered my absence already and sent her to find me?

"Keep quiet, madam, and I will explain," she said, still whispering.

Explain what? I did not trust her, not with that dark look on her face and the candlestick held like a club in her hand. She was going to force me back upstairs, back to my execution. The thought took no more than a fraction of a second to go through my mind, but I reacted to it with the instinct of an animal. Lifting the chair in front of me, and with the strength born of panic, I attacked her. She ducked under the chair. The next thing I knew, the top of my scalp seemed to lift clear off my head.

I came to, lying in a heap on the floor, my head throbbing. I touched the place above my ear where it seemed to hurt the most, and I winced as I felt a small bump the size of a wren's egg. Pushing myself upright, I sat holding my aching head until the room stopped whirling.

The blue cloak was missing from the four-poster bed; Carla was gone.

Miserable, my teeth jarring with pain, I got slowly to my feet. My poor, muddled head—how it ached. I never thought to ask myself why Carla, as a servant, had not been fixing puddings and tea rather than Lady Violet. But my mind could only assimilate what seemed obvious; Carla would never have struck me with the candlestick if she were not an ally of the Blackmores.

Tired and thirsty, I longed to climb into the four-poster bed and close my eyes and forget. But I couldn't stay. I must go. Carla surely had gone to warn the others, and the instinctive need to keep moving urged me to the door. I opened it and shuddered as, again, the hinges scraped in the silence.

In the corridor a shaft of feeble sunlight had penetrated the one window and it fell on the planked floor in a cross-paned pattern of yellowed ivory. The rain had ceased then, and I wondered why it should matter.

I walked slowly toward the window where dust motes swam in the pale light. Dust motes. Ordinary, commonplace, they would go on sliding down sunbeams long after I had died and become dust myself. Odd how pain and fear had turned me introspective—I, who had never pondered much beyond the feelings of the moment. Now I felt infinitely old, infinitely wise.

The sudden slamming of a door brought me out of my reverie. I moved quickly into the shadows, listening. Footsteps. Heavy booted footsteps. I pressed against a door, my heart beating wildly.

Far down the corridor a door opened and a moment

later banged shut. Then another door opened. I leaned forward and peered into the distant shadows. It was Landeville; I recognized his black riding coat. He was going from room to room, searching for me. There was no good in trying to run. I was too weak and he would have little trouble in catching me.

He was coming closer. I could hear him cursing. When he slammed the next door shut, I pushed the one I was standing against open. Thank God, it hadn't squeaked. I closed it and glanced about quickly. A wardrobe and another four-poster bed, this one, amazingly, made up with a dusty, faded spread. I could hide in the wardrobe, but I was sure Landeville would open it. Gathering my skirts together, I got down on the floor and rolled under the bed.

It was none too soon. A minute later the door opened and from beneath the fringed border of the spread I saw a pair of long black mud-spattered boots. They remained quite still while the breath swelled and swelled in my lungs. The boots moved, turning sideways, and paused. Landeville was looking around.

Surely he would hear the wild, erratic beat of my heart! It clamored so in my ears the entire room seemed to throb. From one agonizing moment to the next I expected to feel the grasp of Landeville's hand as he pounced upon me and dragged me from my hiding place.

The boots moved again, clumping across the floor. Hinges squeaked and there was the sound of wood hitting wood. Just as I had thought; he was looking inside the wardrobe.

"Damn the wench!" he muttered. "Damn Ian, having me to do his dirty work."

Once more the boots began to move. They were approaching the bed. I watched, all eyes, mesmerized like a trapped fox from its hole. Closer and closer they came, pausing at last not two inches from my nose. I could see where the left boot was cracked and the mud caked at the toes. Landeville had only to shift his feet and I would be discovered. I felt as if my body were shrinking inch by inch out of sheer, stark terror, while in my mind's eyes I saw the knife with which Landeville had so neatly, so diabolically cut the apple in two. Would a knife of such surpassing keenness hurt unbearably? Would he plunge it straight to my heart—or cut my throat? "Easy and quick," he had said.

They say that a drowning man reviews his whole life in the moment or two he feels will be his last. Not I! I could think of nothing but that knife. Everything, every thought, every memory was blotted out except for the vision of the sharp rapier blade grasped competently in Landeville's thick fist.

In my fear-benumbed, fantasy-thronged mind, the seconds became minutes, the minutes hours. And then suddenly Landeville moved. He turned and as I watched in disbelief, the black boots marched across the floor. The door opened and shut. He was gone.

I lay there for a long time, my head cradled in my arms, breathing in the stuffy dust of centuries, while my heart gradually returned to its normal beat. Again I had an almost irresistible longing to remain, safe, hidden. But I knew I could not. When Landeville did not find me, he would retrace his steps and make a more thorough search. So I slid out and got to my feet, hastily brushing the lint from my skirt and tidying my hair, gestures performed more from ingrained habit than any real concern for my appearance.

When I came out into the passage, all was silent again. The sun slanting at a sharper angle now, its rays a deeper yellow. Noon? I thought of the roast fowl I had seen Landeville feasting on, and my stomach swelled with the memory. Hungry and thirsty, so parched a cup of tea—even Lady Violet's—would have done me well.

Moving softly, I went through moted sunlight and dark shadow, my ears alert for the slightest sound. I had gone only a few feet when I came to a staircase going down. I descended cautiously, holding to the rail and when I reached the landing, I paused. There was another long, shadowy corridor here. Stairs and corridors, and more stairs, dusty, ill lit, a labyrinth of a never-ending nightmare. Would I ever reach the ground floor?

Haltingly, I moved along the passage. There were several alcoved windows, all shuttered. I paused before one where a slat had broken away and peered out. I could see nothing but a patch of lemon sky. A bird flew across it, flapping dun-colored wings.

I crept on, and presently I thought I heard men's voices. Ahead of me was a landing and the broad staircase I had been seeking. The conversation seemed to be coming from below. I stole up to the carved banister and looked over.

Sir Ian and Maurice Peale were standing in the center of the great hall speaking to a short stout man.

Red face, white hair. The constable!

"Constable Meacham!" I cried. "Constable!"

Laughing and weeping, I raced down the stairs, suddenly revived, unmindful of my aching head. I was saved! *Saved!*

When I reached him, I threw myself at the poor man, hugging and kissing him, exclaiming how glad I was to see him, babbling on and on about knives and ghosts black boots and how I should never, never be able to thank him enough for saving my life.

I could not blame the man for staring at me, an embarrassed and bewildered look on his flaming face. I must have presented a wild sight, too, with my hair tumbling past my shoulders, my cheeks stained with tears and grime.

"My dear Mrs. Blackmore," he said, somehow managing to disentangle himself from my embrace. "Calm yourself."

"Yes, yes—I am sorry, but you see, there is so much to tell; I do not know where to begin. Except that I am *not* mad. There are . . . that is . . . that is to say, Sir Ian has taken my husband prisoner and it is possible that he has been murdered. And this man—Maurice Peale—has helped him."

Sir Ian and Maurice stood by silently, glum and wooden-faced.

"For a map," I went on. "Yes, yes, a map of a diamond mine. And now, Mr. Meacham, they are trying to kill me."

The constable looked shocked. "I can't countenance murder, you know," he said sternly, all law and justice and authority. Bless him, I thought. "Is this true, Sir Ian?"

"Not at all," Sir Ian replied calmly. "I'm afraid Mrs. Blackmore has taken that odd fancy into her head. No truth to it at all."

"It's a lie!" I exclaimed heatedly. It was all I could do

to keep from screaming. "Sir Ian is not telling the truth. There was—*is*—a plot, Mr. Meacham, to make you and myself as well, think I was mad. But the Blackmores *were* here, and the furniture was hired and the servants—"

Maurice Peale interrupted. "Why did you come, Constable?"

Mr. Meacham seemed somewhat deflated by this inquiry, although it was put mildly enough. "Bess—my wife—was beside herself, when the young lady ran off." he said. "She insisted, and I—"

"Oh, Mr. Meacham!" I exclaimed, overcome again. "They have behaved so dreadfully."

"Now, now," he soothed. "I'll take you away. Where is your cloak?"

Maurice Peale cleared his throat. "I am afraid it's rather late for that. She knows too much. She can't go." Mild inconsequential-looking little Maurice, speaking in a soft voice, had never seemed more menacing.

The constable picked at the brim of his hat. "But what am I to say?" he asked.

"You should have thought of that before you let her out of your sight," Maurice said. "If you remember, you were paid well to keep her in Tenwyck."

Chapter 12

There is something very unreal about the sudden shock of betrayal. One's mind simply refuses to accept it.

I stared at Mr. Meacham, who stood with eyes fixed on the floor as if there were something between his feet of extraordinary interest. This was the man who had taken me in, been so kind, so understanding, and who had now come to my rescue. My own father could not have been more concerned. There was some mistake. There *had* to be. Mr. Meacham could not possibly be in Sir Ian's pay.

"You are wrong, Mr. Peale," I said through dry lips. "This man—his wife—"

"My wife," the constable spoke, still without looking at me, "my wife knows nothing of this. She must never know. It would be most upsetting, most upsetting."

"Most upsetting," I repeated dumbly. "Then it is true?" still hoping, still expecting denial.

Mr. Meacham remained silent, eyes averted.

"How . . . how could you have done such a thing?" I demanded angrily.

"I am sorry," he muttered.

Sorry. What a feeble word!

"And you were part of the plan from the first?"

He did not answer, but I knew it was so. When I had knocked at his door, seeking help in the pouring rain on that long-ago night, he had been expecting me. No surprise my sudden midnight appearance, my pale anxious face. The sympathetic speech that followed, the offer of hospitality, the long delay in the morning before we started back to Rommany were all part of a prearranged plan. But worst of all was the memory of the ruined, deserted house, myself standing in the great hall, my mind teetering on the brink of madness and Mr. Meacham going on with the deception, the lie.

"Why did you do it?" My voice was hoarse with disgust.

The constable did not speak. After a moment, Maurice Peale spoke for him. "For money," he said and smiled. "A constable in these parts gets little pay. Isn't that right, Mr. Meacham?"

The constable's throat worked. He played with his hat. "I did it for Bess," he mumbled. "She's never had anything."

I tried to understand, I really tried. A man living in genteel poverty, wanting to give his wife a pretty dress, a bauble, wanting to pay for a good servant, an outing—whatever reason—had suddenly been offered the chance at a bit of extra cash. But to sell his dignity, his self-respect at the expense of harming someone—me? No—it baffled me beyond comprehension.

"Your wife would be more than upset," I said bitterly. "How could you?"

"They told me no harm would come to you," he answered.

"They lied. They are going to kill me. There is a man here—"

"What nonsense!" Sir Ian took hold of my arm, his fingers pressing painfully into my flesh. "Eustacia, my dear. As usual you are letting your imagination run away with good sense."

"But—" I protested.

"Now, Mr. Meacham," Sir Ian went on, his fingers tightening cruelly around my arm, "you have nothing to worry about. It has all worked out for the best. This lovely lady's husband has consented—in fact is eager—to join us, as I knew he would all along. Mrs. Blackmore, here, is somewhat put out with him because he has not consulted her on the matter. Am I not right, Maurice?"

"Perfectly. It is nothing more than a marital squabble." Maurice showed his bad teeth in a smile. "You know how those things go."

Anger rose to my head in a white frothing tide. "Where

is Duncan, then? Why don't you bring him here and have him speak for himself? I demand to know why?"

"Mr. Blackmore is on the ship. Can you deny that you were told of it?" Maurice asked me.

"No, but—"

"There you are, Mr. Meacham. A dispute between man and wife. Simple as that. If I were you, I would not trouble myself further. I give you my word. No injury has been done to this lady's husband. And she, as you can see, has worked herself into an excitable state over nothing."

"They have killed John Hempstead!" I shouted.

Startled, the constable looked questioningly at Maurice. "She is much distraught," Maurice said, tapping his forehead knowingly. "But we shall see to her comfort—never fear."

"Yes," Mr. Meacham said, obviously relieved. "Mrs. Blackmore is easily perturbed, it is true."

It was unbelievable how completely the constable had been taken in. "They are lying, I tell you. They have kept me locked up."

"Now, now," Sir Ian chided. "Eustacia, my dear, you know that isn't so. Inventing such stories. And distressing our constable, here."

"Quite all right," Mr. Meacham muttered, giving his hat one last twirl before setting it on his head. "I shall be on my way, then."

"No!" I begged. But he had already started for the door and I was prevented from running after him by Sir Ian. "Mr. Meacham—please!"

Maurice opened the door and without looking back Clem Meacham—my last hope, my last link with the world—went out into the afternoon sun. And suddenly the fight went out of me, leaving me limp and deflated, overcome by a feeling of helplessness.

"You must not look so disheartened," Sir Ian said in a low voice.

"Don't you think I have cause to?" I replied bitterly.

"I promise you shan't be harmed," he continued in the same intimate tone, and then moved away as Maurice Peale returned from barring and locking the door.

"I wonder what we can expect next," Maurice said.

"First the girl, then Landeville with news of the ship's delay, and now the constable."

"I think you can rely on the man holding his tongue," Sir Ian said.

"I should hope so."

"Meacham isn't acquainted with all the details," Sir Ian said. "He believes it just a matter of persuading Duncan to go on an expedition without Eustacia's interfering."

"So I gathered. But I think he knows—or guesses—a lot more than he pretends. I wonder if he's thinking of blackmail in the future? Venal men never let a trick go by."

"No, not Meacham. He doesn't dare open his mouth. He's got too much to answer for. And he's afraid of his wife, as you saw."

I thought vaguely of escape while the men were absorbed in their conversation, but where would I run? I hadn't the strength to take the stairs, and the door had been bolted and locked.

Maurice said, "It's a pity Landeville had to get back to the ship so soon."

His words cut through my lethargy. Landeville was gone. At least I did not have to anticipate the knife. And Sir Ian had said that no harm would come to me. But could I trust him? He had looked at me so hungrily. . . .

"I shall see to the girl, then," Maurice was saying in that disconcerting way of referring to me as "girl" or "she," never by name.

"Eustacia is my responsibility," Sir Ian said, taking my arm.

Maurice raised his brows. "You did not seem to think so yesterday."

"Look here, Maurice. I owe you a great deal—there's no question of that," Sir Ian's voice was edged with annoyance. "But it seems to me that you have gradually been taking over this enterprise. And I resent it. By God, I resent it!"

"I beg your pardon, Sir Ian, but I haven't been taking over the 'enterprise,' as you call it. You've simply been letting it go."

We had come to the staircase and Sir Ian paused, glaring at Maurice. "I won't comment on that statement because it is not worthy of comment. And I won't argue. But let me make it plain to you; *I* am in charge."

"Very well," said Maurice quietly. "We shall see."

"It's not that I don't appreciate your advice," Sir Ian said, suddenly apologetic, "but we must have somebody in authority. You can see that, can't you?"

"Of course." Maurice gave me a meaningful glance. "I leave the disposal of the girl to you—and your ironing it out with Lady Violet."

Once again I was installed in the attic room. Before Sir Ian left, I said, "May I have a drink of water, please?" My lips were cracked dry with thirst.

Sir Ian touched my hand, and for a moment I thought he meant to embrace me, but Maurice was hovering at the door and he said, "I'll send Daphne with food and water."

She came soon after, bearing a tray with cold tea, a sausage roll, and a picked-over chicken caracass which I guessed was the remains of the roast fowl they had all shared earlier. It was not an appetizing sight, but I fell upon the food as if it were my last meal, thinking in the back of my mind that it might very well be.

Daphne, arms akimbo, watched me. "You are eating like a greedy street Arab," she said.

"I feel like one," I said between mouthfuls. "Wouldn't you, if you hadn't eaten in two days?"

"There's been many a time when I haven't eaten for two days. But then you wouldn't know about that, would you?" There was a sneer in her voice.

"No," I answered honestly.

"No," she mimicked. "No. You think, like Lady Violet does, that because I was poor I ain't got brains," she went on, dropping all pretense of her acquired accent. "Well, I've got feelings, just the same as anybody."

"Feelings?" I said, swallowing. "If you have feelings then, how can you stand by and see them kill me?"

"What are you to me?" She twisted a blonde curl into place. "Nothing!"

"Then you expect me to have feelings about you, when you have none for me?"

She knotted her smooth brow, as if pondering. Either the logic of that statement was too involved or she chose to ignore it, for she said, gruffly, "Finish. I must take the tray back."

I drank the last of the tea, bitter dregs and all. Wiping my greasy hands on the hem of my petticoat, I said, "Daphne, save my life. Help me get away.

She laughed.

"Help me escape and I'll see to it that you receive a good sum of money."

"Money?" she said scornfully. "Maurice has *lots* of money."

"You'd be written up in the papers," I argued. "People would point to you and say, 'There goes Daphne Peale—she saved someone's life.' You would be famous."

She looked at me, pursing her pink Cupid's-bow lips. "That would be going against my husband, wouldn't it?"

"He would forgive you."

Her curls danced as she shook her head. "No, no he wouldn't. And I could never do anything he didn't like. I couldn't go against him. Not Maurice. He's the only one who has ever been kind to me. I was—never mind. He washed my face and gave me clothes and hired someone to teach me better English and he *married* me. He's mean sometimes, but that's because he's got lots on his mind. But he *married* me, and. . . ."

As Daphne spoke, I rose from the chair, the tray in my hands. I'm not going to die because Maurice married you, because you are selfish, I thought. With a quick glance, I calculated the distance to the door and then I dropped the tray. The tea mug rolled to Daphne's feet.

"See what you've done," she complained, stooping to pick it up.

I bolted for the door, flung it open, and was out into the passage before she could scream.

I ran blindly, pell-mell, down the low-ceilinged corridor, my strength renewed by food and drink. Suddenly a door opened and Lady Violet stepped out, barring the way.

"So our little bird wants to fly," she said in that cold, hard voice I had learned to dread.

"Stand aside, Lady Violet," I said, my breath coming in gasps. "Stand aside or—"

"Or what?" she said coolly, taking a revolver out of the

pocket of her skirt, a long-barrelled, ugly, terrifying weapon.

"I do not like you," she said. "I do not like the way my husband looks at you—or the way you look at him."

"I have never—"

"Please do not play the innocent virgin with me, my dear, all demure and proper. You have the eyes of a whore."

"No," I said shocked. "No!"

"I think I shall get rid of you myself. You managed to elude Landeville, and my husband is too much of a coward, or too infatuated to do what he must. That leaves me to act."

She raised the revolver with both hands and drew back the hammer. At the sound of the click, mindless panic seized me, and I turned and fled.

I heard the bullet's whistle, hot and lethal, before the sound exploded in the narrow corridor, shivering the walls, rattling the window.

I stumbled and fell.

Someone screamed.

The screaming, together with the bullet's echo, continued to reverberate, to bounce under the low ceiling as I lay face-down, thinking, *it is over, it is over, I need not be afraid any longer.* I felt no pain, no distress, only a kind of relief, a surprising tranquillity.

But the darkness, the void I anticipated did not come. Instead, there was the sound of running footsteps and voices. Sir Ian shouting, "What in God's name have you done? Give me that gun!"

I turned my head and, sensing a shadow, opened my eyes.

"Are you hurt?" Sir Ian asked, kneeling beside me.

"I—I don't know," I said. Had the bullet passed through me without my feeling it?

A woman was sobbing close to me, and Maurice Peale's voice, unfamiliarly agitated, was saying. "You're all right, Daphne, love. All right. It's just a flesh wound."

Sir Ian helped me to rise. I saw Daphne then. She was sitting on the floor, supported by her husband's arm, her face buried in his shoulder. The sleeve of her gown, just above the elbow, was stained with crimson.

Lady Violet had disappeared.

"How did this happen?" Sir Ian asked.

"She—Lady Violet tried to shoot me," I said, incredulous to find myself alive and unharmed. "I . . . I tried to run away and she shot at me."

"Missed and hit poor Daphne," he said. "You are very lucky my wife has poor aim."

"Yes," I said looking fearfully past his shoulder. "Though she might try again."

"You need not worry about that. Come, I will take you back to the room."

"But—"

"Trust me. Violet does not know it, but she has inadvertently saved you."

"How?"

"You shall see."

Again I asked myself: Does one trust a thief, a murderer? But what choice did I have?

Maurice was binding up Daphne's wound. "How is it?" Sir Ian asked.

"Hardly more than a scratch, thank God," Maurice replied. "There now, Daphne, you're a good girl."

Sir Ian led me back to the attic room. "I shan't lock you in," he said, "but you will turn Peale against you and spoil it all if you attempt to escape. You can't get out of the house in any case, and we need Peale's help." He went to the door and looked out, then turned to me and again I saw that warm, moist look in his eyes. "I shall return in a short while," he promised and closed the door behind him.

I don't think I realized, even then, what price I would be asked to pay for my life. I was still too naïve, too young and untried to know that cowards could be as ruthless, devious, and unprincipled as men of steel. More so, perhaps, since they were constantly trying to hide their weakness.

An hour must have passed before the door opened again and Sir Ian came into the room.

"It's all settled, then," he said, sitting beside me, and reaching for my hand.

"What is settled?"

"You are to go with us to Africa."

"But Lady Violet. . . ."

"You need not concern yourself with her." He bent and kissed my hand.

"And Landeville and Maurice Peale?"

"Peale has left it up to me, and I feel sure I can make Landeville see it my way."

"And what of my husband?" I asked, edging away from him. "If he is on the ship, as you say—"

"I can find a way to persuade him also." He drew me close. His hot breath reeked of brandy.

Wriggling free, I sprang to my feet. "I do not understand."

"Why, it's quite simple. I have fallen in love with you, and I want you with me."

"As your ... your mistress? I shall never consent to such a ... such a ..."

He leaned back against the wall and smiled. "I think you will. You see, it is either you or Violet."

"Then take Violet."

"No—again, you mistake me. It is either your *life* or Lady Violet's."

I stared at him.

"Violet, you see, came within an inch of killing Daphne, an act for which Maurice finds it hard to forgive her. He agrees that Violet is a dangerous person—all jealous women are—and he is willing to have her—shall we say, done away with? And for you to take her place."

I was appalled. "You would kill your own wife?"

"You might have noticed that there is little love lost between us. She has become a possessive shrew, unhappy with me, unhappy with herself."

It was a true assessment of Lady Violet, yet it did not lessen my shock. "Then I am to agree to her murder?"

"No. *Your* self-preservation." He got to his feet and touched his lips to my hair. "I *do* want you—you can't know how much." And when I again pushed him away, "In time you will grow to like me."

"And if I don't agree?"

"Then I'm afraid there is nothing I can do for you."

I knew he was speaking the truth. My life or Lady Violet's. "May I think it over?"

"There is not time. Maurice might change his mind."

With a coolness that surprised me, I weighed the pros

110

and cons while Sir Ian's eyes watched and waited. That Sir Ian would take Duncan's place in my bed was a revolting enough prospect, but to have a human life hanging on my answer sickened me even more, though Lady Violet, I was sure, would have had no such scruples were she in my place. And if I died, they would all go scot-free, wouldn't they? I did not want to die, certainly not to save Lady Violet. And if I went with Sir Ian, I would be free of the house. Surely at some time during our journey from Rommany to the seaport where the *Destiny* was berthed I would elude my captors or, failing that, cause a commotion, an outcry to attract attention. I knew I would never give myself to Sir Ian. I couldn't. In the meantime, however. . . .

"I have decided to go with you."

"Good," said Sir Ian, coming to me and putting his arm about my waist. "I knew you would. Suppose we seal our bargain with a kiss?"

I closed my eyes and steeled myself not to show the revulsion I felt as he bent his head and brought his lips to mine with a rough, moist greediness.

The kiss seemed to go on and on, my breath draining away when suddenly I heard the door behind us open.

Sir Ian looked up and his face blanched. "Where in the . . .?"

I turned. Standing there, one hand on the door, the other holding a revolver, was a wild-haired Duncan, his eyes savage with anger.

Chapter 13

"Duncan!" I cried, flinging myself at him. "Oh, Duncan. Thank God, you are alive!"

"Very much so. Step aside, Eustacia, if you will."

"Duncan . . ." Why was his voice so cold and hard, so frightening? "Duncan," I pleaded.

"Not now, Eustacia," this terrifying stranger, in rumpled clothes with an ugly bruise under one fierce eye, said. "There's Sir Ian to deal with first. If you will, Ian." He waved the revolver at him. "Please to join the others."

Sir Ian wet his lips. "Now, look here, Duncan, be reasonable."

"I *am* reasonable. Just as reasonable as you have been," Duncan replied. "Veda?"

Veda? I glanced past Duncan and saw the half-caste girl move from the shadowed doorway to stand beside Duncan. But, of course! She had told me Carla was not her real name.

"Yes, Mr. Duncan," she said, looking up at him with large adoring eyes. She *was* in love with him. It was written all over her face. A sick knot formed in my stomach.

"I want you to get a horse," Duncan said. "There must be at least one in the stables. Ride into Tenwyck and fetch the constable."

"Not the constable!" I exclaimed. "He is in with the lot of them. He was paid to keep me from returning to Rommany."

"Thank you, Eustacia," Duncan said, his eyes never leaving Sir Ian's face. "I suppose nothing would surprise me by now. So the constable is just as corrupt, as rotten as the rest of you! With what did you pay the good man? No, don't tell me; Maurice Peale, Mr. Moneybags, must have arranged it. Well, Veda, my girl, do you think you can find your way to Blethane? It's on the same road—five miles to the north by the left fork."

"I'll find it, Mr. Duncan," she said in her soft, melodious voice. I suppose that if Duncan had asked her to ride to London she would have done it gladly. So willing to please, so lovely. And how wretched I must surely look by comparison—as wretched as I felt.

"Tell the constable there to bring several men," Duncan instructed. "And have him wire the magistrate at Bristol, asking him to round up the crew of the *Destiny*. Can you remember that?"

"Yes, Mr. Duncan."

"You'll need the keys Lady Violet was obliged to give me," he said, handing her a bunch on a ring.

"Now, Ian," Duncan said when Veda had left. "Get along, with you."

Sir Ian gave me a quick glance and I averted my eyes. Shrugging, he went past Duncan and hesitated on the threshold. Duncan prodded him with the muzzle of the gun. "One twitch," Duncan said, "and I shall shoot you—with pleasure."

I started to follow, but Duncan said, "Wait here, Eustacia."

I did not want to "wait here," I did not want to remain in that horrible room, *waiting*. Duncan had not asked if I had been harmed; did not know what I had suffered; did not, in fact, seem to care.

I did as he asked, though, returning to the mattress on which I had spent so many painful hours, feeling utterly dejected. Duncan was alive just as I had hoped and prayed he would be. But our miraculous reunion had been far from a happy one—no kisses, no embraces, not a single word of endearment. Somewhere in the back of my mind a small voice nudged like a scold, branding me selfish and ungrateful for not thanking God instead of feeling my own disappointment. But I could not shake my misery. What had happened to Duncan? Was he in love with Veda, then? Hot, bitter tears coursed down my cheeks as I leaned against the wall.

"Eustacia?" In my dream I was running through a maze of dim passages. "Eustacia?"

I blinked in the light. Duncan, holding a lamp, was bending over me. "It's all over," he said. "They have been taken away."

"I . . . I must have fallen asleep," I said in a thick voice. "What time is it?"

"Past midnight."

He set the lamp on the floor and gathered me close to him.

"Oh, Duncan," I murmured against his shoulder, my unhappiness suddenly gone, now that I was safe again in his arms. "I did think they had killed you."

"They would have, but for Veda. They had me bound and gagged in one of the attic rooms. Veda found and released me."

A thousand questions burned on my tongue. Did you— *do* you love Veda? What does she mean to you? Why did she attack me with the candlestick? But I could not spoil what I had now—Duncan's dear face close to mine, his lips caressing my cheek. Later perhaps I—or we—would sort it all out.

"Come, my darling," Duncan said, taking my hand. "Let us go home."

Home. Was there ever a more beautiful word?

Burning with fever, I remained in bed for a week, slipping in and out of the same horrible nightmare where I found myself fleeing down endless dusty corridors, often pursued by phantoms, ghosts who took shape at the last cataclysmic moment either as Lady Violet or Sir Ian or a grinning Maurice Peale.

The doctor Duncan had fetched said that rest and food would eventually bring me around. And he was right, for gradually my strength returned and I began to think more rationally about my experience at Rommany. There were still so many unanswered questions (Veda was uppermost in my mind), but Duncan seemed disinclined to discuss what had happened, so I kept my thoughts to myself.

One morning, soon after my recovery, we were sitting at breakfast when Duncan, who had been immersed in a newspaper, suddenly put it down. "Just exactly why were you kissing Ian?"

The question, coming out of the blue, startled me. I gaped at Duncan for a moment or two, then commenced to stutter, "W ... w ... why ... I—"

"If you thought me dead," he went on, his voice tinged with irony, "you certainly lost no time with the amenities of mourning."

"Duncan! How—how could you—how could you say such a thing?"

"Well, my dear, explain then. You have my full attention."

I began, haltingly, recounting my stay at the Meachams and my loss of memory.

"I know all that," he interrupted impatiently. "That scalawag Meacham, could not talk fast enough. He went on and on about how well he had cared for you. He hoped to save his skin, I suppose. But get to the point, my dear."

"Well—Sir Ian gave me a choice. I . . . I would be killed or I could go to Africa with him as his mistress."

"And you chose to be his mistress?" he asked, a stern frown between his eyes.

"No, Duncan," I pleaded. "But I thought if ... if I could put him off by saying yes ... and ... and he wanted a kiss to seal the bargain. He meant nothing to me, I swear."

"Nothing?" I could tell by the sudden glimmer in his eyes that he was teasing me and probably had been all along.

But I did not like being teased, especially about something which had been most unpleasant. "Why should you point a jealous finger at *me?*" I said, vastly annoyed. "When you—you and Veda had an affair?"

"What?" he exclaimed incredulously. "I and Veda? I thought you had met her and were aware of her identity."

"No—she was very secretive. The only thing she told me was that she had met you in Bombay."

"And so you believed . . . ?" He shook his head. "I've known Veda since she was small. She is John Hempstead's ward. He adopted her when her mother, a Hindu woman, and her father, a British soldier, died of typhoid. Veda was eight years old at the time. John cared for her as though she had been his own daughter. I thought I told you she was in school."

"Why, yes, I remember you speaking of John's ward, but you said nothing about her being a half-caste."

"I suppose not," he said dryly. "I had never thought of Veda as having any sort of label. To me she is a sweet, dear girl. She was entirely devoted to John when he was alive and, I might add, has since confided to me that she is madly in love with John's nephew, Harold."

"Harold?"

"He came to our wedding, my dear, and he also called upon us here when we returned from our honeymoon."

"Of course. He was growing a moustache. And he said that he was sorry we had missed his uncle's funeral. But why did I not meet Veda, then?"

"She was supposed to have returned to her school in France immediately after the funeral."

"And she didn't?"

"No. Actually, the little minx had obtained employment as a maid in Ian's household."

It seems that the day after her guardian's funeral, Veda, looking through the window of an upstairs bedroom of the Hempstead house, noticed a well-dressed man across the street standing in the shadow of a doorway. "He was staring at the house in such a way as to arouse Veda's suspicions," Duncan said. "So she drew on a shawl and came downstairs and continued to observe him through a side window. When he started to walk away, she slipped out and followed him. Fortunately he was on foot and did not live far. The man, as you may have surmised, was Ian.

"When Veda returned home, she inquired of the Hempstead butler if a man of Ian's description had ever called at the house. He said yes, he believed such a person had come by a week before his master's death, requesting to see him, but that Mr. Hempstead was out at the time."

"Ian must have come back another day, then," I said.

"He confessed to me that he killed John Hempstead."

"Yes, I guessed as much as soon as he began to hound me in earnest about the map. And he did return one afternoon when all the servants were gone. Veda, of course, knew none of this. She merely had an intuitive feeling that this man had something to do with the death of her guardian. She thought that if she could obtain employment in the Blackmore residence, she might find some proof to justify her suspicions.

"I won't go into the devious scheme Veda concocted to lull Harold and his father into believing she had been safely packed off to school. Suffice it to say that she was hired as a maid by Lady Violet."

"I was surprised that she had," I said. "Pretty girls are anathema to Lady Violet."

Duncan smiled. "She did not much like you, did she?"

"Lady Violet hated me," I replied.

"She probably would have felt the same about Veda, except for three things. One, Veda caught her at an opportune moment, just when the third lady's maid had left her employ within a month. Two, Veda, being foreign, came exceedingly cheap. And last, Lady Violet, who is a terrible bigot, believed that Veda, because she spoke with an accent, had a poor understanding of English and therefore could be trusted.

"Veda had been at the Blackmore house only two weeks when Lady Violet informed her that they were going to Rommany, explaining that she and her husband were planning a practical joke on a relative. You can imagine how it shocked Veda to discover I was the relative in question. She kept out of my way, she told me, for fear of being exposed as a spy."

"She had no idea what Ian was really after?" I asked.

"Not then. Veda said she first started to feel things were very wrong when she noticed that she and a halfwit stableman were the only two servants taken by the Blackmores from the London house. The rest were supposedly hired at Rommany."

"They were the crew of the *Destiny*," I said.

"So Veda subsequently discovered. Nevertheless, after the furniture was trundled away and Veda and the stableman paid off and returned to London, Veda began to see in retrospect that there was much more than a joke involved at Rommany. She came back then, managed to pry open a shutter—and you know the rest. By the way," he added, "she does apologize for hitting you with the candlestick. It was an accident, really. She panicked when she thought you were going to scream. Afterwards she went to get some water with which to revive you, but when she returned you had gone. She said she wants to explain in person as soon as you are able to receive company."

"I shall be happy to have her any time," I said, thinking that it was I who owed the apology for the shameful way I had pictured her, a siren pursuing Duncan.

"My solicitor wants to see me at eleven," Duncan said, pushing his chair back. "Would you like to come along?"

"Oh? Why—yes, of course. What does he want to see you about?"

"I have no idea."

Upstairs in the narrow, cramped bedroom, I sat before a mirror, adjusting my hat. "The map," I said. "Did you ever really give Ian the map?"

"No," he answered, peering over my head as he tied his cravat. "I bluffed. I knew he would kill me once I did, so I kept procrastinating. But, of course, I couldn't have given him the *whole* map. You see, John Hempstead had the other half."

"*Had?*"

"I was never able to find it after he died."

"Ian got it?"

"No, he would have told me if he did."

"And so you have half a map. Where?"

He turned me around and lifted me to my feet. "Eustacia, my love," he said, taking me into his arms, "if I never hear the word *map* again, it will be too soon. Enough of such talk. I will tell you someday, in good time. But now for more important things." He kissed me, a long, thoroughly satisfying kiss, and when I was finally released, breathless and happy, I was quite willing to forget about maps, too.

Chapter 14

The trial of Sir Ian, Lady Violet, the Peales, Mr. Meacham, Landeville, and the crew of the *Destiny* stretched out for weeks and was an ordeal I shall try to forget. In the end, the lesser participants in the plot were sent to gaol. Lady Violet, for her part in the murder of John Hempstead, was sentenced to life imprisonment. She received the news with cold fury in her eyes. And although he threw himself on the mercy of the court, Sir Ian was sentenced to death by hanging. Some said these were harsh penalties for aristocrats, but then John Hempstead, a member of a prominent family himself, was well liked, and feelings ran high.

It was a tragic ending. And ironic. And it altered the course of our lives. For with Sir Ian's death, Rommany came to Duncan.

We knew, of course, when Duncan's solicitor had spoken to us that morning, that if Ian should be judged guilty, Duncan, the only surviving Blackmore, would fall heir to the Blackmore title. But we had not thought Sir Ian would be executed and had not concerned ourselves with thoughts of the estate. And if we had, I never would have dreamed that Duncan would want to *live* at Rommany. After all, he was quite wealthy and could have most any house he chose and, failing that, could have easily built one suitable to his position and taste.

"I'm fully aware of the bad memories Rommany has for you," Duncan said, after listening to my objections. "But it has been in the family for over three hundred years. I can't give it up."

"I'm not asking you to give it up."

"I know, I know. But listen, my sweet," we were sitting side by side in the small parlor of the Kensington house. "I plan to renovate Rommany from top to bottom. You shan't recognize it when I am through. It will be a showplace—really, darling." His eyes glowed with the kind of enthusiasm Duncan reserved for very new, exciting projects and I guessed his fascination with Rommany had more to do with the challenge it presented then its place in family history. "Please say you agree," he begged, hugging me, kissing my cheek.

How could I not?

He was my husband, and I, as his wife, wanted to make him happy. Perhaps he was right. Perhaps Rommany, once restored, the roof and chimneys repaired, the shutters rehung, the bare floors covered with colorful carpets, the rooms newly papered and furnished, would look different, even attractive. And hadn't I admired it the first night I was there with the fire leaping in the grate, the rosy flames reflected in the shine of satinwood?

"Very well, Duncan," I capitulated halfheartedly, for, despite my optimism I still had grave reservations.

But Duncan, ignoring my lukewarm acceptance, hugged and kissed me again, delighted as any schoolboy.

He did not want me to see the house until everything was finished. I could select whatever wallpaper, fabrics, and furniture I liked from the London shops but for the rest he wanted it to be a surprise. It was a rather bewildering task for a young girl to undertake, so I asked Mama to come and help me. Duncan provided us with the measurements and a diagram of the rooms and carte blanche as to expense. The house was so huge I thought it a waste to bother with more than we needed. The ground floor alone boasted of two dining rooms and two drawing rooms, the larger dining room and drawing room (as I had guessed earlier) having been set aside for "state" occasions. (It seemed the original Sir Blackmore had hoped to be visited by royalty.) But Duncan said the house must be complete, that we should have children and grandchildren and a host of friends. ". . . And I want no one turned away for want of a bed."

Mama came and stayed during the month of February

and a good part of March, and helped me choose breakfronts and tables, sofas and rugs, hangings and beds, lamps and bric-a-brac until my head fairly whirled. By the last week in March we had finished and the furnishings were lodged in a warehouse awaiting delivery to Rommany.

Since it would take another three weeks before the house would be ready for occupancy, Mama suggested I come home with her on a visit. Though the reason for my recently acquired title was hardly a secret—the Blackmore scandal had been given prominent play in the newspapers from one end of Britain to the other—my parents, in their own inimitable way, chose to ignore the sordid story and were openly proud of my having become Lady Blackmore. They insisted my showing me off to their neighbors by giving a large dinner party in my honor during which I became embarrassingly ill.

It was not the food, I discovered—I was in the family way.

When he heard the news, a delighted Duncan came immediately to Newberry. Now Rommany would have an heir, he said, and then he and Papa proceeded to celebrate by getting disgracefully drunk.

To my surprise, Mama did not scold. "All's well that ends well," she said to me with a smile.

Duncan had been accepted at last—so much so that Mama was later to forget her initial objection to Duncan, and, to my astonishment, take full credit for the match.

We came to Rommany in early April, traversing the fourteen miles from Colchester through lush new green countryside. It was a far different landscape from the drab November one I remembered, and I took heart. Even so, I was not prepared for the complete change Duncan had made in Rommany. As we rounded the sweep in the drive and the house came into view, I could hardly believe my eyes. The buff-colored brick walls were set off by cream shutters, thrown back from gleaming windows, the gardens had been cleared and new flower beds laid out, blooming now, vivid with yellow daffodils and red tulips.

The interior was even more splendid. I went from one room to the next, exclaiming, pleased that the furnishings

Mama and I had chosen had so completely transformed the house. The old Rommany—the Rommany of my nightmares—no longer existed.

Happiness, too, served to blot out bad memories. Except for an occasional headache and an uncomfortable dream, I seemed to have suffered no ill effects from my horrible experience. In the years that followed I rarely thought of Lady Violet or diamond mines or a map. I was too busy, too occupied, taken up with the numberless duties of hostess (for, true to Duncan's word, Rommany did become a showplace and we entertained lavishly) and as a mother. Ernest, our eldest, was born that July, and two years later we had Amelia, so like me in her coloring; the honey-gold hair, the blue-gray eyes. And then, in quick succession, three more boys! Stuart, Roger, and David. They were healthy, boisterous children and I loved them all dearly, my sons and my lovely daughter.

I don't know where the time went, the months, the years, all so hurried, so full. The house lost some of its glossy elegance under the rough-and-tumble of four boys, but neither Duncan nor I really minded the sometimes muddied carpets or the occasional spill on a tapestried chair, or even the fading wallpaper. Somehow homely shabbiness lent a new, mellow dimension to Rommany and to our lives.

Duncan had found an outlet for his energies in county politics and the business of managing the estate. He had grown a little heavier, quite gray at the temples, now, but was still a handsome, well-set-up man, still had the power to move me when he walked into a room.

Veda had married Harold, and they became our dearest friends, traveling down to Rommany from London for all the holidays. We looked upon them as family; Veda, charming, warmhearted; Harold, stalwart, heavily moustached, carrying on the business which he had inherited from his uncle. And their children, too, as they arrived one by one, Benjamin, Dora, and John, were included in our warm relationship.

So it went, Christmas passing into Easter, Easter into midsummer with hardly any interval between, it seemed, the seasons rolling up the years. Then one day, quite suddenly, I realized that Amelia had grown up and it was time to send her away to school. We had sent Ernest, who would in time inherit the title and the estate, to boarding school at a tender age and later to Eton, from where he was planning to enter Oxford, but Amelia had been kept at home with the younger children under the tutelage of a governess. Now that she was fifteen and had learned everything a governess could teach her, she must be "finished" properly.

Apart from a desire to have Amelia turned out as an accomplished young woman, there was another reason for my wanting her to leave Rommany. She had grown overly fond of Douglas Woodhill, a local youth, entirely unsuitable as a prospective husband. I knew that it might be premature to worry about Amelia's marriage, but I could not take the risk of seeing this childhood friendship develop into a misguided love.

I thought to enroll Amelia in the same school I had attended in Ulster as a girl, but Duncan said it was much too far away—he had a tendency to spoil his only daughter—and much too rigid, so, instead, Amelia entered Miss Lockridge's Female Academy in London, an institution which Duncan found commendable because it gave several scholarships each year to less fortunate girls, on merit alone. "It helps remind the others that money and position are not everything," he said.

At first sight I was not overly impressed with the academy. Though it was housed in what had formerly been the Mockford mansion, a lovely Palladian structure, the neighborhood in which it stood had long ceased to be fashionable. Nevertheless, the school, according to Harold Hempstead, was one of the best and highly recommended by a number of peers whose daughters had been—or were currently—under Miss Lockridge's care.

After Amelia had recovered from an initial homesickness, she settled down quite nicely at the academy, did well in her studies, was apparently liked by her teachers and fellow students as well.

The year went smoothly, and as the summer holiday approached, Amelia asked if she might bring a friend home on a visit. The girl was an orphan, one of those on scholarship, Amelia wrote, and had nowhere to go except to an old crotchety godmother.

"Of course, she is welcome. We have plenty of room," I replied to Amelia's letter, thinking of Douglas Woodhill and how Amelia's schoolmate would provide a good diversion.

So I was quite prepared for our visitor. What I was not prepared for was my reaction to her. The moment I set eyes on Trina Blake I was filled with an inexplicable, totally baseless dread—the same sort of foreboding I had experienced long, long ago when Duncan and I had first approached Rommany through the darkness and the rain.

Part II

AMELIA

(1886)

Chapter 1

"You don't like her very much, do you?" I asked Mama.

We were conversing in low tones in the bedroom Mama shared with Papa. I had come there after installing Trina in one of the guest rooms, thinking I had better clear the air before things got too uncomfortable.

"Oh, dear, is that the impression I gave?" Mama replied, her hand fluttering to her forehead, a gesture I knew from past experience to be the harbinger of one of her "bad" headaches.

"No, Mama, it is just my own feeling."

To a stranger, Mama's welcome may have appeared gracious and courteous, but to me, who knew her so well, the momentary widening of gray-blue eyes, the almost imperceptible stiffening of the spine had clearly signified disapproval.

"You are always imagining things," Mama said, leaning back on the pillows. "Do draw the curtains, Amelia. There's a good girl! I can't understand why you seem to think your friend displeases me. After all, we've hardly had the chance to get acquainted."

Poor darling Mama! I did love her so, and I had guessed at once that Trina's shabby, though neat, appearance had caught her by surprise. Mama had always been *so* transparent. Even as a small child I remember the way I could tell how she felt by the expression in her eyes. And when she sent me away to the academy, ostensibly to finish my education and to make a "fine lady" of me, I knew all along that the real reason was to separate me from Douglas. As if anybody could!

"Perhaps you are right, Mama," I agreed. "But tell me truthfully—*do* you object to Trina Blake?"

"Of course not," she said quickly. "It's just that there is something about her. . . ." She paused, then gave me a small smile and reached out for my hand. "Oh, well, never mind. We shall do our best to make her stay at Rommany a pleasant one."

And I knew she would try to do just that, though she would have been far happier if I had brought home Sir Gillespie's daughter or the earl of Rochester's niece.

"She's not had very much," I said. "Her father earned a poor living as a clergyman when he was alive, and her mother had no money of her own. Her mother's people, I think, went bankrupt in the wine business. Anyway, Trina is without relatives and must live with this dreadful godmother, Mrs. Cozzens. She's sixty, and very gloomy. Wears black all the time for her dead husband."

"What's wrong with mourning for a dead husband?"

"Nothing, I suppose. Except he died thirty years ago."

Mama smiled and I laughed.

"You've a kind heart," Mama said. "And I count that for something."

"You've a kind heart, too." I bent down and kissed her on the cheek, warm and dry to my lips.

She held my hand for a few moments, and her eyes suddenly became moist. "I couldn't bear to have anything happen to you."

"Whatever do you mean?" I said, surprised. "I'm home, and Trina and I have made all kinds of lovely plans for this summer. What could possibly happen to me?"

"I don't know," she said in a vague voice. "I don't know."

Looking at her white face in the dim light, her eyes roaming the room, my heart suddenly constricted. My father, when he was in a bantering mood, claimed my Irish mother was fey, prone to superstitious notions. It was a family joke. But now I wondered. Did Mama see something with those large, beautiful eyes of hers I did not, something strange and frightening for the future? Or was it my imagination, the imagination she had chided me about earlier?

"Is your head worse?" Perhaps pain had brought on this sudden, alarming concern.

"Oh—not much."

"Can I get you something?"

"No, thank you, darling. Run along, dear, and ask Mrs. Chalmers to hold dinner back an hour. Your father said he would be late."

Mama leaned heavily on Mrs. Chalmers to run the house. She was a countrywoman of Mama's, formerly lady's maid to my grandmother, a tall, spare woman with a quantity of iron-gray hair which she tried (not always successfully) to confine under a white lace cap. I had never heard Mrs. Chalmers raise her voice, never heard her laugh, had never seen her smile. Yet she was fanatically devoted to all of us—and fair. (I could remember more than one occasion on which she had stoutly defended me against an unjust accusation.) She had been with us ever since I could recall and was as much a fixture at Rommany as the great front door. And I am sorry to say that for the most part I did look upon her exactly as I did the great front door, present, solid, indispensable. It was not until later, when tragedy descended upon us, that I came to realize for the first time how fond I was of her, how much she had meant to me. But this was the summer of my sixteenth year and I was still somewhat of a child, spoiled, expecting everyone to be pleasant and pleased with me.

I found Mrs. Chalmers in her rooms. She was at her desk, going over a ledger, her lips pursed, a frown between her eyes. A tray holding a pot of tea and a plate of scones sat on the round table at her elbow. I gave her Mama's message.

"Very well, Miss Amelia," she said with a tone of heavy patience. Mrs. Chalmers was a punctual soul and any deviation from strict routine brought on what we called her "martyr" voice. "I shall inform Cook."

"Mama has told you, I suppose, that I have brought a guest home?" I asked.

"Yes, Miss Amelia," she answered. "I had a glimpse of her as she came in the door."

"And what do you think? She is pretty, isn't she?"

Mrs. Chalmers studied her pen for a moment. "I daresay she is, but. . . ."

"But what?" I asked, leaning over and selecting a scone from the plate. We had missed our tea and I was hungry.

"It isn't for me to say, I suppose, but I'll say it anyway. She gives me a peculiar feeling."

"What kind of peculiar feeling?" I asked, biting into the scone, crisp and flaky, not soggy like the ones at school.

"She's unlucky."

My eyes went wide. Mrs. Chalmers may have been as Irish as Mama, but there the similarity ended. Mrs. Chalmers was the last person in the world to bandy words like "luck" about. "I don't know what you mean," I said.

"You mustn't talk with your mouth full," she reprimanded, getting to her feet. "And I haven't the time to sit here and discuss whys and what fors. I must see to Cook."

I wiped my fingers on a scrap of handkerchief and went out and down the stairs. The great hall was empty and I sauntered across it and up the main staircase to my room, feeling depressed and lonely. What a curious thing for Mrs. Chalmers to say about Trina. Unlucky. Perhaps our housekeeper was getting old and a little odd.

An uncharacteristic quiet pervaded the house. Ernest, my older brother, had gone on a tour of the Continent with a friend and was not expected at Rommany until the first week in September. Stuart, six years younger than I, would begin his holiday from boarding school the following week, and my two youngest brothers, Roger and David, were out with Miss Weatheringham, the governess, on a nature walk. Most of all I missed Papa, whom I had so looked forward to seeing. Throughout my childhood he had been my special ally, lending a sympathetic, kindly ear to my woes, real or imaginary. He rarely "approved" or "disapproved," leaving such decisions or pronouncements to Mama, and he was far more tolerant than she. Though he never said as much, I felt *he* did not mind my friendship with Douglas Woodhill.

I sat down at the window and drummed my fingers on the sill. Two hours until dinner. I could go and talk to Trina, I thought, but somehow I felt reluctant to do so. Even though I had stoutly defended her, she and I were not really close friends. It's not that I had lied when I told

Mama I felt sorry for her. I did. Trina was an orphan, and her life with Mrs. Cozzens must have been terribly dreary, though Trina rarely spoke of it. She had only said, "I hate to see school term end," in a tight little voice, as if she were trying to keep from crying. It seemed such a contrast from me and the others, chattering like happy birds, eager to get home. I felt a twinge of guilt mingled with compassion, and so I had impulsively invited her to Rommany.

Later, when I reflected on it, I wondered if my invitation had not been prompted by more than altruism. For in having a girl companion to accompany me Mama would not be worrying overmuch about my seeing Douglas. Not that she had strictly forbidden our meeting, but I knew she frowned upon it. Before I left for the academy she had said, "You are growing into a lovely young woman, Amelia, and I hope you will learn to put all childish attachments behind."

But Douglas was more than a "childish attachment." I loved him. I think I loved Douglas from the time I was eight and looked down from the saddle of my pony to meet his dark gypsy eyes. Even now, though so many years have passed, that steady, solemn boy's stare is still fresh in my memory.

It was a day in April, I remember, warm for the season, sunny and fragrant with lilac. Papa had invited me to ride with him to High Farm where he had business with the Woodhills, long-time tenants of the Blackmores. Tyson Woodhill's wife Molly had come into some money through the death of a distant cousin—a squire somebody or other—and the windfall, coupled with Tyson's excellent husbandry, had enabled them to negotiate with Papa for the purchase of High Farm as a freeholding. Though my father hated to lose the Woodhills as tenants, he was glad for their sakes. "I always like to see a good man get up in the world," he had told Mama.

We arrived at the farm shortly after eleven. Tyson Woodhill met us at the gate. Papa turned to me and said, "You needn't come indoors. Here's young Douglas. Perhaps he'll show you around while Mr. Woodhill and I discuss our business."

It was then I looked down and saw Douglas. He took

hold of the pony's bridle. "She's lovely," he said, his hand patting her flank appreciatively. "Is she yours?"

"Of course she is," I replied haughtily.

Douglas smiled. He had very white teeth and they contrasted strikingly with the brown of his skin. He was tall for his age (twelve, I later learned) and carried himself very straight, with his shoulders thrown back in contrast to Ernest, who had a tendency to slouch. I didn't think I had ever seen a boy quite so handsome.

"Shall we give the pony a drink of water, then?" he asked.

"If you like," I said, my voice still starchy.

He led us around the house and across a yard where chickens pecked in the hard, packed soil, to a stone trough under a pump. The pony drank loudly while we both watched intently, suddenly shy of each other. Finally she had her fill, lifting her muzzle from the water, snorting and shaking her head.

"Would you like to try the stack?" Douglas asked politely.

"The what?"

"The haystack. Sliding down the haystack. Haven't you ever done so?" Douglas's accent was not as pronounced as the other farm children I had met (they said that Molly Woodhill, having had some pretensions at education, had seen to that), so it wasn't that I did not understand him. It was simply that such a form of entertainment had never occurred to me.

"No," I said. Then, after a moment, "I believe I should like to try."

It was a wholly surprising, delightful experience. I can still hear myself shouting with glee, hear the ring of Douglas's laughter. Afterwards I got scolded for tearing my riding habit and was forbidden to repeat such unladylike behavior. But that stack slide was the start of my friendship with Douglas.

It was a curious friendship considering the difference in our stations and ages. Yet Douglas never patronized, never rebuffed, accepting me on my own merits without making me feel I was a child four years his junior or a daughter of the manor.

Perhaps the word "friendship," at least at the early

stages, was a euphemism, for we saw each other infrequently. Sometimes months passing between each meeting.

I rode over to High Farm with Papa whenever I could, of course. On one of those occasions, aware that Douglas was an avid reader, I brought him books from the Rommany library, books which I am ashamed to say, were seldom read by the Blackmore clan. On another occasion, I invited him home to afternoon tea. I think Mama was somewhat dismayed, but gracious, and later had to admit that Douglas comported himself in a far more gentlemanly manner than Ernest, who had slopped tea all over his cakes.

After that tea, because Papa no longer had business with Tyson Woodhill, our visits stopped.

Ten months passed during which I thought often of Douglas. I learned by way of servants' gossip that he was attending Parson Bell's school in the village, an unheard-of situation for a farmboy of twelve, since all hands were needed at home to help with the work. But, according to Mrs. Chalmers, Molly Woodhill favored her second son, and in spite of her husband's grumblings, insisted that Douglas be educated.

"Claims he's a born scholar," I overheard Mrs. Chalmers tell Salton, the butler, in outraged tones. "Hmmph! What's a farmer to do with education? I tell you, no good comes of people acting above themselves."

If I had been free to do so, I would have gone over to High Farm myself. But I was not allowed to ride past the stone arch unaccompanied by an adult—the adult in most cases being the current governess in residence. In the spring of that year it so happened that we acquired a new governess, a shy creature, afraid of horses. One afternoon I persuaded her to allow me to take the pony out alone, promising faithfully to be back within an hour, and I trotted off, heading straight for High Farm.

I found Douglas working alone in a field not far from the house. His face broke into a broad grin when he saw me. "Amelia! I didn't think I should ever see you again," he said as he helped me dismount.

"Nor I. But I can only stay a little while."

"Come, let us sit under the tree. I have so much to tell you. I'm going to school now."

We sat under an elm, drinking cold tea from a stone jug, eating the leavings of his noonday meal, and talking, talking as if we had known and been seeing each other every day of our lives. Old friends, as comfortable as old shoes.

"My father has bought Green Oaks," he said. "Tom Peeble died, and his widow let the farm go for cheap."

"Does that mean you will be moving?" I asked, somewhat dismayed. High Farm was fairly close to Rommany, but the house at Green Oaks was some five miles distant, a long way for a girl on a pony.

"I think so. The house here is old. The roof's going, and it's become much too small. At Green Oaks we can spread out, and Granny can have more room for her herbs and things."

Granny Woodhill, famed for her Christian piety and her skill at healing, was somewhat of a legend in the country.

"We shall still work High Farm, though," Douglas added.

There was a pause and then I asked, "Why haven't you been to call on us?"

He plucked a stone from between his knees and turned it over in his strong, brown hands. "I'm afraid I'm not very welcome at the house."

"That's not true," I hotly denied.

"Oh—your folks were mannerly enough. It's just a feeling I had."

"Mama," I said. "You mustn't mind her. She really doesn't mean to be . . . to be standoffish."

"Perhaps not, but still . . ." We both watched as a black crow, its head bobbing, pecked at a furrow. Douglas threw the stone at it and the bird flew off with a cry. Then turning to me, he asked, "Can you keep a secret?"

"Of course," I assured him, delighted that he had chosen me as a confidante.

"I'm writing a book."

"A book?" I repeated astonished. "About what?"

"It's a novel about country life. Someday I'll be famous," he added, his eyes staring darkly into the future. "And then no one will ever look down at me."

"*I* shall never look down at you, Douglas," I said, impulsively taking his hand.

He broke away from his dream to smile. "You're still a little girl, Amelia, but soon you will be a young lady and then—well, then things will seem different."

"No," I protested vehemently, "I shall never feel differently about you."

He laughed. "Here," he said, picking several blades of grass and giving me one. "Have I ever shown you how to make a whistle?"

I managed to get away once a week all that spring and summer, and then our governess, who had apparently been corresponding with a suitor in London, left to get married, and she was replaced by a woman of sterner stuff. Miss Weatheringham was keen on all sports, including riding. It was not that she frowned on my going to High Farm; she simply went with me, her presence confining conversation between Douglas and me to the weather and to polite inquiries about our respective health.

I did not have the opportunity to speak privately again to Douglas until the following Christmas, when there was an unexpected dip in the temperature and Turner's Pond froze over for the first time in years. Skates were found and Ernest and I, in Miss Weatheringham's charge, went to join a merry group already skimming expertly (or so I thought) over the ice. Douglas was there, too. It was my first time on skates and I was awkward, but under Douglas's guidance (for once Miss Weatheringham was content to sit on the sidelines) I learned quickly. Hand in hand we skated round and round, laughing and talking, our breaths little puffs of steam in the cold, brittle air. Douglas's cheeks shone with ruddy health. His dark eyes glistened as he told me that he was going to try for admission to Cambridge.

"I shall be happy if you pass the examinations," I remember saying, "but I shall miss you dreadfully, even if I don't get to see you all that often."

"I shall miss you, too," he said.

He did pass his examinations, and I did miss him. He wrote me long, eloquent, expository letters describing the school, his tutors, his fellow classmates, interesting letters, but a poor substitute for his company.

I saw little of him for the next two years and then Ernest, home from school on summer holiday, formed an unexpected friendship with Douglas. It began over a few pieces of pottery and a half dozen bronze coins unearthed by a farm laborer in the neighborhood. The farmer had shown them to Douglas, who in turn had consulted with Ernest. They both recognized the coins as Roman, and for the next few weeks, whenever Douglas could be spared from the farm, they dug—or rather excavated—a large pit on the spot where the finds had been made.

As for me, I suddenly developed an extraordinary interest in Roman history and succeeded in convincing Miss Weatheringham that my education could be broadened by watching the boys as they worked. Several afternoons a week Ernest and I would ride out, carrying a hamper strapped to the pony. And how my heart would lurch with excitement when coming up over the hill I spied Douglas already at the site. I would perch on the edge of the pit, eyes glowing, reading from a book on ancient artifacts, or simply sit, content to be silent.

As the days went by I made a shattering discovery. I was in love! I was in love with Douglas, had been for years without realizing it. Watching him laugh, frown, drink from a cup, talk, I was filled with wonder—and dismay. For Douglas still looked upon me as "little Amelia," taking no notice of how I had grown or my new, painful, adolescent shyness.

Nevertheless I took what joy I could from the moment. One evening, to my delight, Ernest had Douglas come home with us for dinner. "Papa is so glad you could come," I managed to whisper as we sat down at the table.

It was during the meal that Douglas told us he would not be returning to Cambridge for the new term. His father's health was failing, and he was needed at home. "It's only for a short while," he explained. "And I really don't mind. My father's worked so hard all his life, I feel it's the least I can do."

I remember expressing proper concern at this unfortunate and sad interruption in Douglas's schooling, but in my heart I was selfishly pleased. Douglas would not be going away! He and I could continue, as we had been, digging for old Roman treasure. And since Ernest would soon be leaving for Oxford, I would have Douglas all to myself. Day after day, alone with Douglas! In my mind I could already see him laughing, running down the hill to meet me, his brown arms bare to the sun. We would spread a blanket under a tree and unpack the picnic things, and he would smile at me with his eyes. . . .

At that instant, I recall looking across the table at Mama. She was gazing at me with a rather shocked expression in her eyes, and I knew she had guessed my secret.

And that was how I got sent to the academy, and why I was now, scarcely an hour back at Rommany, plotting; my mind racing hither and yon, trying to devise a way to see Douglas again.

But I had Trina! Of course! In my ramblings through the past I had nearly forgotten. First thing tomorrow, we would ride out, for I must acquaint her with all of Rommany, including the countryside. And what better excuse could I give for dropping in at Green Oaks than to show Trina what a prosperous farm looked like?

I got up from the window seat and went to find Trina, feeling somewhat guilty because I had neglected her these past few hours.

She was sitting in a chair, gazing out at the lawns. As I came into the room, she turned and smiled. Her eyes had a curious shine to them.

"I love your house," she said, her face glowing. "Rommany is perfect."

I should have been pleased and flattered, thanking her for the compliment, instead of staring at her dumbly. For a subtle change seemed to have come over the girl before me, a girl who I had always considered pretty in a rather unobtrusive way. But now she was beautiful, her features lit with a strange incandescent light, her blue eyes glittering. It was a face I found oddly disturbing.

Chapter 2

Trina rose to her feet. "Is something the matter?" She was her old self again, blue eyes in a white heart-shaped face, black hair parted in the center and caught in a smooth unswept bun at the back of her small head. Modest, neat—a pretty but ordinary girl.

"Nothing. I'm sorry if I seemed to stare." It was the light, I told myself, the light from the window, a reflection of the early evening sky still stained by the rose-mauve of the dying sun, which had made her seem strange. "It's just that"—I fumbled for words—"that I am not accustomed to having people praise Rommany with such enthusiasm."

"You must forgive my enthusiasm, then. But Rommany is . . . well, rather overwhelming to me."

I had never thought of Rommany as overwhelming—large, yes; full of good solid furniture, yes; comfortable, yes—but never overwhelming. I looked round the room with new eyes.

We called it the Green Room because of the wallpaper, pale green ivy climbing in profusion up olive-green columns, and the window hangings, tasseled and fringed, green velvet draperies. I had always thought the effect rather charming, but now, perversely, for some reason I could not fathom, there seemed too much green; the wallpaper, the draperies, the bed canopy—there was even green figured into the carpet, something I had not noticed before. The overall effect, it suddenly occurred to me, was bilious and far from agreeable.

"You don't mind all this green?" I asked Trina.

"No—I love it. I am eager to see the rest of the house."

"Of course," I murmured. "Oh—I had almost forgotten. Dinner will be late. I hope you don't mind."

"Not at all," she said. "Do you dress for dinner? I don't own a proper evening dress."

"I can lend you one of mine," I said, and the next moment we were both laughing. Trina was a good four inches shorter than I.

"Never mind," I said, "I won't dress either. We're—"

I paused, listening to noisy laughter coming down the corridor. Roger's voice shouted, "You do so!"

"It's my brothers," I explained to Trina. "They've been out for a walk. Come along to the schoolroom and meet them."

The schoolroom was at the end of the corridor, a large, airy place with a many windowed view of the rose garden. Its furnishings were nondescript: scarred tables, a ponderous oak desk on a dias for the governess, two revolving globes (one dented from the day I, in wrath, had thrown a book at Ernest and missed), glass-fronted bookcases and mounted butterflies on the walls. I had spent a great deal of my growing-up years there, resentfully doing sums and improving my grammar when I would have preferred galloping my pony out of doors instead. And yet whenever I thought of the schoolroom, it was with a twinge of nostalgia, as if I had lost some small unretrievable item there.

When I turned the doorknob, Truffles, Roger's cocker spaniel, began to bark, then seeing who it was she ran to me, her tail wagging, her long ears straining back with affection as I patted her smooth, silky head. The moment Trina entered the room from behind me, however, she began to bark again and suddenly began nipping at her heels.

The next minute was all confusion, with David hugging my knees and Miss Weatheringham exclaiming, "Quiet, Truffles! I say there, quiet!" and Roger wanting to know if I was going to stay the summer, and the dog yapping on and on. Finally Roger scooped Truffles up in his arms and took her from the room.

"I'm so sorry," I apologized. "This is my friend, Trina Blake—Miss Weatheringham. And this is David."

David, aged seven, chubby, red-haired and freckled (a throwback to his Irish ancestry, Papa claimed), bobbed his head. Then tugging at my skirt, he said, "D'you see my canary? In the corner. Look!"

What with the noisy fuss I hadn't noticed the wrought-iron cage containing the tiny yellow bird. Swinging to and fro on a perch, the canary watched us intently with beady eyes.

"Does it sing?" Trina asked, going up to the cage and tapping at the bars. The bird ruffled its wings, then suddenly flew at Trina's finger.

"Oh, dear," I exclaimed. "Did it hurt you, Trina?"

"No," Trina said. Her back was to us and I could not see her face.

"Are you sure?"

"Certainly." She turned and held out her hands, then brought them together, cracking her knuckles. "See?" She laughed. "That's a savage bird you have there, Master David."

David scowled. "Her name's Louise, and she's not savage. She's never done anything like that before, has she Miss Weatheringham?"

"There, there," the governess soothed. "It's long past Louise's bedtime. That's her trouble." She threw a napkin over the cage, and in a minute, Louise settled down.

"Perhaps she's not used to strangers," Trina said in a conciliatory tone.

"Perhaps," David agreed grudgingly.

Roger came back into the room. A year older than David, he had Papa's dark eyes, and Mama's honey-colored hair. Always a solemn child, old for his years, he shook Trina's hand gravely when I introduced them and asked politely if she had had a pleasant journey.

"Quite pleasant. But my arrival seems to have caused a commotion," she added ruefully.

"What sort of commotion?" I smiled and took her arm. "Really, Trina, if you stay long enough you will see what a real commotion we Blackmores can make. Books flying, dishes crashing, people shouting—that sort of thing. Am I not right, Miss Weatheringham?"

Miss Weatheringham, who, like Mrs. Chalmers, never had the faintest notion when her leg was being pulled, said, "I believe you exaggerate," in a rather hurt voice. "The boys are really well-behaved."

"Are you?" I asked David and Roger, twinkling my eyes.

They both laughed.

"We must get ready for dinner now," I said, kissing each of them on the cheek. "But we shall see you tomorrow."

Then, amid a chorus of goodnights, Trina and I left.

Papa was in a jovial mood. Apparently he had successfully convinced his friends, the owners of various estates in the county, that Gladstone's reform act extending the franchise to the rural population (already enjoyed by town dwellers) would not be the ruin of them.

"Progress," he said, rubbing his hands over the fire, as we sat in the drawing room after dinner. "They simply find it hard to understand that progress for one section means progress for all."

Trina, sitting primly on the sofa next to me, said, "I agree with you, sir. I think people are happier, more secure when they feel they have a say in a nation's affairs."

"Exactly," Papa said, observing Trina for the first time with interest. "You are perceptive, young lady."

"Thank you, Sir Duncan," she said modestly.

Mama touched a lace-edged handkerchief to her pale brow. "They always look to you for your opinion, Duncan, no matter how argumentative they may sound."

"True," Papa replied. "But it was not an easy matter persuading Lord Walton to my view."

Mama smiled. Lord Walton, by reputation, was a man who found it safe to say no to any proposal, regardless of merit.

Trina said, "You must have been quite eloquent then, sir."

A faint tinge of color came to Mama's cheek. I glanced at Trina. She was leaning forward, chin tilted, gazing at Papa with the same strange glow in her eyes I had seen earlier when she had spoken of Rommany. Clearly she was impressed with my father and, again, I should have felt flattered and proud. But those eyes, so dazzling blue, so frank in their admiration, unsettled me.

What sort of girl was this classmate of mine?

I went to bed that night musing over Trina, wondering

if I really knew her, but a night's dreamless sleep erased her from my mind, and when I woke in the morning, my first thought was of Douglas and how in a few hours I would see him again. Would he smile? Would he say, "I've missed you, Amelia?" Yes, of course. And would he notice the new, grown-up way I was wearing my hair? Perhaps. And, at some time during the weeks ahead, would he see I was no longer "little Amelia?"

I leapt out of bed and ran to the window, pulling the curtains aside. The sun was peeping over the trees, a brassy arc, bathing the lawns in clear light. My eyes swept the skies—not one single cloud. I smiled and the day seemed to smile back.

It was going to be the loveliest of summers!

When the maid arrived with hot water, I was still sitting on the window seat in my nightdress, gazing down at the small marble fountain on the terrace where a leaping spray of water glistened in rainbow colors.

"Good morning, Miss Amelia," she said, bobbing her head. "It's good to have you home."

Clara always wore her maid's cap a little awry and her apron tied carelessly, despite Mrs. Chalmers's carping. But she was young, strong, nimble-witted—and willing, the last of which, according to Mama, counted far more than neatness.

"Thank you, Clara," I said, watching her pour the steaming water into the basin. "It's good to be back."

"I'll bring your tea along presently," she said.

"There's no hurry. By the way, is my friend awake?" I asked, suddenly remembering. "She is in the Green Room."

"Miss Trina, you mean. She weren't there when I brung her water, miss."

"Not there?" I asked in surprise.

"No, miss. Her bed was all made up, neat and tidy-like, but she'd gone."

"Oh?" Of course, Trina was not accustomed to the service of maids. That explained the bed—but where had she disappeared to? "She's probably downstairs," I said.

I was not doing well as a hostess. Most likely Trina had awakened early as I had done (at school we were roused at six in the morning) and not knowing what to do had dressed and gone in search of breakfast, which we, at Rommany, never took before nine. Though she seemed like a person perfectly able to care for herself (and here I brushed aside a twinge of disquiet at the fleeting recollection of those strange blue eyes), it was my job to see to her comfort.

I hurriedly washed and dressed and went downstairs. Two maids were laying out the silver and china in the small family dining room when I looked in. No, Miss Trina had not been there.

I searched through the drawing room, the anteroom, the library—all the rooms on the ground floor. But Trina was nowhere to be seen.

Then I returned to the first floor and tapped at the door of the Green Room, thinking that Trina might have come back. There was no answer and I went in. The bed, as Clara had said, was made up. Trina's cloak was in the closet, so she hadn't gone out of doors.

Puzzled, I stood for a moment in the corridor, listening to the familiar sounds of early morning, the clinking of crockery as the maids delivered tea, David shouting, Truffles barking. The schoolroom, perhaps?

The shades were still drawn, the canary still sleeping beneath Miss Weatheringham's napkin.

I found Trina at last in the Long Gallery, sitting on a chair and studying the portraits along the walls. The Long Gallery was a room we rarely visited, a place given over to paintings and marble busts of various and sundry Blackmores, japanned chests and old chairs, their tapestry covers torn and faded, a suit of armor; the sort of heirlooms which had belonged to the family for simply ages and which Mama claimed did not "fit in" with the rest of the furnishings. It was a cold, unheated room, rather like a museum, which, in a way, I suppose it was.

"I have been looking all over for you, Trina," I said apologetically. "I didn't mean for you to be on your own—not the first day."

"I don't mind, if you don't," she said.

"Why should I mind?"

"Oh, my going about, perhaps poking my nose into places where I shouldn't."

"Oh, that's silly," I laughed. "We have no secrets at Rommany."

She lifted her brows. "Everybody has secrets."

It was the kind of statement any romantic sixteen-year-old would make; a banal statement really, one that, under ordinary circumstances, would evoke a responding giggle. But somewhere in Trina's words I sensed a double meaning. Instead of laughing, I felt a sudden cold chill squeeze my heart.

"Not the Blackmores," I said, with a little more emphasis than I had meant.

She turned her head and gestured at the portraits. "Can you tell me who some of these people are?"

"Well—let me see." Papa had once taken Ernest and me through and explained all the pictures, but I had only a spotty recollection of what he had said.

"This is Sir Joshua," I began, "the first baronet, sixteen hundred and something." I looked up into the heavy-lidded eyes of Sir Joshua. He wore his hair in ringlets down past his shoulders and had a neckpiece of flounces under an assertive chin. "And then ... hmmm ... well, here is Lady Charlotte. I recognize her because Papa said the picture was done by Joshua Reynolds. She is a beauty, don't you think?"

"Mmmm—rather."

We moved along, pausing before a huge family portrait. The man was wearing the white wig of the eighteenth century, the woman had a red mass of pompadoured hair and coy neck curls. Their children were grouped in various poses around her, while house dogs romped at their feet. "I have forgotten who they were," I said, making a wry face. "As you can see, some of the plaques are missing."

We passed on. "Ah—this is someone more up-to-date." I pointed to a sandy-haired man with pouches under his eyes. "Sir Ian. He was supposed to have been a black sheep."

Trina peered at him with interest. "What did he do?"

"I think he killed a man," I said in hushed tones.

Trina was properly impressed. "He *did?* How terrible! Whom did he kill?"

I thought for a moment. "Papa didn't seem to know

much about it. The two men were cousins, but they hardly saw one another. Papa inherited Rommany from Sir Ian."

Trina stared at the portrait. And suddenly that ardent glow came into her eyes again.

Really, she *was* strange!

I had always thought of her as a girl without surprises. Perhaps she was attracted to older men—Papa, and now the man in the portrait—because she had no father. The only male we ever saw at school was the dancing master, a wispy creature well into his sixties, a man not likely to stir either paternal or romantic notions.

"Shall we start down?" I asked, rather disconcerted. She seemed so far away.

Trina did not hear me and I repeated my question, suppressing the desire to shake her.

"Oh? Yes, of course," she said, at last tearing her gaze from the portrait.

Roger and David, who usually had all their meals in the schoolroom with Miss Weatheringham, were allowed to have breakfast with us that morning in honor of my homecoming. Roger carried off this rare venture into the adult world with his usual stoic calm, but David kept chattering like a squirrel while Mama looked on with an indulgent smile. (Talking with a full mouth was something she would have never tolerated from the rest of us, but then David, the youngest, was her favorite, though she stoutly denied it). In his excitement David had forgotten to feed his canary and when he suddenly remembered, he was out of his chair before Miss Weatheringham had time to restrain him.

"Come back and finish your breakfast," Mama said, still smiling, though Miss Weatheringham frowned. "After you've eaten, you may be excused."

Papa said, "All this fuss about a canary."

To which Mama replied, "It's a pet, just the same as a cat or a dog, isn't it, David, darling?"

"Yes, Mama, and I do love her."

"There you see," Mama turned to Papa. "And speaking of fuss, if I recall you were much put out when Winkie died."

Winkie had been a mongrel, not good for anything but lying in front of the fire. But he had chosen Papa upon whom to lavish his affection, and when he died, Papa had locked himself in the library with several bottles of port and would speak to no one all that day.

"Winkie was a *dog*," Papa said gruffly.

"Now, was he?" Mama said and laughed and Papa and the rest of us joined in.

I remember thinking how happy we are, what a happy family. And Mama looked so pretty that morning, her headache obviously gone, her eyes shining, her golden hair a nimbus of light. She was wearing a pale blue dress, one with tiny pearl buttons done up the front and purple violets embroidered on the collar and sleeves. Later I was to recall that picture of her in great detail, the embroidered violets, the light in her hair, her gay laugh, and wonder what had happened, what had gone wrong.

"And how are you girls planning to spend the day?" Papa asked, turning to me.

"Perhaps we shall just be lazy—or we might go riding," I said casually, not looking at Mama. "Trina could have Missy." Missy was a sedate mare, suitable for a beginning rider, which I assumed Trina to be.

"That sounds like a splendid idea," Papa said.

I felt Mama's eyes on me and sensed that she wanted me to promise not to seek Douglas out. But she said nothing. And for my part I rationalized that a promise never made was one that could not be broken.

"Well, then," Papa said, pushing back his chair, "have yourselves a pleasant day."

Trina did not own a proper riding habit, and when we got upstairs, I searched in my closet for one that might do without too much alteration.

"Here," I said, pouncing on a blue velvet jacket and skirt, "I wore this when I was twelve, but it's still in good condition. See if it fits."

Trina went to the mirror and held the skirt up, tucking it around her waist. "It's a wee bit long," she said, "but if you will lend me a needle and thread I think I can remedy that."

"Mrs. Chalmers will help you. She's a marvelous seamstress," I said, reaching for the bell.

Suddenly a shout followed by a high-pitched scream shattered the air. Petrified, I stood for an indecisive moment, hand outstretched. The disturbance had come from the schoolroom. Miss Weatheringham was not one to scream, but perhaps David or Roger had managed to outrage her beyond endurance. I hurried to the door and stuck my head out.

I could hear David sobbing and then shouting hysterically, "She's dead! She's dead!"

Terrified now, I ran down the corridor and into the schoolroom. David was standing on a chair he had pulled over to the birdcage. Beside him, the usually staunch, unflappable Miss Weatheringham, her face drained to a pasty white, clasped and unclasped her hands.

"What is it?" I demanded, going up to them.

"She's dead," David said tearfully. "Louise is dead."

I saw the canary then. It was lying at the bottom of the cage, a tiny heap of yellow feathers, its neck twisted grotesquely, its beadlike eye staring into space.

I turned away, heartsick. Trina was standing on the threshold, and for a fleeting fraction of a second, I thought I caught a look of triumph in those very blue eyes.

Chapter 3

Trina stepped into the room and the illusion—for that is what it must have been—vanished.

"How did it happen?" She asked. The look on her face was one of sincere distress.

"I don't know," Miss Weatheringham said. She retrieved the napkin from the floor where it had fallen and placed it over the cage.

David went on sobbing.

"Please don't cry," Trina said gently, as she put her arm about him. David, resting his small red head against her, continued to weep.

"We shall get you another," I promised. "The next time Papa goes up to London, he'll buy you another."

David's breath caught. "I don't want annuver. I want Louise."

Trina said, "I had a canary once."

"Did you?" David lifted his tear-stained face.

"It was a *he,*" said Trina. "And he died, too. They are very delicate birds, you know."

This one did not die because it was delicate, I thought. It was deliberately and cruelly killed. However I could not bring myself to say it aloud. David was upset enough as it was.

"We can give Louise a lovely funeral," Trina went on. "As I did with Hubert."

Who would twist a small bird's neck? I wondered. A servant, one who resented cleaning the messy cage?

"Shall we have a *real* funeral," David said, suddenly enchanted.

"Certainly. A candy box for a coffin." Trina's glance went to the window, "And we shall bury her in the rose garden."

"She'd like that," David said and he smiled.

Miss Weatheringham, now fully recovered, nodded. "I must say, Miss Trina, you have a way with children."

"I have never had a brother," Trina said wistfully.

How could I have felt that she was anything but sincere?

The funeral was held an hour later. Mama, the two boys, Miss Weatheringham, Trina and I attended. Somehow I could not bring myself to tell Mama how the canary had died, and to this day I have no idea whether she ever knew. I wanted to talk to Papa about it, but he was closeted with the local auctioneer in the library, and I dared not intrude.

Perhaps, I thought, I was making too much of a canary's death, but even after we lowered the beribboned box into the ground, the memory of the yellow fluffed feathers and the twisted neck haunted me.

What with Louise's sad interment and the alteration of my old riding habit for Trina, it was well after lunch before we left the house for our ride. When we reached the stables, Trina paused at Lucifer's stall.

"May I have this one?" Trina asked. The horse, a huge black stallion, snorted and shot us a wild white-eyed look.

"That's Lucifer," I said. "No one dares ride him but my father. He's got a temper as devilish as his name."

"He seems friendly to me," Trina said, putting her hand out.

And, to my utter amazement, Lucifer, who would have whinnied and reared had I done the same, laid his nose on the bar as gently as Truffles, while Trina stroked his velvety head.

She had a way, it seemed, not only with small children, but with horses as well.

"I don't think Papa would like it," I said after a moment. "Besides Lucifer might behave differently once you get on his back. I think it's best you stick to Missy."

She did not protest, though I noticed the flash of scorn in her eyes when Missy was brought out by the stableman.

"I did not realize you were an experienced rider," I

said. "But if you wish, you may have my mount." The pony had long since been replaced by a large fawn-colored mare named Biscuit.

"No, thank you, Amelia." She smiled. "This will do nicely."

We trotted down the drive and through the stone arch. "Where shall we go?" Trina asked.

"Green Oaks," I said, without hesitation, resisting the sudden urge to kick Biscuit into a gallop, the morning's unpleasantness with the canary instantly forgotten in the excitement of anticipation. Would Douglas be at home? I wondered. I had heard from him only once during the last school term, a short letter saying that though his father's condition had worsened the farm was doing splendidly. He had made no mention of progress on his book, not a word about returning to Cambridge. Had he changed his mind, then, or worse still, had it been changed for him?

A half mile from the farmhouse we came upon Douglas's older brother, William, mending a fence. As we brought the horses to a halt, he came forward to greet us.

"Yer back from school, then, Miss," William said, removing his cap.

"For the summer," I replied. William was of middling height, stockily built, with a weatherbeaten face already beginning to show deep lines. He would inherit the farm when his father died and he took his farming seriously. "How is your father?"

"Not good," he shook his head, "not good at all."

"I'm sorry to hear that."

"Can't be helped," he said stoically.

"And how is the rest of the family?" I was suddenly too shy to ask after Douglas in particular.

"All in good health, thanks to Granny, though she don't seem able to do much for Father. Why don't you stop by and chat with her? She likes company."

"We shall do that," I said.

We left him then and trotted on, presently coming to a gate set between two low buildings. Slipping out of the saddle, I opened the gate and led Biscuit through. Trina followed, looking around at the farmyard. She said nothing, but from the look in her eye I guessed she was wondering why I should want to visit anyone who lived in such a place.

"The Woodhills were once tenants of ours," I said, hoping that explanation would satisfy her. I could not bring myself to tell her about Douglas. It was a secret I found hard to share.

"That man—William," Trina said, "did he not seem a bit disrespectful?"

"How do you mean? Because he did not bow and scrape?" I answered, somewhat annoyed. Last night she had heartily agreed with Papa about equal rights for rural folk, and now she was playing the *grande dame*. "The Woodhills are freeholders. They are their own people."

"I expect you are right." Her eyes swept the house, a large whitewashed building with a thatched roof. Suddenly her gaze froze, and glancing upward, I saw Granny Woodhill's yellow wrinkled face at an open window.

"That's Granny," I said and waved. "She is supposed to have a cure for everything. Would you care to meet her, Trina?"

"No." Her face had gone white. "I ..." her lips trembled.

"Are you ill?" I inquired, somewhat alarmed at the sudden change in her.

"No—not ill. Just feeling a bit queasy." She cracked her knuckles nervously.

"Here, let me help you down." With my assistance she slid from Missy. "Perhaps Granny might have something—"

"No!" she exclaimed. And then in a more moderate tone, "No, I hate to bother anyone. It's simply that I'm not used to riding. I'll be all right in a few moments."

I was tethering the horses when Douglas came round the corner of the house. Seeing me, he stopped abruptly, his face breaking into a smile; a beautiful, sweet smile.

"Amelia!" he cried, striding up to me, taking my hand. "I've been thinking of you all day and wondering when you would come home."

"I arrived yesterday," I said, letting go of his hand reluctantly.

"It's so *good* to see you."

"Thank you, Douglas. But why didn't you answer my last letter?" I chided.

"I didn't have all that much to say, I'm afraid. Things here haven't changed."

"William told us about your father."

"Yes, poor man. He seems to be dying slowly. He has a malignant growth. Nothing can be done."

"I am sorry, Douglas."

"We all are. But . . ." His eyes went to Trina, who was standing quietly next to the horses.

"Oh," I said, "I've forgotten my manners. This is Trina Blake, Douglas Woodhill. Trina's a classmate and is spending the summer with us."

Trina apparently had fully recovered from her queasiness. Her white cheeks had turned pink and her eyes shone. She was looking at Douglas now exactly the same way she had looked at Papa. And it seemed to me that peculiar, ardent expression resembled nothing as much as *hunger*—predatory hunger.

Not Douglas, I thought angrily, *you can't have Douglas!*

"You did not tell me you had such a pretty classmate," Douglas murmured, staring at Trina as if mesmerized.

"I never knew you were interested," I replied tartly. But Douglas did not seem to notice.

"Our Dalmation hound has just had a new litter," he said to Trina. "Perhaps you would like to see the puppies?"

No mention of whether *I* would like to see them. How could he have forgotten my presence so quickly?

"I should love to see them," Trina said, her eyes still on his face.

"They're in the cowshed." Then, as an afterthought, "Amelia, are you coming?"

I had the impulse to say, "Go on by yourselves. I really don't care," but didn't. Instead I tagged behind them across the yard, wondering sourly why I had ever thought bringing Trina to Green Oaks such a good idea.

Like all the buildings on Tyson Woodhill's farms, the cowshed was spotless. Empty now, because the cows were still in pasture, it smelled of sweet hay mingled with the odor of dung. The Dalmation bitch was lying on a bed of clean yellow straw, her nine pups nursing at her black-spotted belly. She bared her fangs when Trina leaned over, but Douglas spoke and the dog stopped growling, though her eyes remained hostile as Trina lifted one of the pups.

"Miss Blake?"

"Please call me Trina."

"Trina," Douglas said, "do you mind terribly if I have a word in private with Amelia?"

Had I heard correctly? A word in private with *me*? But then Douglas touched my elbow and I could have laughed with joy. Ah, jealousy, how it clouded one's perspective!

"I shall not mind at all, Douglas," Trina said, looking up at him with a soft smile on her lips. "As long as you do not stay away too long."

"I'll try not to," Douglas said gallantly.

He took me by the arm and guided me out of the shed and across the yard to a crude wooden bench under a large oak.

I waited for him to speak. A duck waddled past, followed by her brood, tiny fluff-feathered birdlings, all in a row. Against the cowshed wall, a cat dozed in the sun. Douglas stared at the cat and said nothing.

"What is it?" I asked, breaking the long silence at last. "Are you worried about your father?" His face, now that I had a more dispassionate look, appeared drawn.

"Yes." He turned to me. "But there is something else. I had to see you alone for a moment."

My heart leaped in my throat. Was he going to declare himself? Was he going to say he loved me, had loved me?

"You are the only person who would understand," he went on, "and I have needed someone to talk to. A friend." He gave me a brief smile.

A friend. It was not the declaration I had hoped for. Nevertheless, it was far better than nothing. Friendships did sometimes bloom into love, didn't they?

"I couldn't write," Douglas was saying. "On paper it seemed too much like complaining. But it seems that I shall have to remain on the farm. Permanently." His eyes had a hard bright shine.

"But, Douglas, when your father ... your father—" I could not say the word.

Douglas said it for me. "When my father dies, both

farms will go to William. But he cannot operate them alone."

"And you feel obligated to stay?"

"Mother says I have no need to. She insists I go back to school. But I've given my word to my father. I won't shirk my responsibilities."

"There's your reading public," I pointed out. "You have a responsibility to them. The book, the novel!"

"My reading public, little Amelia, as you well know, exists only in my imagination." He smiled faintly. "Maybe when I am old and lame, I can sit by the fire and finish writing the great saga of Green Oaks and High Farm."

I did not know what to say. Above our heads the leaves stirred and their dappled shadows trembled in my lap. I thought of Douglas's ambitions—to get a degree in literature at Cambridge, to write, to become a famous novelist—and now a sick old man had put an end to his dreams. Conscience dictated that I should pity Tyson—so soon to die, and therefore to lose his dreams, too—but I'm afraid my thoughts were all with Douglas. How hard and selfish love can be when one is sixteen!

"I wanted you to know," Douglas said. "Perhaps you won't want to continue your friendship with a man who has no future, except as a peasant." It was said without rancor, but I knew that deep in his heart Douglas was bitter.

"What nonsense!" I said, touching his hand. "I would not be much of a friend, then, would I?"

He turned his dark gaze upon me, his somber eyes searching mine. His face was very close, so close I could feel his breath caress my cheek, could see the pupils of his eyes widen ever so slightly. His hand seemed to burn to my touch. For a heart-beat instant I thought our lips would meet. But suddenly the dog in the cowshed began to bark and a scream shattered the shadowed sunlight.

Douglas was on his feet. "It must be Trina!"

He ran toward the cowshed. And I, gathering up my riding skirt, followed as quickly as I could.

Trina was standing away from the straw litter, stick in hand, her arm upraised over the cringing Dalmation at her feet. She must have struck the dog; its snout was bloodied.

"Here . . . !" Douglas spoke to the Dalmation. He

grabbed her by the scruff of the neck and dragged her back to her pups.

"Did she hurt you?" I asked Trina.

"No," Trina said and shuddered. "But she tried. She suddenly attacked me for no reason."

Douglas said, "It's her pups. They make her nervous. Although I've never known this particular dog to attack anyone. I am sorry, Trina."

"How were you to know?" she asked. "I'm like any city-bred girl, I suppose. I don't seem to have a way with animals."

"But you do, Trina," I said. "Lucifer, who is absolutely *savage*, loved you."

"So he did," she said, adjusting the tiny riding hat on her head and smiling. "Surprising, wasn't it?"

Again I caught an enigmatic undercurrent to her words, something elusive; a threat, perhaps? But that is nonsense, I thought. Why should Trina threaten me?

"Won't you come in and have a glass of Granny's cowslip wine?" Douglas invited.

"I don't mind," I said. "What about you, Trina?"

"Thank you, Douglas," Trina said. "But not this time. Amelia, is it all right with you?"

"Yes," I said. "Of course."

An hour later when we reached Rommany we found the household in turmoil. Truffles had disappeared.

The dog had gone out shortly before lunch and apparently had never come back. Roger, usually so sensible and rational, refused to be calmed by Miss Weatheringham, and after the house had been combed from top to bottom and the grounds searched without result, he had gone to Papa in tears.

Papa, at once sympathetic, had his horse saddled; and with Roger behind him rode over the entire estate, even calling at the outlying farms. Nowhere did they see a sign of the little dog. The odd fact about Truffles's disappearance was that she, like Winkie before her, hated fresh air. She would venture outside only when nature demanded it, then quickly scoot back inside and up the stairs to doze before the schoolroom fire, or, in warmer weather, to curl up on the window seat.

It was late, past suppertime for the boys, before the

search was finally given up. "I shall stop at Tenwyck early tomorrow morning and inquire," Papa promised Roger. "Perhaps someone picked her up on the road and not knowing where she belonged, took her into the village."

Later at dinner, Papa said, "First the canary, now the dog. I have said it before and I will say it again. This family is done with pets. We don't seem to be able to keep them."

"That's not true," I objected. "We've had pets for years, and they lasted a long time. Winkie, if you recall, died of old age."

Mama, looking pale and tired, said, "But two in one day?" Tears—especially our tears—always distressed her.

Trina said, "I feel so dreadful about it. Both Truffles and Louise. Perhaps I'm unlucky."

There was a chorus of protest, although in the back of my mind the word "unlucky" echoed like a struck gong. Wasn't it Mrs. Chalmers who had used that word?

"How absurd," Papa was saying. "When was a pretty girl ever unlucky?"

"Yes," Mama agreed, toying with her wineglass. "We can't have you thinking such a thing." She gave Trina a wan smile, but I noticed how her hand trembled when she raised her glass to her lips.

Sometime during the night I awoke chilled, my blankets all in a heap at the foot of the bed as if I had kicked and thrashed about in my sleep. I had had an unpleasant dream, but what it was I could not remember. An odd heaviness lay on my chest, and my tongue tasted of brass. I got up and poured myself a glass of water from the pitcher. Then, glass in hand, I wandered to the window, drawing the curtains apart.

The dark velvet sky held a sprinkling of stars and the faint, crescent edge of a new moon. Below, all was black shadow; the gardens, the brick paths, the elms and the hedges barely discernible. I looked over the sleeping countryside in the direction of Green Oaks and thought of Douglas. What was to become of him? Of me? Of us?

I knew that Mama had planned to give me a season in London (that is where she met Papa) after I left the academy in hopes I would find a suitable husband. But I didn't want a "suitable" husband—I wanted Douglas. How could I possibly marry anyone else?

And yet I was fully aware of the gulf that divided us. There might have been a glimmer of a chance had Douglas been able to go on with his education. As a don or a professor at Cambridge he might have been acceptable.

But now, with Douglas's future sealed at Green Oaks, there seemed little reason to expect Mama to give her consent. And Papa would bow to her wishes.

Aside from my own selfish considerations, there was Douglas himself. Unhappy, Miserable. He hated farming, he once told me. "I'd rather be a peddler," he had said. I thought of the evening he had first informed us that he would not be returning to Cambridge and how I had received the news with concealed joy. How childish I had been, how thoughtless. Was it possible I could have loved him without feeling his heartache as I did now?

I sighed, leaning against the sill.

Suddenly, far in the distance, I noticed a pinpoint of light. It burned steadily in the darkness, not moving as a light would if it were a lantern on a vehicle or carried by a man walking home late at night. Perhaps a farmer was tending a sick sheep in the field. But then, I reminded myself, no field could be seen from my window, only parkland and trees belonging to Rommany. How strange. I watched for a long while until the tiny yellow glow unexpectedly winked out. Then, hugging myself against a sudden chill, I made up my bed and crawled between the sheets.

I was awakened the next morning by Clara clanking into the room with a can of hot water. Even to my sleep-dazed eyes she looked ill, white as a ghost. And when she dropped the can of water, nearly spilling the contents and scalding her shaking hands, I raised myself on the pillows. "What is it, Clara? Is something wrong?"

"I don't think I ought to say," she bit her lip.

"You can tell me," I coaxed. "Is it personal?"

"I don't know what you mean," she said.

"Are you ill, then?"

"No. It's something . . . I . . . oh, you'll think me balmy."

"No, I won't. Please tell me," I begged, all curiosity.

"I . . . you won't believe it unless you see it with your own eyes. I'll show you."

I threw on a dressing gown and followed her out into the corridor. We went up the back stairs to the second story, where the servants had their bedrooms. Clara paused at a window. It faced east, and the morning sun shone brightly through the paned glass so brightly that I did not see what was on the sill until Clara said, "Don't touch it."

It was a black candle, half-gutted, standing in a congealed puddle of wax.

"How careless of someone," I remarked, thinking Clara had been worried about a possible fire.

"It's *black*, Miss Amelia. We have no black candles in the house. Don't you see?"

I didn't see. I would not *allow* myself to see. "No," I said.

Clara lowered her voice to a shaky whisper. "Only them that has traffic with the devil uses black candles. Like *witches*, Miss Amelia, like witches!"

Chapter 4

I told Trina about the black candle and Clara's reaction to it as we were going down to breakfast.

"But that's superstitious nonsense," she said, matter-of-factly. "Witches went out with the Middle Ages."

"That's exactly what I said to Clara. Someone must have played a joke. The stableboy or one of the younger maids."

"It was a bad joke," Trina said. "Tasteless."

If I had harbored any suspicions of Trina—no matter how vague and nebulous—they were dispelled by her dry factual tone.

Breakfast that morning was an unusually silent meal, and afterward Mama asked if she could see me alone in the library. It was obvious she had something on her mind, and I waited for her to speak. There was a long silence. Then she said, "Do you think Trina will be happy here?"

"Happier than she would be at home. Why do you ask?"

"I just wondered. I wondered if she might not find some other place—how shall I put it?—more interesting?"

"Mama, she *has* nowhere else to go. I've invited her here, and she loves Rommany. I can't ask her to leave."

"No, of course not." Her hand fluttered to her forehead. "That would be rude."

Mama didn't like her. She didn't like the way Trina looked at Papa for which she could hardly be blamed, since I had resented Trina's looking at Douglas in that same way. And yet I came to her defense for reasons I

159

cannot rightly explain even now. "She doesn't mean any harm," I said. "And Roger and David seem to like her."

"So Miss Weatheringham has informed me. Trina has asked permission to read to the boys before bedtime."

The news surprised me. Trina hadn't said a word about it to me. "Don't you see, Mama, she probably feels she is not entirely welcome . . ."

"But she is," Mama insisted.

". . and so she is trying to make herself useful."

Mama drew herself up, a delicate pink staining her cheeks. "That is entirely unnecessary. Guests at Rommany should never feel they have to be useful." The grand hostess in Mama had come to the fore.

"Perhaps Trina likes children. I think she plans to be a governess."

"Oh . . . ?" Mama pressed her fingers to her brow.

"Are you getting a headache, Mama?" I asked after a moment's silence.

"No . . . no." She folded her hands in her lap. "I had a letter from Grandmama yesterday. She wants us to come for a visit."

"Had you been planning to go?"

"Not this summer. Papa is too busy, what with one thing and another. And then we do have our houseguest." A faint smile. "But I thought of sending the boys, including Stuart when he arrives home, with Miss Weatheringham."

"Poor Miss Weatheringham," I said, thinking of the long journey by train and boat to Newberry.

"Papa has business in Bristol, and he will see them part of the way."

"The house will be so empty."

"That is what your father said. But I think I've convinced him how beneficial such a visit would be for the boys, not to say how happy it would make your grandparents."

"I shall miss them."

"Perhaps I can persuade Uncle Harold and Aunt Veda to come down for a fortnight."

"Would you? I should like that." Harold and Veda Hempstead were not really uncle and aunt, but they were such old, good friends of my parents, I never thought of them in any other context except as kin. They had four children, three boys and a girl, the eldest of whom was the same age as I. We were fond of them all, and whenever they descended upon Rommany the house took on a festive air.

"I thought you might be pleased." She gazed at me speculatively for a long moment. And then it came, like a sudden bolt of lightning. "Have you been seeing Douglas Woodhill?"

"Just once." I couldn't lie—not outright—so I colored the truth a bit. "We stopped by Green Oaks to inquire after Tyson Woodhill."

"Ah," she sighed heavily. "Poor man. What a pity. And he's your father's age, still a young man." I had never thought of Tyson Woodhill as a young man. "I suppose that means Douglas must stay at home now."

"Yes, Mama."

"Well." She seemed to be searching for words, and I thought she would say, "I forbid you to go to Green Oaks again." But she didn't. "See that you don't make a nuisance of yourself there," she said. "Your visits might be misinterpreted."

"Yes, Mama."

"And—Amelia—I rely on you to use your head."

"Yes, Mama." All those unspoken words inside me. Why couldn't I say, "Mama, my head has nothing to do with Douglas—it's my heart that's concerned"? But there seemed too many barriers between us.

Truffles was never found. Theories were advanced as to the little dog's disappearance, all of them logical and none of them satisfying to Roger, who continued to mourn for her. However, he cheered up considerably when he learned of his prospective visit to Newberry. Roger, after all, was still a small boy, and the idea of a long ride on the train and a sail across the sea, plus a promise that Grandmama would try to find a replacement for Truffles, had finally brought a smile to his long face.

Trina surprisingly, seemed upset by the news. "Shall they be gone all summer?" she asked.

"I expect so," Mama replied. "It would hardly be worth the long journey if they were to stay just a few weeks."

"Then I shan't see them again," Trina said, disappointment in her voice.

She *is* fond of the boys, I thought. "Perhaps you can visit us again at Christmas," I said on impulse, feeling a sudden rush of warmth.

"If I am invited," Trina said.

Mama said nothing.

"Of course you are," I quickly supplied.

"Lady Blackmore?" Trina asked softly.

Mama, who had been fussing over a vase of flowers on the side table, lifted her eyes. "Yes?"

"*Am* I invited, your ladyship?"

Trina was wearing a gold locket she had once told me had been left to her by her mother. She was toying with it now, the gold glinting in the gloom of the hall.

Mama stared at the locket without speaking.

"Am I invited, your ladyship?" Trina coaxed in a soft voice.

Mama looked at the locket and said nothing.

"Your ladyship. . . ?"

A long, uncomfortable silence followed. Trina stared at Mama and Mama stared at the locket. The two of them seemed to be worlds away, frozen in time, facing one another on a far distant plane. What was happening? Why this silent confrontation charged with such hostility? I wet my lips, wanting desperately to break the unbearable tension.

And Mama suddenly said, "Of course you are invited," in an odd, strained tone.

She moved back to her flowers and a moment later, in her usual voice said, "What have you girls planned for today?"

The unexpected question, the swift change of Mama's facial expression and mood startled me so I could not find an answer.

But Trina promptly replied. "The weather looks like rain. I suppose we shall have to remain indoors."

Had I imagined that small scene between Trina and Mama? It couldn't have lasted more than a minute or two. Perhaps I had read into Mama's reluctance to offer Trina an invitation a meaning that was not there.

"It doesn't look promising," Mama was saying. "Certainly not for riding."

"No," I agreed, bringing my mind to the present, and thinking that my planned visit to Green Oaks would have to be postponed again.

"I shall sew," Trina said. "Amelia has promised me one of her old evening dresses . . ."

Had I?

". . . and I plan to alter it."

Perhaps I had done so that evening when she had asked me if we dressed for dinner, although I could not remember. It worried me, not remembering.

Trina and I went up to my room and I suppose because I felt guilty, I gave her one of my favorite frocks, a hyacinth-blue silk. "It goes with your eyes," I said.

"Are you sure you want me to have this? It's so lovely."

"Of course I'm sure."

She hugged the dress to her waist. "Oh, but it is a beautiful gown! I've never had one so lovely." There was a feverish glitter in her eyes—not tears, but something I found vaguely disturbing—as she kissed my cheek. "Thank you, Amelia."

After Trina left I wandered down to the library for a book. Through one of the long double windows I saw that the rain had begun to fall. It swept across the drive in gray sheets, shrouding the hedges in heavy mist. I thought of Green Oaks, miles away, and how the rain must sound as it pattered through the leaves of the great oak, striking the wooden bench where Douglas and I had sat. I wondered what he was doing at this very moment, what he was thinking.

With a sigh I turned from the window.

There must have been at least a thousand books in the library at Rommany. My father loved books, although he rarely read now, and his collection of first editions was said to have been among the finest private collection in England.

Now as I studied the floor to ceiling shelves, the row upon row of red and gold bound volumes, a title seemed to leap out at me. *The Compleat History of Magick, Sorcery and Witchcraft* by a man named Boulton.

I can give no explanation for my sudden attraction to

that particular title, except, perhaps, that the business of the black candle was still at the back of my mind.

I pulled the book down and flipped open the cover.

Published 1751. London. The pages were old, yellowed and cracked with time. There were woodcut illustrations of hideous crones, malevolent-visaged half men-half beasts, dark silhouettes of humped women gathered in rings about a goat-masked image of the devil. The book repelled, yet fascinated me, and before I realized what I was doing I was sitting in a chair, deep into a middle chapter.

I read of black masses, of evil spells, of covens, of compacts with the Devil! "They [witches] often threaten with injury those with whom they quarrel ... they inflict or procure infirmities, langours, madness ... deaths of men and beasts. They trample and spit on the cross and do the same to the consecrated host."

Finally I came to a description of an unbelievable ritual which even I, in my naivete, recognized as obscene, and I slammed the book shut in disgust.

I doubted if Papa was aware that this book had been left on the open shelf. I knew he kept certain volumes, books he felt young eyes should not see, under lock and key in a glass fronted cabinet. But somehow Boulton's work must have slipped past his notice, and feeling like a sneak thief, I hid *Witchcraft* on the back of the shelf where, if my dusty fingers were any judge, the maids never cleaned, and arranged the other books to cover the gap.

After selecting Scott's *Ivanhoe*, which I had read three times, but which would not give me nightmares, I went upstairs. Before sitting down to read I washed my face and hands, as if in so doing I could cleanse myself of Boulton's graphic, profane narrative.

A week passed. It rained all but one day. Papa and the boys and Miss Weatheringham left for grandmama's, and the gray, dreary weather, combined with their absence, seemed to have thrown a pall over the house. To add to the gloom, fires suddenly became difficult to light. The kindling would sputter and die before the flame could take hold, sending great billows of smoke into the room.

Ordinarily Mrs. Chalmers tried to keep the daily irritants of running a household from Mama, but the smoking, sputtering fireplaces were impossible to hide.

Mama seemed to think it was a matter of clogged flues, and discussed the problem with Mrs. Chalmers. Too many birds, she said, had built their nest in the chimney pots. Mrs. Chalmers disagreed. She maintained that the wood and coal were of poor quality. Mama, who rarely argued with Mrs. Chalmers, remained uncharacteristically stubborn in her view. They quarreled. For the first time I could ever remember, the two women exchanged angry words.

It happened at the breakfast table. We—Trina, myself and Mama—had been sitting in the dining room awaiting our breakfast—late for the third consecutive day—when Mrs. Chalmers came through the service door, her lips in a white line. She explained that the scullery maid, whose job it was to get the kitchen fire going, seemed unable to do so.

"First the fireplaces and now the stove," Mama said crossly.

"*I* have no trouble," Mrs. Chalmers replied in a voice she had never, never used to Mama before. "It's the maids. They're all country louts, don't know the first thing about lighting a proper fire. Overpaid, spoiled, like all the help that's hired in this house."

Mama got very red in the face. "I am still mistress here, Mrs. Chalmers, and I shan't have you speaking that way to me, no matter how many years you have been with us."

"It would do you good to listen, for a change."

"Mrs. Chalmers!"

They went on quarreling, oblivious of our presence.

Horribly embarrassed, I looked over at Trina. She sat watching Mrs. Chalmers and Mama, the faintest of smiles curling her lips.

Mama and Mrs. Chalmers made it up, of course, but I could not forget that smile of Trina's. Had she been amused? Had it pleased her to see disharmony at beautiful Rommany?

The quarrel was not the only thing which disturbed me. Everything seemed changed; the corridors smelled dank; doors stuck and refused to open, or, perversely, would not stay shut once closed; the mirrors and the windows would cloud over with mist no matter how frequently cleaned. And always it was cold, a cheerless, penetrating cold.

Especially at night. After sunset the house seemed to close in on itself, solitary, brooding, the long nocturnal silence broken only by the creak of a board or the sibilance of the wind whispering at the casements.

One night, unable to sleep, I suddenly remembered a ghost story a governess (I had forgotten her name) had told me when I was quite young. Something about one of the Blackmore ancestors coming back from the grave, wandering about Rommany, sighing dolefully. The tale had given me nightmares, and when Mama heard of it, had immediately dismissed the governess. I had never seen her so angry. "There are no such things as ghosts," Mama had said. "And if anybody should know, it is I."

But now I wondered, although I suspected that these thoughts were pure foolishness brought on by the dreary weather. Having been cooped up in the house for days on end, I had allowed my imagination to run wild. And, of course, when the sky finally cleared and the sun shone brilliantly warm, my superstitious pessimism vanished.

Future events, unfortunately, were to prove that my imagination had not been quite that wild. But I did not realize it then, and so I set out with Trina that first bright morning after a week of rain with a joyous heart.

We galloped all the way to Green Oaks. I in the lead. My mare, though I urged her on, could not go fast enough. It seemed like centuries since I had last seen Douglas and the distance more miles than I could count.

We reached the farm just as Douglas was leaving with a calf he was to deliver to a man in Tenwyck. So we had time for only a few hurried words, hardly more than a "Hello," and, "Have you been keeping well?" It was difficult to hide my disappointment.

After he'd gone, Molly Woodhill came out and invited us into the parlor.

I might have accepted the invitation, except that Trina spoke, and thanking her, refused, explaining how we both had been housebound and had planned a long ride. Listening to Trina, it came to me that this was not the first time she had found some excuse for declining to enter the Woodhill house. Why this reluctance? I wondered.

As we trotted homeward, taking the long way back across the fields, I had it on the tip of my tongue to ask her when she suddenly said, "You're in love with that boy, aren't you?"

Caught by surprise, my face flamed. "What a ridiculous idea!"

"Oh, Amelia! It's written all over you."

I turned to her aghast. "No! Do I . . . *did* I look silly?"

"Not at all. But I am right, am I not?"

There was no point in denying it. "Well—yes. But, Trina, please don't mention a word of it to anyone, especially to Mama."

"I won't. But you're a fool."

"All lovers are fools," I said sententiously

"That's not what I had in mind," Trina said, holding the brim of her hat against a sudden gust of wind. "How will you ever know if Douglas wants to marry you for yourself or because you come with a large dowry?"

I thought it rather a cold thing to say. "Douglas is not that sort of person," I replied stiffly. "He is very proud."

"Proud?" she snorted. And then, "Has he asked you yet?"

"No—no." The answer came hesitantly. "I don't even know if he loves me."

She laughed. "Can't you *make* him love you?"

I stared at her. Her cheeks, whipped by the wind, were a deep pink, her eyes a clear fathomless blue. "How could I do that?"

"Why," she said, "it's quite easy. But it's not for me to tell." And with that she kicked her horse into a gallop, leaving me behind.

Two days later the Hempsteads arrived in the late afternoon. I was delighted to see them, but disappointed because they had not brought Benjamin or any of the younger children. Benjamin was spending the summer with a cousin in Bournemouth and the others—Adrian, John, and Deborah —had all come down with the chicken pox, one following the other. They were on the mend now, but Veda thought it best to leave them at home.

"Nanny is most reliable," Veda explained as we sat in the drawing room, awaiting the announcement for dinner, "and I simply had to get away."

Veda was dark and small and graceful in all her movements. I think her mother had been a Hindu ranee—something like that—a fact which, to me, gave her a romantic aura, though in reality she was a practical little soul.

"When we got your invitation I seized upon it."

Harold, sitting on the sofa next to her, corrected, "Two invitations. The first for both of us, and the second for Veda only."

"Why, yes," Mama said, suddenly flustered. "It was because—because, as I explained, Duncan had gone and I thought you might find a houseful of women dull, Harold."

"I should never find you dull," he said gallantly and smiled. Harold was far from a handsome man; he had a large nose jutting out over a thick, bristly moustache and a high forehead from which the hair was already beginning to recede. But his smile radiated such warmth and good feeling one forgot about his large nose and balding head.

"In any case," Harold went on, "I expect Duncan will be back soon. He can't have that much business in Bristol. He hates the place."

"He did not say how long he planned to be away," Mama said.

Harold turned to me. "I understand you have a guest."

"Yes," I said, "Trina Blake. She's at the academy with me. She's dressing for dinner. Perhaps I ought to go and see what's keeping her."

Before I could get to my feet, however, the drawing-room door opened and Trina came in.

I gaped at her, perhaps the others did also, but I was too caught up in surprise to notice. She was wearing the hyacinth blue silk I had given her, altered to fit her like a glove. The dress with its modified bustle (the latest in fashion) and tight bodice boldly outlined her figure, while the neckline (which she had lowered) revealed far and away more bosom than was acceptable for our modest tastes at Rommany.

Unabashed, Trina went up to Harold who had risen to his feet upon her entrance.

"So you are Uncle Harold," she said, dimpling, giving him her hand, her head cocked slightly. And in her eyes there was *that* look, a look as old as time.

Chapter 5

Trina must have sensed disapproval, for a few minutes later she excused herself, saying she felt cold, and ran upstairs for a shawl. During the meal, with the shawl wrapped high about her neck, she kept silent, eyes downcast, only speaking in soft tones when spoken to; a model of propriety.

Her ability to switch from enchantress to prim schoolgirl was so swift, so amazing, so thorough, I often wondered in those early days whether I was imagining the brash side of her. Perhaps, I would think, I have misjudged the girl. Perhaps her delight in meeting new people is so wholehearted she cannot help the hungry look in her eyes.

I could not blame her for liking Harold Hempstead. I was fond of him, too. Among the countless visitors who came to Rommany (and we had some rather exotic ones through the years) the Hempsteads stood out as my favorites. Neither of them had one ounce of snobbishness. In their London drawing room they played host to literary folk, artists, musicians, persons who had no pretense to birth, much less to wealth, as well as the socially prominent. Furthermore, they thought well of Douglas. Veda and Harold had met him during the days when he and Ernest were digging for Roman treasure, and had prasied him as a fine boy, intelligent and handsome.

Mama shared my feelings for the Hempsteads (though for different reasons, I suspect), and the day after they arrived, casting about for entertainment, she suggested we attend the local fair, a popular event held twice a year on the outskirts of Tenwyck. As a rule we rarely went because Papa hated fairs. He said the people who put them on were frauds, dressing up in seventeenth-century costumes, trying to revive old ways for the sake of luring customers who must pay twice the usual price for their wares.

But to the rest of us (even Mama) the fair was a joy, a carnival of wonders, and I looked forward to it with excitement. My only regret was that the boys could not be there to share the fun—nor Douglas.

So, at ten o'clock, with the sun already hot in the sky, the five of us set out in the carriage. Harold, squeezed in between Veda and Mama, his face wreathed in smiles, said he felt like a bee come to rest on a summer bouquet. And indeed we all looked fresh and dewy; Mama pale but pretty beneath a pink and white straw hat, Trina and I in sprigged muslin and small white hats with gloves to match, and Veda in blue.

People already crowded the aisles between the booths when we arrived. Inside the entrance we agreed to separate, Harold going off to inspect the stalls which sold handicrafts, Mama and Veda to look at bolts of cloth, and Trina and I to do as we liked.

"Shall we watch the Punch and Judy show?" Trina suggested.

"Yes, let's."

About fifty people were herded together in the small narrow space in front of the Punch and Judy booth. There was not a bit of shade, not the slightest stir in the air. The blinding sun's rays beating down from the white-blue sky together with the press of bodies served to increase the oppressive heat.

After a few minutes of stretching my neck in an effort to peer past a stout man's beefy shoulders, I said, "Shall we go, Trina? I'm thirsty."

"Oh, Amelia." Her face fell. "Must we? I've never seen a Punch and Judy show. Can't we. . .? I tell you what! You save my place and I'll get us some lemonade. I saw the stand back there."

Before I could object she edged past the fat man and disappeared.

The sun grew hotter. I had left my parasol on the seat of the carriage, but, in any case, it would have been impossible to open in such a crowd. Moisture beaded my forehead and I felt sticky drops of perspiration rolling down my back. My eyes pulsed and ached in the strong glare. The raucous voices of the puppets, the shrill laughter, the deep guffaws of the audience flowed and ebbed, reaching me through a queer miasma.

I craned my neck but I could not see Trina. What was taking her so long? Perhaps she had to wait her turn at the lemonade stand. Too many people. Far too many people. All this crowd and no room to breathe. We should have come to the fair in the late afternoon when the air had turned cooler and most of the farm folk had gone home.

My head seemed eggshell light—not my own head, but a stranger's. And my tongue, dry as a sandy blotter. I had to sit down. I *must*. Little black dots began to jump before my eyes and I began to feebly push through the throng.

Somehow—miraculously, it seemed—I managed to get free of the crowd. Leaning against a nearby fence I mopped my damp brow with a handkerchief. The black dots had gone, but my knees were still trembling, my brain still a bit muddled. It was a weird feeling as if everything around me, the wooden slats of a barrow, a tall iron pole, the sky, had been squeezed together then stretched into long, angular lines.

The pole, for instance. It had been propped against the wall of a portable cookhouse, but now it seemed suddenly taller and as my eyes slid down its length I saw a white-gloved hand reach out from the window and attach itself to the pole. I looked up at the top again and it had tilted toward me. Funny, I thought. And the next instant something snapped in my brain—and I jumped.

The pole came crashing down, missing me by inches.

I clung to the fence, not daring to breathe, a whole series of pictures flashing through my mind—the falling pole, the white hand, myself lying on the ground with a smashed bloody skull.

"My God! What happened?" It was Harold, followed by a group of curious people, locals who had heard the crash.

"I don't know," I said in a dazed voice. *I might have been killed. Four inches closer, and I might have been killed.*

"Are you hurt?"

Trembling, I shook my head. Harold put his arm about my shoulders to steady me.

"It's the grease pole," a man said—the fat man who had been in the puppet-show audience.

"The grease pole?" Harold asked.

"It's a tradition," the man explained. "On the last day of the fair, all the men have a go at climbing it. The one who can get to the top in the shortest time gets a prize—a brace of fowl or a goose."

They were all staring at me, a ring of inquisitive eyes. I heard Trina's voice, "Let me through, please." The crowd parted and she appeared, a mug in each hand.

Her face was flushed with heat. "Oh, Amelia. . . !" Her hand shook as she handed me one of the mugs.

The lemonade was tart and cool, and I drank half of it in one long draught.

"It's all my fault," Trina said, pale and contrite.

Harold dabbed at a drop of lemonade on my chin with his handkerchief. "Now, Trina, why should you think that?"

"Because it was I who persuaded Amelia to stay." She explained how we had been watching Punch and Judy. "If we had gone when she asked, then this would never have happened."

"That's nonsense," Harold said. "How could you know an iron pole would topple over just as Amelia was passing by?"

"That doesn't matter," she said. "I was selfish. Amelia was uncomfortable and she wanted to leave."

Harold said, "Trina, my dear, you weren't being selfish. If Amelia had wanted to leave that badly, she would have done so. Am I right, Amelia?"

In some subtle way it seemed the blame (if it could be called that) had been shifted to me. But I said, "Of course, Uncle Harold."

"Now enough of this *mea culpa*." Harold linked one arm in mine and the other in Trina's. The crowd had drifted away and someone in the cookhouse began to grind a hurdy-gurdy. "If I recall," Harold said, "there is a woman here who makes the most delectable strawberry tarts. Shall we sample a few?"

It was not until we were seated in the carriage again

and starting for home that I noticed Trina was without her gloves.

"Trina," I said, "what happened to your gloves?"

She looked down at her hands. "Oh, dear! I hope I didn't lose them." She opened her purse, a tiny reticule hanging by a chain from her wrist. "I thought I put them in here when I paid for the lemonade. I must have dropped them in the crowd."

"Shall we go back and look?" I asked.

"No. They were old and much mended anyway. Now my godmama will *have* to buy me a new pair."

The following day—the last day of July—began with a chill haze, but by noon the sun had burned the mist away, throwing a bright hot light over the glistening trees and hedges. Mama and the Hempsteads had gone to look at a house on the other side of Tenwyck that a friend of Harold's was thinking of buying, and I suggested to Trina that we ride over to Green Oaks.

"It's so hot and I've a bit of a headache," she said. "Would you mind terribly if I don't go?"

"Of course not," I said, trying not to look pleased. "I'll stay, if you like."

"You will do nothing of the sort. I know you want to see Douglas."

"But I—"

"Your Mama won't know. We'll keep it a secret."

On Trina's lips the word "secret" had an unpleasant ring. Furtive. And although I never spoke of my visits to anyone, I didn't like to think of myself as seeing Douglas on the sly.

"That won't be necessary," I said. "If Mama should get back before I do, you can tell her the truth."

Trina raised her eyebrows. "All right, then."

On the way to Green Oaks, I saw William in the field talking to one of the hired hands and I waved to him, but he did not return my greeting. Though William had always been friendly and courteous in the past, I sensed he was beginning to look on my frequent visits with a jaundiced eye. He was a hard-working man himself, and I expect he resented my taking Douglas from his tasks even for a short time. Knowing this, and knowing that my appearances at Green Oaks were bound to be the talk of the parish, and that such gossip (much embellished) would eventually reach Mama's ears, I still could not stay away.

Once inside the farmyard gate, I dismounted and searched the premises for Douglas. Unable to find him I knocked on the farmhouse door. To my surprise Granny Woodhill, who seldom left her room beneath the eaves, opened the door. Her eyes squinted out at me through a mass of wrinkles. "Ah, so 'tis you."

"Yes, Granny. Can you tell me where Douglas is?"

"Where's t'other 'un?" she replied in the high, shrill voice of the deaf.

"The other one? Oh, Miss Blake. She's at home."

"What? What? You'll have t'speak up!"

"At home!" I replied loudly.

"At the manor? Not gone?" She shook her head. "She's a bad 'un."

"Now, how would you know that, Granny? You haven't even met her."

"I can tell. I can tell." Again she shook her head.

But I hadn't come to Green Oaks to discuss Trina. "Douglas!" I shouted. "Where is Douglas?"

"He's out to High Farm. Left early this mornin'."

"Thank you, Granny."

Douglas was cultivating a row of new corn just below the empty farmhouse. When I hailed him, he dropped his hoe and came to meet me.

"I can stay only a minute," I said, declining his hand and offer to help me dismount. "I just wanted to say hello."

"Where's Trina?" he asked, his eyes searching past me.

Why was everyone so concerned with Trina? "She didn't feel like riding today."

"Oh? And how is she liking Rommany?"

"She loves it."

"Her family," he began, his eyes wandering back to the horizon.

"She has no family," I said rather tartly. "Her mother and father are dead."

"They left her well off, then, I suppose."

"No." *Oh, Douglas, what about me? Look at me, darling, I am here. I love you.* "She's on scholarship at the academy."

"Clever girl."

"Very," I said bitterly.

He gazed thoughtfully at the house.

"Douglas," I said, "we went to the fair yesterday." I told him about the grease pole, making a light, and I thought, funny story of it. He didn't laugh, didn't even smile. I wondered if he had heard a single word I had said. He stood, one hand holding the bridle, a slight frown between his eyes. A light wind had come up and it ruffled his dark hair, a lock of it falling over his brow. How I longed to reach out and brush it back! Instead, I said, "Are you planning to do anything with the old house?"

"Here? At High Farm? It will take a lot of doing, what with the roof half gone." The farmhouse was ancient, said to have been built some two hundred years earlier. "Not many of the old thatchers left who'd know how to repair it."

"Your father could lease it," I said, pursuing the topic, anything to divert his interest from Trina.

"No, I don't think we'd lease it. William will soon be married, and if the house were fixed up, I think he would want it for his own."

"I didn't know that William was walking out with anyone."

"Franny Keever."

The Keevers were tenants of ours, good people, but there were so many Keevers I could not recall which was Franny.

"She'll make him a fine wife," Douglas was saying. "Franny's a hard worker, has a head on her shoulders, too. It's about time William was getting married. A farmer needs a wife."

And what about you? I wanted to ask. Is it so utterly hopeless to think that some day you and I will marry?

Sitting there on the restive mare, dimly conscious of the scent of new-turned earth, I suddenly saw more clearly than ever before how immense was the abyss which divided Douglas and myself. Perhaps Douglas had seen it too, long ago. He wasn't like me—foolish and sentimental —a girl whose head was stuffed with impossible dreams.

Was he like William, thinking of a wife society would accept as nearer his own station? Not a person like Franny

Keever, because Douglas was well educated, but someone in between, a girl who had no family to question her choice, no money with which she might lure an aristocrat. A girl, in short, like Trina.

The thought chilled me to the marrow.

"I think I'd best be going," I said in a muffled voice. If I should lose Douglas to Trina, what would I do? Give up everything, take the veil, go into a nunnery, or failing that, simply die?

"Amelia," Douglas began, looking up at me in an odd way. "Take care of yourself." He lifted my hand to his lips "Little Amelia." He smiled.

Encouraged by that smile I gripped his hand. Perhaps all was not lost. Surely that look in his eyes meant something? "Douglas—" But I was suddenly too shy. His fingers slipped from my hand. "Good-bye, then," I said.

When I got back to Rommany I saw Harold's stick and hat on the side table in the hall. They were home—Mama and the Hempsteads. I was wondering how Trina had explained my absence when she opened the drawing-room door.

"You're here," she said. "I'm sorry, Amelia, but I had to tell your mother."

"That's quite all right. Where is she?"

"Upstairs."

I climbed the stairs and knocked on Mama's door. Best to take the bull by the horns. I would rather face her displeasure at once than have to sit through a long tea, wondering what she was thinking, what she would say.

I tapped at the door again and without waiting for an answer, turned the knob and went in. At first glance both the anteroom and bedroom were empty. Then I saw her—and my heart turned over.

She was lying in a crumpled heap on the floor next to the dressing table, her face white as wax, her hand clutching a long-stemmed rose.

"Mama!" I ran to her and knelt at her side.

She wasn't dead, thank God! A small pulse, barely perceptible, beat in the hollow of her throat.

I sprang up and rang for Becky. Then I went to Mama's dressing table and shoved bottles aside until I found her smelling salts.

Her blue lips twitched when I put the bottle under her nose. "Mama," I whispered.

She opened her eyes, yellow-tinged, puzzled.

"You fainted," I said.

"Did I?" Tears swam in her eyes.

"Come, I'll help you up." She held to my arm while I pulled her to her feet. I was surprised at how light she was. "I think you'd better lie down," I said, leading her to the bed.

I plumped up her pillows and she lay back on them. "The telegram," she said in a vague voice.

"What telegram?" I asked.

"The telegram," she repeated with a distracted wave of her hand. "On the floor."

I searched the floor twice over. "I can't find a telegram, Mama."

There was a knock on the door. "It's Becky," I said, going to it.

"I . . . I don't want to see her," Mama pleaded.

I cracked open the door. Becky, square-jawed, with the long-suffering look of someone snatched hurriedly from important business (her own tea, by the look of the crumbs on her chin) said, "Yes, Miss Amelia?"

"Could you bring Mama a cup of tea?" I asked. "She isn't feeling well. And please tell the others to go ahead without us."

"Yes, Miss Amelia."

I shut the door.

Mama said, "I had it in my hand when I came upstairs. Oh, Amelia." Tears filled her eyes again.

"What did the telegram say?"

"It . . . it said your father had an accident. And he . . . he . . ." She bit her quivering lip. "And he died."

Everything seemed to go black, and for a terrible moment I thought I would faint too. Papa dead? No, I couldn't believe it. There was some mistake, a horrible mistake.

"You see," she went on. "I was in the garden—yes, in the garden." She swallowed. "I thought I'd cut a few roses. They bloom so fast in this heat. Just a few roses . . . and this man . . . this man—"

"What man?" I asked, my voice sharp with fear.

"*I don't know.* I'd never seen him before. And he had a peaked cap on. I—I couldn't see his face too well. He rode up on a bicycle and gave me the telegram."

"Gave you a telegram? Why didn't he deliver it at the front door?"

"Yes, yes. I thought it strange. But I took the telegram and thanked him and I came up here to open it. And it said . . . it said—your husband has met with a mortal accident."

"That is all? Not how or why?"

"No." Tears spilled down her cheeks.

"Who sent it?"

"The telegram was not signed."

"Where did it come from, then?"

"I . . . I didn't think to look. I read it and then everything . . . I must have fainted."

My eyes wandered around the room. "But there is no telegram, Mama. Are you certain?" I had never seen Mama in such a state—weak, barely coherent, her face ghastly—not even when she was suffering from one of her migraines.

"Yes, yes, I'm certain." Her hand fluttered to her brow.

Another knock at the door. It was Becky with the tea tray, her eyes moist with curiosity. "It's all right, Becky. I'll take it."

As I poured the tea, Mama said, "I . . . I don't know why this should have happened to me." She shook her head slowly from side to side. "So much to live through. He disappeared in the rain and I couldn't remember. All that terrible time, and now I sent him away because I was afraid."

"Sent him away?" I asked, alarmed at her incoherence. "Who? Papa?"

"You don't understand," she said. "You're still a child."

"What were you afraid of Mama?" My own heart constricted with apprehension.

"Your father was in danger. I sent—"

At that moment, Papa walked into the room.

I stared at him in disbelief as if a phantom had suddenly come through the door. And then Mama began to laugh—high, shrill laughter intermingled with harsh, breath-catching sobs. It was terrible.

Poor Papa, dumbfounded, exclaimed, "What is it?"

I ran to him, hugging and kissing him, weeping now, too. "I knew it was a mistake," I sobbed. "I knew it all the time."

He disentangled himself from my hold and went over to the bed where Mama was still laughing and crying. "Here! Eustacia—*please!*" He took her by the shoulders and shook her until her face turned red and her laughter suddenly stopped.

"There's a packet on the shelf over the basin," Papa said, turning to me. "A blue packet. Get it."

I found the packet—Dr. Ogilvie's Sedative Powders—and brought it to him. He tore it open and tapped the powder into the cup of tea I had poured earlier. "Drink this," he commanded. "It will help you, darling."

Obediently, like a small child, Mama drank, one hand clinging to his arm. Then she sank back on the pillows.

"Now," Papa said. "Can you tell me what this is all about?"

Mama started to talk, but she was still upset and got her sentences twisted around. So I had to tell Papa the story. When I had finished he said, "But can't you see, my darlings, the telegram must have been delivered in error."

"I had guessed much the same, Papa," I said.

He thought for a moment. "The fellow who brought it—you say he was a stranger?"

Mama nodded.

"Being unfamiliar with the neighborhood I shouldn't doubt he got his names and houses mixed. That is all. And, Eustacia, my dear," he took her hand, "you know how you worry whenever I leave. I was on your mind, and when you saw the telegram, you were sure it contained bad news—about me. You put two and two together and got five. Am I right?"

"Perhaps," she said, frowning.

I touched Papa's hand. "Mama said she didn't open the telegram until she got upstairs."

"You are right," Mama agreed. A small bright spot of red had appeared on either side of her chalk-white cheeks. "That is—I *think* I did."

"You see, Eustacia," Papa said. "You aren't sure. You

must have opened it downstairs, very likely dropping it in the garden."

"Yes—yes," Mama said, clasping her brow. "It could have been so."

I left my parents and went down to the rose garden to look for that ill-starred telegram. But though I searched through the thorny, sweet-smelling bushes and the greensward between, I could not find it. Perhaps, I thought, the wind had blown it away.

Chapter 6

There is nothing like the shock, the dismay, of watching an accident in progress and knowing that one is helpless. Afterward, when Dr. Jemson had left and Veda's leg was set and her hysterics were finally under control, I found myself seeing the fall in my mind's eye, again and again, as if in slow motion: Veda, standing at the top of the stairs, staring down at Harold, who was listening to Trina in the hallway below, a look of rapt adoration on his face, and then Veda starting down the stairs and tripping on the hem of her gown and, as we watched helplessly, falling the length of the staircase.

It was a miracle that she was not killed; as it was, the break in her leg, below the knee, fortunately proved to be a simple fracture.

Papa, Trina, and I ate dinner that night without the Hempsteads or Mama, who was still feeling distraught; a tardy meal, taken in gloomy silence. Trina was the first to excuse herself and, after a short interval, I followed suit.

Ascending the stairs I came upon a comb, Trina's, one of a pair she usually wore in her hair. Picking it up, I went down the corridor and knocked on her door. "Trina?" There was a muffled reply. "You've lost a comb."

A minute later the door partially opened. "How negligent of me," Trina said, taking the comb. "Thank you, Amelia."

She did not invite me in, but from where I stood I could smell the pungent odor of singed cloth. "You haven't caught fire?" I asked, peering over her shoulder at the fireplace. I thought I saw what looked like a small doll dressed in red cloth just an eyelash blink before the flames leaped to consume it.

"I'm afraid I dropped my handkerchief in among the hot coals," Trina said ruefully.

"Do be careful," I advised. "We can't have another accident."

"Oh—I shall be careful. Never fear."

Troubled, I went to my room and slowly undressed. I crawled between the sheets and cradling my head in my arms, stared wide-eyed into space. Something eerie was going on at Rommany. A black candle, a phantom telegram, Veda's fall. What did it mean?

In a little while I began to doze and in a half-dream, half-thought saw Trina's fireplace, the dancing fire, and a scrap of vivid red curling, withering in the flames.

I came fully awake with a start. That shade of crimson—where had I seen it? Yes, of course. It was the color of the gown Veda was wearing when she fell.

And I suddenly remembered the passage I had read about effigies in Boulton's *Witchcraft*, and of women who made pacts with the Devil to obtain their heart's desire. Women who cast spells, women who dispensed deadly potions, women who *created images of their enemies*.

I was sure now that Trina had fashioned a doll in Veda's image.

Was it possible? *Trina*? A witch?

I threw the covers from me. It was utterly mad to think of it. Witches had long since gone out of fashion; no one today believed in those hoary superstitions of the Middle Ages. Frightening inventions to scare the wayward, they had never existed. Nor did they exist now. Witches? Impossible.

I drew on my robe and went to the window. Pulling the curtains aside, I knelt on the window seat. A half moon rode the skies, spilling its creamy light over the treetops and lawns, painting long fingers of shadow on the terraces below. Far in the distance a cock, mistaking the lunar light for dawn, crowed. A homely farmyard sound. The night settled in; peaceful, quiet, a tranquil scene, a Rommany scene, familiar and reassuring.

Yet—there had been a disturbing light on the horizon

not too long ago. And the black candle in the alcove. Signals, one witch to another?

No. What a wild, improbable fantasy. I did not believe in such nonsense. Did I? No, of course not.

What of Truffles and the canary, and the Dalmation, then? Female animals, all, they had made some show of antagonism toward Trina. The dog had vanished, and the canary had had its neck twisted. The Dalmation had been saved from harm only by the timely appearance of Douglas and myself. Coincidence? Or had Trina wreaked vengeance on the dumb brutes who sensed her inherent evil?

But she was just a girl. A *schoolgirl*, for heaven's sake!

Yes, but—a girl who could enchant with a smile. A girl who could make a man's eyes shine with ardor. Had Trina said a few esoteric words, burned a powder, cast a spell?

Preposterous! I did not believe in spells.

Supposing I did. Supposing, I said to myself, for the sake of argument I did believe. Supposing Satan had emissaries among us; people like Trina, for instance, who could on the surface appear modest, retiring, "sweet," as Harold had called her, but who were actually workers of mischief. That might explain the fires refusing to light, the stuck doors, the argument between Mama and Mrs. Chalmers. Mrs. Chalmers hadn't liked Trina from the start. "She's unlucky," she had said. Had she suspected what I did now?

And Mama—that hesitancy I sensed when I first brought Trina home, the sigh of relief when Papa and the boys left, her remark, "I sent him away." Did she suspect, too? Did she *know*?

All the annoying incidents and scenes, the strange, worrisome encounters which I had subconsciously stored in my mind came tumbling out, one following the other. And among those disturbing recollections the day at the Tenwyck fair stood out like a stark, vivid picture; the blue sky, the long pencil-slim black pole falling, the white glove. Trina had "lost" her gloves that day. Or had she discarded them because they had been soiled with telltale grease?

And then, suddenly, I saw a light in the distance, the

same small yellow light I had seen before, and a burst of wind touched my arms and I shivered.

Whose light was it? Why, in this wind, did it remain so steady? Across the miles it seemed to beckon, like an unblinking yellow eye.

Was it a signal?

Would there be a second black candle upstairs?

I was in my robe and out the door, lamp in hand, before I realized what I was doing. Standing in a small pool of light, I hesitated, listening. Not a whisper, not a rustle, not the smallest stirring. Around me the dark shadows thronged, kept at bay only by my feeble light. The corridor, so familiar to me all the years of my life, now seemed fraught with the unknown.

Was that a footstep?

No, only a board contracting in the cool of the night.

Should I go back to bed and forget this nonsense?

Coward! Afraid of your own shadow. Then how will you ever know?

I took a firmer grip on the lamp and went down the corridor in slippered feet and up the back stairs to the alcove.

A black candle, unlit, was there as I expected it might be. Yet seeing it gave me a queer turn. There was something very sinister about that thick taper of gutted ebony —and it was still warm to the touch. It had been lit this evening; wax had trickled down and congealed on the sill. I put the candle and the drippings in the pocket of my robe, and pressed my face to the window. The distant light had gone.

Early the next morning I got up and dressed quickly before Clara arrived. Slipping quietly out, I went down in search of Mrs. Chalmers, carrying the black candle safely hidden in my knitting bag.

She examined the black candle in silence.

"It's just like the one Clara found," I said at last.

She nodded. Affirmation or denial?

"Do you think it might have been put in the window by one of the servants?" I said, cautiously sounding her out.

"Not one of mine," she replied stoutly. "They have no truck with black candles. Who do *you* reckon it was?" she asked, throwing the question back at me.

"Miss—Miss Trina," I ventured.

"I wouldn't be at all surprised. She's been troubling you for some time, hasn't she?"

"Yes." What a relief it was to say so!

"Would you like to tell me about it, my dear?"

I tried to keep my voice steady, tried to keep everything in sequence, but I couldn't. I got it all out though, the doll resembling Veda, the grease pole at the fair, the canary, the episode with the telegram in the rose garden.

"You were so right, Mrs. Chalmers," I said in conclusion. "Trina Blake is unlucky for us." I had been careful not to use the word "witch."

"It certainly seems that way," she said.

If Mrs. Chalmers had been a less formidable person, I would have hugged and kissed her. She believed me. She did not call me a fool, a silly goose. She did not think my story was superstitious nonsense. Good, solid, kind Mrs. Chalmers.

"I told you from the start she gave me a peculiar feeling," she said.

"What shall we do?"

"Leave it all to me, my dear. I know how to handle the likes of her."

"What mischief do you thing she's up to?" I asked. "Is it black magic? What is she?" I wanted to hear Mrs. Chalmers say it.

She thought for a moment before she replied. "I don't know if I could rightly put a name to her sort. But I do know there's forces in this world, evil forces which come out of hiding from time to time."

"But why here at Rommany?" I said, troubled.

"Now, Miss Amelia, no need to be afraid. No godfearing person should be," she lectured sternly. "Simply go about your affairs as if nothing were amiss. I will deal with Miss Trina Blake. All I ask is that you do not speak of this to your mother. It would upset her unnecessarily."

"As you say," I agreed. She had never appeared more determined, more capable. Suddenly I felt immensely relieved. I had been so right to come to Mrs. Chalmers, something I should have done long ago.

The Hempsteads left shortly after lunch without my having had a chance to speak to Veda privately. Dr. Jemson was opposed to her going, but Veda prevailed. I was glad for her sake that she had. Now it remained only for Mrs. Chalmers to persuade Trina to leave, and then I would be able to breathe easily again.

But that long-drawn breath of relief never came. That night in the servant's hall, Mrs. Chalmers got a chicken bone lodged in her throat while having dinner with the staff, and before the stableboy could saddle a horse to fetch Dr. Jemson, she died.

It was a horrible shock to us all. Papa, quickly summoned from the drawing room by a hand-wringing Clara had tried valiantly to dislodge the bone, but it had been too deeply embedded. When he had returned to us, announcing the housekeeper's death, Mama went white as a ghost, but she did not faint. I helped her up to her room; once there, she dissolved into tears. I wept with her, realizing for the first time how much that dour woman had meant to me, too.

But more than that (something I could not share with my mother) I was overcome with remorse and a kind of sickening horror. If I had not gone to Mrs. Chalmers with my story that morning, she would still be alive. For now there was no longer the slightest doubt in my mind—none whatsoever—that Trina was a witch. She had known (sensed? guessed?) that Mrs. Chalmers was planning to send her packing. And though Trina had never been out of sight all evening, I was convinced she had used some occult power to kill the housekeeper. Trina knew how to deal with her enemies.

Had she decided I would be her next victim?

Perhaps, silently, without fanfare, war between us had already been declared. And what weapons did I have to defend myself—or any of my loved ones, for that matter? None. I had never been religious. Papa claimed he was an agnostic; Mama (who unlike most of the Northern Irish was an Anglican) went to church regularly, but neither church attendance nor religion had been pressed upon us. Miss Weatheringham, it is true, had taught us our prayers, and we did sing hymns each morning and evening at the academy, but the words had meant nothing to me. Now, for the first time in my life, I felt a desperate need for God. Surely He in his wisdom could see I needed help?

But then, I thought, why should He help someone who came to Him only in trouble? And wasn't it said that God helped those who helped themselves?

Mrs. Chalmers was buried in the Blackmore plot under the elms at the local churchyard. She had no relatives, except a niece living somewhere in Dublin who was married to a cobbler by whom she had a tribe of children. She never wrote to her aunt, so we did not know how to reach her. At any rate, I think Mrs. Chalmers would have preferred lying in that quiet mossy place, still part of the family even in death.

All during the preparations for the funeral, the cortege that followed and afterward, I had kept my distance from Trina. If she suspected my coolness, she said nothing. Perhaps she assumed I was too overcome with grief to be very communicative. Good, I thought, let her assume whatever she wished. It gave me time; time to think, time to decide how I could get her to leave Rommany with the least possible fuss.

Finally more in desperation than anything else, I went to Papa to whom I had brought so many of my problems. An error, a grave error, but I did not realize it until I said the word *witch* and saw the look of shock in his eyes.

"You can't mean what you are saying, Amelia," he said, amazed. "I believed you to be an intelligent person, one we have gone to great pains to educate."

"It isn't a matter of education, Papa. You do admit there is evil in this world," I replied, summoning Mrs. Chalmers words as argument.

"Most certainly. But witches?" He smiled. "My dear child, more evil has been done hunting down so-called witches than those poor unfortunate wretches could have possibly perpetrated on their own."

"And you don't think Trina fashioned that doll out of malice toward Veda?" I said, with a sinking feeling of defeat.

"Are you quite sure there *was* a doll?" he asked kindly.

And, in fact, I was not quite sure.

"Look at it sensibly, Amelia. Trina is an unfortunate girl, without family, a charming girl. If she were unpleasant or rude . . ."

Hadn't I said something like that to Mama?

". . . we might have an excuse for asking her to leave. But as it is, we simply can't. Do you see, Amelia?"

"I thought so, too. But now, Papa—"

"*Now,* Amelia, if I may speak bluntly, I have the feeling that you might be a bit jealous of her. Am I right?"

My face flamed, but I held my tongue. What was the use? Protesting would serve only to convince Papa he was right. Jealous! If that were only the half of it!

"I suggest you put all this witch-foolishness from your head," Papa said. "And enjoy your friend's stay. Here." He reached in his pocket and brought out several pound notes. "Why don't you and Trina ride into Tenwyck and buy yourselves new parasols?"

I wanted to say—but I'm afraid to go anywhere with Trina. Instead I took the money and thanked him.

That night I had a frightening experience. It all started with a nightmare. I dreamt that I was walking slowly down the main street of Tenwyck dressed only in my shift. People along the way, shopkeepers at their doors, housewives at the windows, children at the curb, stared at me, some with shock, others with lewd amusement. I was horrified. I wanted to run, but could not; a mysterious force seemed to hold my bare feet to a slow, molasseslike gait. The crowd along the way grew, men and women tumbling from their houses, laughing. An old woman shook her stick at me and cursed. But though their lips moved and they gestured, and their bodies trembled with laughter, no sound came; everything was eerie silence.

It got darker and the crowd thinned. I came to the end of the street. Stretching before me, smooth and black as ink, was Turner's Pond. How could that be? But I saw the wooden markers along the outer edge, thin, straight sticks driven into the bottom to gauge the depth. On I went, in that slow, inexorable gait, straight for the pond. The icy waters closing over my bare feet were a bone-shattering shock.

And I opened my eyes.

I don't think I shall ever forget the stunning horror of that moment. I was not in my bed. I was standing ankle deep in Turner's Pond!

How did I get there? Was I still dreaming?

The cold night air touched my face and wound itself about my limbs. Over the rim of the woods beyond the pond, a full moon was rising, throwing a path of pale ivory over the still black water. A cock—the same cock perhaps that I had heard before—crowed, but now the sound was like a trumpet of doom. Shivering, I shrank back, the mud oozing between my toes.

I was not dreaming. Somehow, walking in my sleep, I had come this long way over fields and through woods to Turner's Pond. Not far from where I stood, the bottom dropped away. If I had not wakened. . . .

Stupefied with terror, I stepped out of the water and a sudden new fear gripped me. My white nightdress was like a beacon in the darkness, an easy target for anyone watching. And someone *had* to be watching. I had never sleepwalked in my life, and I knew what had happened to me was not of my own doing. Had I been brought here?

By Trina?

Was she hiding in the woods, behind this tree or that bush, spying on me with narrowed blue eyes?

I stood very still, tense, waiting. But no figure emerged, no one spoke. The wind ruffled my hair and whispered in the summer grasses. My gaze darted this way and that along the ground. A hare raised its long-eared head above a small tuft of sod and stared unblinkingly at me.

A hare—nothing more?

It continued to stare at me, its eyes glittering strangely. How odd, I thought, he's not afraid. I turned my head away, but found it slowly swinging back. The hare's eyes glowed in the dark, solemn, hypnotic. I tried to move my hand, to make some sort of gesture so that it would scamper away, but to my horror I found I could not move a finger.

The hare's blue-green eyes grew more intense, glittering like twin orbs of fire. I felt myself being pushed back and back toward the pond again by the strange power of those awful eyes.

I dug my toes in and clenched my fists, resisting, fighting with heart and breath, with the very blood which pulsed through my veins.

Slowly, ever so slowly, I saw those feral eyes lose their glow, grow dimmer. And then, with a quick jerk of its long-eared head, the hare turned and disappeared into the tall grass.

Shaking, quivering from head to toe, I put a trembling hand to my face and found my cheek wet with tears. What had happened? Was that hare not a hare, but a familiar, a creature which did a witch's bidding? I did not know. I could not guess. Only my fear was palpable and real.

Bunching the skirt of my nightdress in one hand, I began to run across the field toward Rommany. But soon, gasping painfully, with the breath whistling in my ears, I was forced to a walk. It was a long, long journey, the longest I had ever taken in my life. Each hurried step was an agony, each moment an eternity of fear. Now and again I would throw a quick look over my shoulder. But nothing followed; no beast, no strange shadow, only the moonlight showing the way. At last Rommany came in sight. I found the front door open (had I unlocked it when I went out?) and, half-fainting with shock, I climbed the stairs to my room.

Chapter 7

When I awoke, the morning sun was streaming in the open window, the light glancing off the mirror, making patterns on the carpet. I lay on my pillow, listening to the merry chirp and chatter of birds. Had last night—the horrible wakening in the pond, the terrible eyes of the hare—been a dream? But no—there, flung over the back of a chair was my nightdress, its hem crusted with mud.

All the cold terror I had felt at the brink of the pond returned when I thought that but for my strength of will I should be in that pond now, floating face-down, dead.

Nothing could shake my conviction that Trina had been at the back of my waking nightmare. How had she done it? She would try again, I was sure. She was not one to accept failure; it would only spur her on.

Ought I to go to Papa?

But how could I when our last conversation had produced nothing but a reprimand? He would say that illness had probably made my nightmare so realistic and suggest that Dr. Jemson look in on me.

Mama?

Perhaps if I tried a different approach she might be of help.

She was at her little desk, writing a letter with the old-fashioned quill pen she preferred.

"Am I interrupting?" I asked.

"I was just dashing off a note to Veda. But it can wait. Is there something you wanted?"

"Yes, Mama. I was thinking—couldn't we—you, Papa, and I—go to Grandmama's?"

Her eyebrows, pale golden arcs, went up. "Why, I thought I explained that your father could not get away."

"His business could not be *that* important."

"He seems to think it is."

"But we *must* go!" It was going badly already.

She stared at me for a long moment. "Is it Trina?"

Her sudden perceptive question sent me stammering, "Y . . . y . . . yes. Partly. You see, she and I do not get along."

"Oh? Papa told me you were talking some nonsense about Trina—calling her a witch. Am I right?"

In some subtle way, Mama seemed to have changed. Baffled, dismayed because I could no longer guess what she was thinking I replied. "But—she is!"

Mama looked at me, her eyes reflecting pity. Or was it disgust? "Mama," I pleaded, "don't you remember when I first brought Trina home you had some doubts about her?"

"I do remember. And when I got to know her better, my doubts were laid to rest."

"But, Mama—had you not noticed how she looks at Papa?"

"Looks at him? Why, she gives him the same looks she gives me. My dear Amelia, I have a feeling your wish to be rid of Trina has nothing to do with this witch foolishness."

"I don't know what you mean," I said through lips gone stiff.

"You want her out of the way so that you can be free to see Douglas Woodhill as often as you like."

"That's not so! Has she been tattling on me?"

"Not at all. I merely asked her where you were the day the Hempsteads and I returned from looking at Blythe House, and she told me you had gone to Green Oaks. I questioned her further, and she did not lie. It seems you have been there quite a few times since you've come home."

"Yes—yes, I have," raising my chin.

"You must realize by now that I do not approve of that friendship."

"I have guessed it, but—"

"Hear me out, Amelia. I haven't wanted to make a fuss

over this, but you leave me no choice. I must forbid you to see Douglas Woodhill again."

"Mama, you can't! You don't understand. Please—"

"I *do* understand. You and Douglas are no longer children. If this goes on, there is the danger that you might fall in love with him."

"But I already have!" The words were out before I could stop them.

She pressed her lips together and said nothing.

"What have you against Douglas Woodhill?" I swallowed the threatening break in my voice. "I know, I know. He's not suitable. He is—beneath me. Isn't that what you want to say?"

Still without speaking, she carefully laid the pen down and with her long patrician fingers rearranged the note paper on the desk.

Her continued silence goaded me on. "I suppose if he was Lord Popinjay's son, you'd think him the best catch of the season!"

Her lips moved, but she did not speak.

Reason left me. The fear of the last few weeks, the agony, my longing for Douglas, everything that had troubled me rushed to my head. "Well—I don't *care*! I love him, do you hear? I don't care what you say. I love him!"

A faint flush stained her pale cheeks. "You will get over it."

"Never! Never, *never*! I will never get over it. Don't you—*can't* you understand. Haven't you ever been young and in love?" It was the eternal cry of daughter to mother. I did not look ahead to the years when I myself might have a daughter. How could I? Who does at sixteen?

Mama's eyes grew bright. "Enough of this, Amelia! You forget yourself."

"Oh, Mama." Defiance melting into tears. "You've had it so easy with Papa and everyone's—everyone's blessing. And I. . . ." My voice choked and I began to sob.

Mama stretched out her arms and drew me down upon her lap. "Poor darling, poor darling," she crooned while I wept on. "I've not had it as easy as you may think."

"I—I am sorry, Mama," I said, feeling blindly in my bodice for a handkerchief.

Mama gave me hers, and after I had blown my nose, helped me to my feet.

"Come sit down," she said, leading me to the little sofa which stood against one wall. Her arm was trembling. Or was it me? "There is something I must tell you, although I had hoped it would never be necessary."

I had one last dab at my nose and looked into Mama's troubled eyes, brimming with compassion. A queer constriction squeezed at my heart. "What is it?"

"You can never marry Douglas."

"Why not?" I asked, almost inaudibly. Her pity frightened me.

"Because he is related to you."

Stunned, stricken, I could only stare at her, those words like an echo in my brain repeating, ". . . he is related . . . he is related . . ." A half brother? Dear God, why hadn't I been told?

". . . my salts," Mama was saying. "You look so white."

"No . . . no."

Nevertheless she brought them. The aromatic spirits stung my nostrils, stripping them raw, but they cleared my head.

"Better?"

"Yes, Mama. But—but how—how do you mean?"

She set the vial aside and folded her hands. "Your great-uncle, Sir Edward, had a son out of wedlock by Douglas's grandmother; and so the Woodhills are related to us."

My father rarely spoke of his family, and Sir Edward was only a dim figure to me—one of the many anonymous portraits in the Long Gallery. But I knew Douglas's grandmother. "You mean Granny? Granny Woodhill? Not Granny!"

"Yes, Alice Woodhill."

Granny—old and wrinkled—and Sir Edward? It was not as bad as I had first thought, but still shocking. "How? I mean—"

"She was a servant here, and Sir Edward got her with child."

"How—shameful." And so long ago. Did Douglas know? I wondered. But even as I asked myself the question, I knew the answer. Of course he did. The look in his eyes, the way he kissed my hand, his clinging to the childhood endearment, "Little Amelia." He would not allow himself to love me.

Still. "If Great-uncle Edward and Granny had a child, then," I said slowly, my brain digesting the complications of relationship, ". . . then that would make Douglas a cousin—removed. Cousins do marry, Mama."

"Not often. Against better judgment, with unhappy results. You see, Sir Edward's branch of the family was quite erratic."

"You mean mad?"

"No, not exactly."

"And you think Douglas might have inherited this—what you call—erratic trait?"

"I can't rightly say. But I know your father feels very strongly about this. He is adamantly opposed to family intermarriage."

So that was why Papa, though he liked Douglas, had never defended me against Mama's opposition. "Douglas," I said, "is not . . . not erratic."

Mama leaned back on the sofa and sighed. "Amelia, has Douglas ever spoken of love or marriage?"

"N . . . no."

"I think you may find him cognizant of the facts and in agreement with your father and myself."

That was what I feared. Yet I must hear it from Douglas's own lips. "Do I have your permission to speak to him about this?"

"I can see no harm in it now."

No harm? Oh, Mama do you think it matters? Do you think I can turn off my love just because old Granny had a tumble in bed with a man who was supposed to be a great-uncle? My throat swelled and tears burned behind my eyes. I lowered my head, fussing with the handkerchief in my lap, folding and refolding it. I was right; she didn't understand, she would never understand.

"About Trina," Mama was saying.

Trina! During the emotional storm over Douglas I had forgotten.

". . . try to make up with her, will you, my darling?"

"Mama, you don't know . . ." I wanted to tell her of my horrible experience, how I had nearly drowned in Turner's

Pond. But one look at her face and I knew it would be a waste of words. Somewhere along the way she had lost her dislike of Trina and had fallen under her spell. She would never believe me now.

"Yes, Mama." I said. There must be something I could do to stop Trina, I told myself. I had faced the hare—that creature of darkness—and won, hadn't I?

But for the present my main concern was with Douglas.

I lost no time in going to see him. Since I no longer had to practice subterfuge, I went boldly, choosing an hour when I knew he would be taking a pause from work—four o'clock—and rode over to High Farm first. I found him sitting under a tree, drinking from a stone jug. When he saw me approaching, he got to his feet and smiled. His boots and breeches were dusty and there was a streak of dirt across his forehead where he had impatiently brushed his hair back with his hand, a gesture which was as familiar to me as it was dear. For all his rumpled, unshaven appearance, he was still the handsomest man I had ever seen, and the white dazzling smile in the dark face still had the power to melt my very bones. Cousin indeed!

"A pleasant surprise," he said, handing me down from the mare. "Share my loaf with me?" He broke off a piece of thick, coarse bread and I took it. Then he spread his jacket out and we sat down together.

I had a few moments of shyness and held my tongue while he spoke of the fine weather. But when he paused, despair suddenly made me bold and I went right to the heart of the matter.

"Douglas," I said, "did you know we were cousins of a sort?"

He looked at me, then away. "Yes, I knew."

"And you didn't tell me? How long have you known?"

"Several years." He turned back and his eyes were deep and dark, full of pain.

"Oh, but Douglas, don't you see, it doesn't matter—it doesn't matter at all!" And I flung my arms about him. For a few ecstatic moments he yielded. I felt his arm go up and tighten as his mouth found mine. The hot blood rushed to my face as I clung to him, limp with desire. But, suddenly, he was pushing me away.

"No, Amelia. It *does* matter." He got to his feet, his

dark brows drawn together in a frown. "It is something that is just not done. No ... no." He shook his head. "Amelia—don't cry." He took my hands and lifted me to my feet. "We can go on being friends."

I bit my lip. "No—I can't. It would ... I can't."

"Well, then, perhaps we should not see one another again," he suggested reasonably.

The tears froze on my lashes as I stared at him. What was he saying? Not see one another again? *Douglas* suggesting that we not see each other? He had suddenly become a stranger, someone who had gone over to the enemy and for a moment I came close to hating him.

"I couldn't bear that," I said in a muffled voice.

He looked down and moved a stone with the tip of his boot. "I should miss seeing you, too."

Small comfort, but better than dismissal.

There was a long, awkward silence. Then Douglas said, "And how is your guest?"

Trina!

The agonizing possibility of losing Douglas forever had erased everything from my mind. Especially Trina. She frightened me no longer. How could anything, anyone frighten me when I had this pain in the pit of my stomach? Douglas was lost to me; we would never be sweethearts, never marry. All the witches in the world could carry me off on their broomsticks and I wouldn't turn a hair.

And yet. . . .

"You haven't answered my question," Douglas said.

And yet there was Papa and Mama. Trina had beguiled them into thinking she was nothing more than a sweet well-mannered schoolgirl, but I was sure she meant to harm them. Could I stand by immersed in my own unhappiness and do nothing? What if I should lose them too?

"Amelia. . . ?"

I gave Douglas an oblique glance. "I was thinking— thinking how best to phrase an answer." Whatever Douglas was now, a lover lost, or never gained, he had always been my friend. I trusted him, had always done so. During the years of our friendship he had listened to whatever confidences I had shared with him patiently, with understanding.

"Douglas," I said, "be honest with me. Haven't you noticed something odd about Trina?"

"Odd?" He seemed to turn the word over in his mind. "No, not especially. She's a pretty girl with unusually blue eyes, but I wouldn't—"

"No, no, that's not what I mean. Does she give you a . . . a . . ." How could I say it? ". . . a funny feeling?"

"I hadn't noticed," he said. "Is there something wrong with her?"

"I am sure of it." I lowered my voice, though there wasn't another soul in sight. "You heard that Veda Hempstead fell down the stairs—and Mrs. Chalmers died?"

"Certainly. You told me about it. But what has this got to do with Trina?"

"It's her work. Douglas, please believe me, she planned it. Veda was meant to die." I told him about the doll and concluded by saying, "It may sound silly, but I am convinced Trina is a witch."

There were a few moments of stunned silence. "Do you know what you are saying?"

"But, Douglas, she uses *black* candles."

"You actually *saw* her?"

"Well—no." I was making a poor case of it, as I had done with Papa and Mama. But how does one put into words (and what a feeble thing language can sometimes be) what I *felt* with such certainty. "But so many things have happened at Rommany ever since she came. Truffles disappeared, and the canary was found with a wrung neck, and the fires wouldn't light, and—"

"All because of Trina Blake?" Douglas interrupted the flow in a voice of disbelief.

I swallowed and began again, more slowly. "Mrs. Chalmers knew what she was. She was going to speak to her. And that is why she died."

"Mrs. Chalmers got a chicken bone stuck in her throat, Amelia."

"Because Trina had willed it. She cast a *spell!*" I said, angered by his stubbornness. "Douglas, I read this—this book and in it the author describes how witches get rid of their enemies. Why, only last night—"

"A book? What book?"

"It is called *Compleat Witchcraft*, an old book, written by a man named Boulton."

"I see," he said knowingly, sounding very much like Papa. "And that's where you've gotten those loony ideas."

Loony! Appalled, angry, again I came close to hating him. Was this the Douglas who had never mocked me, who had called himself my friend?

"Look, Amelia," Douglas said, "Trina is a charming girl, perfectly harmless, except that she might—perhaps has already—broken a heart or two." He smiled an engaging smile, a smile which turned me cold.

Charming! Harmless! So—she had enchanted him, too.

Chapter 8

I rode back to Rommany with a heart as heavy as stone. Because Granny Woodhill had allowed herself to be seduced by Sir Edward I had lost Douglas. (That Douglas would not have existed otherwise, my mind refused to see.) And why should all this happen to me? Trina at Rommany. No one believing me. Papa and Mama closing ranks in her defense. Douglas claiming Trina was "charming," refusing to hear me out, calling me "loony." That last—an ultimate betrayal.

The mare, sensing home and her evening meal, broke into a canter. "There, now," I said, checking her with the reins. She snorted in protest, but obedient to my will, slowed her pace. I was in no hurry to reach the house, in no hurry to see or speak to anyone.

The hawthorn along the lane had seen the best of its bloom, but there still were enough pink and white blossoms to scent the warm summer air. Small brown birds hopped from hedge to hedge and somewhere a willow warbler sang, a full-throated, liquid, heart-rending melody. I thought of summers past when riding this same way I would drink in both fragrance and song with joy. Now there was pain—and a hovering uneasiness.

As we passed Turner's Pond I thought, as I had so many times before—can they all be right and I wrong? Had Mrs. Chalmers, under that strict, hard demeanor, been as superstitiously foolish as any kitchen maid? Douglas had touched a sore spot when he asked if I had seen Trina with a black candle. I had never *seen* Trina do anything, except gaze at the menfolk with pulsating, come-hither eyes. Yet it was Mama who had first said, "... there is something about her." What had happened? When had Mama changed her mind?

I thought back over the weeks and recalled Mama's bright, almost vivacious smile when she had unexpectedly come down for dinner the day after receiving the spurious telegram, the day after Veda's fall. It had been very hot, and the rest of us had spent the afternoon on the terrace. Yes, it was then that I noticed her attitude toward Trina had altered. She had thanked Trina again for the roses, I remembered. ...

The roses. Of course, I could see it now—Trina had asked permission to take Mama a bouquet, and I had shown her where the garden tools were kept. Surprisingly, she had remained in Mama's room for much of the afternoon. What had they talked about? What had Trina said to charm Mama? I closed my eyes, trying to remember what Trina had looked like that afternoon. She had worn her usual costume, a dark blue skirt trimmed with bands of gray, a clean white high-collared blouse, her gold locket about her neck as ornament. That locket had fascinated Mama. I recalled how she had stared at it one day in the hall while Trina twisted the delicate gold chain with her fingers.

Was it possible that Trina had hypnotized Mama? I knew a little of mesmerism because Miss Peters, our history teacher, had mentioned a French physician, Charcot, who was currently trying this method on mental patients. A bright object was often used to put the sick into a somnolent state, making them more receptive to suggestion. A bit of mirror, a polished coin—a gold locket? Could a mere girl be skilled in hypnotism?

But Trina was not a "mere" girl, I reminded myself.

I rode through the stone arch and down the long drive. When Rommany came into view, I drew the mare up. The sun had gone behind a cloud and the house was in shadow. It looked gray and forbidding, not the home I knew and loved. No smoke curled from the capped chimneys, no face appeared at the windows, no sound came from within. And for a few moments I had the illusion that I had mistaken the way and stumbled upon the wrong place, a strange, bleak house. It frightened me.

But then the sun came out again. The illusion passed, but not the fear. Chilled, I brought the mare round to the stables and then, still reluctant to go in, I dismissed the groom and brushed Biscuit's coat down myself.

When I finally entered the great hall, Becky was instructing one of the maids to clear the tea things from the drawing room. Becky, having been lady's maid and second in command, had now taken Mrs. Chalmer's position as housekeeper. A tall, thin woman, capable, with many years of service, she was easy to get along with, providing one remembered to flatter her from time to time.

"You've missed your tea, Miss Amelia," she said. "But if you like I'll have a fresh pot brewed."

"No, thank you," I said, starting up the stairs. "I don't care for any."

"Your friend has been asking for you," she said.

"Friend?" I paused, my hand on the rail, and turned my head. "But I told Trina I was going out."

A small, reproving smile curled her lips. "You *thought* you told her, Miss Amelia."

"Perhaps she's forgotten, Becky," I said wearily.

"She does not seem like a forgetful sort of person," she said in a tone which implied that I was. "She, at least, remembers to address me correctly."

"I'm sorry. It was force of habit, Mrs. Grayson." Since her elevation to housekeeper, it was inappropriate to use her Christian name. The "Mrs." was merely dressing. I don't think Becky ever had a husband, and for that matter I could not recall Mrs. Chalmers having had one either. I often wondered why it was perfectly all right for a governess to be a "Miss," whereas a housekeeper found it unsuitable.

"It is not my place to speak, Miss Amelia," Becky-cum-Mrs. Grayson said, "and I don't mean to criticize, but aren't you neglecting your house guest?"

A quick, angry retort flew to my tongue. It was *not* her place. "Has she complained?"

"Not at all. She is a sweet person, very amiable, very pleasant—and very noticing. Why, only this morning she remarked how smoothly things were now run at Rommany."

Trina, sugaring up Becky Grayson. "And you think highly of her?"

"Very highly. And I might add, the entire staff feels the same."

Well they might, I thought bitterly. Trina had seen to that, whether with charm, or with flattery, or with the gold locket. She had won family and servants over completely.

But I was wrong on that score, for there was one person whom Trina had not bewitched: Clara.

I had asked that some hot water be brought up so that I could wash after my dusty ride and a half hour later, Clara tapped at my door. She came in with an averted face and, as she tipped the can and poured the water into the basin, I noticed that her eyes were red and swollen.

"Have you been crying, Clara?" I asked.

A series of loud sniffles answered me. A tear coursed down her bony cheek.

"Can't you tell me what is wrong?"

"Oh . . . oh. . . ." And she dissolved into harsh, rending sobs, her meager bosom heaving with the effort to control them.

"Has Becky—Mrs. Grayson—been scolding you," I asked kindly, offering her my handkerchief.

She declined it, using her apron, blowing her nose loudly.

"What have you done?" I coaxed gently.

"Nothin', miss, nothin'. That's jest it. Nothin'. Miss Trina said one of her ribbons was missin'."

"She accused you of stealing?"

"Not outright, but she might as well have, because I'm the only one as tidies her room."

"Perhaps it was misplaced."

"Miss Trina said she couldn't find it. Nowhere." She bit her lip. "She don't like me."

"And—you don't like her?" I smiled in encouragement.

"I'm afraid of her, miss," she said simply.

"Clara," I said, putting my hand on her arm. "I can understand that, believe me." Her large reddened eyes looked into mine. "I'm afraid of her, too."

"Are you, miss?" Her voice lowered to a hoarse whisper. "Do you remember that black candle I found?"

"Yes—I do."

"I think she is ... is a *witch*! I think—"

A knock on the door startled us both.

Trina's voice called out, "It's me—Trina. May I come in?"

Clara's flushed face drained to the color of putty. She snatched up the can and scuttled to the door. "Pardon, me, miss," she said as she brushed past Trina.

Trina came into the room wearing a gray gown with a prim white collar. A small smile sat on her face, a cat's smile. "Whatever is wrong with *her*?"

"She is disturbed," I said with forced casualness. "Seems she has been scolded for stealing a ribbon."

"*My* ribbon?" Trina's smooth brow crinkled. "I hope not. I merely mentioned to Mrs. Grayson that Clara must have misplaced it while cleaning my room. She's a simple girl, but I think she's honest."

"She *is* honest," I said.

"I am sure you are right. It is all a misunderstanding." Trina sat down and smoothed her skirt. "I shall speak to Mrs. Grayson again and see if I can right things."

"It will help, I am sure," I said with asperity. But Trina did not seem to notice.

"How did you find Douglas?" she asked.

"Quite well," I answered. *He thinks you are charming—and harmless.*

"I have tried to put in a good word for him."

"You have?" I asked, surprised, but on guard.

"Someone must. He's a fine young man and educated, too. I pointed that out to your parents."

In spite of what should have been better judgment I found myself softening. "And what did they say?"

"They listened to me with interest."

"Ah—no—it is hopeless."

"Why do you say that? I had a contrary impression."

"It is hopeless because ... because we are cousins."

"Tut," she said, fingering her locket. "Is that all? Why, my mother and father were cousins."

"Were they?" I leaned forward, one part of me warning that she was using Douglas to reach me, the other part desperately needing an ally. "I wish you would tell Mama and Papa that."

"I shall," she said softly. Her eyes were sparkling blue sapphires. "I shall."

What occurred next happened so quickly I hadn't time to draw a defensive breath, much less allow myself the luxury of a thought. Suddenly it was as if I were standing at Turner's Pond again gazing into the fiery hypnotic eyes of the hare. I felt the same surge of evil power pushing at me, forcing me back ... back. ...

"I am your friend," the soft voice went on in singsong fashion, "... your friend ... your friend. ..."

A sharp, brilliant light, too painful to bear, danced across my face.

I closed my eyes, but the intense light burned on the inside of my lids. *I must not give in. I can't. I mustn't.* I took hold of that small voice within me and hung on, hung on for dear life. *I must not give in.* Blood rushed to my face. I ground my teeth.

Time passed. A minute, an hour, I could not tell.

Then suddenly the terrible tension in the room seemed to snap. I opened my eyes. Trina met my look for a brief second, then turned away. All the color had fled from her face and there were beads of moisture on her brow. My own hands were clammy, and I could feel a damp spot between my shoulder blades. Neither of us spoke.

Down below a door slammed. The clock on the mantel chimed the half hour. The silence, heavy with meaning, resumed.

Trina moved at last, interlocking her fingers and cracking her knuckles. "Your wash water is getting cold," she said. "I'll leave and let you dress for dinner."

After she had gone, I sat for a long time, unable to move. Exhausted, wrung out by struggle, my mind nevertheless remained clear and active. I was perfectly aware of what had happened. Trina had tried to hypnotize me and failed. So far I had been able to hold my own against her. How much longer I could do so, I did not know. Nor did I have the slightest notion what she was planning. If I had had an inkling of how her dark mind worked, a hint as to the size or shape or form of my peril, I might have been less afraid. But the very vagueness of the threat which hung over my head, the uncertainty, worked like yeast inside me, and the more I thought, the more terrified I became. Still sitting in my chair, I began to shiver and shake like an old woman with palsy.

An unexpected knock on the door startled me. I cried out, "What. . . ? Who. . . ?"

"It's Mama. May I come in?"

I sprang from the chair. "No—Mama." I looked about wildly. She must not see me this way. "Not just yet. I'm in the midst of washing." I ran to the basin and made splashing sounds with the water.

"Oh—very well. We missed you at tea."

"Yes. I'm sorry about that."

"Try not to be late for dinner, will you, dear?"

"No, Mama."

I took off my dusty riding habit and washed my face and arms in the tepid water. Then I put on a yellow gown of dotted muslin. When I had finished brushing and pinning up my hair, I felt somewhat better.

Recovered from earlier panic, I saw where I was not as strong as I had thought. If my last encounter with Trina had left me weak and gibbering, what could I expect in the future? Alone, I would be utterly unable to defend myself or those I loved. I must seek help. While Clara seemed to be the only one at Rommany who had not fallen under Trina's spell, she was too frightened to be of much use. I had to find someone unafraid, capable of combating evil. Someone versed in dealing with malevolent forces. Someone with God on his side.

Who but the vicar?

After a sleepless night, I set out for Tenwyck early the next morning. In order to accomplish my mission alone, I had told Mama a lie. I had said that I felt badly concerning the way I had behaved toward Trina and, wishing to make up for calling her a witch, I had decided to buy her a gift. "A paisley shawl, perhaps," I had told Mama, "or a length of good wool for a skirt." It was to be a surprise, and I begged Mama not to tell Trina.

Though I did not attend church regularly, the vicar and I were acquainted; he had dined with us on several occasions. Papa enjoyed lively discussions with learned men and the vicar, though not lively, was undoubtedly a scholar, well read on a number of subjects. He had come to

Tenwyck two years earlier, when the village had grown into a town because of a new railway spur and there was need of a larger church. A gray-whiskered man, unmarried, he rattled around in the ten-room vicarage, looked after by a housekeeper.

It was she who answered the door when I knocked. "Is Vicar Smythe in?" I asked.

The old woman stared at me with something like shock in her eyes. Heavy jowls hung from her wrinkled face, and I noticed that her arms—bared by rolled-up sleeves—were loose-fleshed, too, as though she had once been stout.

"Why—yes."

"I would like to have a word with the vicar," I said firmly.

"Ah—yes. Forgive me for staring, Miss. . . ?"

"Blackmore. Amelia Blackmore."

She nodded. "You do look so like your mother."

"You know my mother?"

After a slight pause, she said, "Just in passing. The vicar is closeted with a parishioner at present."

"May I come in and wait?"

Again that stare. "Why," she said, visibly collecting herself, "why certainly. I'm forgetting my manners." She smiled. She had kind eyes, I noticed.

I was ushered into the parlor, a large, gloomy room whose windows were overhung with ivy. "I was baking bread," she said. "Perhaps you'd like a slice and some tea while you are waiting."

"Thank you, Mrs. . . ?"

"Mrs. Meacham."

"Thank you, Mrs. Meacham, but I've had a hearty breakfast." Not true, since I had been too nervous to eat. "A cup of tea will do nicely, though."

In a little while she bustled back with a teapot under a knitted cozy and a china cup and saucer on a tray. "You are from Rommany, then?" she asked, setting the tea things down on a little gate-leg table.

"Yes, I am."

"I hope all is well," she said with motherly interest as she poured my tea.

I looked at Mrs. Meacham in her clean white apron, her arms where patches of dusty white flour still clung, her eyes mirroring concern; and I had an enormous temptation to cry. She was a stranger, yet I longed to tell her all, tell her that nothing was right at Rommany, that under its roof evil was growing like an insidious cancer, that I did not know what to do and I was afraid. But I remembered only too well the skepticism, the disbelief, the reprimand not to talk "nonsense" with which my earlier outpourings had been met.

"Very well, thank you," I said, taking the teacup from her hands.

"Well, then." Mrs. Meacham smoothed the cozy over the teapot. "I must see to my bread. There's one more batch in the oven. I'll let you know as soon as the vicar is free."

"Thank you."

Fifteen minutes later Mrs. Meacham returned. "Vicar Smythe will see you now if you will come this way, my dear."

I rose, swallowing an anxious lump in my throat, and followed her across a small entryway. She tapped on a paneled door and after a low "Come in," Mrs. Meacham turned the handle and I entered a book-lined study.

At our dinner table the vicar had seemed small of stature and undistinguished—a rather nondescript man. But here in his own domain, seated behind a large, neatly ordered desk in a high-back chair, he appeared dignified, almost imposing, and for a moment I faltered. But then he spoke in his pleasant clerical voice. "Good morning, Miss Blackmore. How nice to see you. Won't you be seated?"

I sat down on the chair indicated, folding my hands in my lap. My heart was thrumming so, I was sure he could hear it.

"And to what do I owe the pleasure of this visit?"

How to begin? I had rehearsed my speech over and over on the ride into Tenwyck but now under the vicar's curious gaze every word of it fled from my nervous tongue.

"I wished to speak—to speak to you on a—on a matter of grave importance," I said striving to overcome a quivering jaw.

He nodded in encouragement.

And then I heard myself saying, "Do you believe in witches?"

I could hardly blame him for looking startled. "What I mean," I went blundering on, "is, well, there is something—*someone* at Rommany who I'm sure is in league with the Devil."

He pursed his lips. "My dear child—"

"Please, Mr. Smythe," I begged tearfully. "Please, let me have my say. I—I will tell you why I think so."

He sat back and folded his hands across his stomach. I took a deep breath, and marshaling my thoughts as best I could, tried to make my account brief and factual.

"You say you have discussed this with your parents?" he said when I had finished.

"Yes, but of course they disbelieved me, since they are under Trina Blake's spell."

If he had smiled or even blinked his eyes I would have thanked him kindly for his time and left. But he did neither, and I took heart.

"I see," he said, after a long pause. "You must understand, Miss Blackmore, that Tenwyck is still backward in many ways, and I hear tales of satanism and ghosts and goblins more often than I would care to mention."

Perhaps I had misjudged him after all? But then he went on. "I don't give much credence to superstitious talk. My vocation as minister of God forbids it." A faint smile. "However, you seem to be an intelligent young lady, educated, brought up by a learned father." The smile again. "Although I fault him for not bringing you to church."

I had expected that—a reference to the Blackmores' poor church attendance—and so steeled myself for a sermon. And I was ready, too, to promise faithfully that I should be present in the Blackmore pew every Sunday, every holy day without fail. I would be the most pious of parishioners—if only he would remove Trina from Rommany.

But the sermon did not come.

"I am much interested in your story. Mind you, I don't say that this person is a witch, that she is not influenced by evil; but neither do I discount it. We live in a world that is far older than Christianity. Long before we were here, the Druids worshiped in our groves and made use of strange boulders and stones in their rites. And on the continent the peasants assembled regularly for Black Mass.

So, who am I to say? But—I shan't give you a lecture on antiquity. I would like to meet this Miss Trina Blake. Perhaps you can arrange for your father to invite me to dinner so that I can observe her without arousing suspicion."

"Yes—oh, yes!" I cried, wonderfully relieved. "I will speak to him and suggest it the moment I get home."

He escorted me to the door. "Is there anything I can do in the meantime?" I asked, suddenly thinking it might be days before the vicar came to Rommany.

"Why, Miss Blackmore, pray," he said simply. "You would be surprised at the efficacy of prayer."

"Yes, I shall do so," I said, not at all as certain as the vicar that any prayer of mine could have much effect.

Before leaving Tenwyck I stopped at the draper's and bought a roll of woolen cloth for Trina, thus giving some truth to my earlier lie. Then I rode slowly home.

It was nearly noon when I arrived at Rommany and the butler, Salton, unusually solemn-faced, let me in.

"Did you meet the doctor on your way?" he asked.

"The doctor?" I asked, suddenly alarmed. "Why?"

Mrs. Grayson came to the head of the stairs and seeing me burst into tears.

"Is it Mama? What has happened to Mama?" I demanded. "Where is she?"

"She has fainted," Mrs. Grayson said, coming down the stairs, dabbing at her eyes. "Clara is with her."

"Fainted? Why?" My lips were dry.

"Your papa," she said. "Your father has—has had an accident."

"An accident? I shall go to him at once."

Salton put his hand on my arm. "Miss Amelia," he said in a sympathetic tone which, nevertheless, had an ominous ring to it. "You must be strong."

"What is it?" I cried. "For God's sake, what is it?"

Mrs. Grayson began to sob again.

"Miss Amelia," Salton said gravely. "I'm afraid you are too late. Your father is dead."

Chapter 9

After the initial shock, I wondered how I could remain so calm. Perhaps it was trauma, or perhaps, strange as it may sound, it was a profound sense of relief. The worst that could happen—had happened. The unknown disaster I had been waiting for with such unbearable suspense had finally occurred. Death. It was almost like my own death, coming after a long, agonizing illness.

"What sort of accident?" I heard myself ask in a distant, detached voice.

"Clara found him in one of the attic rooms," Salton said. He had a mole on his cheek, the left one. Odd that I had never noticed it before. "Apparently he had gone up there to look through some old papers in a trunk and fell, hitting his head on the edge of it."

"Papa fell?" I repeated numbly. "How could that be?"

"We think he may have had a seizure of some kind," Salton said. "The doctor will be able to tell."

Mrs. Grayson sniffed and touched her shiny pink nose with a dainty handkerchief. "Would . . . would you like to go up and see your father, Miss Amelia? He's in one of the guest rooms."

Dazed, I followed her up the stairs. She opened a door and I saw Papa lying on the bolstered bed. I moved over to his side on tiptoe, as though he were sleeping. And indeed, except for a gash at the side of his forehead, he looked as if he had stretched out only moments earlier for a short nap. His face was smooth and peaceful and strangely young. With the tip of my finger, I touched his cheek. "Papa," I said. "Papa."

Surely he would wake in another moment! His eyes would open and he would smile. "Ah," he would say, "I must have dropped off...."

I stared at the handsome waxlike face, the hands folded in an attitude of prayer. *He's dead, Amelia, he's dead. He will never open his eyes again.* I thought of the little girl who had taken his hand, crossing the cobbled street in Tenwyck, the sobbing child leaning against his breast, seeking and finding comfort for childish hurts, the eight-year-old who had ridden side by side with him to High Farm on a long-ago April day. I thought of all the little kindnesses he had shown me through the years and the words of gratitude and love I had never spoken.

Dropping to my knees I put my head on his arm and felt his rough sleeve on my cheek. I could not weep for the pain.

Mrs. Grayson tapped me gently on the shoulder. "You'd best see to your mother," she advised.

Clara, her red-rimmed eyes large with distress, sat at Mama's side. "O—Miss Amelia!" she said, her voice breaking.

"How is Mama?" She lay very still, her face as white as the pillow beneath the mass of her golden hair.

"We've tried everythin'," Clara whispered. "Even to burnt feathers. She hasn't stirred."

"Here—let me." Clara moved away and I sat down in her place. Lifting Mama's icy hands I began to chafe them.

"It was you who found my father?" I asked, speaking in a low tone.

"Yes, miss. I was in my room and heard a loud thump on the ceilin'. When I went up to look, I saw him. Lyin' on the floor."

"And he was...?"

"Dead. Yes, miss. I could tell by the weight of his head, Sir Duncan was gone."

Oh, Papa, I thought, to have taken your last breath in the musty attic upstairs. Alone. No one to smooth his brow, to say a last word, no one to hold his hand. How unseemly for Papa to die in that manner, how cruel that he should die at all. Salton had spoken of an "accident," of a heart seizure. Not for one moment did I believe any such thing. It was Trina who had killed Papa. Perhaps at the last moment he had found her out; perhaps he had asked her to leave Rommany. And angered, she had killed him.

"Before that thump on the ceiling, Clara," I said, "did you hear any other sounds?"

Her voice sank to a frightened whisper as she replied, "Footsteps, Miss Amelia. Footsteps. Heavy ones and lighter ones."

Her head bobbed.

We stared at one another in silence. And then Mama groaned. Turning quickly to her I said, "The brandy, please, Clara."

Mama's eyelids fluttered. I lifted her head and brought the cup to her lips. "Have some of this, Mama."

She sipped, and a shudder ran through her body. Her eyes opened and she smiled. "Amelia." She looked at Clara, at the bureau, at the windows, at me again. "I must have fainted."

"Yes, Mama."

"You see, it was the telegram."

I sought valiantly for words but found none.

"Why do you look at me like that?" Mama asked fearfully. She grasped my hands. "Your father. . . ." Her eyes grew wide. "Oh, my God! Duncan . . . Duncan. . . !" She gathered me to her, and with our arms entwined about one another, we both broke into tears.

Dr. Jemson found us some ten minutes later, still weeping. "Lady Blackmore," he said. "I am so sorry."

Mama wiped her eyes and gave him her hand.

Dr. Jemson, a short, stout bewhiskered man, kissed her hand gallantly. Aside from his medical skill, he was noted for his old-fashioned courtliness, a fact which made him especially popular with his elderly female patients. In the past I had found him archaic and a bore, but today I welcomed the sight of him, fussy manners and all.

"Such a loss," he murmured, "such a loss."

Mama covered her eyes with her handkerchief. "It's too hard to believe."

"Death is never easy, my dear lady." He smiled sadly at her.

Anxious, trying not to notice his depressing banality, I said, "You have examined my father, Dr. Jemson?"

"I have. From what I could tell, he had a cardiac seizure and fell, striking his temple on the iron hasp of the trunk."

"But he wasn't *old* enough to have heart failure!" I cried in protest.

"My dear," Dr. Jemson said, patting my shoulder. "Death calls us at any age. Only yesterday I was at the bedside of the draper's son. Poor Edgar was only twenty-eight, and he died of the same ailment."

"But Papa was never sick a day in his life." It was Trina who did it, I wanted to shout—Trina, with those terrible blue eyes.

"Neither was poor Edgar. Hale and hearty, and then. . . . It is hard, very hard. But who are we to question the will of Almighty God?"

Mama rolled her head from side to side. "Duncan— Duncan. How can I go on living without him?"

"Now, now, Lady Blackmore," Dr. Jemson gently reproved, "you must try to pull yourself together. I would advise"—he delicately cleared his throat—"I would advise sending for Ernest."

Ernest. It had never occurred to me until then that my brother would take Papa's place as Sir Blackmore. In a way it seemed inappropriate, almost ludicrous. Ernest was only eighteen, two years older than myself. Thin, gangly, freckled Ernest, the head of the family? Oh, Papa. . . .

"Ernest is on a walking tour of Switzerland," I said, wanting to cry again.

Mama twisted her handkerchief. "Yes. We have no way of reaching him until the end of the month."

Dr. Jemson adjusted his eyeglasses. "He left no address?"

"None, except his hotel in Zurich," Mama said, her chin quivering. "You see we did not know . . . we did not know—"

"Of course, of course," Dr. Jemson nodded. "Have you no male relative then, Lady Blackmore, a brother, your father. . . ?"

"My father is a semi-invalid," Mama said, "and I am an only child."

"Ah, yes. A friend of the family, perhaps?"

"There's Harold Hempstead," Mama said. "But I dislike leaning on him. His wife has a broken leg."

"Yes, I know. Then perhaps you would wish me to make the—ah—the arrangements?"

"Arrangements?" Mama gave him a puzzled look.

"The funeral, Lady Blackmore."

A slight flush appeared on her cheeks. "No." She looked down at her hands. "I think Mr. Hempstead would want to do that."

The doctor provided Mama with a packet of powders; then, advising her to have courage, he took his leave. I followed him out into the corridor. "I should like a word with you, Dr. Jemson," I said in a low voice.

"Yes, Miss Amelia. Did you wish a sedative for yourself?"

"No. It's ... I hope you will forgive me for asking again. But are you certain my father died of a heart seizure?"

"Not completely certain, no. It might have been the fall which killed him *after* the seizure. Only an autopsy would tell. But I don't believe your mother would sanction such a move simply to settle a fine medical point."

"No," I said. "I suppose not. But Dr. Jemson, do you think it possible Papa might have fallen because he was—well, pushed?"

He peered at me over the rims of his spectacles. "Pushed? My dear, what are you trying to tell me?"

"He may have quarreled with someone."

His eyes got large. "In the attic?"

"It was Clara, you know, who found him. Before that, she said she heard Papa's footsteps upstairs and—and with them another pair of footsteps."

"Clara? The maid?" His chin indicated the closed door. "Miss Amelia, I have found that in time of tragedy, accidents, sudden death, the memory of witnesses, especially that of the servants, cannot be relied upon. They tend to be very confused, sometimes inventive with their recollections. Now, you are a sensible girl. Who would want to—I hate to use the word, but that is what you have implied—who would want to *kill* your father? He was well liked. He may have had a detractor or two, gentlemen who differed with his politics. But you don't *murder* a man for that. Do you see?"

"Yes, Dr. Jemson." I had learned by now not to

denounce Trina unless I felt reasonably sure of a sympathetic ear. Dr. Jemson might be sympathetic, but for the wrong reasons. As a physician, he would think sorrow had deranged me.

"I'm sure I need not tell you how such speculations would affect your mother," Dr. Jemson said.

"Perhaps you are right." Better to agree. What sense would there be in making a fuss? I still had the vicar. Certainly *now* he would see how right I had been about Trina. And with the vicar on my side, I had a better chance of proving my case—even to Dr. Jemson.

Mama sank back on the pillows, closing her eyes. "Ah, brandy—brandy always makes me light-headed." She appeared wan, tired. The groove between her brows had become deeper, giving her fine nose a pinched look. "Amelia ... Amelia, you must wire Miss Weatheringham and ask her to bring the boys home."

Had she forgotten why she had sent them away?

"Yes, Mama."

I would send a telegram, of course, a telegram informing my grandparents of Papa's death, but I would also say that Mama had thought it best for the children to remain with them. If there were explanations to be made later, then I would think of something. I could not risk having David and Roger home while Trina was still with us.

The funeral arranged by Harold was an impressive affair, befitting the eighth baronet of Rommany. Whether Papa, who was never much for show, would have approved, did not matter. The somber pageantry, the mutes with their long staves, the horses plumed in black, the muffled carriage wheels, the glass-walled hearse bearing its walnut coffin heaped with flowers had a therapeutic effect on Mama—on myself. While we were in that long procession rumbling past the people who lined the streets of Tenwyck, the men with their heads uncovered, the women eyeing us with sympathy, we did not have to think of tomorrow, of next week or next month and how empty Rommany would be without its master. I did not even have to think of Trina, though she rode in the carriage with us veiled in black sitting very straight, her gloved hands neatly folded.

But after the services, when Vicar Smythe approached me, Trina again was uppermost in my mind.

"My dear Miss Blackmore," the vicar said, "such a tragedy, such a loss."

"Yes." I looked around and for the moment, at least, we were alone. "I would like to speak to you." I lowered my voice. "You heard how my father died?"

"Yes—a seizure."

"*She* is responsible!"

He blinked his eyes.

"Miss *Blake*!" Had he forgotten already?

"The young lady you spoke of? Yes, yes. Perhaps I will meet her when I dine with the family tonight."

"She will be there. And, Mr. Smythe," I added hurriedly, "one of our maids, Clara—*very* reliable—heard two pairs of footsteps in the attic just before Papa died. I'm almost sure Miss Blake was up there with him."

"You say the maid heard this? Perhaps I can have a word with her, also."

But the vicar never got his chance to speak to Clara, for when we got home we found that she had left Rommany. Apparently she had gathered her few possessions together and slipped out while the rest of us were at the funeral. My first reaction was one of dismay. I had hoped to have Clara as a witness (despite Dr. Jemson's disparagement), for I was bound to prove to the vicar that my father was murdered. Had Clara fled in fear? Had she been afraid that she would die like Mrs. Chalmers? In my heart I could not really blame her. Had I been in her place, I might have done the same.

Mrs. Grayson, for her part, was convinced that Clara had run off as a thief.

"I am having Salton go through the silver," she said. We were in Mama's room helping her out of her heavy black silk dress. "I should have dismissed that girl when Miss Trina complained her ribbon was missing."

My face turned hot. "Clara was honest! Even Trina said it was misplaced."

"Begging your pardon, Miss Amelia," Mrs. Grayson said

with asperity, "but does an *honest* servant leave employment without notice, without a single word to anyone?"

"She was frightened."

"And well she might have been if she took anything that did not belong to her. Your ladyship," Mrs. Grayson began to unhook Mama's corset down the back, "I would advise you to check your jewelry."

Mama put her hand to her forehead. "I am tired, Becky. I can't discuss it now." Her voice was vague, weary, distant. "Get my dressing gown, please. I think I shall have one of Dr. Jemson's powders and lie down for a bit before dinner." Mama had invited a crowd of people to come home with us after the funeral.

I got her powder and a glass of water while Mrs. Grayson helped her into her gown.

"Run along, Amelia," Mama said as she stretched out on the bed. "Make my excuses to our guests."

Mrs. Grayson drew the curtains and we went out together. "Had Clara any relatives?" I asked.

"None that I knew of. I believe she once said she was brought up by an aunt in Dorset."

"You have no idea where she may have gone?"

"No, Miss Amelia. I would soon have her back if I did."

I pretended to go along the corridor to my room, and when Mrs. Grayson had disappeared down the stairs, I quickly made for the servants' staircase.

Clara shared a room with one of the parlor maids, a small room, sparsely furnished; a double bed, two chests of drawers, a lamp, a washstand. Both chests contained black stockings, aprons, parts of uniforms, though one was bare of underthings. I surmised that these articles were the few possessions Clara had gathered in fear and haste. She had left nothing behind—no letters, no writing of any sort, no address by which she might be traced.

From Clara's room I went up to the attic where Papa had died. I had been there several days earlier to see whether I could discover some clue, some small indication that Trina had been there with him. By that time, however, the servants had already tidied the room, even sweeping the dusty floor, and I found nothing. Still my search had been hasty, done in a state of apprehension, and I might easily have missed a clue of significance.

A small room with a single fly-blown window, it had no furniture but a few cane bottom chairs, the rattan eaten away by mice, and the trunk, a large old-fashioned iron-hasped one. The trunk was not locked and I opened it. Inside I found a jumble of documents, letters, bills, tracts, all smelling of dust and decay. Why Papa had come here to search through this miscellany was a mystery to me. I knew he had kept his important documents—his will, the deed to Rommany—in a safe in the library. It didn't make sense.

I closed the trunk, and in doing so my eye caught sight of a tiny shred of dark blue material stuck on one of the hinges.

I loosened it and turned the scrap over and over in my hand. Dark blue—exactly the same color, the same texture as the skirt Trina habitually wore. It couldn't have been torn from the maids' clothing. Their uniforms were either gray or black. Mrs. Grayson always wore gray, and Mama had no cause to come to the attic. The tiny bit of cloth could belong to no one but Trina. To me it was proof positive! Trina had been in the attic. She had killed my father.

The vicar, as promised, came to dinner that evening, and when the long, interminable meal had finally finished, I drew him aside. "I have further evidence," I whispered. "If you could manage to get away, I shall be in the card room." I indicated it with a slight nod of my head.

"Evidence? Ah, yes. Very well."

I waited a good half hour, the rolled-up handkerchief containing the blue scrap of cloth turning moist in my hand.

At last the vicar came into the room. "Well?" I asked anxiously, scanning his face.

Carefully adjusting his coattails, he sat down and cleared his throat.

"What do you think of Miss Blake?"

"My dear child." He fixed me with solemn eyes. "My dear child, I honestly cannot say I see anything extraordinary about your Miss Blake."

"But," I protested, "but her demeanor is sheer hypocrisy. She's not the innocent girl she pretends to be."

"I'm afraid I cannot agree with you."

I stared at him. "She has charmed you, too!" I blurted.

"My dear Miss Blackmore," he exclaimed, sitting up, his face shocked. "Take hold of yourself."

"How can I?" I said, fighting angry tears. He had been my last hope. "I know she killed my father."

He made an impatient sound in the back of his throat. "God will forgive you for accusing an innocent girl of murder, for He knows you speak out of grief. The girl—and I have closely examined her—is no more cognizant of witchcraft than you or I."

"But you do not think she would show her true self, do you?"

"Naturally not. But there are ways, subtle ways of questioning, of learning the truth. Now, I give you my word—my solemn word—that this Miss Trina Blake is harmless."

Harmless! Why did they all say she was *harmless*? How I hated the word!

I bit my lip. "I am willing to concede, simply for the sake of argument, that she is harmless as a witch. But not as a murderess." I unwrapped the handkerchief and presented it to him. "This scrap is from Miss Blake's skirt. I found it on the hinges of the trunk in the room where my father died. Miss Blake had no cause to be up in the attic—none whatsoever. My thinking is that she followed my father there and, catching him unawares, deliberately pushed him."

The vicar stared at the handkerchief, a look of distaste in his eyes. "A few strands of blue thread do not a murderess make," he said sanctimoniously. "There must be a motive. Now, why should Miss Blake want to kill Sir Duncan?"

Because she is evil, I longed to say. But since the vicar did not believe she was, I replied, "Perhaps—perhaps my father wanted to send her away."

"And you suppose Miss Blake killed him for *that*?"

"But don't you see, Mr. Smythe, it all ties in with Mrs. Chalmer's death, with the canary—"

He shook his head. "My dear, you have invented a fantasy. A scrap of cloth that might have been in the attic for years or, at best, torn from a manservant's trousers. And poor Mrs. Chalmers and the canary. No, I am sorry, but your theory makes no sense." And then in his best, most soothing pulpit manner, "Young girls are often prone to fantasies, so do not feel badly. I knew a very fine miss who swore she was engaged to the Prince of Wales. But she got over it, and so will you."

Oh, the fool! The fool!

"There now," the vicar smiled, mistaking my despair for sorrow, "things will look up. Do come to church next Sunday. You will find solace in God, like so many others have. Now—shall we return to your guests?"

With the exception of Harold Hempstead—who was anxious to rejoin Veda and his children—my parents' London friends remained at Rommany for two more days. During this time Mama was mostly confined to her bed, and it fell upon me to play hostess, to consult with Mrs. Grayson as to menus, to preside at the table, to see to everyone's comfort. Thus I had little opportunity to speak to Trina, much less to be alone with her.

But never for a single moment was she out of mind. She followed me in my thoughts even as I conversed with Mrs. Grayson, or arranged the flowers in the great hall, or sat in the drawing room pouring tea. She haunted me in the silence of the night, creeping into my restless dreams, her voice calling, her limpid eyes smiling in triumph. Wherever I went, whatever I did, I was reminded of her presence. And every day, at every meal, she was there, her face wearing its proper expression of mourning, a face as false as a mask.

To say that I was apprehensive would only be putting an inadequate name to the emotion I felt—a dreadful nagging fear. Each morning when I woke, I wondered that I was still alive. I alone now knew Trina's real self. And *she* knew I knew. Of that I was certain. Would I disappear like Truffles and Clara, or would Trina kill me, too? How? Where? When? Sometimes I thought I would go mad thinking on it. And there was no one to whom I could unburden myself, no one to listen, no one to come to my aid.

The last guest left on Wednesday, toward the close of the day, and for the first time in a week I found myself alone with Trina. We were sitting in the drawing room over the tea things, empty cups and crumb-strewn saucers.

Trina said, "I have not had the opportunity to tell you how sorry I am."

"Are you?" I asked, calmly pouring myself another cup of tea from the cold pot. Inside, though, I was shaking.

"Of course I am. Why do you say that?"

Her eyes were an artless blue; she looked so innocent, so truly concerned, I hesitated. But only for a moment. "Trina, when I invited you here, I never dreamed you would turn against us."

"Turn against you?" she said, surprised. "I have done nothing of the sort."

I set the cup down. I was sick unto death of playacting. "You killed my father," I said in a low, intense voice.

Trina studied the remains of a tart in the saucer on her lap. When she looked up, she was smiling. "So I did," she said, as if I had simply accused her of forgetting to pass the sugar.

I stared at her, unable to utter a word. I had expected equivocation, denial, counter accusation, not this simple, almost bland confession. It was worse than evil—it was evil with a smile.

"He was a good man," I said, finding my voice at last, clenching my teeth to keep from shouting. "He was good to you. Why did you do it?"

Calmly she adjusted a ruffle on her sleeve.

"Why did you do it, you witch!" I hissed, trembling all over.

Her blue eyes darkened and a faint flush stung her cheeks. "Why?" she asked. "I'll tell you why. Two reasons, if you must know." Then, her voice rising, she said, "one, for revenge, and the other for the map. He would not give me the map, so I pushed him and he fell."

"What map?" I asked, bewildered, frightened. "What revenge? What have we ever done to you?"

She drew herself up, her eyes flashing with hate and malice. "My name is not Blake, but Blackmore. *Blackmore*, do you hear, you stupid bitch. Blackmore! The same as yours. I am your cousin. My father was hanged, and my mother died in prison three hours after I was born. Now do you know what I am talking about?"

Chapter 10

A shattering, stunned silence. Presently a bee began to drone at the open casement. I could hear it thumping against the glass, thumping and buzzing angrily.

"You are no Blackmore," I said, shaking inwardly with fear and rage.

"Indeed, I am," she replied with cold arrogance.

"You are wrong! You are inventing it. I have no relatives on my father's side."

"You have *me*," she said with that terrible smile on her lips. "Do you remember that portrait in the Long Gallery, the portrait of Sir Ian? The black sheep of the family, I believe you called him."

I stared at her dumbly.

"Sir Ian was my father," she said.

I kept staring at her. The deep blue eyes, the black hair, the white skin. "There is no resemblance," I said at last. "None whatsoever."

"I favor my mother, Lady Violet. Unfortunately, she did not live long enough to have her portrait painted."

"You lie," I challenged, but there was no heat to my voice. Papa had said very little about Sir Ian, had glossed over his picture, in fact, now that I recalled. Could it be? I scrutinized her face once again. "Why—if that is so—why do you go by the name of Blake?"

"Because my godmother refused to have me called Blackmore. She said it was a disgrace. I know differently. My mother left a letter to be given to me on my sixteenth birthday. In it she wrote that my father had been falsely accused of murder by Duncan Blackmore, sent to gaol, and executed."

"Papa falsely accusing someone? Never!"

"You see," she went on relentlessly, "your dear Papa wanted the estate and the title. And so—"

"Stop!" I covered my ears with my hands. It *couldn't* be true! "I don't want to hear any more!" Sobbing, I rose and stumbled blindly across the room.

With tears streaming down my face I ran up the long staircase. "Mama!" I cried breathlessly, bursting into her room. "Mama!"

She turned her head languidly on the pillow. "Why are you screaming so?" she asked in a vague, pained voice.

"Is it true Papa sent a man to gaol?"

She looked at me with clouded eyes.

"Did he?" I demanded. "His name was Sir Ian. Trina claims she's his daughter and that she is my cousin and that her mother left her a letter and ... and she killed Papa!"

"My dear Amelia, I can't make sense of such garbled speech. Please—darling." Her hands covered her face. "I've just taken a sedative. Later—come later ..." Her voice trailed off and she closed her eyes.

"But, Mama!"

She was asleep.

I stood gazing down into her face. Why have you failed me, Mama? I wanted to sink to the floor, to put my head on her bosom and cry. I wanted to be little again, to go back through the years to my childhood and have her take me in her arms and comfort me, to tell me that Trina had lied about Papa. But I wasn't little, I thought bitterly, and Mama was too lost in her own grief to take notice of mine.

I know now that I judged her unfairly. Poor Mama. She was in shock from Papa's death and struggling against an evil force as well—struggling and losing. Yet, looking at her then, I could think of nothing but my own pain.

I went to my room and after locking the door securely behind me, sat down at the window. I stared out but saw nothing. Lies, lies, Trina had told me all those lies to hurt. Revenge. The only part of her confession I believed was

that she had murdered my father. Tomorrow, I told myself, I shall see the vicar.

But it was my word against hers and, as I should have
known, hers prevailed.

I had sent a note to the vicar, asking him to come immediately to Rommany. I wanted the interview to take
place in Trina's presence. Face to face with her accuser,
she might find it more difficult to deny her story.

Mr. Smythe arrived shortly before noon. It was a hot
day—the last of July, I remember—and his face was shiny
with perspiration, but he smiled and greeted us pleasantly
enough. We received him in the drawing room, Trina demure in her white blouse and dark skirt. Smiling.

Then, without waiting for the vicar to settle himself
comfortably, she spoke. "Amelia, here, has accused me of
killing her father," she said in a high, sweet voice.

The vicar, mopping his face with a handkerchief,
paused. "I beg your pardon?"

Trina repeated her statement.

The vicar, turning pink with embarrassment, cleared his
throat and muttered something I did not catch.

"Do you deny it?" I asked Trina, trying to keep my
voice steady, dispassionate.

Trina ignored me. "Now, Mr. Smythe," she said, fixing
him with clear blue eyes, "I know that Amelia is upset,
her father having died so suddenly, but when she has
recovered she will realize her mistake and apologize, I am
sure. Why should I want to murder my benefactor? Sir
Duncan was so kind to me. I loved him like my own father. We got along well. You have only to ask the servants—or her ladyship. They will all testify to that."

"But you confessed!" I asserted, throwing calmness to
the winds, outraged, confounded by the way she had
mixed truth with fiction.

"Confessed?" Her eyebrows arched.

"In this very room. You said you murdered Papa for revenge and a map." Turning to the vicar, I repeated what
Trina had told me. I could see by the shocked and perplexed look in his eyes that he found my story somewhat
bizarre.

And Trina, of course, in her cool, matter-of-fact manner (in contrast to my own highly emotional one) refuted

all of it. "You will forgive me, Amelia, but my ancestry is no secret. The school has my records and my godmother will be glad to vouch for the fact that my name is Blake. My poor dead father—hardly a baronet—was a humble clergyman." This last with a disparaging twist of her lips, so that in wryly calling attention to her impoverished orphaned state, she could not be accused of self-pity.

"Then all you told me was a lie," I challenged.

"I told you no lies," she said with patient dignity. "How could I, when I have said none of the things you keep insisting I did?"

I appealed once more to the vicar. But I could sense by the expression on his face my case was already lost.

He hemmed and hawed, hooking his fingers in his waistcoat pockets and then asked to speak to Mama. I guessed what he would say. He would tell her that I was afflicted with fantasies to the point where I was ill, possibly mentally unbalanced.

"Her ladyship is indisposed," I said coldly.

"Well, then, my dear Miss Blackmore," he cleared his throat, "there is nothing I can do for you. Perhaps Dr. Jemson might help you."

Would I never learn?

Boxed, trapped by Trina's deviousness, I held my tongue.

Trina said, "Amelia, if I am the cause of your distress I think perhaps I should leave. I can see I have outworn my welcome. Tomorrow, early, if someone will take me into the train station at Tenwyck, I shall be on my way."

Was she telling the truth? Was it a trick?

She must have seen the dubious look in my eye, for she added, "The vicar is my witness. I promise I will leave Rommany tomorrow."

To be rid of her! Oh, what a relief! No matter that she would get away with murder (and how could I ever prove it?), the important thing now was that she would be gone from Rommany.

"Very well. I shall have the stableboy bring the gig round after breakfast," I said. Perhaps she really meant to go. Revenge accomplished, why shouldn't she?

Trina and I took our lunch together, speaking only for the sake of the servants. Mama had not come down. She was feeling poorly, she had said when I looked in at her. "It's just one of my headaches," she had assured me, refusing to let me call Dr. Jemson.

The day grew hotter, more humid and stifling. After lunch I shut myself up in the library. It was cooler there. And I wanted to be alone, to think. Second thoughts about letting Trina go had begun to plague me. Was I doing the right thing? Should I speak to the magistrate in Tenwyck, the constable? But then the vicar had not believed me, why should they?

I knew I would never draw a comfortable breath until Trina was safely out of the house. And there was still an afternoon, an evening, and a long, long night to be got through somehow. Would Trina try something else, something destructive to me or Mama, or to all of us at Rommany, a final *coup de grace* before she went on her way?

I went to the bookshelf and fumbling behind the volumes brought out the book on witchcraft. "Know thine enemy," someone had once said. I opened the book at random.

. . . witches were organized into covens, composed of twelve members, mainly but not exclusively females. The coven assembled once or twice a week in a meeting called an esbat. At these meetings the witches performed acts of Devil worship. In addition there were sabbats, large regional meetings to which initiates were brought. These were generally held on the nights of April 30 (Walpurgisnacht), October 31 (Halloween), July 31 (Lammas), and February 1 (Candlemas).

I turned a few pages, my eyes skimming the words.

". . . witches can cause diseases." Diseases. I thought of Mama upstairs. She had been ill ever since Papa had died. Was it more than grief that ailed her?

". . . witches can raise storms, make rain, or on occasion cause drought . . . can do harm even unto death. Men should fortify themselves with prayer and the sign of the cross."

I shut the book. My mind still refused to accept much in those pages. But that Trina had powers, I did not doubt, for I had seen with my own eyes how she had charmed both male and female alike, and how she had rid herself of Mrs. Chalmers and Clara and how she had tried to do the same with Veda and me.

"Prayer," the vicar had recommended. And the book, too, had claimed that this might be effective. But again I wondered, could one minuscule drop of humanity such as myself, one young, sometimes frivolous girl raise her voice and reach the ear of God? But I was alone, utterly, completely alone in this, and I had nothing else with which to fight Trina.

There was a large Bible on a stand near the window. Since it was too heavy and cumbersome to move, I stood over it, turning the pages until a portion of the Seventeenth Psalm caught my eye.

". . . incline thy ear to me, hear my words . . . hide me in the shadow of thy wings/ from the wicked who despoil me/ my deadly enemies who surround me."

I looked out through the ivy-framed window. A single white cloud, like a lost sheep, moved languidly across the pale blue sky. Would God answer my prayer? If only I could remain clear-headed, strong, I would not ask for miracles.

A knock on the door brought me from the window. It was Mrs. Grayson, who held a tray bearing several covered dishes. "Your mother is asking for you, Miss Amelia.

"Thank you. I'll go up. Is that her lunch you have there?"

"Yes—but she wouldn't eat any of it."

Alarmed, I said, "She didn't touch her breakfast either. I think you ought to send someone for Dr. Jemson."

"I've suggested it to her ladyship, but she claims it is nothing and not to bother."

Was this Trina's work? The illness, the refusal to eat? "*I* say we should bother." Fear gave my voice an edge. "And please give me the tray. Perhaps I can persuade her."

"As you wish," she said coldly.

Mama was awake, staring at the ceiling when I came in. Her head turned and she looked at me with blank eyes as I set the tray down on her bedside table.

"Come, Mama," I said, "I've brought you something to eat."

She glanced at the tray. "I told Becky I was not hungry."

"Nonsense," I said lightly, "a few sips of Cook's broth will do you good. You must keep your strength up."

"Oh—it seems so pointless." She shifted her head on the pillow. "The children. Why have they not come?"

Prepared for the question, I did not hesitate. "Grandmama thinks it best to keep them with her until you are feeling better," I lied, and wondered if God would mark that against me and withhold His help.

"Perhaps she is right," she said wearily.

"Are you in pain, Mama?" I asked, plumping up her pillows.

"No—I'm tired, that's all. I seem to want to sleep all the time."

I unfolded the white napkin and tucked one edge into the neck of her nightdress. "Come, Mama," I said, lifting the bowl of broth and skimming the top, "have some of this."

After several spoonfuls, she grimaced. "I don't care for any more. It has an odd taste."

I sipped at the broth. "Seems all right to me. A little salty, perhaps—"

"No, take it away."

I removed the dishes and the tray and set them down on the bureau. "Would you like a wet cloth, Mama?"

"No, I—" She had gone suddenly white.

"What is it?" My heart leaped with fear. Poison was my first thought. Trina, somehow, had gotten hold of the tray and poisoned the broth.

"Ah—it's my head again. A sharp pain over the right eye."

"Not your stomach?"

"My stomach is fine. It's my head, I tell you," she complained rather peevishly. "Get me one of the powders.

"But, Mama, I fear you've taken too many already."

"A powder, if you will!" She pressed her forehead with both hands.

I mixed the powder and she drank it to the last dreg in one thirsty gulp. "Thank you, my dear," she sighed, sinking back on the pillow. "Now, if you will leave me."

"Mama—perhaps I'd better stay."

"No. Please, Amelia, don't annoy me. I wish to be alone." She closed her eyes.

I moved to the windows and opened them wider.

"Please draw the curtains, darling. The light hurts my eyes."

"But it is so hot."

"Draw the curtains," she repeated, her speech slurred.

I did as she asked. Then I picked up the tray and hesitated. Mama's face, white as wax, looked peaceful, deathlike. "Mama?" I whispered apprehensively, moving closer. She was sleeping, her chest rising and falling in a barely perceptible flutter.

I deposited the tray in the kitchen and then wandered out into the great hall. The hands of the tall walnut case clock said four. I stood for a few minutes listening to the ponderous tick-tock, watching the brass pendulum swing in perfect rhythm, back and forth. How slowly time passed!

I went out through the front door and strolled down the drive, my skirt trailing limply in the dust. The sky had changed. The white fluffed cloud, now a dirty gray, had been joined by a great mass of ugly leaden ones, tinged with ominous purple. Not a breath of wind stirred. Every jade-green leaf on the motionless chestnuts and poplars, every blade of grass stood out in brilliant relief. No birds were to be seen or heard, not a sound of insect life. All nature seemed wrapped in foreboding, a smothering, sullen silence.

When I came to the arch I sat down on a stone abutment and wiped my damp forehead with a handkerchief. I planned to say nothing of Trina to Dr. Jemson, nothing of my most recent suspicions concerning poison. I would let him decide for himself what ailed Mama.

And it was then that I suddenly thought of Granny Woodhill. Famed throughout the neighborhood for her skill as a midwife, for her knowledge of herbs, the farm folk sought her advice on a variety of matters. They claimed she could cure dropsy, gout, pains in the joints, consumption, toothache, and a host of other ailments. There were also dark whispers belowstairs that she could make love philters as well as potions to ward off evil. Perhaps I should have fetched Granny Woodhill instead of sending for Dr. Jemson. But Mama, who did not hold with the practice of herbal medicine, would have refused to see her.

But *I* can see her, I thought. Granny was the one person who would not mock me. And she disliked Trina. Hadn't she once said, "She's a bad 'un?" Perhaps she had guessed at the corruptness behind Trina's pretty blue-eyed mask.

The heat had brought a flush to my face and I fanned it with my handkerchief. The sky had grown darker. Rain seemed imminent. How I thirsted for it—fresh, cool rain, for a world washed clean.

I continued to sit there, hot and uncomfortable, when the sudden crackle of a twig in the silence startled me. Slowly I turned my head.

A huge black dog, yellow fangs bared, green eyes blazing with hate, stood on the cindered path. I blinked, thinking it might be an illusion, but no, the dog was still there, an ugly menacing creature. Terror gripped me as it growled ominously, drawing a wrinkled muzzle back. I had never seen the dog before. Where had it come from? And so suddenly! Was this more of Trina's work?

I sat frozen, stiff with fear. The dog growled again, snapping at the empty air with a horrible clicking of rapacious teeth. In another moment it would attack, springing at my throat, tearing me to bloody shreds. When they found my torn body would Trina smile, secretly, triumphantly?

At the thought something seemed to snap in my mind.

"The Devil take you!" I shouted, anger sweeping over me. I had not battled and fought through so much to give in to Trina now. Not while I had the strength to breathe, the will to stay sane and alive.

I snatched up a stone. "Move on! Or I'll kill you!" I flung the stone at it—and I saw the menace fade from its eyes. I picked up another stone. The dog pivoted about and slunk away with its tail between its legs.

I leaned against the arch, weak and trembling. Had I won another victory? Perhaps the dog had simply been a mean animal, one made savage by hunger. But in my present state of mind I could not be sure of anything.

I took one last look down the empty drive and started back to the house. Dr. Jemson's tardiness worried me. Usually quick to respond to a summons from Rommany, he was taking much longer than I had expected. Perhaps he had been called out on an emergency. It never occurred to me until later that he might not have received my message.

Tea time came and went. Whether Trina partook of Cook's bountiful array of dainty sandwiches, cakes, crumpets, and tarts served as a matter of course each late afternoon in the drawing room, I did not know. I had gone straight up to Mama's room, refusing refreshment for both of us.

Mama seemed hardly aware of my presence. When I spoke to her, she answered in monosyllables. Her cheek was cool to my touch, but her eyes still held the glazed look of illness. She asked for water and I gave her some, but she did not complain of hunger. When Mrs. Grayson knocked on the door with an early dinner tray for Mama, I told her to take it back. She was horrified—indignant and argumentative—but I stood my ground, keeping to an earlier decision that neither Mama nor myself should taste food while Trina remained in the house.

"Has there been any word from Dr. Jemson?" I asked.

"None," she said.

"Then send someone again, if you will. And—Mrs. Grayson, we shall not need your services for the time being. I shall prepare Mama for bed myself."

"I can't allow that," she said, bristling. "I've always helped her ladyship at bedtime."

"Yes, of course. But if you don't mind—not tonight." And with that I closed the door. I knew there would be an uproar down below—no tea, no dinner, and now this. But it couldn't be helped. Somehow, after Trina had gone, matters would be made right again.

Through the window I could see the twilight sky. A faint glimmer of light pulsed amidst a swarm of black clouds, pulsed again and was gone. In a few moments, even as I watched, night closed in. Complete and final. The damp, dark heat pressed at my temples, yet I felt cold and sick with dread. "God give me strength," I whispered.

At nine o'clock I got a wet cloth and washed Mama's face and hands. Then I helped her out of her robe, turned her pillows, and tucked her in. Through all this she remained limp and passive, never uttering a word.

I longed to change into more comfortable nightclothes

myself. Dare I leave her? But with the door locked, I reasoned, Mama would be safe until my return.

Once in my room, I undressed quickly. I sloshed cold water over my face and arms and rinsed my teeth. With a clean nightdress, my hair brushed out and tied back by a ribbon, I felt cooler, but tired, so terribly tired. I put my head down on the cool marble top of the dressing table for a moment and closed my eyes.

A rumble of distant thunder brought me to with a start. Dumbly, I gazed at my image in the mirror.

The small clock on the mantel said eleven. I had slept nearly two hours! Slipping into my robe, I hurred down to Mama's room. The key rattled in the lock as I twisted and twisted it again. It took me another moment to realize that the door was unfastened. But I remembered distinctly *locking* it! Distinctly!

Cold with apprehension, I opened the door slowly. Looking through the small sitting room I saw that Mama's bed was empty. Her nightdress was neatly folded on her pillow. Her robe still lay at the foot of the bed where I had placed it earlier.

"Mama?" I called, going through the anteroom. "Mama . . . ?"

Mouth agape I stared slowly around, refusing to accept what I saw. Only two hours ago Mama had been too ill to wash her own face. And now—gone. Gone, but where?

Hastily, with trembling hands, I searched through her wardrobe. If she had dressed, what had she worn? I could not tell. More importantly, where was she now?

I ran down to the drawing room. It was empty as were the other rooms on the ground floor. The servants had retired, and the house was deathly still. I stood in the hall, my thoughts racing hither and yon. Then, suddenly on impulse, I hurried back up the stairs to the Green Room.

A turned-down bed, smooth pillows, blankets untouched. Trina's portmanteau yawned on the floor, packed, ready for departure on the morrow. But Trina, like Mama, was gone.

Chapter 11

Oh, God, what a fool I'd been! I should never have left Mama. Never, never! Not for a single moment. I should have known that a locked door would mean nothing to Trina.

I stood in the center of the room, clasping and unclasping my hands, sick with fear and guilt.

Where should I look? Where to begin? Trina had not exaggerated when she had said Rommany was vast. There was a whole wing of rooms (in addition to the one we occupied), rarely used except when there was an overflow of guests. And the attic storerooms upstairs, high under the eaves, how many I could not begin to guess. Rooms and more rooms, large and small. I had always thought of Rommany as well defined, a known territory, but now it seemed my home had suddenly expanded into a terrifying warren.

I couldn't search it alone.

I hurried out into the corridor and went directly to Mrs. Grayson's apartment. Gone. Not in her sitting room or her bed. Was this her free night? I couldn't remember. My heart beating wildly I went next to Salton's room. He was sleeping, his bald head covered with a white knitted nightcap. And though I called and shook his great bulk, he would not wake beyond an incomprehensible mumbling.

Close to panic, I turned and ran up the backstairs to the third story. The parlormaid was missing from her bed, and the other maids, four of them, were impossible to rouse. "Lizzie! Agnes! Mary!" Why such a deep sleep? Had they been given something?

Once again I found myself in Trina's room. Surely, I thought, looking about frantically, there must be some clue as to where she and Mama had gone.

The bureau drawers and wardrobe were empty of clothes, all packed neatly. There remained only a few items on the dressing table—a hairbrush, a comb, a hand mirror and a small book calendar. The latter's pages were opened to July and the 31st was circled in black.

Today, July 31st.

Oh, God—*no!*

July 31st. The sabbat. Lammas. ". . . covens assembled at these large regional meetings to which initiates were brought."

Was Trina part of a coven? As a witch, wouldn't she be? I remembered the tiny light in the woods and the black candle on the window ledge. It made sense, now, terrifying sense. Of course. Trina had been signaling to other members of the coven. And tonight, Lammas night, they would meet. Was Trina bringing my mother to this unholy congregation as an initiate? Or was Mama to be used for some other, diabolical purpose? Perhaps Trina had taken Mama in order to lure me into a trap. Alone, Trina had thus far been unable to overcome my resistance. But with her sister witches to help her. . . .

I was seized with a terrible urge to run to my room, to my bed, to burrow under the covers, to hide, to blot this horror from my mind. But it was only a momentary weakness.

Think! I said to myself.

Where would such a sabbat be held? A church? The only church for miles around stood in Tenwyck, but it was situated in the heart of town, cheek by jowl with the vicarage. Someone—a restless sleeper, a late passerby, the vicar himself—might notice lights, hear voices. No, it had to be a secluded place, a place dark and secret. In the woods, perhaps? But with the impending storm, would that be a likely choice?

Hurrying down the corridor, I stopped in my room to throw a long cape over my nightdress and slide my feet into slippers. I had little time to spare for, according to what I had read, at midnight the sabbat's preliminary revels would end and the serious business of initiation begin.

But where would the witches congregate?

I put my hand to my head. Think! A secluded place. An abandoned place, perhaps? The deserted house at High Farm! It was just two miles away. Part of its roof had fallen in, but enough of it remained intact to make fairly good shelter from the elements.

Grasping the small lamp from the bedside table, I hastened down the long staircase and let myself out into the black storm-threatened night. A wind had come up, chilly, with the cool scent of rain. On the western horizon, eerie lightning flickered among the moving mass of cragged clouds. I walked quickly round to the stables. The animals were restive. They snorted and whinnied, tossing their heads, stamping their hooves impatiently. Lucifer's stall was empty. So Trina had taken Papa's horse, a demon animal, but of flesh and blood. Somehow it heartened me to realize that Trina's power, evil as it was, had limits, and that she must transport herself like any mortal.

I got Biscuit from the stall and led her outside without saddling her. Extinguishing the lamp, I left it there by the stable door. Then I mounted the mare and we galloped down the drive. No one seemed to have noticed us. I saw no light go on in any of the windows, heard no voice calling out. Not even the stable dogs had been roused from their sleep. Only the fidgety horses had been awake. Was the whole of Rommany under a spell?

I thought it strange, too, that the storm, brewing all afternoon, had not broken yet. Had the witches been able to delay it until they were finished with their obscene celebrations? It seemed that way, and yet if God were that omnipotent, why should a handful of witches be able to command the forces of wind and drought and storm as Boulton claimed? I did not know. It was a theological argument beyond the abilities of my frightened brain. The important thing—the only thing—was to get to Mama before it was too late.

A quarter of a mile from High Farm, I drew the mare up and dismounted. Tying her to a tree, I started out on foot across a field in the direction of the house. Were it not for an occasional stab of lightning, I would never have found my way, for the night was as black as mourner's crepe. Using the house's high chimney (outlined starkly now and again) as a guide, I stumbled on over sharp tufts of grass and clods of dirt, the wind whipping and twisting my skirts about my legs, slowing my pace. This particular field had been left to lie fallow so, with all its impediments, the ground under me was still fairly negotiable. But when I came into the next field, planted with corn, now shoulder high, it was like entering a black tunnel. I could no longer see the chimney, and I became panicky lest I blunder about in the dark all night, never coming closer to my destination.

But luck was with me, and in a short time I emerged at the old orchard bordering the kitchen garden of the farmhouse. My heart quickened when I saw several horses—Lucifer among them—tethered to the gnarled apple trees. I had guessed correctly, then. As I moved through the trees Lucifer, temperamental under ordinary circumstances and made more uneasy by the brewing storm, greeted me with a loud whinny. I tried speaking to him in low, soothing tones, but this only seemed to increase his excitement. He began to rear, his eyes rolling white in their sockets. The other horses, taking their cue from Lucifer, added their voices to his, neighing, pawing the ground, straining at their reins.

Suddenly above the commotion I heard voices. Through the leafy trees I saw a swinging yellow light and I shrank back into the shadows.

"I tell you there's someone here," a man's deep voice said, a voice I did not recognize.

"It's the storm that's spooked the beasts," a woman replied tipsily and giggled.

"A lot you know. Here—let me have that lantern," the man said gruffly.

I dodged behind a tree trunk, drawing in my skirts, pressing my face to the rough bark. Holding my breath, I waited for what seemed to me the inevitable. They would find me; I would be caught and dragged ignobly from my hiding place.

"If it's some prying farmer," the man said grimly. "I shall have his head."

Lightning flared blue-white.

The woman tittered. "Most likely my husband's missed me from our bed."

"You did not forget to give him the potion?" he asked anxiously.

"Of course not," she replied coyly. "Are you jealous?"

"Not when I can have the best of you. Here—give us a kiss."

There followed a silence, and then the woman giggled. "No, no, enough, enough. Not here, love. They shall miss us. We ought to be getting back."

"All right, then. But first let me have another look around."

I squeezed my eyes shut as the lamp beam swung my way.

A long moment went by—then another.

"Perhaps you are right," the man said at last. "I can see nothing but the horses."

I waited until I could no longer hear their footsteps, then with my heart still beating loudly, I slowly crept across the neglected garden to a window where an arrow of light fell through a missing slat in the shutter.

I pressed my eye to the meager opening and saw the back of a figure clad in a cowled black robe. Across from him, facing me, sat a man who also wore a black robe. Though the cowl was thrown back to the shoulders and candlelight gleamed on his face, I could not recognize him. He and the figure whose back was to me were eating greedily with their fingers. By craning my neck, I saw others, dressed similarly, seated at a long, trestle table on which black candles smoked amid bowls of food. Neither Trina nor my mother were in sight. I stood on tiptoe, twisting my head but the chink in the shutter was not wide enough to observe more, except the corners of the fireplace and the old-fashioned brick oven. They were in the kitchen, then.

Cautiously I skirted the house. In the past Papa and I had been inside the house at High Farm only twice, and then we had been received in the parlor. So I had no idea which doors led to the kitchen or if I might find a window with an unobstructed view. As for a plan to rescue Mama—I had none. My main concern, at the moment, was finding her.

Feeling my way along the walls I came to a small lattice-windowed door. I twisted the handle and a babble of voices reached my ears. Peering round the edge of the door I saw that a small darkened room separated me from the kitchen. Lightning played over empty shelves, a jar of moldy preserves, a broken butter churn, a sawhorse on which rested a few articles of rusting farm equipment. It was a former dairy room, used also as a pantry storeroom.

My breath tight in my lungs, I stepped over the threshold and tiptoed across the hard-packed floor toward the band of light. I squeaked the door open a fraction of an inch, and my hand flew to my mouth.

Mama!

Dressed in a crimson robe, her honey-colored hair streaming down her back, she was sitting at the end of the table next to Trina. Her face had a blank, wide-eyed, tranced look. Drugged? Mesmerized?

Mama! I wanted to cry, *oh, Mama, I'm here!*

I opened the door a little wider. By shifting my eye from side to side, I counted twenty-five people—and I was able to pick out familiar faces. I recognized the stout man I had encountered at the fair, though his wife was not with him. He was sitting next to the missing parlormaid, Delia. The scamp. And oh, my goodness, there was Cook, she of the marvelous tarts and cakes. And—Mrs. Grayson! Becky Grayson, smiling and nodding and chatting. How long had they been part of this unholy crowd? Before Trina came to Rommany?

And then my eye going round the table once again paused. Shock upon shock! The vicar! Mr. Smythe? But yes, he was there, his spectacles awry, gnawing with relish on a chicken bone. And I never suspected. A parlormaid and a former lady's maid and a cook, perhaps. But a vicar? Had anyone guessed? Had even Mrs. Meacham with her aura of fresh-baked bread realized that his holiness was a—a witch? "I don't give much credence to superstitious talk," he had said with a sanctimonious air, ". . . my vocation as minister to God forbids it." Was it possible for a man to serve two masters? Perhaps Mr. Smythe could alter his personality at will, slipping from one form of worship to another, thus insuring himself a place in the hereafter whether it might be on the right hand of God or on the left hand of the Devil.

But the vicar's congregation—all the good folk who believed in him! A man in a high place, trusted, looked up to. And myself, seeking him out for help against Trina. It maddened me to think how I and the others had been duped. Well, Mr. Smythe has attended his last sabbat, I thought grimly. For once I had accomplished my mission I planned to inform the Tenwyck elders of their vicar's gross betrayal.

But as I stood there, my eye to the crack, fuming with righteous indignation, the shattering realization suddenly came to me that I was but one against twenty-five—one slip of a girl planning to confront twenty-five stalwart fanatics. Each one of those black-robed communicants (especially the vicar) would fight tooth and nail to keep their secret. They might, they *could* kill me. Why should I matter to them? To Trina? Mrs. Chalmers had died because she had guessed Trina's evil identity. And here I was an eyewitness to their sacred sabbat. How could I expect to take Mama from them without dying in the attempt?

There was no question about it. I had been a fool. A mindless, blundering, daft fool to think that I, single-handedly, could save Mama. If only I had gone for Douglas! Even if he discounted my tale of witches, he would have accompanied me without question, knowing Mama was missing.

But it was too late now.

The vicar was rising to his feet. He lifted his hand in a grandiose gesture of command and the talk subsided. "Enough of feasting. Let us prepare for the ceremony."

Everyone rose and amidst a great deal of clatter and the babble of excited voices shoved the table and benches against the far wall. This done they arranged themselves in a long line, their backs to the table. Mama remained sitting on the edge of the bench, her face wooden, her eyes blank, a frozen scarlet figure.

Total silence fell once more as Trina stepped forward. Her black robe was embroidered down the front with silver thread and girt with a silver sash. A silver-threaded ribbon, glittering like her eyes in the candlelight, banded her forehead. Exotically beautiful, she was a far cry from the humped crones pictured in Boulton's book. But because of it, to me she seemed even more perfidious, more wicked.

The congregation watched as Trina drew a large circle on the floor and then within it several cabalistic designs. When she had finished a makeshift altar was placed in the center of the circle and on it a burning black candle. Candles were also set at each quarter of the circle. A horned headress was produced, from where I could not see, and solemnly placed on the vicar's balding pate. He walked to the altar, looking immensely tall and frightening. Then the assembly, except for Mama, joined hands, making a larger circle outside the chalked one.

"We are gathered here," said the vicar in pearllike tones, "to do homage to the Lord of the Universe."

"We are! We are!" the crowd responded.

He twitched at his robe and it fell to the floor, revealing a pallid nude body.

I shut my eyes quickly, green nausea rising in my throat. I remembered only too well the obscene references in the book I had read, the obsequious vile homage to those who represented themselves as Satan.

Why did God allow such abominations to exist?

I heard the shuffling of feet, quiet laughter.

After an interminable length of time, silence fell again and I opened my eyes. The entire company was stark naked! I had never, in all my life, seen a single person divested of clothing, and I did not want to see them now. But I swallowed my revulsion and kept my gaze on Mama, still robed (thank God!), sitting like a wax image on the bench.

"We have an initiate tonight," the vicar said. "A bride. One who will add luster to our congregation. She is not a virgin, but then the Lord of Darkness makes no such squeamish requirements. Am I right?"

Laughter answered him.

"Our good sister Trina has brought her. Thank you, good sister."

There was a round of applause.

"And now if you will. . . ."

Trina went up to Mama and took her by the hand. Mama rose without a murmur, and like a doll-figure lost in a distant dream, walked into the circle up to the travesty of an altar.

"Behold!" the vicar intoned and he loosened the scarlet

robe. It fell from her shoulders. She stood there as motion-less as an alabaster statue, staring into space.

"Ah——!" they all sighed in one breath.

I wanted to sink into the ground. I wanted to die. It was as if I stood there myself exposed to their collective lasciv-ious gaze.

"Oh, Satan, we all bow in reverence to you." The entire company including the vicar, prostrated themselves, faces pressed to the floor.

Impulsively, before a cautionary thought could stay me, I dashed from my hiding place, past the prone bodies, grasping Mama's arm with one hand and scooping up the red robe with the other. The next minute, without quite knowing how it happened, so quickly, so *easily*, we were back in the dairy room. An iron bolt came to hand, and I slid it into place.

Throwing the robe about Mama, I pulled her to the outer door.

It was locked!

But how? Who?

I pulled at the handle, twisting it frantically again and again. It was not locked. Somehow the door had jammed. But no matter how I tugged and sweated and strained, I could not budge it.

A howl went up in the kitchen. Mama's disappearance had been discovered. Loud, shrill voices, and a moment later the vicar's rising above them. "Silence, I say! Silence! She can't be very far."

There was the sound of running feet—then what I feared, happened. The doorknob rattled. "It's locked! She's in here!" a woman cried.

The door shook as the mob threw themselves against it, yelling and screaming, pummeling the wood with angry fists. But, miraculously, the door stood fast.

Sweating with fear I moved closer to Mama and took her hand. Her skin was icy cold. "Mama!" I whispered. She did not turn her head, did not answer. "Mama . . .?" I may as well have addressed a stone. Dare I wake her from her trance? The shock would be ghastly and if she fainted I would be burdened by her lifeless body, leaving me more helpless than ever.

The pounding and the outraged shouting of obscenities

went on. Why, I thought suddenly, if they have so much power, could they not simply snap the iron bolt with a word, an incantation? Perhaps I had overestimated their abilities as I had done earlier with Trina. Or perhaps it had something to do with me. Trina had tried more than once to bring me under control and had failed. Physically I was no match for that raging mob, but thus far their witchcraft seemed unable to reach me. I was safe as long as the door held.

That gave me hope.

I left Mama and moved across to the outer door again. Bracing my feet, I pulled and pulled until my arms ached. But anxiety and the day's fasting had left me too weak. It was like trying to move a wall of stone.

I began to search the corners of the room for a heavy prop of some kind with which to reinforce the inner, beleaguered door. But all I could find was a hoe with a cracked handle, a rusted farm bell and an empty cask.

Suddenly the voices died and silence, an unnatural, eerie silence settled over the house. I waited, tense, my ears straining, while lightning flashed and distant thunder grumbled and rolled sullenly across the sky.

Trina's cool voice said, "Your ladyship? Do you hear me? Open the door, your ladyship. Pull back the bolt and open the door."

To my horror, Mama stepped to the door and put her hand to the bolt.

I sprang at her before she could slide it back. "You mustn't!" I cried.

A shout went up on the other side. "There's someone in there with her!"

"Quiet!" Trina commanded. "Is it you, Amelia?"

I said nothing, holding my breath.

"All right then," Trina said with malice. "You shall pay for this. Your ladyship . . .?"

"Mama, don't listen," I begged. "Mama, look at me."

But Mama's attention was riveted on the door.

"Pull the bolt, your ladyship," Trina's voice coaxed again. "Don't let anyone stop you. Pull the bolt."

"No!" I grabbed hold of Mama's arm. She shoved me aside with such shocking force it took me a moment or two to recover. And then I did something which I had never done in my life to anyone, let alone Mama. I struck at her with my open hand, a violent blow which sent her reeling against the wall. I heard a cracking sound as her head struck it, and I thought—oh, God! What have I done? Have I killed her? But she kept to her feet and in the next flash of light I saw her eyes blinking rapidly.

"Where am I?" she asked.

I hugged and kissed her and hugged her again. "It's all right, Mama. Don't say anything. You ... you have been walking in your sleep."

"But where am I?" she insisted.

Trina, apparently with her ear to the door, said, "You're locked in a room in a farmhouse, your ladyship. Your daughter is angry with you because you have come between her and Douglas Woodhill."

"You lie—you witch!" I shouted. And then in a whisper, "Mama, I will tell you everything. For now, trust me, please. We must get out of here."

There was a mumble of indistinct words on the other side, then someone, the vicar, I think, said, "The outer door," and my heart froze. They had finally guessed. I ran to it now and my hands, searching frantically for a bolt, found a wooden bar hanging at one side. I brought it down across the door, locking it in place. I was just in time, for a moment later the first of the angry congregation had come round the outside and were pushing and pulling at the handle. Others followed. I could hear their voices, shrill with anger.

"What is it?" Mama cried, horror-struck. "What is it?"

"Mama, they're witches," I said, shivering, holding her about the waist.

A stone was hurled through the window accompanied by the tinkle of broken glass and howling of the mob. Only the cross-barred panes prevented anyone from entering through the gaping hole. Another stone, another howl; like beasts, only worse. And then, a few moments later, a thudding noise at the door, as if a battering ram were being used.

It could only be a matter of minutes now.

I would be killed and Mama assaulted.

What was I to do? I had no magic powers. In olden days a crucifix, the sign of the cross, a prayer or the tolling of a church bell served to disperse the covens. But I had no crucifix and I had tried prayer. And there was no church bell.

But wait! There was a *bell*. The farm bell once rung by Molly Woodhill to call the men in for their evening meal. It was there on the sawhorse. I ran to it and grabbing hold of the clapper began to strike the sides of the old bell.

Clang-clang clang!

The bell's brassy timbre sounded nothing like the deep-tongued carillon which rang from the tower of Tenwyck's church. Nevertheless I went on grimly swinging the rusty clapper. *Clang-clang-clang!*

After I had been at it a few minutes I sensed that the tumult at the door had abated. I paused. They were talking in low voices, plotting something new, no doubt. The bell had not dispersed them as I had hoped. Still the desperate need for action—*anything*—prompted me to commence ringing the bell again. I could not simply stand there limp and acquiescent, waiting for ultimate disaster.

An eternity went by—although it could not have been more than ten minutes. My hands ached, grew numb, still I went on tolling the antiquated bell. The clamor jarred my nerves, grated my ears, stupefied my brain. Mama clasping her own ears screamed, "Leave off! Leave off!"

But I was as one possessed. Disgusted, sickened, angered, frightened out of my wits.

Above the clanging bell I could hear the crowd shouting and hammering, mad, wild with frustration.

Then suddenly the noise outside ceased. The bell echoed through the room as I listened. Silence. Utter silence.

"Run!" I heard the vicar shout, "Run!" There followed the sounds of rushing feet, the muted calling of names.

And then—silence once more.

Was it a trick, a ruse to make me unlock the door? Were they waiting in their black robes, clustered about in the dark shadows, smirking one to the other, certain that I would fall into their trap?

Thunder crackled overhead and the window panes shook as a stark white bolt of lightning danced crazily through the room. A few moments later above the dying mutter of thunder I heard my name called.

"Amelia? Amelia?"

I knew that voice. I would know it anywhere. "I'm here, Douglas!" I cried, running to the door and lifting the bar. "I'm here!"

The door flung open and he came across the threshold just as the rain burst from the sky.

Chapter 12

For a long time I could say nothing. Douglas held me close and gradually I ceased to shudder.

"When I told Granny the farm bell was ringing," he said, "she guessed— I don't know how—you were in trouble."

"Yes—Mama. . . ." I turned and gasped.

She was lying in a corner, a scarlet heap, having quietly fainted dead away.

We were trying to revive her when William Woodhill and Granny came through the door. "Here, let me," said Granny. "Step aside." She crouched beside Mama.

"Can you bring her around?" I asked anxiously.

"Best not to," Granny replied, gnarled but gentle fingers brushing Mama's hair from her face. "Let her be for now. Here, Douglas, give me your coat." Douglas got out of his jacket and Granny covered Mama with it. "Soon as the rain lets up, we'll take her home in the cart."

William helped his grandmother to her feet. "Now, Miss Amelia," she said, "can you tell it without gettin' all weepy?"

"Yes—I'll try." So once again I found myself explaining how I had impulsively invited Trina to Rommany and how through the weeks evidence, bit by bit, had built up convincing me that she was a witch. I told them how I had gone to the vicar and how he had presided over the sabbat. I skipped over the ceremony. It was too shameful to repeat to anyone. But I did describe how I had locked Mama and myself in and how the coven had tried to break the door down.

"I know'd she was a witch the minute I seed her," Granny said when I finally left off talking. "But Douglas here wouldn't pay me no mind."

"He would not listen to me either," I said ruefully.

Douglas said, "All right, all right. Draw and quarter me, hang me, but I still don't believe in witches."

I gaped at him. "*What?* After all I've been through!" Anger shook my voice. "You think I made the whole thing up? The vicar and Trina and Mama here in a dead faint, and—"

"Wait—wait, Amelia. I *do* believe you. I believe that those people who met here *think* of themselves as witches. But as for black magic, sorcery—no." He shook his head.

"Here, here," said Granny. "Douglas is as stubborn as the miller's mule."

"Granny's right," I said hotly. "And how can you explain all that's happened?"

"Coincidence mostly."

"Coincidence," I said scornfully.

"Yes, coincidence. Fear. Suggestion. Let's take it from the beginning. The canary and the dog. The canary's neck was obviously twisted by Trina. She got rid of Truffles— killed the poor dog, no doubt, and buried her in the woods somewhere. Veda fell down the stairs. Considering the long, hobbled skirts you women wear, it's a wonder more of you don't have that kind of fall. Now, wait, Amelia. Mrs. Chalmers got a bone stuck in her throat and died. She could have done so even if Trina had never existed. Then there was Clara. She was frightened. She ran. Whether she was afraid of Trina or the housekeeper who accused her of stealing, we do not know. You walked in your sleep . . . ."

"But I never have."

". . . you saw a hare and your apprehensive mind thought it was a familiar. Now, as for your father, you yourself have told us that Trina freely admitted to pushing him. If she were a witch, that kind of physical contact would hardly be necessary. In fact, none of the things I've mentioned, as far as I can see, were due to black magic."

"And Mama's trance?"

"Hypnotized, obviously. Suggestion, as I have said. And you, Amelia, simply are not open to it."

"I suppose," I said bitterly, "*you* were indifferent to Trina's charm? And, of course, never fell under her spell."

He grinned. "Yes, she does have charm. She's beautiful, but her charm is that of a ... oh, the word 'viper' comes to mind. I sensed something wrong there. Something cold and without feeling—and it worried me."

Granny spoke up. "T'is true. The boy didn't let on for fear of scarin' you worse, but he's fretted 'bout you all this summer."

So Douglas had thought of me, had cared, had worried. I looked at him, my anger melting like snow under sun. "I thought you had deserted me."

"Never. I could never do that."

I wanted him to go on saying that, over and over again. No argument there. And though I would always believe Trina was a witch (nothing could shake me from that) I would not belabor the point. Douglas was too dear to me to let Trina come between us again.

I smiled at him and he smiled back, a gentle, sweet smile. Granny looking from his face to mine, started to speak just as William said, "The rain's stopped."

On the ride back to Rommany, Douglas thought it best not to make the affair of the sabbat public. "It would rouse the whole countryside," he said. "And to what purpose? We don't hang or burn so-called witches anymore. The last I believe went to the gallows in seventeen hundred and sixteen."

"You mean we are to let that ... that wicked congregation go? Just like that?"

"They haven't actually harmed anyone, have they? As far as we know the only law they've broken is trespassing on private property. We could get the constable after them, I suppose, but think of the embarrassment and pain it would cause your mother if she were to be dragged through an inquiry and a trial."

He was right, of course. Mama had suffered enough. "But what about the vicar?" It seemed a travesty of justice to let him go on posing as a man of God.

"Mark my word," Douglas said, "by morning he will be long gone. And Trina Blake, too. As for the others, I shall have a word in private with those you can name. You can count on my putting the fear of God—or the Devil—into them so that they will never dare take part in such foolishness again."

Douglas had been right. Neither the vicar nor Trina were heard from again. Mr. Smythe's absence—discovered the next morning by Mrs. Meacham when she went to summon him for breakfast—alarmed her at first. But subsequently noticing that some of his clothes and a large suitcase were missing, she concluded the good man had left of his own free will. His disappearance caused a great deal of speculation in Tenwyck. There were many who believed that since the vicar had not stolen church money (of which a careful count had been made), his abrupt departure must have been due to a bit of dalliance on his part with a woman parishioner—a married one, to boot, whose husband had found them out. The identity of the woman and husband in question were matters fervently debated long after a new vicar had been installed.

As for Trina, she, like Clara and Truffles, vanished into a void. A riderless Lucifer, muddied and weary, trotted back to Rommany the next morning, but Trina herself never returned. The portmanteau with all her belongings remains in the attic to this day. When I wrote to her godmother, Mrs. Cozzens, at her Chelsea address the letter came back with the message: *"Moved. Address unknown."*

To everyone who inquired, I said that Trina had left because her godmother had suddenly taken ill. But to Dr. Jemson I told the whole story. He advised me to be truthful to Mama up to a point.

"Since your mother seems to remember nothing of that witch gathering," Dr. Jemson said, "I think it is wise to keep silent on that score. It would be a dreadful shock to her, and she already suffers from a nervous disposition."

"Are we to keep silent as to the circumstances of my father's death also?"

He gave me an indulgent smile. "We have no proof Miss Blake killed Sir Duncan accidentally or otherwise."

"She confessed."

He lifted his brows and adjusted his pince-nez. "In writing? Well then—you see how our hands are tied. If I were called upon to testify, I could say only what I know: Sir Duncan did have a seizure. That it might have been brought on by Miss Blake I have no way of ascertaining. Now I leave it to your good judgment, Miss Amelia, as to whether you wish to trouble your mother with this information or not."

Mama insisted on getting up as soon as Dr. Jemson had left. "I'm perfectly all right," she said as I helped her into her dress. "I did have the most dreadful nightmare, though," she continued, sitting down at her dressing table and inspecting her face in the mirror. "I dreamt that I was in a strange place and a crowd of black-robed monks were seated at a table and one of them had this queer headdress." She shuddered. "Ah, well, it was only a dream."

"Mama," I said, after a few moments, "Trina is gone."

"Without saying good-bye? I think that was rude. But then, quite frankly, I did not care much for her."

Apparently she had forgotten much more than the sabbat. "Trina said she was related to us," I said.

"Related? How?" She mused for a moment. "I know of no Blakes on either side of the family."

"She said her name is really Blackmore." I repeated what Trina had told me.

"Sir Ian—and Violet," Mama said, biting her lip. "Lady Violet." She turned suddenly to me. "That was it! That was what I saw in Trina's face the moment she walked in the door. Those cold eyes, that white skin. Yes—yes. Very possible. Lady Violet died in prison, but she may well have given birth to a child beforehand. Lady Violet. God, how I hate to think of her!"

"Trina said that her father never really killed anyone."

"He killed John Hempstead."

"Harold's uncle? But why?"

"Because of a map—a diamond mine, or something of that sort in Africa. Your father was supposed to have one half of the map and John Hempstead the other half. John's half disappeared, and your father promised he would tell me about his half one day. But he never did."

"And you never asked?" I exclaimed, visions of darkest Africa, jungles and lions, and ropes of glittering diamonds dancing through my head.

"My dear Amelia, the whole episode was . . . was horrible. I was only too glad to forget it. Even your father was loath to speak of it."

"But the map!"

"Your father never gave it to me, never told me where it was. Perhaps it was all just another of his wild stories. All I know for certain is that Ian, desperately in need of money, was caught by John Hempstead as he tried to rob his house. And then he had this scheme to force your father to go on a treasure-hunting expedition with him."

"Treasure hunting! Why have you never told me of this before?"

"I couldn't." Her eyes suddenly filled with tears. "It was all a nightmare. And I thought I had lost my mind, and ... oh, Duncan ... Duncan!" She covered her face with her hands.

"Oh, Mama," I said, kneeling beside her, feeling contrite. "Please don't cry. I shan't mention it again ever. I'm sorry I've upset you so. Please."

She lifted her tear-stained face and I kissed her.

We held each other without speaking.

"I *have* become a baby, haven't I?" Mama said, sniffling. "Here, give me my handkerchief. Tell me, where did you find me last night?"

"Oh—beyond the stone arch," I said vaguely. On Dr. Jemson's advice I had told her she had been sleepwalking.

"That far? And did I see Douglas Woodhill in this room?"

"Yes, Mama, the Woodhills helped me bring you back."

"The Woodhills?" She stared at me.

I was afraid she would ask why I hadn't gone to Salton for help. She did.

"I was so worried about you," I replied, "I didn't think, and William, Douglas and Granny were on their way back from High Farm and saw my lantern." I was getting deeper and deeper into a morass of half-truths, yet there was nothing to do except plod on. "And they offered their assistance."

"Well, bless their hearts," she said. "And old Granny. There aren't many women who would raise a—a fatherless child alone. You must stop at Green Oaks, Amelia, and give them my special thanks. Perhaps you can take something."

"No, Mama. Not a gift. They may be farmers, but they are as proud as we are."

If she caught the mild rebuke in my words, she gave no sign. "Then perhaps I ought to visit them myself."

"I think that would be nice, but really not necessary."

"No, I insist. And I promise I shan't be the least patronizing, if that's what you are thinking."

I blushed, but said nothing.

We set out the next morning in the gig, splashing over the puddled roads. The storm had washed the air clean, and the fresh breeze blowing across the lawns brought the scent of rich loam and green grass. It was a blessed relief to have the heat over.

To Mama this visit was a gracious expression of thanks. But to me it was a trial. The closer we drew to Green Oaks, the more uneasy and fidgety I became. Would the Woodhills look upon Mama's sudden unannounced appearance at their door as a grand aristocratic gesture? Would one of them inadvertently let fall a word about the horrible sabbat? About witches? About Trina?

Needless to say, by the time we reached the farmhouse I was in a nervous lather. Molly Woodhill met us at the door, surprised and pleased, but not obsequiously so.

"Come in, your ladyship—and Miss Amelia. How nice of you to call."

"Not at all, Mrs. Woodhill," Mama said, lifting her skirts and crossing the threshold.

Molly Woodhill led the way through a warm timber-ceilinged kitchen and a dark passage into a parlor where baffled sunlight smote at closed shutters.

"Forgive me," Mrs. Woodhill apologized, opening the shutters, "but I was not expecting company."

I looked about me at the plain cupboard, the worn, slippery sofa, the rag rug on the floor, the gaping, blackened fireplace and thought—this is where I should live if I were Douglas's wife. But, oh, how happy I should be! With Douglas as my husband, I would gladly live anywhere, a tent, a sod hut, a gypsy caravan, under a weeping willow, if only. . . .

Mama's voice brought me plummeting from the clouds. "We have come to thank your sons and Granny," she said.

Molly Woodhill gave us a puzzled look.

I said quickly, "For helping Mama into the house. She

253

was walking in her sleep the other night. I'm sure Douglas has told you."

"Why—yes." She smiled. She must have been pretty in her youth, I thought. Her eyes were a periwinkle blue, and though hard work had scored her face, it still held its finely molded lines.

"I would like to thank them personally," Mama said.

"William has gone to the fields, but Douglas is in the barn and Granny's upstairs. I'll fetch them. No trouble. Perhaps while you are waiting you would like a glass of my dandelion wine?"

"I should love it," Mama said, removing her gloves with a smile. "And how is your husband?"

"He seems to be somewhat better today."

"I'm so glad," Mama said with genuine sincerity. It pleased me to see how well she and Molly Woodhill were getting on.

"We were much saddened to hear of Sir Duncan's passing," Molly said.

"He always spoke well of Tyson."

"Thank you. And now for the wine."

Mrs. Woodhill returned in a few moments with a decanter of pale yellow wine and two cut-glass goblets on a tray. She poured the wine, then said, "I'll get Douglas and Granny."

Douglas was the first to appear. "This is a pleasure, your ladyship—Amelia."

"I wanted to thank you for helping Amelia the other night," Mama said.

"You're very welcome," Douglas replied graciously.

Granny came hobbling into the room. "Well, I declare! Lady Eustacia."

"Take my chair," I offered, springing nervously to my feet like a jack-in-the-box.

But Douglas had already pulled one forward for her. "Thank 'ee, Douglas."

Douglas moved to the fireplace and stood leaning against the mantel. Tall, broad-shouldered, he wore his work clothes with the same easy grace London dandies affected their expensively tailored suits. Ah, but he was handsome!

"Amelia," Granny said. With an effort I dragged my attention from Douglas. "I was telling your mum here I hadn't noticed how 'twas between you and Douglas 'til the other night."

My face turned scarlet. I dared not look at Mama, nor at Douglas, but kept my eyes on a spot of dull brown in the rag rug.

"I been thinkin' on it now," Granny continued. "I'll tell you all somethin' I ain't told no one 'afore."

I lifted my eyes. Douglas was smiling affectionately at his grandmother.

"Sir Edward Blackmore weren't the father of my child."

A pin could have dropped in that room and been heard with a clang.

Molly Woodhill was the first to recover. "Now, Granny," she began.

"I ain't in my dotage, if that's what yer goin' to say," Granny bristled.

"Then why haven't you told us this before?" Mrs. Woodhill asked reasonably.

"Saw no need to. Better to have folks think I had a bastard by nobility than the scoundrel who's really Ty's father."

A wild, improbable hope surged through me. "Who was he?" I asked, my mouth dry. A duke, a baron, a prince?

"A scalawag. Promised to marry me, then ran off. His name don't matter. He was a manservant at Rommany."

Only in silly, romantic novels did the dark handsome hero turn out to have aristocratic lineage. But it *still* didn't matter. No, it didn't matter at all, I thought, my heart thumping with sudden excitement.

Douglas said, "You are sure?"

From a mass of wrinkles, Granny's eyes looked out at him in scorn. "I was there," she said. "I ought t'know."

I glanced at Mama. She sat very straight, her pale cheeks tinged with pink. Would it matter to *her* now?

"Sir Edward took pity on me," Granny was saying. "He'd been very ill that year, and the doctor hadn't done him much good. I was handy with herbs even then, and I nursed him through. So when I had my trouble I came to him and asked, please could I have an advance on my wages? He gave me twenty pounds and told me not to worry 'bout payin' it back. And when folks talked and said he was the father—why, as I already said, I didn't disclaim it."

"But Granny—" Mama began, then bit her lip.

"Did I do wrong, your ladyship?"

Mama sighed. "It's all in the past. I'm sure by now everyone has forgotten the circumstances of Tyson's birth. You've raised a good son. My late husband thought a deal of him."

"Thank 'ee," said Granny.

"And now, Amelia," Mama said, drawing on her gloves. "I think we've kept these good people long enough."

"If you please, your ladyship," Douglas said, "may I have a word alone with Amelia before you leave?"

Mama after an almost imperceptible pause said graciously, "Of course."

My face stiff to keep it from trembling with excitement, I preceded Douglas from the room. He took my arm and silently led me through the outer door across the yard into the shadow of the barn. There, still without a word, he drew me into his arms, his mouth meeting mine in a hungry, almost savage kiss. "I love you," he murmured, kissing my throat, my cheek, my hair. "I love you—ah, how long I've waited to say that!"

Chapter 13

Mama and I spoke little on the ride back. Once or twice I tried to start a conversation, but she seemed abstracted, inattentive, hardly aware of my presence. When we reached home, however, I followed close on her heels up the stairs and into her sitting room, determined to have the matter out.

"Mama," I said, watching her closely as she sat in front of the mirror unpinning her hat, "Mama, Douglas wants to marry me."

She set the hat down carefully and flicked an imaginary speck from the crown with a long, elegant finger. "Now, Amelia," she began calmly, "if you—"

"Surely your objection no longer holds?" I interrupted, my face flaming, ready to do battle.

"No," she said slowly. "No. But you are only sixteen."

"Douglas is willing to wait. Mama, you—" I bit back the torrent of angry words. Would she go on and on, putting obstacles in our path? "He said he would wait forever."

She turned then and smiled, a sweet, compassionate smile, and in that smile I saw hope. "Oh, Mama . . .!" I ran to her and kneeling, kissed her. "Oh, Mama, I do love him so. I shall die if I can't have him."

"There now," she said, patting my cheek. "That won't be necessary. And you would be much surprised how familiar those words are." She tipped my chin and looked into my eyes. "You realize what life as a farmer's wife would mean?"

"But, Mama, he shan't be a farmer all his life. He is

writing a novel which I'm sure will be a huge success, like
... like a Thomas Hardy novel. And the farm is doing so
well, and his younger brothers are growing up and there's
my dowry."

"And a substantial one it is. Are you sure Douglas is
not marrying you for your money?"

"Oh, Mama." But there was a teasing light in her eye.
"Say, yes, *please*, say yes."

"You are in mourning now."

"One year," I said eagerly. "One year, and then I shall
be seventeen and I shall have finished at the academy."

"And you would be willing to live at Green Oaks? You
can't stay here, you know. The house belongs to Ernest
now."

"Oh, Mama, ever so willing!"

"Perhaps we ought to wait before we decide. A year is a
long time."

"It's terribly long. But I can wait patiently if only you
will say yes."

She rose to her feet with a heavy sigh. "I wish that Papa
were still alive. It's so hard to make decisions."

"He would give me his blessing. I know, I know. He
liked the Woodhills. He liked Douglas, and he never
thought of them as beneath him."

"Do I?" She raised light, arched brows. "Well, I suppose
I might. But if you are determined—"

"I am, Mama!" I whispered, my voice hanging by a
breath.

"Then there is nothing to do but to say—yes."

"Bless you, Mama!" I flung my arms about her laughing
and crying, and hugging her so tight she cried out.

Two years—not one—were to pass before Douglas and
I were married.

Soon after our visit to Green Oaks, Tyson Woodhill suffered a relapse and, after a month of racking pain, died.
But Providence, as if to make up for the Woodhills' loss,
brought the family unexpected financial success. Their harvest that year, a bountiful one, fetched unusually high
prices at market. Then, when the last of the corn had been
trundled off, a Mr. Blessing came along with an offer to
buy High Farm. He had made a fortune in rubber and tea

in the Malays and wished to build himself a country manor. The offer was such a generous one William could not refuse, and with the sale of the property (plus the profits from their crops) the Woodhills found themselves the most well-to-do farmers in the county.

It was then that William released Douglas from his promise to remain on the farm and urged him to return to Cambridge. I thought we could be married at once, but Douglas wanted to establish himself as a Lecturer at the College before taking on the responsibility of marriage. And so the extra long—and for me—interminable year.

But finally, unbelievably, my wedding day arrived. And such a day! Warm and lovely, with a beneficent sun looking down from a cloudless sky so blue it dazzled the eye. As we rode into Tenwyck the trees gleamed green and gold and late roses and pinks scented the morning wind. The church was crammed to overflowing with town and country folk come to see one of *them* marry an aristocrat. I took only passing notice of the craning necks, the gaping faces, the whispers, the murmurings. Nor did it offend me that Mama had not invited any of her London friends (except the Hempsteads), or that Grandmama was conspicuously absent, or that Ernest went through the ceremony of giving me away with a bewildered air. (It was one thing to search for Roman ruins with Douglas, and quite another for his own sister to marry him!)

None of it mattered. My eyes were only for Douglas, so handsome, so elegant in black formal attire. I felt myself the luckiest girl alive.

We started out for Cambridge that evening. Douglas had rented two rooms, four steep stories up from the street, a meagerly furnished flat with a greasy oil burner to cook on and a fireplace for heat. I did not mind, happy as a lark to have Douglas as husband and lover, all to myself.

But in two weeks, when the school term began, the honeymoon came to an end. Douglas was away for most of the day, leaving early and coming home late. In the evening he worked on his novel. I learned very quickly not to disturb him, sitting in a corner, reading, or staring at the peeling walls, wondering how Douglas, who in the past had so much to say, could now go for long hours without uttering a word.

As I struggled with broken latches, chipped dishes and cups (mine were still packed away) and lack of space, I tried not to think of my earlier naïve exuberance when I had believed so fervently that I could live in a hut with Douglas. Oh, how I missed and longed for the spacious beauty of Rommany, the early morning knock on the door and tea brought to my bed.

We were uncompromisingly poor. Douglas refused to touch my dowry, and so we lived on the stipend he received from the college plus the few extra guineas he earned by tutoring private pupils. When I suggested that I give piano lessons to bring in more money, he exploded in anger—no wife of his was going to work!—and we had our first quarrel.

I, who had been waited on all my life, soon learned how to cook, how to mend, how to haggle in the marketplace for the cheapest of cuts, the sorriest of vegetables. The loneliness was hardest to bear, for we had not the means to entertain and were rarely asked out. The day I discovered I was with child, I cried bitterly. Where would the poor babe lay its head?

But I was still proud; my letters home were painstakingly written, full of gay anecdotes, all contrived, all lies. When Mama wrote that she planned to pay us a visit, I, in a panic, promptly sent off a note saying that I had already made arrangements to visit *her* for a fortnight.

Rommany never looked more splendid, never seemed so lovely, her rose-colored brick walls set off by mossy parkland and hedges of olive-green yews. Early spring had brought out the daffodils and narcissi in yellow and cream-white profusion and they seemed to nod their heads in welcome as I rode past.

Mama greeted me with a kiss and exciting news—Ernest had gotten engaged to a Miss Patricia Chumwaite, the only daughter of a wealthy squire. "She's not pretty," Mama said, "but she has charming manners. A lovely girl." The wedding was to take place the following Christmas.

Roger and David, grown taller, clustered about me, tugging at my arms, begging me to come see the litter of pups Truffle's successor had recently delivered.

It was good to be home. Mama fussed, saying I was too pale and too thin and I must take care of myself now that I had the coming child to think of. Miss Weatheringham—her services no longer required now that the boys were in boarding school—was gone (as were the deceitful Becky Grayson, Cook, and Delia the parlormaid), but enough of the old, familiar staff remained to pamper me. They all went out of their way to be kind.

For three days I basked in the warmth of my homecoming, but on the fourth morning I woke with an empty, depressed feeling. It took several minutes to reason out why.

I missed Douglas, missed him with a sudden, surprising, sick longing. I realized all at once how thin and drawn he had become, working far into the night for my benefit, for *ours*. I recalled a dozen and one little acts of love which I, in my self-pity, had overlooked: Douglas rising in the cold morning before me to light the fire and set the water on for tea, his payment to the landlord's boy of a few precious coins to carry my heavy bundles up the stairs, his bringing home a bunch of sweet violets one wet February afternoon, and last, selling one of his valuable books so that I should have the fare to come home to Rommany.

I knew then, not as a romantic schoolgirl, but as a woman, that though our life together might be hard, it would be impossible to live it without Douglas. I loved him. A simple but irrefutable fact.

So I cut short my visit, wired ahead, and caught a noon train back to Cambridge. When the train pulled into the station and I saw Douglas's face light up with a smile of recognition and love I felt like a bride all over again.

Time passed. Granny died. Ernest got married. And Constance was born at Rommany with Dr. Jemson in attendance.

Douglas sent his book off to a London publishing house which refused it. He took it to another house which also turned it down. Again and again the book was rejected until the sixth house finally accepted it. *Holloway's Fancy* was published in March 1890. However, the instant success we had anticipated did not materialize. Few people seemed inclined to buy Douglas Woodhill's book. And though Douglas's editor claimed it was the finest book *he* had ever read and that the public apparently was more interested in trash than literature, I knew Douglas was secretly disappointed.

And then, almost a year after the book was published, a man named Davis wrote a glowing review of *Holloway's Fancy* in the Sunday *Times*, comparing Douglas to Hardy and Dickens and Trollope. Within a week the existing copies in print had been sold out. The novel went into a third, a fourth, a fifth printing. Money—at first a trickle, then a shower—began to pour in.

We were looking about for a larger place, a house, preferably, when we received a letter from Ernest. It was addressed to both of us. His wife Patricia did not like living in the country and since Ernest was thinking of setting up a law practice in London in any case, they had decided to make the City their permanent home. The younger boys were away at school, and Mama was rattling about all alone at Rommany. Would we consider making it our residence? We could have life tenancy, Ernest went on to say—that is, unless he had a son who should inherit after he died.

"Could we?" I asked Douglas eagerly, for I had never left off missing Rommany. "I should be so happy if we could live there and it would be near your own family, and the country air would benefit Constance."

"I'd have to give up the College," he said grudgingly. "And besides I can't afford the upkeep—not even now."

"We could close off a wing. And we don't need all those servants, nor the stables," I pointed out, anxious to convince him. "And Mama would pay her share—no, it is only right. Papa would turn over in his grave if he thought she hadn't. And you are not all that fond of the College, Douglas. You could accept those offers to lecture at London University without committing yourself to a full-time position. And you'd have so much more time to write. And there is Papa's library."

I think it was Papa's library which finally persuaded him.

Life at Rommany, though far easier and more pleasant then it had been at Cambridge, was not without tragedy.

A year after we had settled in I was delivered of my second child—a stillborn son. We buried him next to Papa on a bitterly cold day. Though he had never drawn a single breath, I grieved for him as if he had lived to maturity.

Two years later we had another death. Mama. She had been visiting her aged parents in Newberry when I received a telegram from Grandmama, asking me to come at once. Mama had come down with typhus. When I finally arrived at her bedside, after a breakneck, harrowing journey, she was incoherent and close to dying. She lingered another day without recognizing me. Her last words were, "The map! Oh, Duncan—the map! Where did you hide it?"

And sitting by her bed, watching as the light went out of her dear, tired face, that whole terrible summer came back to me (the Summer of the Witch, as I called it in the deep, dark recesses of my mind), and I had a vivid picture of Trina, her eyes diamond-bright, a malicious smile of triumph on her face. Had Mama suddenly, at the last terminal moment, remembered, too? For her sake, I hoped not.

Perhaps it is true, as some say, that death comes in threes, for I was not done with sorrow. Pregnant again, I had the misfortune to slip on a wet stone in the rose garden, and my second son was born six weeks early. We christened him Duncan and he lived but a month, his small, frail heart which had tried so hard, giving out as he lay in my arms.

Dr. Jemson said I would have no more children. It seemed the last straw. Too much had happened too quickly. Inconsolable, past grief, past tears, past caring, I took to my bed and there I remained week after week. If it had not been for Douglas and Constance, perhaps I should have died there in that somber, airless, shade-drawn room. But between them they coaxed me back to the world of the living.

Douglas prospered. He had written two more novels, both of which received critical and popular acclaim. He was much in demand now as a guest lecturer, and his fees were set high, so that though we were far from rich, we had more than sufficient for our needs. Constance was a loving child, but to my private regret she had three qualities which boded ill for a girl who must some day look for a husband: she was plain, far too bright, and stubbornly willful. Nevertheless we doted on her, Douglas especially, though he was not one to demonstrate his affection openly.

Ernest and Patricia remained childless. While Mama was alive they made a point of visiting us at least twice a year. But with her death, those visits stopped. Ernest was too busy with his law practice, Patricia too involved in good works. Neither of them expressed any desire to take up residence at Rommany.

My brother Roger, in his solemn, methodical way, had taken to Presbyterianism, joining the ministry. He had married a thin, sweet-faced woman from Perth, where Roger had been given a church, and there they resided.

As for David, after playing and laughing and gambling his way through Oxford he went into the army and later served with distinction in the Boer War. The perennial bachelor, he would descend on us at Rommany without notice, usually accompanied by a crony or two and set us to laughing with his boundless store of anecdotes until the tears ran.

Harold had given over his business to his eldest son, Benjamin, and he and Veda had retired to a villa in Bournemouth. From there Veda wrote, "The climate, while far from tropical, is certainly more suitable. Now, at long last, I'm not shivering with cold ten months of the year."

Benjamin and his wife Mary proved to be warm, affectionate, like-minded people who soon became good friends. They had two children: a son, Eric, and a daughter, Beatrice (or Bea, as she was endearingly called), born the same year as Constance.

William Woodhill, shrewd as always, realizing that the steady march of industrialization would soon squeeze the small farmer out, sold Green Oaks at a high profit to some people from Manchester named Talbot, and to our amazement, bought himself a large ranch in America—Texas, I believe it was—and moved his family there.

The years went by and then shortly before Constance's fourteenth birthday—to everyone's astonishment, especially Dr. Jemson's—I gave birth to a full-term boy. We named him Gordon. A year later he was joined by a brother, Alistair. At last my family was complete.

Life from then on was good to us. The boys grew like hothouse weeds, nettlesome, boisterous, happy. Douglas's success had brought a mellowness to his stubborn temperament, and I had learned to cope with his long silences and my own tendency to easy anger. We were closer to one another now than we had ever been. It was on the whole a happy household I ruled over, except that now and then glancing covertly at Constance I would feel a twinge of anxiety. There were times when she seemed unhappy, and more than once I caught a strange look on her face, a look—how shall I put it?—of fear.

Part III

CONSTANCE

(1911)

Chapter 1

To me Rommany will always be a dark place, dreary, full of shadows and haunting echoes. From earliest childhood I felt uneasy within its walls; at times, frightened. My own home. Ridiculous. Yet I can still recall a recurring nightmare—the symbolization of Rommany at its worst. In it I would find myself moving slowly, against my will, down a long, endless corridor, alive with silence and ominous shadows; an unpleasant dream which never failed to increase my disquiet.

In retrospect this anxiety seems very strange because by nature I was not a timorous child. Once outside Rommany I became quite venturesome, possessed of a continuous and often perilous curiosity. I climbed trees, fought with Cook's son, fell into Turner's Pond, and perpetrated other wild follies which gave my parents much concern. On my eighth birthday, I remember, scorning the pony I had been given, I insisted on trying a new mare who promptly threw me, jarring loose two teeth. Unfeminine I might have been, perhaps rash, reckless, even harebrained, but far from fainthearted.

Why then this fear of Rommany?

If I could have spoken of my apprehension more freely to my parents, perhaps it might have helped. But I did not know how to approach them. Not that they were unkind. In fact, the reverse was true. Because I was an only child for so many years, I received more than my share of parental consideration. When I grew old enough, Father managed to find the time from his books to take on my education himself. A man of few words and long silences, he nevertheless possessed a smile of singular warmth. I thought him handsome, brilliant and kind. I adored him.

And I loved Mother, too. More open in her display of affection, I sometimes felt very close to her. True, she did have a quick temper, one I often provoked, but she was equally quick to forgive and forget.

So all in all, I cannot fault my parents for my incomprehensible fear. I simply found it difficult to talk to them about it. With loving parents, why should a child be afraid?

I could not blame the deaths of my brothers or grandmother for casting a shadow over the house—not for me, at least. I was too young to understand little except that Duncan and Howell and Grandmama had all gone to Heaven where they sat with the angels, happy forever.

Part of my fear was tied to the ghosts at Rommany, though I cannot remember exactly when I became aware of them. They were not the wraithlike, white-sheeted kind, dragging chains and groaning, the sort one reads of in fanciful literature. No, these were *presences*—three of them—invisible, but palpably *there*. I heard them rarely, but often enough to distinguish one from the other: a deep, sorrowful sigh, the shuffle of a pack of cards, and the sound which frightened me most of all—the crack-crack of human knuckles.

I knew there were three—not one—simply because I *felt* their different, distinct personalities.

I spoke only once of these "ghosts" to Mother. I was seven at the time, I recall, and it was the card-shuffling sound I asked her about. She exclaimed angrily, "What nonsense! Has Tessie been filling your head with claptrap?"

Tessie, the current servant girl, was sacked, but the sounds went on and I, ashamed of my fears, never mentioned them again.

As I grew older, however, these shadowy phantoms receded into the background and finally seemed to fade away. Then an incident occurred when I was ten, and I realized that the ghosts at Rommany had never left me at all.

Being a lonely child, without sisters or brothers, a cousin of mine, Dora Woodhill, was sometimes invited to

Rommany to keep me company. She was an aggressive, loud-voiced, clumsy girl who habitually broke my playthings. We quarreled more often than not. But she was better than having no one, so I was always glad to see her. On this particular day, a wet, windy March afternoon, I remember, she suggested we "dress up" and pretend we were grown ladies. The logical place to find "dress up" clothes, of course, was the attic. Alone, I never would have dared venture above the first story. But with Dora, strong-willed and noisy, I felt somewhat brave.

The room at the head of the stairs was the only one occupied on the entire second floor. It belonged to our maid (the cook slept in a room adjacent to the kitchen), and though sparsely furnished it, at least, looked lived in. The other rooms were bare as a bone.

"Where is the attic, then?" Dora wanted to know, puzzled because I obviously was as much a stranger to the geography of my own home as she.

"It must be upstairs," I whispered, looking about me anxiously. The corridor, dim and cold, lost in shadows at the far, far end was exactly the corridor of my nightmare. "Can't we play at dools instead?" I suggested hopefully.

"Oh, come along," she said, impatient, tugging my arm. "I want to dress up."

The next flight of stairs became steeper and more narrow as we climbed. The uncertain light filtering down revealed thick dust smooth as gray velvet on the steps which no one had trod on for a very long time. I clung to Dora's hand, my own clammy and cold as we reached the landing. Rain drummed against the dirty panes of a stainedglass window, and peering through a rubbed spot I saw the stable yard far below. We must be under the rooftop, I thought with a shudder, and felt inexplicably trapped.

"It's so cold up here. Let us go down," I urged.

"Whatever for?" Dora asked, dragging me along the gray-lit passage. "Why don't we try this one?" she said, opening a door.

The room was small, airless, smelling of mice and rot. Silvery cobwebs hung trembling from the low, peaked ceiling.

"Look here!" Dora exclaimed, letting go of my hand. "A trunk!"

I stood by the door, poised for flight as she lifted the trunk's heavy lid. "Nothin' but papers," she said, disappointed, slamming the top down and raising a cloud of dust. "Now, where d'you suppose . . .?" She gazed about her. "Look here! A traveling bag in the corner."

It was an old-fashioned portmanteau.

"C'mon, don't stand there, Connie." She tittered. "Oh, my! Haven't you got the funny look on your face. I do believe you're afraid. 'Fraidy cat! 'Fraidy cat!" she taunted.

But not even her jeers could bring me into the room. Motionless, torn by shame and fear, I remained stubbornly on the threshold. Something terrible had happened here. I sensed it, knew it in the innermost reaches of my wildly beating heart.

Dora worked the straps from the leather bag and pulled it open. She brought out a comb, a brush, a book.

As she did so an icy, evil emanation seemed to flow across the dusty, bare boards toward me. My limbs grew cold, colder, achingly cold.

"It's a calendar!" Dora exclaimed. "July, eighteen eighty-six."

And then it came—the soft crack-crack of knuckles.

Panic—blind, irrational panic—seized me, and without a word I turned and fled, stumbling along the shadowed corridor to the staircase. Down I went, sliding, slipping, half tumbling, down and down, clattering past the stained-glass window, glaring at me like a crimson malevolent eye. More stairs and more.

When at last I came to the familiar first story, I did not pause for breath but raced along the hall until I reached my mother's room. Bursting through the door, I flung myself into her arms. There I babbled and wept and babbled until Mother finally managed to calm me.

"Have you quarreled with Dora again?" she wanted to know as I sniffed and hiccoughed into her handkerchief.

"No, Mother it's—it's—"

"Why, look at your dress! It is all dirty. Where have you been? And where is Dora?"

"In the attic," I said.

"What on earth were you doing up there?"

I told her. "And Mother—I got so frightened."

Did I imagine her face suddenly losing its color? "Frightened?" she asked. "Of what?"

"I don't know. There was only a trunk and an old-fashioned traveling bag, but. . . ."

She stared at me, stared *at* and through me.

"Mother," I said, fear gripping me anew. "What is wrong?"

She gave a little start. "Nothing," she said composedly. "It's just that I don't like you and Dora wandering about in the dust and cobwebs. Furthermore, I object to you girls prying into trunks and suitcases without my permission."

"But—"

"That's enough. Fetch Dora and wash up. We'll have an early tea."

"Mother—I can't. I can't go up there and fetch her."

"Nonsense. Stand at the bottom of the stairs, then, and call to her."

We never spoke of the attic again. I had the strong feeling that Mother knew something about that room, something that frightened her too, something which she would rather not talk about.

So I tried to look elsewhere for an explanation.

Our cook's name was Mrs. Meacham. She once worked as housekeeper to a bachelor vicar, long gone from Tenwyck's church, and because his successor was married and had no need for her services, Grandmama, out of pity, had hired her. She was incredibly old, but still spry enough, a good cook and a marvelous baker. We had formed a warm friendship early on over her sticky raisin buns, a delectable, yeasty concoction which I found irresistible. Shortly after the attic incident I was sitting in the kitchen, sipping tea and nibbling one of those buns, watching her as she peeled potatoes.

"Did you know my mother when she was my age?" I asked.

She rested her gnarled hands on the bowl for a moment. "No. She was older, a young girl—Miss Amelia. The first time I laid eyes on your mama was when she came to the vicarage one summer's day to consult with the vicar. Gave me a start, it did—she looked so like your grandmama."

I was hardly more than three when Grandmama died,

and my one dim recollection of her was of a mass of tawny hair streaked with white and wide, tired eyes. Try as I might, I could not associate that picture with Mother's shiny golden hair and bright features. Perhaps Mrs. Meacham's memory through the years had turned even more vague than my own.

"Why did my mother come to consult the vicar?" I asked, working a raisin from a back tooth.

"I have no idea. The vicar never discussed his parishioners' affairs with me. I did not expect him to. Besides, I don't see that it is any concern of yours, young lady."

She selected another potato from the basket and I watched as the thin peel began to unwind under her knife. After a minute of silence, I said, "And when was the first time you saw Grandmama?"

"Lady Eustacia?" She inspected the paring knife held in her swollen-jointed fingers. "Many, many years ago."

"Did she come to the vicarage too?"

She finished peeling the potato, plopping it into a kettle of water before she answered. "No—not exactly."

"Well, then, how did you meet her?"

"My, my aren't we full of questions today." She wagged her knife at me.

With the intuitive perception all children possess I knew I was being put off and I wondered why. It was a simple enough question.

"Was it here at Rommany?" I persisted.

"No. No—it wasn't. It was in Tenwyck, and I wish you'd leave off badgering me, young miss."

I finished the bun in silence and began to lick my fingers.

"Use the tea towel for that, Miss Constance," Mrs. Meacham admonished, profferring me the towel.

I wiped my hands. Smoothing the towel out on my knees, I said, "Have you ever been up to the attic, Mrs. Meacham?"

"My old bones don't permit climbing. And besides, why in God's name should I go up there?"

"I've been. It's a scary place. I think it's haunted."

She turned, her jowls quivering. "Fiddlesticks!"

"Oh—I didn't see a ghost or anything like that. It's

just," I shuddered, remembering. "It's just a *feeling*—a cold feeling."

"I should think so. The attics aren't heated."

"Yes, but it's a feeling I get sometimes . . . sometimes in the drawing room or in the great hall. As if something bad had happened."

Her hands paused for a fraction of a second. Then she went on with her work, the knife deftly slipping round and round the potato. "What a lively imagination you have. Nothing *bad* happened, my dear."

I knew with a certainty beyond shaking that she was glossing over the truth, perhaps hiding it, just as Mama had done. I was deliberately being kept in the dark. And because of it my curiosity grew like a festering sore. Though I was fearful of that forbidden knowledge, afraid that it might prove more than I could bear, I still wanted—no, *needed*—to know.

I had told Mrs. Meacham that I sometimes felt strange in the drawing room and hall. But there was another room—the Long Gallery—which made me uneasy, too.

I had been there only once, and, again, it was Dora who had led the way. A large room, dark-paneled, shuttered, the Gallery held relics of the past, old suits of armor, gilt tables, inlaid chests, and several worn velvet footstools. The walls were lined with portraits. One especially haunted me—Sir Edward Blackmore, whose fierce eyes glowered from beneath tufted brows.

I had not wanted to linger, but Dora, in her usual overbearing way, persisted. "Now, here is a handsome one," she said, dragging me along. "Sir Ian."

I looked up at the sandy-haired man. "I don't think he's one bit handsome," I said. His smile was false, and I did not like his puffy-lidded eyes. They were mean.

Later I asked Mother about Edward and Ian. Sir Edward, she told me, was a great-uncle and Sir Ian, his son, was a cousin of Grandpapa's from whom he had inherited Rommany. I would have left the matter there and not thought of it again, if I had not overheard Mother discussing my questions with Father.

I had come into the little anteroom adjoining my parents' bedroom in stockinged feet, wanting Mother to help me do up the back of my blouse. She and Father were in the bedroom talking, and when I heard my name, I paused.

"I don't know how much of the truth Constance should know," Mother was saying.

"She's too young," my father replied. "But when she is older I think she ought to be apprised of the circumstances under which your father inherited Rommany. Better to hear the truth from us."

Hear what? What truth?

I stood very still, my heart beating in fear and excitement.

Mother sighed. "When I think how different our lives might have been if Granny had absolved Sir Edward long ago!"

Absolved him of what?

"It's a mystery to me," Father said, "why Edward didn't speak up and simply say—'The child is not mine.'"

"Perhaps he did not have the opportunity."

"Well, it hardly matters now, since the truth came out eventually."

There was that word again! Truth.

"Yes," Mother said, "and I'm grateful for that. But if Sir Edward had not been blamed for producing a bastard, perhaps I shouldn't be here."

"Then I'm glad your wily old grandfather cheated Sir Edward of his bride," Father said. There was the sound of a kiss.

Concealed by the shadow of the anteroom wall, I tried to puzzle the conversation out. Apparently Sir Edward— he of the glowering eyes—had been blamed for "producing a bastard" (whatever that was), and my great-grandfather, taking advantage of it, had stolen his bride.

Was Sir Edward's "cheated" spirit one of the ghosts haunting Rommany? Was it he who sighed in the great hall in the murky twilight of a winter's evening, or in the drawing room moments before the lamps were lit?

"But don't you think it ironic," my mother was saying, "that *we* should be living in Rommany?"

"Not at all," Father said. "You forget his son was hanged for murder."

"Ah, yes. And all for a silly map which doesn't even exist," Mother said.

"Ian must have been a bigger fool than his father."

Sir Ian, the one with the false smile. But what was this about a map? A map of what?

Hurriedly, silently, mystified more than ever, I stole from the room.

Chapter 2

At the age of fourteen I made a shocking discovery—my face was considered plain. I had never particularly noticed my face. It was simply *there*, the blunt nose, the wide mouth, the overlarge eyes, and I had carried those features around quite comfortably for many years. Now, suddenly it seemed that the image in the mirror staring back at me belonged to a stranger.

This startling revelation—seeing myself as others saw me—occurred one evening as I sat at my dressing table, arranging my hair. Until my thirteenth birthday I had worn it in two long dark plaits down my back. But then Mother said I was getting too old for that, and showed me how to twist and coil the plaits so that they could be anchored neatly at the back of my head. But it was not the new hairstyle—though it did bring out my features more sharply—which caused me to coldly reassess my appearance. It was Bea.

The daughter of Benjamin and Mary Hempstead, close friends of my parents, Bea was a girl my own age. She and her parents (her brother Eric was at school) had come to Rommany on a visit. They were still in mourning, I remember, for Bea's grandfather, Harold Hempstead, who had died in a horrible accident (trampled by horses from a runaway carriage). But they seemed to have gotten over the worst of their grief and Mother, very proud of our new baby, was particularly happy to see them. I recall how pretty Mother looked as she showed Gordon off in his beribboned cradle, her eyes sparkling, her hair held back by a blue velvet band.

As we stood there admiring Gordon, who *was* quite handsome for an infant, Bea said to me, "What a pity you don't have either your mother's or father's good looks."

"Don't I?" I asked surprised.

"No," she said bluntly, looking me over with her beautiful sloe eyes. "Perhaps you ought to cut and curl your hair."

"Whatever for?"

"So you can catch a husband, silly," she said. "You certainly won't get one unless you *do* something about your appearance."

It was then I left her and went to my room to examine my face. Yes, what she had said about my not resembling my parents was true. Well, not quite. For I did have my father's dark hair, his dark eyes. But they did not seem to suit me as well as they did him. Perhaps if I were a man....

What nonsense!

Did I really care that much? I asked myself, gazing sternly into the mirror. Of course not. Why should I? my image replied flippantly, and I laughed.

But something had changed for me. I had had my first hard lesson in the school of growing up. Being plain handicapped a girl. Worse than that, one need not be pretty for one's own sake, but must be so for others—preferably men, preferably a prospective husband. Bea had already been talking of her future debut into society when she would be presented at parties and dinners and balls for the express purpose of being looked over by eligible males. It brought to mind Tenwyck Market Fair where the country folk crowding about the stalls carefully inspected an item—a hen, a smoked ham, a basket of apples, whatever—before deciding to commence their haggling over its price. The thought that I should someday be on display like that revolted me.

I decided then that I would never marry.

But I was reared in an age when to remain a spinster was unnatural, if not tragic. Furthermore, to deliberately choose a celibate existence was considered an eccentricity bordering on madness. Marriage was the only state, the ultimate aspiration for a woman. To that end pressures were brought to bear. In my own case these pressures were subtle, applied indirectly with kindness and affection, and so were far more effective in achieving their purpose. "You can do as you like when you are married," was a saying often on Mother's tongue. Or, "You will have your own children someday," Father would comment when I complained that little Gordon cried too much.

Implicit always in these remarks was the promise of freedom, the gilded Eden at the end of girlhood's rainbow. Everything I said, I did, I heard, seemed to be directed toward that glittering goal.

And there was example, too: my parents' own happiness, their close companionship. There was no doubt that marriage had its rewards.

By the time I was ready to be sent away to school, I had developed an open mind on the subject. If some rich, handsome well-bred, intelligent young man were to ask for my hand in marriage, I would not refuse. However, I would do nothing (no debuts, no presentations) to seek out this mythical creature. In the meanwhile, however, just in case his eye should light upon me, I gave up the braids in favor of a smooth chignon, allowing one or two curls to escape "carelessly" at the forehead and on either cheek, thus softening my features.

This preoccupation with appearance and marriage had temporarily diverted my thoughts from the dark, fearful side of Rommany. It had been a long time since I had felt a sudden inexplicable chill in the drawing room or had glanced furtively over my shoulder as I crossed the great hall at night.

Then, too, changes had been made in the household, brightening the atmosphere. Mrs. Meacham, having grown too old and infirm to preside any longer in the kitchen, had been retired to a niece's cottage in Sussex. In her place, a Mrs. Platte took command, a baritone-voiced, bona fide widow from Tenwyck who, together with Gordon's nanny, lorded it over four underlings. For Father was doing extraordinarily well with his books, and we could afford a fair-sized staff. It is surprising how even a handful of servants, as unobtrusive as they might try to be, can fill a house.

Their noise and bustle was augmented by Gordon (who

had graduated from crying to lusty verbosity) and the comings and goings of frequent guests.

In the presence of laughter and music and talk and the clatter of feet on the stairs, what ghost could survive?

I was beginning to think that my fears had been childish fancies and that I had, thankfully, outgrown them. But a week before I was to leave for for Miss Young's Academy I discovered that the sensation of a haunted Rommany may have had some basis in fact.

A gardener digging up some dead rose bushes on the far side of the terrace had come upon the skeletons of a small dog and a woman. The dog had been a house pet when she was a girl, Mother told us, but about the woman she would say nothing.

Father informed the constable in Tenwyck, and the next day an inquest was held. Though I begged to attend, my parents forbade it. Nevertheless, a week later I got a full account of the proceedings from the county newspaper, which I managed to pluck out of a wastepaper basket in the library and sneak up to my room.

According to the article, my mother had been the star witness. It gave me a strange feeling to see her name in print; Mrs. Douglas Woodhill. But it was she who identified the remains from the bits of decomposed clothing still clinging to them as having belonged to Clara Grimes, a former servant girl. The girl had left Grandmama's employ without notice some eighteen years back and had never been seen or heard from since. The coroner, Dr. Bagley, new to Tenwyck (having replaced old Dr. Jemson) was hard put to establish cause of death, though it was obvious from the site of Clara Grimes's grave that she had been murdered.

The newspaper article was detailed, switching from narrative to transcript. And here I quote:

Dr. Bagley: "To your knowledge did the deceased quarrel with anyone in the household?"

Mrs. Woodhill: "Not with the family. I had a house guest at the time who implied Clara had stolen a ribbon. But it was never proven. Clara was the soul of honesty. I will swear to that."

Dr. Bagley: "Who was this house guest?"

Mrs. Woodhill: "Her name was Trina Blake."

Dr. Bagley: "Was she related to the family."

Mrs. Woodhill paused and then in a low voice said, "Yes, Dr. Bagley. She was a cousin of mine."

Dr. Bagley cleared his throat audibly. "I beg your pardon, Mrs. Woodhill, but a moment ago you stated that no one in the family had quarreled with the deceased."

Mrs. Woodhill: "That is true. To my knowledge they—Clara and Miss Blake—never quarreled."

Dr. Bagley: "Do you have reason to believe that this Trina Blake may have done away with the deceased? Remember, Mrs. Woodhill, you are under oath."

At this point Mrs. Woodhill looked at her husband who smiled in encouragement. "She may have," Mrs. Woodhill responded, "but I have no proof. None whatsoever."

Dr. Bagley: "Miss Blake *may* have, you say? Did she have a motive, then?"

Mrs. Woodhill responded in a barely audible voice: "She did not seem to like Clara."

Dr. Bagley: "Can you tell me how to find Miss Trina Blake? We shall need her as a witness."

Mrs. Woodhill: "I have tried to locate her myself, Dr. Bagley, but have been unsuccessful. I can give you her last-known address, but I doubt it will do you much good. She did leave a portmanteau behind, however, which you may have if you feel it would help."

The Portmanteau! The paper trembled in my hands. It had belonged to a cousin: Trina Blake. Why hadn't Mother ever spoken of her?

Greedily, I read on.

Dr. Bagley: "By all means. But how was it that your cousin forgot a part of her luggage? Did she leave in such a hurry, then?"

At this point Mrs. Woodhill appeared rather shaken, and asked for a glass of water. While it was being fetched, her husband, Douglas Woodhill, approached the coroner and whispered in his ear. A few minutes later when Dr. Bagley addressed himself to the witness he said, "I apologize, Mrs. Woodhill. I did not know you were in—ah—in the family way."

Mother expecting? And she had not said a word to me. Too young, I thought bitterly, too young to know about babies or family secrets.

One other witness was called, a Mrs. Grayson, formerly housekeeper at Rommany. She also identified the few scraps of clothing presented in evidence as those belonging to Clara Grimes.

Dr. Bagley: "Did the deceased, Clara Grimes, get along with the rest of the staff?"

Mrs. Grayson: "Moderately so."

Dr. Bagley: "About this business of a hair ribbon. Had the deceased been accused of stealing it?"

Mrs. Grayson: "Not directly. But I'm sure she took the ribbon."

Dr. Bagley: "Were there words between Miss Trina Blake and Clara Grimes?"

Mrs. Grayson: "No, sir. Miss Trina never quarreled with anyone. She was a sweet, considerate, mannerly young lady. We were all very fond of her."

Strange, I thought, remembering my terrified reaction when Dora had opened the portmanteau. It was if Dora had uncorked a musty bottle, releasing an evil genie. Standing at the threshold of the attic room I had felt a distinct malevolent aura surrounding that bag and its contents. But now Mrs. Grayson was claiming that the owner of the portmanteau was sweet and considerate. Her testimony was not only at odds with my own intuition but with Mother's statement, that Miss Blake "may have" done away with Clara, as well.

But apparently the coroner saw no discrepancy or perhaps he still hoped to hear from Trina Blake herself.

Dr. Bagley: "Was Miss Blake on good terms with her cousin, Mrs. Woodhill?"

Mr. Douglas Woodhill suddenly interrupted the

proceedings by rising to his feet. "I beg your pardon, Dr. Bagley, but I thought this was an inquest of Clara Grimes's death, not an inquiry into Mrs. Woodhill's personal life."

Dr. Bagley: "Quite right, quite right. My apologies, Mrs. Grayson, you may stand down.

The verdict brought in was that the deceased, Clara Grimes, had died at the hands of a person or persons unknown.

I wondered who had killed the servant girl—whether anyone (except the murderer) would ever know. Perhaps it had been a stranger, another servant—or Trina Blake, as Mother had hinted. It also seemed to me that Mother might have given more information. But then, why shouldn't she tell Dr. Bagley everything?

I crumpled the newspaper into a ball and put it on the fire. Using the poker to hold the pages steady, I watched as the flames licked away, slowly turning the paper to black ash. The fire hissed and crackled in the stillness.

Suddenly I felt an eerie prickling of the hairs on the back of my neck as if someone were standing directly behind me.

The poker dropped from my hands with a clatter as I whirled fearfully round.

A deepening dusk had thrown long shadows into the room. On the shelf a gilded clock delicately ticked the seconds away. My eyes traveled from it to the wardrobe, the bureau, the dressing table. Nothing. No one. I was alone.

A draft stirred the curtains and they made a sibilant, rustling sound as though a woman were walking across the floor in a long, trailing skirt, the kind of bustled skirt fashionable when Mother was a girl.

My heart leaped in my throat. It's only the curtains, I told myself.

But then the fire suddenly sputtered with a shower of sparks and went out. An icy chill had pervaded the room—bone cold, aching to the marrow. The wind whispered at the casement and fell silent. And into the silence came the sound which I feared above all—the sound of cracking knuckles.

With a mouth gone dry in terror, I fled from the room.

My parents remained very tight-lipped about the inquest. They had given me only the barest of facts—that Clara Grimes had apparently been killed by an unknown assailant. No, Mother said, she would not hazard a guess as to why or who. I, of course, told them nothing about the newspaper article, but I thought it rather odd that neither Father nor Mother made any mention, even in passing, of Trina Blake.

A week later I found myself at Miss Young's Academy. I liked it. One might even say I was happy there. Strange, because the school was not the sort of place to gladden one's heart, but perhaps I would have been happy anywhere as long as it was not Rommany. The very banality of the place, the dun-colored walls, the nondescript paintings, the bulky, outmoded furniture, the uninspiring teachers had a calming effect. I did not even mind the snobbery—when it was discovered that my father's family were farmers, shock raised many an eyebrow—because for the first time in so long I slept through the nights without troubling dreams. I felt no fear; not once did I have cause to start in my chair at a sudden chill, to tremble at the sound of a ghostly sigh, or to peer breathlessly into a nebulous shadow. Dull, boring, sometimes irritating, Miss Young's Academy nevertheless offered me safe haven.

During the last year at school the old headmistress retired, and Miss Winters swept into our lives like a clean, fresh breeze. A tall, brisk, red-haired woman, she reorganized the academy from top to bottom, redoing the dreary decor with bright colors and flowered chintz, giving the more incompetent teachers notice, revising the curriculum, demanding higher academic standards. And she brought something else to us—something modern and daring—a typewriter.

"Most of you girls," she said when she spoke to us at assembly, "will get married. But there are some who may—whether out of necessity or out of boredom—wish to seek employment. Now I know you've been taught that a gentlewoman, no matter how straitened her circumstances, does not stoop to working in a business establishment. But times have changed, my dear young ladies. At any rate, I can see no harm in acquiring a skill. Hence this machine. I myself shall be instructing in its use. If any of you are interested, please indicate so in the book I have provided on the table at the door."

Mine was the first name to be entered.

The typing machine intrigued me, and I quickly learned to master it. At first I thought to persuade Father to buy one so that I could type his manuscripts, thus saving him the trouble of sending them off to London to be done. But then I went on to learn shorthand from Miss Winters and I began to think seriously of getting a job once I was through at the academy.

Why not? It was considered fairly respectable now. As Miss Winters had said, quite a few women of good family were gainfully employed. They were the emancipated, the liberated, the bold. They earned their own money. Some of them even had their own flats. The more I thought of it, the more romantically appealing the prospect of working in the City became. London was a far more exciting place than Tenwyck. I loved the flashy shops, the lofty white townhouses standing link-armed behind filigreed wrought-iron fences, the teeming streets where one could see foreign faces and costumes from far-flung points of the empire.

And I would be shut of Rommany. Oh, I would miss my parents and Gordon and little Alistair (born while I was at school) but we could visit one another now and again. Tenwyck Station was not the end of the world.

And so, living in a bubble dream, I pictured myself, smartly dressed, gloved and hatted, going to work each morning. Where? Perhaps a publishing house or a newspaper, where I would be at the hub of excitement. In my mind I could already hear the brassy clangor of machines setting type, the shrill ring of telephones, the buzz of voices. And I would be sitting at a desk with my own typewriter. "Yes, Miss Woodhill," I could hear someone say. Or, "Could you get this out for us right away, Miss Woodhill?"

When I went home at Easter and informed my parents of my plans for the future, the rosy bubble burst. Mother said no—stubbornly, adamantly, finally. To my surprise, Father, whom I thought to be a more liberal turn of mind, agreed with her. A daughter of his, *work?* "Nonsense!"

"What would you have me do then?" I asked, close to tears. We were in the drawing room. Mother was pouring tea.

"Why," she said, pausing a moment, the silver tea pot in her hand, "why you shall have a season in London."

"No! I refuse! I shan't be put on display like a . . . a side of pork."

"The Hempsteads are introducing Bea to society with a gala ball," Mother said, handing me a cup which I mutely refused. "I can assure you she is looking forward to it."

"Bea would. I am *not* Bea. I am Constance! I don't want a ball. I. . . ." To my consternation my voice broke and the tears came. It was hard—hard and bitter—to give up my dream.

Father said, "I don't see why the girl has to go through that sort of thing, Amelia, if she is so unhappy about it."

Mother gave him a wry smile. "You've always indulged her whims, Douglas."

"Now, Amelia. I backed you up when it came to allowing Constance to work. But you know as well as I that you never cared a fig for society. Why force Constance?"

"Because I want her to be happy. I want her to marry some nice presentable young man and have a family. And you know she'll never meet one here."

"I don't care!" I interposed between sobs. "I don't care!"

In the end a compromise was reached. If I agreed to attend the season's social functions for three months, beginning with the Hempstead ball, Father would speak to Benjamin Hempstead about giving me a job in his establishment. I knew the reason Mother agreed to this plan was because she hoped that by the end of the season I should have found a husband.

She was wrong, of course—something I could have told her from the start. But in the meanwhile I spent the most miserable three months of my life. Uncomfortably gowned and coiffed in the height of fashion, I tried to make small talk at lavish dinners, at intimate suppers, at teas, at musicales with whatever male had the misfortune to be seated next to me. I found them all dull, and I am certain they found me equally so.

Dances were the worst. I was clumsy and self-conscious.

I never could get my feet to follow my partner's in time to the music. More often than not, I sat with the older women and the plain unfortunates like myself in a bank of gilded chairs along the wall, fanning my hot cheeks furiously and wishing I were dead. Invariably, at some point during such evenings, Eric Hempstead (who with his popular sister, Bea, also attended these functions), taking pity on me, I suppose, would ask me to dance. Half-gone with champagne punch and whiskey he would dutifully push me around the floor. Already he had earned a reputation for drinking and gambling, and anxious mothers, including my own, warned their daughters against him. But I would have danced with a gorilla rather than suffer the humiliation of not having danced at all.

After what seemed three centuries rather than three months, the season was over. True to his word, Father had spoken to Benjamin Hempstead, and I was offered a job as typist in his offices. My delight at finally realizing my dream was somewhat tempered by the proviso that I reside with the Hempsteads. I did not mind Benjamin and his wife, two pleasant and comfortable people, nor Eric, who had gone off to school again, but Bea was insufferable. She had become engaged to the count of something or other, and she took great pains to let me know how successful she had been in contrast to my own abysmal failure.

In addition, the position I had so happily anticipated proved disappointing. Benjamin Hempstead was an importer of tea and sugar, and I was given the uninspiring job of typing bills of lading. Plodding, tedious work. At night I would go home, my head swarming with figures, my back aching, my fingers numb. The only ray of light in an otherwise dull routine was a friendship I formed with Miss Henry.

A woman of some thirty-odd, she helped with the accounts at Hempstead's. Efficient, quick-witted and enormously well-informed on a host of subjects, she was also an ardent suffragette and a member of Emmeline Pankhurst's Women's Social and Political Union, an organization which had won a reputation for boldness and militancy.

Miss Henry invited me to a meeting one night and I was immediately caught up in the fervor and excitement of the society's plans to obtain the vote for women. Listening to impassioned speeches about proposed demonstrations with a mixture of fear and delight, I felt as if I had at last come to my vocation in life. But I never got to break a single window or light a single bomb or spend one night in jail, things which I was eagerly prepared to do. For Father, hearing of my association, came posthaste to London and literally dragged mc back to Rommany.

So I returned fo my home, the shadow-thronged, haunted house of memory. And it seemed as I stepped across the familiar threshold once more into the gloomy great hall dimly lit with gaslight that I would remain within those walls forever.

Chapter 3

Day followed day and month followed month. I was nine-teen, and then, apparently without any interval, I was twenty, twenty-one.

If I had been a different person, strong-willed rather than willful, I would have packed my bag, scribbled a farewell note and left Rommany—in effect, run away. An admirer of such staunch feminists as Mary Evans, Mary Wollstonecraft, and Emmeline Pankhurst, I could not find the resolution to emulate them. Though my intellect re-belled against convention, against the strict edict that an unmarried female must remain within the bosom of her family, in my heart I was afraid. Perhaps my long, secret fear of Rommany had sapped my courage, or perhaps some preordained fate held me there. Whatever it was, I had long since given up any thought of flight.

Mother still worked at finding me a husband, though, badgering my two uncles and her London friends to bring down "that nice Mr. So-and-So for a weekend." She even took to combing the neighborhood for likely bachelors and in desperation invited the son of the people who had bought Green Oaks (now a lofty, brick mansion surround-ed by parkland) one evening to dinner.

His name was Wilfred Talbot. He seemed pleasant enough, well-mannered and conversant on a number of topics. Talk at the table had centered around the Parliament Act then being debated in Commons. The proposed law would strip the House of Lords of their power over fiscal matters, and Wilfred had agreed with Father that such an act was long overdue. When he also concurred with me that women should have the vote, I was impressed enough to accept his invitation to go riding in his new automobile the next day.

I remember dressing very carefully for the occasion, discarding one outfit after another until I decided on the one which I thought suited me best. It was a dusty rose skirt and blouse with white lace at the throat and the wrists, and a row of tiny pearl buttons up the front. My hat—one of those enormous pie shaped affairs with yards and yards of tulle and veiling—was decorated with pink and mauve roses. As a hurried last-minute gesture, I dabbed powder on my nose and the tiniest bit of paint on my lips.

Perhaps I overdid my primping, for no sooner had we lost sight of Rommany's chimneys then Wilfred threw his arm about my shoulders, drawing me close. I suffered this familiarity in confusion and silence, not knowing what to do. Should I demand to be released and how should I phrase this demand without sounding prudish?

"Pretty day," said Wilfred, watching the road ahead.

"Yes—isn't it?" I squirmed, and his arm tightened.

My discomfort grew. His breath, smelling unpleasantly of onions, seemed to whistle in his nostrils. I tried adjusting my hat but his arm stayed firmly in place.

In a few minutes we turned off the oiled road on to a bumpy dirt lane bordered by high hedges. We chugged along for another half mile. Then Wilfred stopped the car.

Before I had the chance to speak he had me crushed in a bear hug, his wet, odorous mouth seeking mine. There was no self-debate this time, no question of should or shouldn't I; my reflexes took over and I delivered a resounding slap to his face.

Shocked, he let go. "Well, I'll be damned! I thought you believed women should have the vote and that sort of thing."

I did not pause for rebuttal. I was out of the car and running back down the lane, tripping over my skirt, hanging on to my hat with both hands to keep it from flying off. I reached the oiled road and kept on at a brisk walk. Presently I heard the motorcar putt-putting behind me.

Wildred drew up. "Can't I give you a lift home?"

"No," I replied, furious. "And if you ever show your

face at our door I'll have my father horsewhip you." I was too angry to weep.

He drove away and I went on walking. When I was still a half mile from Rommany it began to rain, so that by the time I reached the front door I was drenched through, my pretty rose outfit ruined.

I think it was then that Mother resigned herself to my single state. Or perhaps she had simply run out of "eligibles." Strangely enough, once Mother had given up trying to marry me off the tension went out of our relationship and we became quite companionable.

We took to sitting before her bedroom fire in the cold autumn evenings whenever Father worked late over his book, sometimes roasting and cracking chestnuts. It was on one such night that Mother began to speak of the Blackmores. Now, at last, I found out how Sir Edward had been mistakenly blamed for fathering Tyson Woodhill and as a consequence had lost Caroline. She also told me that Sir Ian, his son, had been convicted of murder.

"He killed John Hempstead," Mother explained, "when John surprised him ransacking his library. There was some talk of a map—a map to a diamond mine. But your grandmother was so vague about it, I'm inclined to believe that such a map was a figment of her imagination."

"Did Sir Ian have any children?" I asked.

"A daughter," she replied, after a short pause.

"Who? You never mentioned her."

"No. She was—she was not a very nice sort."

"What was her name?"

Mother leaned forward and picking up the poker jabbed at the long on the grate, sending sparks up the chimney. "Trina," she said.

A little pulse began to beat in my throat. Should I tell her about the newspaper article? But I had kept the secret too long. "Trina Blackmore?"

"She went by the name of Blake," Mother said, resting the poker on the hearth. "The scandal, you know."

"Was she ever here at Rommany?" Of course I knew the answer, but I wondered what Mother would say.

"She stayed here a month, one summer. It . . . it wasn't a pleasant time for me. And if you don't mind, Constance, I'd rather not go into it."

"I'm sorry, Mother."

I finished the last chestnut and dropped the shell into a bowl at my feet. "Mother," I said, breaking a long silence, "did Trina Blake have the habit of cracking her knuckles?"

She stared at me, her face suddenly drained of color. "How did you know that?"

"Because I have *heard* her," I said with fierce intensity, releasing the pent-up fear of my childhood at last. "Please don't look at me like that. I've *heard* that sound!"

Her hands tightened on the arms of the chair for a moment, then relaxed. "Nonsense! You heard no such thing. An old house has noises, boards that creak, windows that rattle. Really! I am surprised at you, Constance. Even if I believed in ghosts—which I do not—let me point out that Trina is the same age as myself and is probably very much alive somewhere."

"But do you know for certain?"

"There are a good many things I don't *know* for certain, but assume to be logically so. Now," she got to her feet with an air of finality, "shall we go down and see if we can pry your father loose from the library?"

The topic was thus dismissed, closed. Mother, after allowing me a narrow, limited look into the past had shut me out once more. Yet despite her assertions to the contrary, and her unwillingness to discuss Trina Blake, *I* believed Trina was dead and that her ghost haunted Rommany. What had she done? Had she killed Clara Grimes? And if so why had she thought it necessary to murder a servant girl? For a hair ribbon?

Troubled by these questions, I approached Father. Yes, he had met Trina Blake before he and Mother were married. No, he had not known her well.

"Mother seems reluctant to talk about her," I said. "Do you have any idea why?"

"Constance," Father said firmly, "if your mother has no wish to rake up old coals I don't see why I should. It's all in the past. Best forgotten."

It *was* in the past, yes, but not forgotten—not by me—for Trina Blake remained stubbornly in my mind. According to most occult reasoning, only the dead who thought they had been wronged in life came back as ghosts, roaming their former haunts. That would account for Sir Edward (the deep, sorrowful sigh?) and Sir Ian (the shuffling cards?) returning to Rommany. But why should Trina's spirit walk the corridors of Rommany instead of her victim's, Clara Grimes?

In January we received dreadful news. Benjamin Hempstead, climbing a ladder in his library, slipped and fell to his death. He had been a kindly man, likable, still in his prime, and we were shocked and saddened by his passing. My parents and I went up to London for the funeral, a simple one (those were Benjamin's written instructions) with only close friends and members of the family present. Bea, escorted by her fiancé the Count de Grasse, was subdued, her sharp tongue uncharacteristically silent. She looked very beautiful in a gown of black moiré, cut and fit with an elegance which spoke well of her dressmaker. I caught a glimpse of her eyes when she lifted her veil at the graveside; they were filled with tears, and for the first time in all the years I had known Bea, my heart softened toward her.

Eric, now head of the firm and the family, would not be returning to Edinburgh University to finish his medical studies as planned, though from what we had heard he had never been much of a student, having given most of his attention to the bottle rather than his books. During our stay, however, he remained sober, if not somber, dressed in black, his lank dark hair brushed smoothly back and his large eyes (his best feature) liquid with sadness. At dinner one evening, he made one or two quips which seemed inappropriate for the occasion, but on the whole, we agreed, as we journeyed back to Rommany, Eric had conducted himself better than expected.

Two weeks after the funeral, our neighbor, Mr. Blessing, stopped by the house on his way from London. A gruff, red-faced man, semi-retired now from the tea trade, Mr. Blessing had had business dealings with the Hempstead firm over a period of years and knew the family well.

"Have you heard the rumors?" he inquired as he sat in the drawing room with us, twisting a large snifter of brandy between rough, veined paws. "Ugly rumors, I might add."

"Rumors? About someone we know?" Father asked, opening a carved walnut humidor. "Have a cigar, Mr. Blessing? I'm sure the ladies won't mind."

He shook his head in refusal. "Rumors concerning Eric Hempstead."

"Really?" said Father. "What's he done now?"

"They say he was responsible for his father's death."

Mother was shocked. "Why, that's incredible! *Eric?*"

Father, snipped at the end of his cigar, asking, "Responsible? How do you mean?"

"They say Benjamin was deliberately pushed from that ladder and that it was Eric who did it," Mr. Blessing answered. "He had a mass of gambling debts, you know, which Benjamin had refused to pay."

"Nonsense!" Mother exclaimed, her cheeks flaming. "It's all gossip. Idle tongues clacking away. Besides, I understand he's turned over a new leaf. Mary Hempstead writes that he's down at the office each morning promptly at seven-thirty, has cut out his drinking, and hasn't looked at a card since Benjamin died."

Father touched a flame to his cigar. "That's a new tack for you, Amelia, defending Eric. You never seemed to think much of him before."

"What's that got to do with accusing him of murder?" Mother retorted.

"Right you are," Father quickly agreed. "Mr. Blessing, where did you hear this talk?"

"At the club," Mr. Blessing replied.

"At the club," Mother repeated scornfully. "Haven't they got anything better to discuss?"

Mr. Blessing's florid face turned a deeper color. "Now, Mrs. Woodhill, that talk, you must admit, is not without some foundation. Benjamin was in good health. He must have climbed that ladder a thousand times. And Eric—"

"No," Mother said. "Eric could not have done such a thing. Douglas, do you honestly think . . . ?"

"Of course not," Father said, puffing on his cigar and losing himself in a cloud of smoke.

"Poor Mary," Mother went on. "A sudden widow and now these accusations against her son. Constance," she turned, appealing to me, "would *you* believe Eric capable of murdering his own father?"

I don't know, was the first answer that came to mind. *Eric had always puzzled me.* But then, remembering those evenings when he had obligingly plucked me from a bouquet of wallflowers to stodgily—albeit drunkenly—guide me in a waltz about the ballroom, I replied, "I think basically he has a kind heart."

"There, you see!" Mother exclaimed triumphantly.

The next thing we heard was that Eric had put the firm of Hempstead and Company up for sale. His mother had written, giving us the news. Her letter, couched in defensive terms, read in part: "Eric is not suited for business . . . tea and sugar are simply not his forte . . . Benjamin himself had always hoped Eric would be a physician . . . after all, the healing arts. . . ." And so on. But between the lines both Mother and I sensed pain, if not panic.

This latest development naturally served to fan the flames of those ugly rumors. Something odd in that, Mr. Blessing remarked on another afternoon, selling out so soon.

Mother felt she ought to be with Mary and asked me to come along since Father could not get away.

We arrived at the Hempstead home, a handsome edifice in Belgravia, towards dusk. Mary herself opened the door, and, overwhelmed by our appearance, wept on Mother's shoulder.

There was little we could do, of course, except give Mary comfort. Hempstead and Company had been in the family for generations, and its prospective sale, she said frankly, grieved her. But, she added quickly, lest we think she had turned against her only son, she couldn't blame Eric. "Young men are no longer content to follow in their father's footsteps. Isn't that so, Amelia?"

"Quite right," Mother agreed sympathetically. "I certainly don't expect either Gordon or Alistair to take up writing."

"It's not as if we are ill provided for," Mary went on. "I have an ample annuity, and Bea's dowry was fixed years ago."

Later, in private, Mother commented dryly, "A good

thing Bea comes with a substantial dowry. The count, I understand, hasn't a penny to his name."

Bea, at the time of our visit, was in Switzerland, attending a school reunion. She had done her "finishing" at a very fashionable establishment where she had formed close ties with several members of the sophisticated—and slightly notorious—Edwardian set.

"I thought she ought to go," Mary explained. "The count was called away to Bordeaux on business and I saw no point in Bea's sitting about and moping."

Mary always referred to Bea's fiancé as the count. Being a sweet-tempered, maternal woman without a mean bone in her body I don't think it ever occurred to her that the constant repetition of her prospective son-in-law's title was a source of irritation to me and that there were moments when I thought, "If she says that again, I shall scream!" Instead, an unaware Mary talked on and on—the count this, and the count that—while I suffered her in silence.

Eric, on the other hand, had little to say. He came home each afternoon from the firm's offices around three, and though he was polite enough to Mother and me, I felt he looked upon us with a wary skepticism. If he said anything at all, it was to remark on the rain, or the cold, or the fog, or whatever the state of the weather.

But one evening when we were alone in the library he took to teasing me.

"Doesn't that beau you left behind miss you?" he asked, lounging in his chair, an amused look in his eye.

"Certainly," I replied airily. "But I can't always be with him."

"Just so," slumping even more in his chair. "Lucky to have you at all." He gave me a tense, nervous smile.

A long silence followed during which I observed him from the corner of my eye. I thought he looked unhappy and wondered what gnawed at his soul. Were those ugly rumors warrantless as Mother had stoutly claimed?

"What are you thinking?" he suddenly asked.

"I am thinking about you," I answered honestly.

He rose abruptly from his chair. "Don't bother," he said, looking down at me. "I'm hardly worth it." And with that he went out, closing the door behind him.

Bemused, I returned to the book I had been reading earlier. Presently I became aware that the room had grown chilly and lifted my eyes from the page. The library was a long, narrow room with book-lined shelves going all the way up to the ceiling, perhaps a story and a half in height. The ladder from which Benjamin had lost his footing was still in place, and I could see how someone falling from it could have easily broken his neck as Benjamin had done. It occurred to me, then, as I sat there, alone, conscious of the deep shadows beyond the lamplight, that Benjamin's great-uncle John had died here also.

I had never learned the details of John Hempstead's murder although Mother had said she believed Sir Ian had shot him. I wondered why, of all the wealthy houses Sir Ian could have robbed, he had chosen this one. Perhaps it had something to do with the map my mother believed was a figment of Grandmama's imagination.

I got to my feet and closed the book, replacing it on the shelf. As I stood there with my back to the room, it seemed that the air, uncomfortably chilly until now (despite the fire), had quite suddenly grown icy cold. It was the sort of freezing cold which, at Rommany, always preceded the ghostly sounds I so feared.

Not here, I thought, it *can't* be here.

Motionless, my back rigid, I waited as one waits for the drop of a shoe or the fall of an ax. A long moment went by, and then into the half-lit, cold silence, came the brisk slapping sound of fingers nimbly shuffling a pack of cards, the distinct, unmistakable ruffle of pasteboard.

Not here! I wanted to scream. *It couldn't be here!*

The phantom pack tapped a phantom table, and the shuffling recommenced.

Grinding my teeth, I whirled about. The sound abruptly ceased.

Was it my imagination? Or perhaps there was something wrong with my hearing, since, to my knowledge, no one else had ever complained about these ghostly noises.

This defective hearing was an entirely new notion, and I turned it over in my mind, tentatively, hopefully. I might very well be suffering from some inner ear disturbance, a disturbance brought on by changes in the temperature which caused me to hear things when the atmosphere turned cold.

The next afternoon, unknown to Mother, I made an appointment with a specialist in Harley Street, and two days later I went to see him. A pompous man with a smug smile, he gave me a thorough examination, tapping and peering and testing. It all added up to a simple, disappointing verdict: I was in maddeningly good health, my hearing perfectly normal.

The following June, Father decided to take a holiday.

"You know," he said, handing me a sheaf of pages (I typed his manuscripts now), "your mother and I have never had a proper honeymoon. Hard to believe, isn't it?"

"Yes," I said, smiling. Father was always so earnest.

"Well, as the old saying goes, better late than never."

Privately I was rather surprised. I had never thought of Mother and Father in terms of anything as romantic, as *young* as a honeymoon.

"You're getting very prim," Father said, acutely divining my thoughts.

I blushed a deep red and pretended to be absorbed in the pages he had handed me.

"I'm teasing you, Constance," he said, patting my arm. "Never mind."

After Father left the room, I thought: *Am* I getting prim? Set in my ways, staid, growing old, old before my time?

"While we are gone, Constance," Mother said, "the household will be under your guidance."

She and Father had planned a tour of the Continent. Paris, Rome, Vienna. How I envied them! "You needn't worry yourself, Mother," I assured her, trying to hide my jealousy. "I shall take care of things just as if you had never left."

"I know you will, Constance. You have a level head. Otherwise I shouldn't be going."

A level head. Oh, God, how I wished I were scatterbrained, frivolous and pretty, too young to be entrusted with running a household.

"Your father has placed an advertisement in the London *Times* for a tutor." Gordon had driven off the most recent tutor by hiding a garden snake in his bed. "I'm sure you are aware what qualifications we expect in an applicant, so the hiring is left up to you."

"Yes, Mother," I said, feeling more and more like a maiden aunt, one of those dried-up ladies, indispensable, a cut above a good servant, always grateful to be "useful" because it gave her a reason for existing.

"Perhaps I could teach them myself," I suggested.

"No, Constance. You are capable enough, very capable. But they need a man's strong hand."

A man's strong hand. If only I could be a man, what limitless possibilities would be open to me. Perhaps I should be like Uncle David and go into the army. Traveling the world, riding through white, blinding sands of the Sahara on the back of a camel, or strolling the spice scented shores of Madagascar, or reclining in the shade of palm trees in the jungles of Malaya, or. . . .

"Constance! *Constance!* Are you listening?"

"Yes, Mother."

"We will leave the names of the various hotels where we plan to stay so that you may write and tell us how things are going."

"Yes, Mother."

They left on a Sunday amid a flurry of kisses, good-byes and last-minute instructions. I held Mother close for a long moment, suddenly feeling ashamed of my envy and secret resentment. "Please do have a lovely time," I said fervently. "And don't worry."

I watched them drive off in the Daimler, chauffeured by George, our new gardener and odd-job man, with a curious sinking feeling in the pit of my stomach. It was as if I were still a child and they were abandoning me to Rommany, without a thought for my anxieties and fears.

But I had little time to be either anxious or afraid, confronted as I was with the tasks at hand. During the following week over a dozen letters arrived in answer to Father's advertisement for a tutor. Sorting through them I picked the five which seemed the most promising and wrote to the applicants, setting dates and times for interviews.

The first to arrive at Rommany was a short, stout man in a bowler. Sitting on the edge of a chair in the library, peering warily around, he informed me after the first few minutes that he hadn't realized how remote Rommany was from a metropolis which offered theater and concerts. He didn't think the position would suit him.

The second to apply was an elderly gentleman whose thin, fragile-boned head trembled so on his long, reedy neck I wondered how he had ever survived the journey down from London. I knew the boys would make mincemeat of him in two days and so, tactfully and kindly (I hoped) told him I was afraid he wouldn't do.

The third applicant, scheduled to be seen by me on a Wednesday at one o'clock, was two hours late. I was sitting in the window seat overlooking the drive, impatient, and short-tempered (the boys were taking full advantage of Mother's absence) when a hired hackney drew up to the door. A young man with coppery hair and a valise in his hand sprang out and spoke to the driver. A moment later the hackney turned about and clattered back from whence it had come.

Nervy, I thought, dismissing the hackney and bringing his bag. Mr. Leonard Seagram had assumed I would hire him, had he?

I let him cool his heels in the library for a half hour before I went down.

He was sitting on a chair near the window and got to his feet as I entered.

"I am Leonard Seagram," he said. "I've come to see your husband."

"Mr. Woodhill is abroad," I said with cold dignity. "I am Miss Woodhill, his daughter."

"Ah—I thought you looked too young to be the mother. My sincerest apologies."

He was a handsome man, his most striking feature that deep copper hair I had first noticed. "That's quite all right," I murmured stiffly, taking the chair behind Father's desk. "Won't you sit down, Mr. Seagram?"

"Thank you. I must apologize—again—this time for my tardiness. The train was delayed for two hours at Colchester. I hope you won't hold that against me?" He smiled rather hopefully.

"I'll try not to," I said softening. He had the nicest eyes

I had ever seen; frank and artless, they did not seem to be the eyes of an arrogant man.

"Now," I said, "as to your qualifications."

"Yes. As I wrote, I was schoolmaster at Chemwick for two years. I was let go because they wanted a married man instead of a bachelor. At least that was the official reason, but actually the headmaster's brother-in-law wanted the job." He reached in his coat pocket and pulled out a letter. "They've written me a fine testimonial, though."

I took the letter. Mr. Seagram had evidently been "an excellent teacher, a firm but not unjust disciplinarian, well liked by the boys. . . ." I glanced up through my lashes.

Leonard Seagram was watching me with a mixture of anxiety and hope in his eyes.

". . . a well-read gentleman, with a thorough knowledge of Latin. . . ." The letter went on to a second page. My eyes continued to read, but I had become suddenly conscious of Leonard Seagram as a person, a man.

It was not his handsomeness so much as an indefinable masculinity, an aura of maleness about him which had caught me unaware. Long before I had finished reading the lengthy testimonial, I knew I would hire him.

Chapter 4

Fortunately Mr. Seagram was well qualified, so I had no trouble in convincing myself that I had chosen him from among the others for his ability rather than his masculine attractiveness. Not that I had reason to regret my selection. Within a day he had set both boys and schoolroom in order, a task seldom accomplished with such swift thoroughness by his predecessors.

When I jokingly remarked that he must have been very sure of my hiring him since he had brought his valise and dismissed the hackney, he smiled sheepishly and said, "The reason is embarrassingly simple. My valise contains all my worldly possessions. I've carried it about since leaving Chemwick. As for the hackney, I thought of saving the return fare by walking back to the railway station should you have decided against me."

That Mr. Seagram might have been short of funds had not occurred to me. I said, "I would be very happy to advance you part of your first month's salary."

"Thank you, Miss Woodhill," his cheeks taking on a faint, prideful flush. "But I shall be able to manage."

I made it a point not to go near the schoolroom lest Mr. Seagram think I was interfering. He and the boys ate all their meals there (Mr. Seagram himself had suggested it. "Let them have an occasional dinner in the dining room as a reward," he had said. "It will act as an incentive.") So, except for a rare meeting on the stairs or his coming into the library for a book, I saw very little of him.

But he was there, making his presence known in a dozen little ways; his deep voice echoing down from the schoolroom, an elusive, passing fragrance of pipe tobacco and shaving lotion, a written request in square masculine letters left on my breakfast plate, a heavy step in the corridor. After the void left by my parents Rommany seemed lived in again, the very shadows I so dreaded kept at bay.

Mr. Seagram had been at Rommany a week when he came into the library to ask if the "schoolroom" could join me for dinner. "I think Gordon and Alistair are ready now," he said. "They've been bending to their work with a will."

"I should be delighted," I replied. "I hate eating alone."

Gordon and Alistair, except for one fit of giggling and a hushed conference as to which fork to use for the fish course, were models of deportment.

"You've done wonders with them," I remarked to Mr. Seagram after they had gone upstairs, leaving us to our coffee. "My parents will be very pleased."

"And you?" he asked smiling, "are you pleased?"

"Very much so," I replied, looking away from the intense earnestness of his eyes.

"Then I'm glad."

A small silence while I busied myself with another teaspoon of sugar, my third. Or was it my fourth?

"I've long been an admirer of your father's books," Mr. Seagram said.

"You know them?" I asked, looking at him again feeling safer because the topic had turned from me.

"Indeed. I have read every single novel he's written."

"You didn't mention that when we had our interview," I chided.

"No. I felt that you might take it as flattery meant to influence your judgment. But now I feel free to tell you how much pleasure Douglas Woodhill's books have given me. I liked his first especially, *Holloway's Fancy*. It put me in mind of Hardy."

"Yes. I thought so too. *The Return of the Native*."

"Exactly. Man pitted against his environment."

"And the tragedy of misfits like Eustacia Vye."

From Hardy we went on to discuss Father's latest book, and then from there to Poe and Kipling. Mr. Seagram's testimonial had not exaggerated; he was not only widely read, but an interesting conversationalist as well.

"Miss Woodhill," he said after we had been talking for some time, "I hope you won't think me forward if I voice an observation."

"Not at all. What is it?"

"You have extraordinary taste for a . . . for a—"

"A woman?" I supplied.

"A young girl," he corrected. "Most people your age, male or female, read nothing but trash."

"Does it surprise you? Perhaps you think it unbecoming for a woman to admit to reading other than light romantic novels."

"On the contrary. That's what I admire so much about you."

My heart did a funny little dance.

"Your opinions are worth listening to. None of this coy, shallow chitchat I've been used to in girls."

"You are most complimentary," I murmured, speaking into my cup.

"Now, I've embarrassed you when I hadn't meant to. I'm sorry. Well—I'd best go upstairs and see what devilment those two have managed for me."

After he left I lingered at the table, sipping coffee, going over and over our conversation, recalling the way the light fell on his hair, the timbre of his voice, the intense gaze of his eyes. He had said he admired me. My mind, of course. I felt flattered, yet, at the same time, vaguely disappointed.

The next day I had unexpected visitors. Eric and Bea Hempstead. Neither of them had been to Rommany in years, and their sudden appearance came as a complete surprise.

"We decided to invite ourselves on the spur of the moment," Bea said, removing her hat, a dainty cream tulle and maroon velvet toque. "You won't have a telephone installed, so we couldn't call and let you know."

"There are no facilities for telephones in these parts," I pointed out. I noticed Bea had discarded mourning. The dress she wore matched the maroon of her hat. As unflattering as women's styles were in that year of 1911, on Bea they looked marvelous, outlining to advantage her slim, lovely figure. "Nor electricity," I added. "We are very countrified at Rommany."

Eric was on crutches. He had broken his foot in a

cricket match the week before and looked very pale and hangdog as he stumped his way into the drawing room.

"Sorry to descend on you this way," he apologized. "But I didn't think you would mind."

I did mind. Eric, when I was not condemning or feeling sorry for him, made me uncomfortable, and Bea (except for that brief time at her father's funeral) I had never liked. But the habit of hospitality was too strongly ingrained, and I said, "Of course not. You are welcome to stay as long as you like."

"Good," Eric said, wincing as he lowered himself into a chair. "I knew you would feel that way. The country air is just what I need. And Bea came along as chaperone."

"Well, I had nothing better to do," Bea said with her customary outspokenness. "And speaking of things to do—what sort of amusement has Rommany to offer?"

"Very little," I replied dryly. Perhaps Bea would get bored soon and return to London, taking Eric with her. "Father keeps several horses, if you care to ride."

"Not much. It seems rather silly trotting about with no purpose in mind."

She moved restlessly from the fireplace to the window and thence to a table where she stood idly fingering a beaded lampshade. I wondered why she and Eric had come to Rommany when they might have gone to their grandmother's in Bournemouth. Surely the sea air was just as beneficial as Rommany's? And the social life was so much more exciting.

"Shall we have tea?" I suggested, breaking a long silence.

"I'll have a small whiskey, if you don't mind," Eric spoke up. *Oh, dear, I thought, is he drinking again?* "I'm feeling a bit off."

His sister threw him a look of scorn. But his pale forehead was beaded with sweat, and he appeared to be in pain.

"I'll ring for Jenny," I said.

Bea and I had tea, and Eric, to my surprise, after he had drunk his one whiskey, joined us.

"I sold the firm last week," he said, reaching for a biscuit. "At a whopping good price, I might add. Glad to get rid of it."

"What shall you do then?" I asked.

"Haven't decided." He popped the biscuit into his mouth.

"Laze about, I suspect," Bea said.

"Probably," her brother agreed. "By the way where's Gordon and Alistair? Thought it was rather quiet. You haven't done away with them, have you?"

"No," I said, suddenly thinking of his dead father. Had Benjamin been murdered? "They're upstairs with their tutor."

Bea fumbled in her purse and brought out a gold case from which she extracted a cigarette. I watched in shocked fascination as she fitted it to an ivory holder, and then casually lit it. Ladies did not smoke, my father claimed. But Bea was the sort who could languidly break convention and still command respect as a "lady."

"Mother tells me you have a hard time keeping tutors," she said.

"This one seems to have the boys well in hand," I said, trying not to stare. "He's strong on discipline."

"Oh—one of those," Bea said, blowing a smoke ring through her well-shaped lips.

Later I went upstairs and told Mr. Seagram I had guests. "Old friends of the family," I said, "and I think it would be nice if you and the boys joined us for dinner."

He thanked me and said he thought Gordon and Alistair would be pleased.

The three of them came down to the drawing room while we were having our pre-dinner sherry. The boys, combed and polished, looked very grand and grown up in their suits, starched white collars and dark ties. But—whether out of nervousness or by design—Alistair in coming across the room tripped over Gordon's foot and stumbled to his knees. The next moment he was on his feet again and before anyone could move, he flew at Gordon, pummeling him with his fists and screaming. Gordon, not one to stand by when attacked, returned his younger brother's blows with gusto.

The entire scene could not have gone on for more than twenty seconds before Mr. Seagram grasped Gordon and Alistair by their respective collars and separated them.

"That will do!" he exclaimed authoritatively. "And no dinner."

A wail of protest rose from their throats. "I'm sorry, no dinner," Mr. Seagram repeated firmly. "And now if you young gentlemen will precede me upstairs, I'll take a moment to apologize for your behavior."

The boys, flushed but obedient, went through the door.

"Can't you have dinner with us anyway?" I asked. "You needn't be punished too."

Bea, sliding gracefully between us, said, "Yes, by all means, do join us for dinner."

A remarkable change had come over her. Gone was her languid, bored air. Instead she seemed to vibrate with life, her eyes glowing, her fine nostrils quivering like a thoroughbred filly at the starting gate.

"I'm Beatrice Hempstead," she said in silvery tones, while I stood in the background murmuring a belated introduction. "But friends call me Bea."

He smiled down at her as he held her elegant, slim hand. "Charmed, I'm sure."

Their gazes seemed to lock and hold interminably.

"Bea's engaged!" I said with a sudden fierceness, which astonished even me.

"Congratulations," Mr. Seagram said, letting go of Bea's hand (at last!) and looking over at Eric who, glass in hand, had been sitting silently by the fire.

"Mr. Seagram," I said, "this is Eric Hempstead."

"How do you do?" Eric said. "You'll forgive me if I don't jump to my feet. Bad foot, you know."

Bea, very casually, had taken Leonard's arm. "You will dine with us?"

Mr. Seagram looked over at me, a question in his eyes.

Oh, how I wanted to say, "I think it would be best if you went up and saw to the boys." But I couldn't. Not only would my resentment of Bea show, but it was exactly the sort of prissy statement a staid old nanny would make.

"Please do, Mr. Seagram," I said and smiled and kept on smiling until I thought my face would crack.

"I say," Eric exclaimed. "Where's dinner?"

Just then Jenny opened the drawing-room door and announced the meal.

Perhaps Bea's flirtation with Mr. Seagram would have

been less painful to me if she had been one of those "coy, shallow" girls he so disparaged. But Bea had long ago acquired the knack for disguising what she lacked in intellect by an attentive, flattering silence. She sat next to Mr. Seagram at the dinner table and gave him the full benefit of admiring eyes and dazzling smiles and murmurs of, "You are so right," whenever he spoke. I knew that Mr. Seagram meant less than nothing to her—a tutor, hardly above a butler on her social scale. But he was a man, young and handsome, speaking an educated, cultured English, and she could no more resist setting her cap for him than she could resist breathing.

I sat through that endless meal, tongue-tied, miserable, just as I had sat years earlier at parties and balls. Eric tried to draw me into the conversation, but I was angry with him, too. Why had he found it necessary to play cricket and break his foot? And, having done so, why had he come to Rommany?

Mr. Seagram excused himself immediately after dinner and a few minutes later Bea, yawning and bored, went up to her own room. Then Eric, stumping clumsily along on his crutches, followed me into the library where I sat down at Father's desk, intending to go over the menus for the next day.

"You mustn't mind Bea," he said, sinking into a chair.

"Why should I mind?" I said, what little food I had eaten resting like a stone on my stomach.

"She's quite harmless, I assure you."

"I don't know what you are talking about," I said, crossing out the lentil soup and inserting tomato aspic.

"Oh, come now, Constance. You were as transparent as glass in there."

The pencil dropped from my fingers. "Explain that, if you please," I said coldly.

"Why—you're balmy about that tutor."

Furious, my cheeks burning, I exclaimed, "You're wrong! I am no such thing! And if you want to be critical, look to your sister. Engaged to be married . . . and . . . and she's acting like a . . . like a—"

"A hussy? Yes, I suppose under that ladylike exterior she is one. Perhaps you ought to take lessons."

His eyes were teasing, but I was in no mood for banter. "I'd sooner learn how to pick pockets."

"Hmmm. I daresay you would." He leaned back in his chair, carefully placing his injured foot on a stool.

I checked off the last item on the menu, then looked across at Eric, who sat staring at his bandaged foot. "How is it you didn't bring your mother, too?" I asked sarcastically. "She must be lonely."

"Not at all," he answered matter-of-factly, either unaware of the barb in my question or ignoring it. "Her sister's come to visit. The one with the five children." He made stepping motions with his hand. "Plenty of company."

"Well, then," I said, pushing back my chair. "I think I'll turn in."

"Yes. It is getting rather late. Perhaps I shall, too."

"Breakfast is at nine."

"Oh?"

At the Hempstead house, which was half as big as Rommany, there were twice as many servants and as a consequence, breakfast was served to anyone who wanted it no matter what the hour.

"We have a small staff," I explained.

"I see," he said, grinning.

"Part of country living, you know," I said, trying not to sound too sour.

I took the menus and went across the hall through the dining room and service door to the deserted kitchen. A lamp burned with a soft yellow glow on the old-fashioned dresser and I propped the menus up against a tall pewter mug. Then, using the servant's back staircase I went up to the first floor. When I reached the landing, I saw Eric down the corridor. His back was to me and he was hobbling along on his crutches. He had removed his coat and had slung it carelessly over his shoulders where it now balanced precariously. I was just about to say something when the coat suddenly slipped to the floor. He didn't see me as he stooped to pick it up, but I had a clear view of him.

Looped about his shoulder and under his arm was a holster. And from it protruded the handle of a gun.

Chapter 5

Eric's secretly carrying a pistol on his person surprised, but did not shock or frighten me. I was curious, of course, in a mild sort of way, wondering why he found it necessary to go about with a gun under his arm. Protection? From what? From whom? Perhaps it was simply a toy.

Eric's eccentricities, however, were not uppermost in mind that night as I undressed for bed. I kept thinking of Leonard Seagram, the dinner table, the talk, the way he had looked at Bea. Had he found her irresistibly beautiful as so many men had before him? Or was he accustomed to having women gaze adoringly at him?

Eric had accused me of being "balmy" over Mr. Seagram. The thought that the tutor might have read that in my face, too, made me want to die of shame. Of course I wasn't "balmy" about Mr. Seagram. What nonsense! I prided myself on my good sense, my superiority to the scatterbrained nitwits who simpered every time a male entered a room. Naturally I found Leonard Seagram charming and handsome, nice to look at. Who wouldn't?

The clock on the mantel spoke the hour. Midnight. No use getting into bed. A seasoned insomniac, I knew it would take hours before I felt sleepy. So I sat down at the window instead and gazed out at the night.

Mr. Seagram couldn't possibly be entranced by Bea, could he? He had thought me intelligent. Had he noticed that Bea was not? How I wished I was pretty! How I wished I could smile and have him say, "You are the loveliest creature I have ever met."

High overhead a full moon glided silently through a

drift of smokelike clouds. Wasn't it John Milton who had written, "nor walk by moon,/ or glittering starlight, without thee is sweet"?

Ah, Constance, I chided myself, settling my chin firmly on my hands, you are getting disgustingly sentimental. And yet—a queer little pain had settled around my heart.

I was jealous of Bea. That was a plain and unalterable fact. I did not envy her the count, never had, nor did I really envy her her good looks. It was only when Leonard Seagram smiled at her that I turned green, wanting to shout at her, to rail, to weep.

Yes, I *was* strongly attracted to Rommany's new tutor. Yes, I desperately wanted him to be attracted to me. Was I in love? *Admit it, Constance, admit it.* But I couldn't. It was too hopeless. Leonard Seagram and I? Hopeless.

The moon disappeared behind a cloud and the night suddenly seemed to lose its tranquility. Far in the distance a light glowed for a long moment, winked and went out. A cold breeze brushed my cheeks, raising bumps along my arms. I shivered and reaching up, closed the window.

As I turned to go to bed, the lamp which I always kept burning on the mantel went out, plunging the room into utter blackness. I grasped the curtains for support, my childhood fear of the dark creeping through my veins like an insidious serpent, coiling its way upward, cold, cold.

I waited—waited for the crack-crack of knuckles, the sigh, the shuffling cards.

A board creaked above me, and slow, careful footsteps trod across the ceiling.

The pent-up breath went out of my lungs in a sigh of relief. Footsteps did not frighten me. It was probably one of the servants. While the cook slept in an apartment next to the kitchen and George, the chauffeur, was housed above the stables—or garage as we now called it—the three maids, Daisy, Jenny, and Esther, had rooms upstairs.

Well, I thought, crawling between the covers, she— whoever it is—will soon settle down. Just as I was drifting off to sleep myself, I thought I heard the door open, but I was too far gone to do more than wonder vaguely about it.

Father had installed two water closets on the first story, each with a high heavy-clawed bathtub, though hot water still had to be brought up—on request—by the maids. However morning tea was routinely served in our rooms. So when Jenny came in the next morning bringing the usual tray, I asked, "Was it you, walking about upstairs in the middle of the night?"

"No, miss, not me." Jenny had gray eyes and a saucy nose and would have been a pretty girl were it not for her protruding teeth. "Midnight is long past my bedtime."

"Oh—perhaps it was Daisy or Esther then."

"Walking about, miss? Hardly. A cannon couldn't rouse them two once they got their heads on a pillow. You don't suppose—" She put her hand to her mouth and her eyes got round. "You don't suppose it were a ghost?"

"Certainly not," I said firmly. "Most likely it was only a creaking board. You know how they do here at Rommany." Suspicion of a haunting upstairs would drive Jenny and the others from the house quicker than a shout of fire. And I couldn't have the staff quitting, especially now with my parents gone and guests in the house.

"Yes, miss," she agreed, though it seemed without conviction. "We had a haunt in the last place I worked. Terrible, it was. Wailed and carried on. Was at Wolley Hall. I didn't stay long, I can tell you, miss."

"Rest easy, Jenny. We have no apparitions here at Rommany." A lie. I knew we had ghosts, though the odd thing, as I have said, was that no one else did. No one. For a long time I had thought of myself as mentally unbalanced. Then I happened to read somewhere that it was not uncommon for just a single person in a household to be aware of its haunting, to see or hear a wandering spook, while others remained totally oblivious to it. Thus far, the servants had never complained, and I had no intention of giving them cause to.

After Jenny had left, though, I began to wonder again about the creaking footsteps. My ghosts had never walked—not so they could be heard. Perhaps it had been the cook or George, after all. But why anyone should be wandering around in the middle of the night baffled and disturbed me.

As soon as breakfast was over, I went into the kitchen to speak to Mrs. Platte. Using the utmost tact (good cooks are temperamental, inordinately touchy and hard to come by, Mother had warned me before leaving), I asked her if she had been up to the maids' quarters during the night. She hadn't. Whatever for?

George, though he also denied it, did arouse my suspicion. It was not anything he said, but his manner. A tall, thin man with a drooping underlip, he had the habit of staring into space when spoken to. His hands were never still, fidgeting with his cuffs, his pockets, his tie. He answered my questions in a low, sullen monotone, as if begrudging each syllable which passed his lips.

"No, Miss Woodhill," he said. "I ain't got cause to be in the house after dark. I sleep in the garage." He pronounced it "gayrahj."

George had come to us from Colchester with an amibiguous letter of reference, but his knowledge of motorcars was such as to persuade Father to hire him. Except when it came to the Daimler, which he tinkered at and polished and hovered over like a brood hen, he seemed reluctant to perform his duties.

"Well, then, thank you, George."

"You're welcome, I'm sure, Miss Woodhill," he answered, sliding his eyes to the clock on the wall.

I wondered if he could be having a secret affair with one of the maids. But if that were so wouldn't it be more discreet, if not safer, for he and the girl in question to rendezvous in his quarters rather than on the second floor where they might be discovered?

Perhaps, I thought, I've been worrying myself needlessly. It might have been—just as I had told Jenny— creaking boards and nothing more.

But that night I heard the footsteps again. It was long after everyone had gone to bed and I was deep in the pages of Stevenson's *Kidnapped* when the ceiling above me creaked with the stealthy sound of walking feet. The first thing that came to mind was that George had lied to me. Either he was stealing from us (though what he could pilfer from the second story I had no idea) or he was on his way to one of the maids' beds. Both possibilities angered me. My parents had never tolerated thieves or libertines at Rommany, and I, in their place, would not do so either. If George was up to mischief, I would sack him, no matter how well he polished the Daimler.

Determined to catch the man red-handed I jumped out of bed and drew on a robe. Then lighting the emergency candle which stood on the mantelpiece, I went through the door and down the corridor. Outrage carried me up the narrow staircase.

Holding the candle high, I peered into the room shared by Jenny and Esther. They were asleep, Jenny with her mouth slightly open and snoring softly, and next to her, Esther, her mousy brown hair swaddled with calico strips. Daisy, too, was asleep, and I gazed about her small cluttered room looking for some telltale sign of George. There was none. Daisy stirred, mumbling incoherently, and turned her face into the pillow.

Closing her door, I turned, frowning, as my eyes probed the shadows along the length of the corridor. The feeble candlelight played over the narrowing vista of dark paneled wood and closed doors. Except for the faint sibilance of Jenny's snore, the air was hushed with the kind of peculiar silence that comes when a house is deep in slumber.

As I stood there debating what to do, a door hinge squeaked and the candle flame jumped.

"Who is it?" I whispered, clutching the candlestick. "Who's there?"

The black shadows swirled about me, echoing softly.

I was not afraid of George. If he tried to attack me I would fend him off with my candlestick and scream and scream. I was rather brave when it came to people. It was only the unseen which terrified me.

The door hinge whined again, and a sudden draft swept across the candle. Before I could protect it with my hand, the flame snuffed out and darkness dropped over me like a black cloak.

Bravado vanished. Surrounded by breathing, inky darkness, I began to tremble as the harrowing thought came to me; suppose it was one of *them*? Suppose Sir Edward or Sir Ian or Trina Blake had taken to pacing the empty rooms of Rommany?

Clutching the dead candle, I groped my way blindly back to the staircase and with fear nipping at my heels hurried down, not daring to look over my shoulder. Once in my room, however, my terror abated and I felt rather foolish. What real harm could a ghost do me? I asked myself. But it was a question too often asked, a question I could answer only rationally after the fact. As I did now. How silly I had been to run! A few more steps, a bold, challenging inquiry and I might have discovered George (or whoever) at his game.

The next morning I managed to catch Mr. Seagram in the schoolroom before the boys made an appearance. "Did you happen to hear anyone moving about last night? Upstairs, shortly after midnight?"

He frowned, then shook his head. "Why—no, Miss Woodhill. But I'm a fairly sound sleeper. Had you thought it might be Gordon or Alistair?"

"No—no, I hadn't. The step was a heavy one, a man's." And it couldn't have been Eric's, since I would have heard the thumping of crutches. But Gordon, I remembered, with a habitual instigator of pranks, an ingenious practical jokester. "But now you've mentioned the boys, I believe it's quite possible. Gordon might have slipped into a pair of father's shoes and tried to frighten the maids."

"I wouldn't be at all surprised." He thought for a moment. "Rather than confront Gordon, I'll lock him and Alistair in their room tonight. They won't know. I'll do it after they are asleep. Then if Gordon is guilty, he'll realize soon enough we're on to him." He smiled, his eyes twinkling, as if the two of us were joined in a conspiracy.

A heartwarming, reassuring smile.

Yet the question continued to bother me. Later in the library I put it to Bea and Eric.

"Footsteps at midnight?" Bea's eyes widened. "Really, Constance, you *are* getting to be quite the spinster."

I went hot all over. "You forget I'm responsible for this household."

She shrugged. "*I* didn't hear anything. Did you, Eric?"

"No." He was sitting in the deep upholstered chair he seemed to prefer, his leg stretched out on a stool.

"There you are," Bea said. "Now that's settled, I think I shall go riding, after all. Perhaps I can get Mr. Seagram to accompany me."

"He was hired to teach the boys, not to escort bored guests on outings," I reminded her.

"So he was," she said, opening the door. "But I'm sure he will make me an exception."

"Bad manners," I grumbled between my teeth, sitting down at the desk.

"Bea's manners are tailored to fit each situation," Eric said blandly. "She's bored."

"Then why doesn't she go?"

"Where? Home? It's more boring there. The count is away again, and since Bea is an engaged lady, she can't attend parties without him. Besides, she is still supposed to be in mourning."

"So I noticed," I said acidly.

"The only thing she's given up is wearing black. Come now, Constance, Queen Victoria's been dead a long time. The old customs don't hold as much anymore."

"Don't they?" I asked pointedly.

He looked puzzled for a moment. "Was that meant for me? I suppose so. You're thinking of my selling Hempstead and Company."

"In any case, now that you have all that money, you can do as you like."

"For your information, I haven't 'all that money.' It goes into a trust which I can't touch until I'm thirty." He made a wry face. "Meanwhile, I must make do on my allowance."

"A pity," I said, removing the cover of the typewriter. "Hadn't you known that all along?"

"No. Frankly, I didn't. Or else—"

"Or else what?"

"Or else I would have not been such a prodigious spender." He grinned.

I rolled a sheet of paper into the typewriter and began to type a speech Father had given to a literary society some months earlier, a copy of which he had wanted to send on to a friend. For an hour the only sound in the library was the tap-tap of typewriter keys. It was not until I had finished inserting the copied sheets in an addressed envelope that Eric spoke again.

"Those footsteps you were speaking of—they trouble you?" he asked.

"Somewhat. Mr. Seagram thought it might be Gordon."

"And what do *you* think?"

"I don't know."

He grinned. "Maybe it's Sir Ian looking for the lost map."

"Map? What map?" I asked indifferently—an indifference that was all fraud.

"The map which is supposed to link the Hempsteads with the Blackmores. Surely you are acquainted with the story?"

"I am. I've heard vague rumors of a map. That fairy tale, legend, whatever. Diamonds, wasn't that what it was supposed to be? Had it any basis in *fact*?"

"I don't know," Eric said, giving me a sharp look. "I thought *you* did."

"I'm as ignorant about the matter as you," I answered, starting to sort the morning's mail.

"Didn't your grandfather mention it in his will?"

"No. As far as I know, not a word." I slit open an envelope.

"Neither did mine. Funny," Eric mused.

The greengrocer's bill. Had we consumed all those turnips?

"You don't seem very interested," Eric said.

"Should I be?" I said, looking up. I could not tell him how the subject drew me while at the same time filling me with a vague uneasiness.

"Certainly. It could mean a fortune. You wouldn't have to sit at that desk. You could spread your wings and fly."

I had to smile. "And you?"

"I could pay my gambling debts," he said dryly. "Isn't that your assumption?"

"Would I be mistaken if it were?"

"Yes. But I don't suppose you believe me."

I didn't. How could he have paid them if the money from the firm was tied up in trust?

There was a knock on the door and Jenny came in. "Begging your pardon, miss, but Mrs. Platte wishes to speak to you privately."

Now what? I thought, as I got to my feet.

Mrs. Platte was standing with her back to the dresser, close-set eyes blazing, stout arms akimbo, a pouter pigeon with ruffled feathers.

"My key to the wine cellar is gone!" she exclaimed.

The wine cellar was an euphemism. There were no cellars at Rommany, but the wine was kept in what had long ago served as the buttery—a room on the cool side of the house, just off the kitchen.

"Perhaps you have mislaid it," I suggested tactfully.

"I never mislay anything," she retorted. "Someone's pinched it."

"Have you spoken to the maids?" All three of them were present, ostensibly occupied with various tasks; Jenny polishing the silver, Esther mending a sheet, Daisy scouring pans. But I knew their ears were hanging onto our every word.

"It weren't any of *my* girls. They aren't drinkers," she replied haughtily. Mrs. Platte was a teetotaler, and she viewed the serving of spirits at Rommany as a breach of God's law, a lapse made tolerable only by the hope that her nightly prayers would save the Woodhills from certain perdition.

"Have you questioned George?" I asked.

"Indeed I have. Says he hasn't seen it." She lowered her voice. "But between you and me I ain't too sure. He's sly, that one."

"Yes—but before we accuse anyone of stealing the key, I think we ought to check the cellar. You've kept up with the wine list?"

"Certainly."

"Father has an extra set of keys in the library. I'll fetch them."

I went back across the hall thinking that perhaps I ought to dismiss George. But what reason could I give? Unless I had definite proof of his thievery, I could never explain to Father.

I opened the library door and paused in surprise. Eric, the knee of his injured leg resting on a chair, was closing the top drawer of Father's desk.

"Oh," he said without turning a hair. "It's you. Where does your father keep his matches? I was going to help myself to a cigar."

"They're on the mantelpiece," I said.

It was not until I was halfway back across the hall with the keys in my hand that a sudden thought struck me. As far as I knew, Eric did not smoke, never had.

Chapter 6

Mr. Seagram beckoned from the schoolroom. "May I have a word with you, Miss Woodhill?"

"Yes, of course."

"The boys have gone outside for an hour's recreation," he said as I crossed the threshold, "and I thought I would take this opportunity to speak to you."

"Have they been misbehaving again?" I asked, seating myself on the window seat. "You see, they came rather late in Mother's life, and I'm afraid she has indulged them."

He smiled, looking very young and boyish. "No, it isn't the boys. It's another matter. Rather embarrassing." He pulled up a chair and sat down opposite me, his face and voice now grave. "It concerns Miss Hempstead."

Miss Hempstead! A knife twisted in my breast. I knew it, I could have foretold it. He was attracted to Bea, he was in love with her. He wanted my advice.

"She's a lovely person," he said.

"Indeed," I muttered through stiff lips. He was wild for Bea. He wanted to elope with her. He was giving notice.

"But she doesn't seem to realize that I have duties to perform and that I *enjoy* performing them. I can't drop everything and go riding simply because it suits Miss Hempstead's whim."

I stared at him stupidly, not quite believing my ears.

"I realize she is a guest. But—could you speak to her, Miss Woodhill?"

I groped for my voice. "Why . . . why, yes."

"Perhaps you could explain my position."

"I'll try." A tremulous smile, my heart suddenly light as a feather. "But . . . but Bea's used to having her own way. She won't listen to me. She . . . she thinks I'm jealous."

"On account of me?" he asked surprised.

"Well—yes," I admitted, brushing an imaginary speck of lint from my skirt.

"You flatter me. I only wish it were true."

But it is! It is! I wanted to shout. "Miss Hempstead leads a very social life in London and naturally finds the country a little dull," I said, suddenly finding it in my heart to be generous.

"Have you known the Hempsteads for long?"

"All my life. Their family and mine have been close friends for three generations."

"By any chance, could they be the same Hempsteads who were in the papers a few months back?" A stray shaft of dust-moted sunlight had caught his hair, burnishing it to spun gold. I looked away.

"Papers? I don't know. Benjamin—Eric's father—died six months ago," I explained.

"Yes, Benjamin Hempstead. I'm sure I read of his death. There was some insinuation that he might have been killed by someone looking for a map."

"You must be mistaken. He fell from a ladder."

Mr. Seagram smiled. "Perhaps I have got it mixed up with someone else, then."

I shook my head. "I'm not sure, now that I think of it. You see, there was some gossip of a diamond mine map when John Hempstead—that's Eric's great uncle—was killed." I told him about Sir Ian. "But the map is really a myth. What I can't understand is how such a story would get into the papers."

"Sensationalism, pure and simple. Some enterprising reporter, wanting to sell papers, mixed fact with fancy, the past with the present. It was that kind of tabloid, you know, now that I think of it. A scandal sheet. Strong on rumor and weak on truth."

"What kind of rumor?" I asked, suddenly recalling Mr. Blessing.

"Oh—that the son, Eric Hempstead, might have had something to do with his father's death."

"I heard those rumors. My parents claim that they are libelous."

"And what is your opinion?"

"I have no reason to believe otherwise."

"I'm sure you are right."

His eyes were serious. Depth-haunting, as the poets would say. I wanted to drown in them.

"The boys should be back," he said, breaking an awkward silence.

I had been staring again. God, what must he think? Blushing, I got hastily to my feet, Mr. Seagram rose politely. And then, in my flustered state, I tripped like a bumbling schoolgirl over the rungs of his chair. His hands caught hold of my arms to steady me, and for a long, breathless moment he held me thus, my face very close to his. I saw his eyes widen imperceptibly, and I longed for him to draw me closer, longed for his kiss with a mixture of fear and desire.

But the moment passed as he released me. "Thank you for listening to my complaint," he said.

"Quite all right," I mumbled, and on legs of straw hurriedly found my way from the room.

Mrs. Platte and I had gone over the wine cellar, checking each bottle against the list. Nothing had been taken. But Mrs. Platte still maintained her key had been "pinched," and she would not stop her grumbling until a locksmith was fetched and a new lock put on the door. She might frown on the Woodhills' imbiding, but her sense of duty would not permit the possible theft of a single bottle under her care.

As for the mysterious footsteps, I no longer heard them, though I lay awake several nights listening. Perhaps my inquiries had scared the guilty person (George?) away. Or perhaps those steps had been Gordon's—now safely locked in his room with Alistair each night. That Rommany's phantoms had taken to pacing seemed, in calm retrospect, improbable.

After a week Eric went up to London to have the doctor look at his cast, which had grown troublesome. Bea went with him. Secretly I had hoped they might remain in the city, but before they left Eric said, "I haven't been a nuisance, have I?"

What could I say? "Of course not."

"Then it's all right with you if I return?"

"You know you are always welcome at Rommany."

Perhaps, I thought, he will change his mind. And Bea had said nothing at all.

Meanwhile I enjoyed their absence. The evening of the very day Eric and Bea left Mr. Seagram brought the boys down to dinner. I was pleased to see how well they behaved, how they both seemed to adore their tutor. It was almost as if he had enchanted them. Except for speaking courteously, though briefly, when spoken to, the boys ignored me, a pale, insignificant star to their sun, Mr. Seagram. Had I not been so entranced with him myself I would have felt hurt by their attitude. Perhaps this hero worship was all part of their growing up.

"Mr. Seagram," Alistair (the younger and gentler of the two) said in his soft, small voice, "are we to see the Roman ruins next Sunday?"

"I think so. Weather permitting," Mr. Seagram replied. "Would you care to accompany us, Miss Woodhill?"

The boys turned their gaze upon me, two sets of eyes, expectant, apprehensive. I wanted to go, but I knew how it would be. Alistair and Gordon would resent my intrusion on their day. They would run off or become fretful and naughty, and Mr. Seagram, involved with discipline and instruction, might find my presence annoying as well.

"Thank you, but I have some letters to write." I could not help but smile at the boys, whose faces bloomed with relief. "Some other time perhaps."

Sunday dawned with a light breeze and blue skies. At ten o'clock, Mr. Seagram and the boys left, carrying a picnic hamper packed by Mrs. Platte. I had suggested that George drive them in the Daimler, but Leonard demurred, saying that a motorcar was most inappropriate for a visit to ancient ruins. So they went in the gig, and I watched them rather wistfully as the horse trotted down the drive and disappeared among the trees.

It happened to be the maids' free half day also, and after lunch they changed from their starched aprons and uniforms into their town finery. Mrs. Platte had asked

leave to go into Tenwyck with them. Ordinarily she ro-
tated half days with the maids, so that Rommany would
not be left entirely without staff, but her sister was ill and
she didn't think I would mind.

"Not at all," I said.

George, with my permission, drove them away in the
Daimler, the three maids chattering and giggling, looking
very gay under their flower-decked hats, Mrs. Platte in her
sober black bonnet, sitting upright and tall.

Around three o'clock the fine weather changed abruptly.
A stiff breeze began to blow, whistling across the lawns,
thrashing the trees and hedges. From where I stood at the
library window I could see tiered banks of leaden clouds
moving swiftly across the sky. I hoped Leonard and the
children would start back before the storm broke. The
wind grew stronger, whipping at my hair. Somewhere
above me I heard a shutter banging monotonously.

I hurriedly closed the window and made the rounds of
the ground floor, checking windows and shutters. Then I
went upstairs and into each bedroom doing the same.

I had not found the shutter. It kept knocking, knocking,
knocking. Confounded thing, I thought, standing in the
darkened corridor, listening.

Outside the wind moaned, an eerie, sad sound.

And then it came to me with the impact of a cold, sickening blow—I was all alone in the house! I had been a
fool to let all the servants go, a fool to think I was brave
enough not to mind.

The threat of panic—horrible, all too familiar panic—
quickened my blood. Remembered nightmares, the horrors
of my childhood rushed in upon me, dragging me back
into the terrifying past. The rustle of long skirts, the crack
of knuckles, the shuffling of cards, the heart-heavy sighs—
all the haunting sounds of Rommany seemed to con-
verge upon me there in the darkened space between wall
and wall. Clara Grimes's skeleton, something I had not
dreamt of for years, rose in a sudden, horrifying vision.
The murdered servant girl's grave had been a secret. God
knew how many more Rommany was keeping!

Here, now—I will tell you all, a voice seemed to whisper. I fought the urge to run, to flee down the corridor,

down the stairs, out of the door and away from Rommany, far, far away.

I am not a child any longer, not a child, *not a child*, but a grown woman. What would Leonard Seagram think of me,—the Constance who could converse and act intelligently—if he knew I had been panicked out of my wits by the banging of a shutter?

Gradually, by slow stages, I edged away from the pit.

After a few moments, shaken, but able to move at last, I went along the corridor. The sound of the shutter was louder. The Long Gallery? I put my hand on the doorknob and hesitated.

The shutter went on banging.

I opened the door and, peering down the room's murky length, saw the unfastened shutter. Without looking to the left or the right I walked swiftly to the window. I was reaching out to shut it when the rain caught me in a burst of lashing fury. Tugging with both hands on the frame I pulled it against the storm. But the elements were too strong for me. I could not get the window to move.

Even now I find it hard to describe the sensation which gripped me as I struggled with the window in the beating, wind-driven rain. It was as if I were fighting a malevolent force, an unleashed evil power bent on destroying me. And yet, fearful though I was, I would not give in. Here at last, my blood sang, was something tangible, an enemy I could pit my strength and will against.

The wind laughed hellishly, screaming in my ears, but I was winning; inch by inch, I was winning. And finally, wet and exhausted, I brought the window in and locked it with a queer, satisfying sense of accomplishment. I drew the shutter into place and locked that too.

Then I turned. The only windows in the gallery were situated at each end of the long room, so it may have been the dim light or my earlier quick passage from door to window which had prevented me from seeing what I saw now.

Two pictures had been removed from the wall and were lying on the floor.

Slowly, my stomach knotted with apprehension, I approached them. The canvases had been lifted from their frames. I knelt and turned the portraits over. One was the third baronet of Rommany, Sir Henry Blackmore, painted by Sir Peter Lely; the other, a portrait of Lady Charlotte, painted by Sir Joshua Reynolds. Both pictures were very valuable, painted by artists renowned in their time and even more so in ours. A museum or private collector would pay a fancy price for these two, and it was obvious that someone had been trying to steal them.

Had I frightened the thief away?

No sooner had the word "thief" popped into my head then I thought of George—secretive, sly, resentful George.

But he was in Tenwyck. I had seen him drive off in the Daimler with my own eyes.

And there was no one in the house but me, no one, unless. . . .

I stared down at Lady Charlotte's smooth brow and titian hair and felt the blood drain from my face.

Had a burglar gained entrance to the house? The thought that a stranger might have been in the Long Gallery, watching me from a crack in the door as I moved from room to room, searching for the banging shutter, chilled me to the marrow.

Where was he now?

A hinge creaked and my skin crawled in terror, every muscle, every nerve alert, straining for the sound of a movement, the swift brush of an approaching step.

Wind gusted at the windows, and they rattled in their frames. The sound died and the rain settled into a steady tapping. Nothing else. No other sound. Just the rain.

Still I did not move. My knees ached and I felt vulnerable and afraid. But I knew I could not remain there forever, kneeling, my neck bent as if waiting for the executioner's ax, staring at Joshua Reynolds's handiwork. With a sudden jerk, I twisted my head.

The door was closed, though I clearly remembered having left it open. My eyes darted here and there, probing the shadows as I got to my feet. And then the dark paneled walls lined with staring faces of the past seemed to shudder with a deep, sorrowful sigh. An achingly, *human* sigh.

I was at the door in an instant, tugging wildly at the knob, my hands slippery with the sweat of fear. Oh, God! I couldn't get out! I was locked in! I would never get out!

Suddenly the door sprang open and I was flying down the corridor to the staircase. I had a blurred impression of Leonard, his face startled, coming up the stairs toward me, and without quite knowing how it happened I was in his arms, weeping with fear and relief.

Chapter 7

When I lifted my head from Leonard Seagram's shoulder I was stunned to see Bea, Eric, and the count gaping up at me from the drawing-room doorway.

Mortified, realizing what a pretty sight I must have been in Mr. Seagram's arms, my hair undone from its pins, my bodice damp and awry, my first impulse was to flee to my room. But common sense told me that such a flight would only confirm the supposition of scandalous behavior which I felt sure was going through their separate minds.

"What's the weeping about?" Eric was the first to speak.

"I . . . I've had a dreadful experience," I said. "Mr. Seagram, I—I'm afraid I owe you an apology. Please, if you will come downstairs for a few moments I will explain."

Wrapping the tattered remains of dignity about me, I descended the staircase and entered the drawing room. Leonard closed the door behind the others.

"Well!" Bea exclaimed. "Still water *does* run deep."

"Oh, give Constance a chance," Eric said. "By the by, you have met the count?"

"Yes, at the funeral," I said.

The count came forward and bent over my hand. "Charmed to see you again." A rather short, foppish man of thirty, he spoke perfect English with a nasal French accent. "It's been such a long time." He smiled a knowing smile, sly and approving.

I sat on a straight-backed chair. "About an hour ago," I began, folding my hands tightly in my lap, "about an hour ago, maybe less, when everyone was out, I—I disturbed an apparent burglar at work."

Except for Bea, they all made appropriate shocked exclamations. I knew Bea would not believe what I had to say, and for that matter I wasn't certain that the count and Eric would, either. But it was Leonard I really wanted to convince. I did not wish him to think ill of me, to feel I had thrown myself at him merely to gain his sympathy.

I told the story then, leaving out all mention of eerie manifestations, placing emphasis on the two pictures which had been torn from their frames.

"I thought I had been locked in by the thief and that I was all alone in the house," I said. "And I—well, I panicked. And Mr. Seagram fortunately caught me before I fell down the stairs."

"Quite an adventure," Bea said acidly, her eyes flitting from Leonard Seagram to me.

"I had no idea," Mr. Seagram said. "We had returned home, oh—I'd say about fifteen minutes before you came running out, Miss Woodhill." He explained how he and the boys had started home early and got caught in the rain just as they were approaching Rommany. "You looked white as a sheet, but I had no idea—"

"But we were all *here*," Bea said.

"I didn't know," I said. "I hadn't heard you come in. The rain, I suppose."

Jenny tapped on the door. "Shall I serve tea, miss?"

"In a half hour, if you will," I said. "You've all come back, then?"

"Yes, Miss Woodhill. George brought us home at half past five."

When she had closed the door again, Eric said, "Do you think it might have been one of the servants?"

"Not the maids. Or Mrs. Platte," I said. "They were all in Tenwyck this afternoon. George took them."

"George—that chauffeur fellow?" Eric asked, shifting his leg on the footstool. "So they all have an alibi. Though I should think a clever person might have arranged that jaunt to town and then doubled back."

"It was the maids' regular half day, and Mrs. Platte went along because her sister was ill."

"A sick sister?"

"Mrs. Platte," I said, annoyed at his playing detective as if it were a parlor game, "has been in the family for years. If she wanted to steal, it wouldn't be paintings."

"Quite right," Eric agreed. "But don't you think we ought to call the constable?"

The count, lighting Bea's cigarette, said, "I can't really see where it's necessary, Eric, old man. Nothing's been taken, has it? You know how local constables are—heavy-booted, full of asinine questions, bullying the servants. And the end result? Not very much. That's my experience, for what it is worth."

I looked at the count, and Mother's comment came back to me. ". . . hasn't a penny." I wondered how long he—Bea and Eric—had been in the house before I came running out of the Long Gallery.

Eric said, "You might have a point there. What is your opinion, Mr. Seagram?"

"I should think it would be up to Miss Woodhill," he said.

"Nothing's been taken," I hedged. I thought of Mrs. Platte and how upset she had been by the missing wine cellar key. The attempted burglary of the pictures and the arrival of a constable in her kitchen would disturb her even more. She might even give notice, and where could I find another cook? "Perhaps Count de Grasse is right."

"May I make a suggestion?" Leonard said. "Perhaps a good lock on the Long Gallery door will discourage theft. And now, if you will excuse me, I will return to my charges." He stood up, very tall, very handsome, and I could not help comparing him with the pallid count.

"He seems like a nice fellow," Eric said, after Leonard had gone. "He comes well recommended, I suppose?"

"Very well," I said sharply. "I hope you are not implying that Mr. Seagram is our would-be thief? You heard what he said. He was out all day on an outing with the boys."

"I've annoyed you," Eric wrinkled his nose. "I'm sorry."

Bea tittered. "I do believe Constance fancies Mr. Seagram."

My cheeks flamed. "And what about *you?*"

"Me?" she retorted, laughing outright. "Really, Constance, a *tutor?*"

The count smiled, his lips curving beneath his dapper moustache. "Why don't you let Constance alone?" he chided. And then, turning moist eyes to me, "I may call you Constance?"

It was all most unpleasant, and as the talk turned to other matters, I listened with only half an ear. There was something odd going on. Those portraits in the Long Gallery troubled me; yet no one else had seemed overly concerned. I should have thought Bea—who never traveled without an extensive wardrobe and valuable jewelry—would demand an investigation or protection, but she hadn't. Perhaps it was true then. She—as well as the count and Eric—didn't believe me.

I had another reason to be disturbed by something that happened the next morning. I had come down early, before breakfast, in order to get a letter off to Father's publisher, and, while sitting at the typewriter, I suddenly had the strange sensation that someone was in the room with me. It was an absurd, utterly baseless feeling, and yet, as I tapped away at the keys, it persisted.

The library was one of the few rooms at Rommany where I had always felt comfortable. I had never heard or felt a ghostly presence there. It was a warm room, full of sunshine at this hour, and every corner of it was in bright daylight. The one possible place of concealment was a tall, narrow cupboard, generally used for storage, set in between banked rows of bookshelves.

I looked at the cupboard, stared at it, and the more I stared, the more convinced I became that there was someone behind its closed door. I got to my feet, hesitated a few moments, then resolutely went to it. I had my hand on the knob when the library door opened.

Alistair stood on the threshold in his nightshirt, his face a muddy gray. "I don't feel very well, Constance," he said piteously.

"What's the trouble?" I exclaimed, going to him at once.

"It's . . . it's my stomach. It feels rather queer."

"What have you been eating?" I took his small, cold hand.

"Apples," he said. "Gordon found these old apple trees yesterday and picked some. They were green."

"I shouldn't wonder your stomach hurts."

We were halfway up the staircase when Alistair suddenly bent over with a groan and vomited. I hurried him up to his room, changed his nightshirt and tucked him into bed, while Gordon watched with keen interest.

"You ought to be ashamed of yourself, Gordon," I said annoyed. "Coaxing your brother to eat green apples."

"Didn't hurt *me*," he said with a smug air.

I got some salts from Mother's medical cupboard, and though Alistair groaned and complained, I mixed them with water and made him drink all of it down.

I was wiping his damp brow with a handkerchief when Leonard Seagram came in. "What have we here?" he asked. "Alistair sick?"

"Green apples," I said.

"Devil take it!" he exclaimed angrily. It was the first time I had seen Leonard lose control. "Didn't I forbid you to go near those trees?"

Gordon said meekly, "Yes, sir."

"Well, then, Alistair, I suppose you have learned a good lesson?"

"Yes, sir," Alistair answered wretchedly.

Leonard turned to me. "I'm sorry this has happened."

"Please don't blame yourself."

He apologized for not keeping closer watch on the boys, apologized for losing his temper, while I kept insisting he was not at fault.

When I finally got back to the library I went immediately to the cupboard. There was no one there, of course. If there had been, they would have gone before now. Nevertheless, I inspected the cupboard closely. The packing cases of manuscripts and old books, the reams of paper and boxes of envelopes seemed at first glance undisturbed. But then I perceived several of the boxes had been moved slightly and a packing case was imperfectly closed. I suppose anyone else—Father or one of the maids, for instance—never would have noticed, but I am by nature a meticulous person and since I myself had rearranged the cupboard (as well as the desk drawers) only a few days earlier, I did.

Still, I thought, Esther or Daisy might have come in to clean the library and in a burst of uncharacteristic zeal done the closet too.

Frowning, I sat down at the desk, while my eyes slowly examined the tiers of books. Nothing wrong there. Then I began to open the desk drawers one by one. Papers and pencils and notebooks. But—what was this? An appointment book pushed to the back, and a folio of old prints on top instead of at the bottom? I could not blame the maids for these changes. They were forbidden to touch the desk.

The middle drawer, holding petty cash and a ring of keys, was kept locked, the key to it hidden behind a mezzotint of St. Paul's Cathedral which hung over the fireplace.

My hands trembled as I unlocked and opened the drawer. I saw at once that it, too, had been disturbed. I counted the petty cash three times. Not a penny had been taken. As for the keys, so few doors were ever locked at Rommany I could not tell one key from the other. Except for the wine cellar key, a distinctive, old-fashioned relic with the letter "R" worked in wrought iron at the top, they all looked alike.

The money which Father had left me to pay the servants and run the household was kept in an ugly iron safe, standing in one corner of the library, camouflaged by a tapestry piece. In it were also the jewels Mother had not taken with her and some papers, musty and yellow with age. The combination to the safe I had put under the desk blotter—not the most original or secret of hiding places, but then I (and Father) had not thought it necessary to take elaborate precautions in concealing it.

Again I found nothing missing. The jewels checked out with the inventory list. And the papers—baptismal records, marriage contracts, an ancient, moldering sheepskin document with a plan of the house, a bill of sale, dated 1820— made up the sort of family collection which would be of no interest to a thief.

But was I dealing with an ordinary thief?

The pictures, for instance. Had they been ripped from their frames not because of their intrinsic value, but because something of greater worth may have been hidden behind them?

But what?

The wine cellar key had disappeared, yet every bottle had been accounted for. Jewels intact. The cupboard, the desk drawers searched, but no money taken. Logic dictated that a burglar going through Rommany would not only steal money, but scoop up silver, jewels, paintings, any of the many objects of value lying about the house, as well. Why this search in a desk drawer?

I thought of the footsteps I had heard on two successive nights. "Sir Ian looking for the map," Eric had quipped.

The map. Could someone—not Sir Ian's ghost, but someone very much alive—be seeking the map? That elusive, mythical dream of riches?

Perhaps the legend of the Blackmore-Hempstead map had received wider circulation than I had thought. According to Leonard Seagram, mention of it had been made in a newspaper article. Anyone could have read it. Anyone. The maids—even George.

I shut the safe and tucked the combination inside my blouse. Then I sat down on a chair near the window, staring out at the dark green yews crowding the sill. I wished that I hadn't thought of the map; a thief who stole spoons or paintings would not worry me half as much as someone embarked on this strange, secret quest. It was depressing.

I sat there, feeling the full weight of Rommany, heavy with ghosts, thick with dark memories and hidden mysteries.

My grandfather, Sir Duncan, had died of a heart seizure, so Mother had told me. But I wondered. He was the one, according to Mother's offhand, rather skeptical account, who had drawn up the map with John Hempstead, and John Hempstead (if one believed the newspaper article) had been killed for it. And what of Harold Hempstead, his heir? Run over by horse and carriage at his very doorstep. Accident? The same sort of "accident" which had claimed Benjamin's life?

I went on gazing blindly through the window, my mind's eye turned inward. The shadowed past had begun to take on a dim, frightening pattern. So many deaths; all of men in their prime. Was there a time in each generation when a new search was made for that elusive map, when yet another person had to die for that glittering fantasy? And had that time come again?

Father was not a Blackmore, but he was nominal master of Rommany now, head of the household. Thank God he is away, I thought. No one can touch him as long as he remains in Paris or Milan.

I turned from the window with a sigh, but even as I did so an appalling thought struck me.

In Father's absence, *I* was head of the family.

No, it couldn't be. What did the map have to do with an unmarried female, with me?

But *I* was in charge, was I not? Keeper of the keys? Mistress of Rommany—even if Uncle Ernest remained its legal owner.

True—yet, wasn't this drawing logic to a preposterous conclusion? My theory of maps and murder might be as far from reality as fancy could make it. What good did it do to sit here and scare myself with anticipation of a wholly imaginary doom? No one was going to murder me, not for a will-o'-the-wisp map, were they?

So, trying to shut off further gloomy speculation, I went back to the typewriter. When I finished the two letters, I sealed and stamped them and gave them to Jenny, instructing her to have George post them. As I was speaking to her, the count peeked in at the door.

"Ah, there you are, Constance, *ma cherie*," he smiled fatuously. "We've missed you at breakfast."

"I am sorry," I said. "But there were business matters to attend to."

"All work and no play," he wagged his finger, closing the door as Jenny went out.

I got to my feet, frowning at the closed door, but he did not seem to notice.

"You're too charming a creature to be shut up in a stuffy room," he said, advancing toward me. "Strain those pretty eyes of yours."

"Thank you for the compliment, count, but . . ."

"Jean. Please call me Jean."

". . . but I don't mind. In fact, I rather enjoy it."

"Do you?" He took my hand, caressing it between thumb and forefinger.

I went cold with anger. This was not to be Wilfred Talbot all over again. "Don't touch me!" I commanded, snatching my hand away.

"Ah, well," he said, casually stuffing his hands in his pockets, "perhaps you prefer the man with red hair."

Wordless, I stalked from the room. I could hear Eric and Bea conversing in the drawing room, but I was too angry to join them. I turned my back and went up the stairs.

When I opened the door of my room I was surprised to find George standing in the center of it.

"What are you doing here?" I demanded.

"Mrs. Platte sent me up," he said, his gaze wandering past me to the door. "She said there was a shutter loose, and I've come to fix it."

"She was mistaken," I said, observing him narrowly. "Are you sure she meant here?"

A faint flush stained his sallow cheeks, but his eyes never wavered from the door. "I thought she did. Perhaps she said the Long Gallery."

He was lying; I knew he was lying, and yet I could not bring myself to accuse him of it. "Never mind about the shutter. There are some letters I want posted right away. Jenny has them."

"Yes, Miss Woodhill."

I have to get rid of him, I thought. I'll write to Father and explain. Even if I am unfair, even if he has not been the one prowling around, tearing paintings from their frames, rifling through boxes and papers in the library—the man gives me the cold shivers.

But inexplicably I procrastinated, putting off his dismissal, until the time finally came when my hand was forced.

Chapter 8

Several days after the Hempsteads' return I began to notice a change in Eric's attitude toward Count de Grasse. Whereas Eric had previously seemed on fairly amiable terms with his sister's fiancé, he now spoke coldly to him, if at all. At first I thought it might be due to the count's roving eye, and that Eric, somehow, had got wind of de Grasse's approach to me in the library. But then I overheard a conversation between them at a picnic, and from it learned that the count's casual philandering had nothing to do with their altered relationship.

The picnic had been Bea's idea. Casting around for entertainment, she had suggested we (everyone, including the boys and Mr. Seagram) go on an outing. So I had Mrs. Platte pack several hampers of food, plus a half dozen bottles of chilled wine (requested by Bea; muttered at by Mrs. Platte).

The spot I had chosen was exactly as I had remembered it when I had picnicked there with my parents many years earlier: a meadow of green grass, dotted with late-blooming lobelia and purple wild flowers and a single ancient oak which leaned windward on a slight knoll. At the bottom of the meadow the clear, narrow stream meandered over a bed of smooth stones. Willows and larches draped green, leafy branches at the water's edge. A lovely place, unchanged.

Bea joined the boys wading in the water—throwing off her sophisticated air with her shoes and stockings and screaming with delight at the cold, while Eric, Leonard and I unpacked the lunch.

"Why, aren't you the lazy one," Eric remarked to de Grasse, who had stretched himself out on a blanket, legs crossed, smoking a cigar. "A pity we aren't having this picnic at the chateau, where we'd be waited on hand and foot."

"What's that supposed to mean?" the count asked. "You know very well the chateau's not been in the family for thirty years."

"Oh—forgive me," Eric said dryly. "I'd forgotten."

"Quite all right. You do get forgetful at times, if I recall," the count retorted with barely disguised sarcasm.

Eric set his lips in a grim line as he pulled the cork from a wine bottle. He did not look at Jean.

The ill-will between those two hung on the air like a taut, humming wire. I wondered if Leonard noticed it also.

Mrs. Platte had outdone herself; she had prepared enough food to feed a small army. The boys dug into chicken and pickled beets and cold sausage and bread and cheese as if they had been starved for a week. Everyone ate well, including myself. The wine bottle was emptied and another opened.

After we had eaten our fill, Leonard suggested a walk to the boys, a suggestion greeted with shouts of "splendid idea!" I put a pillow under my head and lay back, looking up into the lacy green, branches of the oak. Wood pigeons called one to the other in the leafy bower above. I could not see the birds, but I heard them rustling as they hopped from twig to twig, making their soft, cooing sounds.

Bea and de Grasse were playing whist. Their voices drifted to me lazily on the summer air. The afternoon drowsed. A white butterfly settled on a pink blossom. The wind stirred, and a ray of sunlight shafting down through the leaves pierced my eyes, and I covered my face with my arm.

I must have fallen asleep then, for when I awoke everyone but Bea had gone. She too had dropped off to sleep, curled up on her side like a small child. Too much wine, too much dinner, I thought, getting sluggishly to my feet. I felt heavy, hot, and sticky.

I went down to the stream and dipped my handkerchief into the crystal water. Mopping my face, I began to stroll along the stream's bank. The sides grew steeper and the path climbed higher, skirting a dense growth of trees.

Suddenly I heard Eric say, "I absolutely refuse to submit to blackmail."

"It would look very bad," Jean replied, "especially to the police."

They were hidden by a tangled growth of shrubbery. Torn between guilt and rabid curiosity, I gave in to the latter and with a prickly conscience concealed myself behind a tree.

"Take your damned letter to the police then," Eric was saying. "And go to the Devil!"

"Look here," the count pleaded. "It's a matter of only a hundred pounds."

"I've paid the money I owe you, and you are not going to get another shilling."

"Perhaps you will change your mind. Let me refresh your memory."

I heard the rustle of paper, and then Jean de Grasse began to read. "Dear Jean: I'm sorry I have been tardy settling our account. Winning at cards does not seem my strong point. And there are others, you know, waiting for theirs—"

"You're boring me," Eric interrupted. "I don't think I care to hear more."

"Ah—but I think you should. Let me go on: However, I plan to appeal to Father. He's not looked upon my debts favorably in the past, but I feel I have a foolproof way to persuade him. And so on. And then, *mon cher* Eric, the poor man, your father, dies—falling from a ladder the same day this letter was written. Really! A ladder he's climbed at least a thousand times before?"

There was a small silence. I shrank closer to the tree.

"If you don't get out of my sight," Eric said in a tight, furious voice, "I shall smash your head in with this crutch!"

I didn't wait to hear more, but like a thief stole quietly back along the stream, shaken by what I had heard.

Whether Eric was guilty of a crime or not, the letter was a damning one. "I have a foolproof way to persuade him," he had written. Had Eric killed his father? Perhaps he hadn't really meant to. Perhaps he and Benjamin had quarreled over Eric's debts and Eric—in a fit of frustrated rage—had pushed his father from the ladder. Or had Eric, in the coolness of his mind, decided beforehand that if the money was not forthcoming he would find a way to "accidentally" dispose of Benjamin?

The idea was horrible.

Was Eric capable of murder? Mother had asked me that same question once, and again I did not know. Eric was a sardonic man who rarely spoke of himself. He had been kind to me on occasion, jibing on others. He had an unsavory reputation, of course—a card player, a man who drank too much and neglected his studies. But did this necessarily make him a murderer? Yet wasn't it hard to tell what a man, pressured by debts, would do when pushed to the edge?

According to Eric, the will had specified he would be limited to his allowance until his thirtieth birthday. Apparently it hadn't been enough to take care of his gambling debts before his father's death, and there was no reason to believe the allowance could do so now. Not unless Eric borrowed from Peter to pay Paul.

Or unless he found another source of income.

And—oddly—as soon as I came to that point in my reasoning, I thought of the map. Odd, because I still didn't believe in its existence. Yet *if* there was a map, that meant that somewhere in diamond country—South Africa, wasn't it?—there was a registered claim. If one did not want to bother with the inconvenience or hardship of mining, the claim itself could be sold, probably for thousands of pounds. Either way, the map—if it existed—as Eric had said, was worth a fortune.

I reached the picnic site, hesitating at the stream's edge.

"Constance!" Gordon called. "We're eating again. Come have a chicken leg. There's only one left."

"In a little bit," I said.

I sat down, resting my chin on my knees, staring at the rippled stream as it murmured its way past me.

Suppose Eric was lying. Suppose he did have the Hempstead portion of the map and had come to Rommany to look for the part that would make it whole. Wouldn't that explain the stolen wine cellar key, the signs of search in the library cupboard, the gun he was wearing? And what of the time I had caught him at the desk drawer?

But the footsteps had definitely not been his. Were there two people searching for the map?

"A penny for your thoughts."

I jerked my head up to find Leonard smiling down at me.

"They're not worth very much, I'm afraid."

He sat down beside me. "Why don't you let me be the judge of that?"

A lock of auburn hair had fallen over his forehead, giving him a devil-may-care appearance. But his eyes were sympathetic and serious. I had a terrible urge to lean my head on his shoulder, a need to have him put his arm about me and hold me close. Ought I to tell him what I had heard among the trees, what I suspected?

"It's a family matter," I said. "I'm afraid you won't find it interesting."

"Try me," he urged; his eyes were asking me to trust him.

Could I?

"What are you two plotting?" It was Bea, her head cocked saucily to one side, a cigarette in her hand.

"Nothing," I said flushing, and hating myself for it.

"We've run out of wine," she said. "And I think it's time we went home."

"I'm going into Tenwyck," Bea said. "Anybody care to join me?"

"Not I," said the count, lighting a cigar. "Walking from shop to shop, standing around while you make up your mind is not my idea of an afternoon."

"Eric? Constance?"

"Lame foot," Eric grinned, pointing to his cast.

"That leaves you, Constance."

I did not want to go—but I saw no way of gracefully refusing her when only five minutes earlier I had said I had finished my work for the day.

Our first stop was the milliner's. It seemed that Bea had been there before, for the proprietress herself, a Mrs. Dobie, came out from the back room to wait on her. "How nice to see you again, Miss Hempstead."

"Have you anything new?" Bea asked, looking around rather skeptically.

"Why yes, I've made up several lovely hats since last you were here."

"Let's have a look, then," Bea said, sitting down in front of the mirror.

Bea tried on five hats, none of which she found pleasing enough to buy. When we were leaving Mrs. Dobie, in a deferential voice, said, "Miss Hempstead, do you think you could pay a little on your account?"

"Oh, yes," Bea said, opening her purse. "Ah, I've left my cheque book at home. Constance dear, do you think you could lend me five pounds?"

"I think so."

I would have thought little of the incident had not the same thing happened at the draper's, the dress shop, and later at the chemist's where Bea purchased a jar of skin emollient. Apparently during her brief stay at Rommany she had run up accounts with at least a half dozen tradesmen in Tenwyck. I wondered if this was a habit; whether she was lax in paying her bills, or, like her brother, unable to live within her allowance (a generous one, I had guessed from the way Mary spoke).

Tired and thirsty, we stopped at a tea shop for refreshment. For all our marching around, Bea's only purchase had been a large, picture puzzle for each of the boys, thoughtfulness which surprised me.

"I used to love puzzles when I was a child," Bea said, placing her package on a chair, and removing her gloves. "Father and I would do them by the hour."

"You miss your father, don't you?"

"Of course I do, silly," she replied flippantly, as if lapsing into sentimentality was something to be avoided at all costs. "He was very good about advancing me money when I ran out. And now—well now, we have that stuffy Bradley—he's the trustee, you know, for the estate, and he's stingy, absolutely *stingy*. You'd think it was all his."

She opened her purse and, as she brought out a handkerchief, a key fell to the floor.

It was the key to the wine cellar, the one Mrs. Platte insisted had been stolen.

There was no mistake. I would have known that key

anywhere with its distinctive size and large iron "R" at the top.

I ignored it. What else could I do? One doesn't accuse a lady of "pinching" a key. But, metaphorically speaking, that wine cellar key opened a new door in my mind. Bea, short of cash, could be looking for the map herself. Why not? To her it would not only be the money involved, but a game, a challenge. Hide-and-seek. Blind man's bluff. Find the map? Had she taken de Grasse into her confidence? Was he her partner? He needed money, too.

"Constance!"

I came to with a start.

"Daydreaming again, about Mr. Seagram, no doubt. What will you have with your tea? There's scones and raisin cake, bread and butter—"

"Bread and butter," I said.

Of course that would explain why Bea had come to Rommany, dull uninteresting, countrified Rommany!

"I shall have a scone," Bea said to the waitress.

If Eric knew about the map, it followed that Bea did, too. Perhaps all three of them together had decided to comb Rommany, looking for the Blackmore portion of the map. On the other hand, that sort of alliance would hardly be possible, not with de Grasse blackmailing Eric. Were each of them slinking about on their own, then?

The situation maddened me. For, of course, I could say nothing without some kind of definite proof. I could not point an accusing finger at Eric, at Bea, at the count, as it now stood, without making a perfect fool of myself.

"Are you in love with him?" Bea was watching me with amused, uptilted eyes.

"In love with whom?" I asked, reaching for the napkin and shaking it out with a flourish.

"With the handsome tutor, silly."

"Of course not."

"Marriage would be out of the question, but you might have an *affaire* with him." Her smile was malicious.

"I wish you'd stop talking nonsense," I said, my face burning with anger and embarrassment.

An hour before dinner that night, I went along the corridor to the schoolroom. Father had written from Milan, asking for a progress report on the boys' studies, and I had forgotten to speak to Leonard about it. The door was slightly ajar, and my hand froze on the knob as I heard Bea's voice.

"... you must admit it's an excellent idea," Bea was saying.

"By all means," Leonard replied. "I would never have thought of it myself."

"And you have me to thank."

"I certainly do. It will solve a big problem—no question of that."

Bea went on talking but I wasn't listening. What had Leonard to thank Bea for? I had a glimpse of their heads bent close, copper and dark.

Crestfallen, I turned from the door and crept back to my room. Bea and Leonard. Conspiring together. They must have been. Bea and Leonard. Oh, God, how it hurt! "I would have never thought of it myself," Leonard had said. To me it could mean only one thing: they had been discussing the map, and Leonard had joined Bea in the search.

I wanted to weep with pain.

Bea with her dark, tantalizing eyes and provocative smile, had persuaded Leonard to her scheme. How could I doubt it?

And how much did I really know of Leonard?

He had come to Rommany with but a single valise, bearing all his worldly possessions. He was poor, the victim of genteel poverty, the worst kind of all. Could I blame him for trying to better his condition?

It was no use telling myself I loved him (there—I had admitted it, at last!), that he had filled a place in my dreams, in my life. It did not help reminding myself that I had thought him above mercenary motives, that I had thought him loyal, scrupulously honest, that I had worshiped him. An idol with feet of clay.

But, after all, what promises had he made to me, what pledges? None.

That night I lay in my bed, listening to the steady tick-tick of the clock. Should I write Father and Mother about my suspicions? Such a letter might alarm them, perhaps cause them to cut short their holiday, the honeymoon they had so looked forward to. Or perhaps they would read my letter with skepticism. "What proof does she have?" I could imagine Father saying. "The Hempsteads? A map? What has got into Constance?"

A board creaked; a mouse scampered on tiny feet behind the wainscoting. The clock ticked on as the house breathed quietly in the dark.

Suddenly I heard a shuffling sound on the other side of the wall. I listened, then rose to my knees and pressed my ear to the panel. A soft, sliding sound, as if someone were carefully closing a drawer. Yes—there it was again! In Mother's bedroom.

When I think of it now I find my subsequent foolhardiness incomprehensible. I was too thoughtless, too stupid, perhaps, to be afraid.

I got into my robe and taking the night lamp stole out of the room. Quietly opening my mother's door, I tiptoed through the dark sitting room. The bedroom was empty. Had I imagined those sounds? But no—one of the bureau drawers was still open!

I set the lamp down. Handkerchiefs, stockings, ribbons, trinkets were all in a jumble. The intruder, in careless haste, had dropped a scarf and an ivory fan to the floor. I picked them up and began to tidy the drawer (how typical of me, I was later to muse—a thief on the prowl, and there I was, compulsively restoring order to disorder).

Hearing a soft sound behind me, I wheeled. "Who's there?"

The shadows mocked me in answer.

"You needn't hide," I said, taking a step. "You—"

And suddenly my head exploded into a thousand fragments and I flung out my arms to embrace the darkness.

Chapter 9

I don't know how long I remained unconscious, but when I opened my eyes, night still lurked in the corners beyond the lamp's glow. It took a minute or two before memory jolted me, and I sat up so quickly the room spun. Digging my fingers into the carpet to steady myself, I slowly regained control and looked around with a dry mouth and a beating heart.

Rigid, ready to cry out at the slightest sound, the only moving part of my face was my eyes, traveling from wardrobe to bed to bureau. No one. My shadow—a humped, distorted image—waited on the wall, waited with me. Waited.

Nothing happened. If someone was still hiding in the room, surely I would have heard or seen them by now?

My head, heavy as lead, ached with a sharp, insistent pain. Running my fingers gingerly over my scalp, I found the bump behind my ear to be surprisingly small. Using the bureau leg, I managed to pull myself to my feet. Then picking up the lamp in hands which shook convulsively. I went slowly out into the corridor.

The house slept in deep, indifferent silence. I stared at the blank doors on either side of me. Should I knock on one and call for assistance? But whom could I trust?

I did not know. I suspected them all. Eric, Bea, the count—even Leonard. And the servants upstairs. All.

The next morning when I awoke it was past ten. Jenny had come in and brought my tea without my hearing her, for there was a tray by my side with the teapot and a small pitcher of milk.

I pushed myself up on the pillows, staring at the teapot with glazed eyes. The pain at the back of my head had settled into a dull ache. There was something I had promised myself I would do, just before I had closed my eyes. I frowned, thinking. Ah, yes—the constable; I must fetch the constable from Tenwyck.

I had a terrible thirst and drank two cups of tea, bitter and cold though it was. A little revived I drew on a robe and went to the mirror. I was brushing my hair, noting the large circles under my eyes, when someone knocked on the door. Thinking it was Jenny come to fetch the tray, I said, "Come in."

It wasn't Jenny. It was Leonard.

I hastily pulled the robe together at my throat.

"I am sorry, Miss Woodhill," Leonard said, apparently as embarrassed as I, "but I thought—"

"It's perfectly all right. I—I overslept."

"I can wait, then, and talk to you later, if you wish."

"No," I said boldly, "if you have something to say, please." I motioned to a chair.

He sat down while I hastily tied my hair back with a ribbon and in doing so carelessly scraped the bump on my head. An exclamation of pain escaped my lips before I could bite it back.

"Something wrong?" Leonard asked, his eyes concerned.

"I . . . no, not really."

He cleared his throat. "I've come to make another complaint, I'm afraid. It's George, this time."

"George?"

"I don't think he can be trusted. I found him in the schoolroom late yesterday. He said he had come to fix a shutter, though there was nothing wrong with any of them."

"Strange," I said. "I had the same experience."

"Perhaps that is his excuse for prowling about. He seems untrustworthy. This morning Gordon accused Alistair of stealing ten shillings he had been saving in a jar. Alistair swore that he hadn't touched them, and I believe him. I can't help thinking it might have been George."

"I've been somewhat suspicious of him for some time now." Before my mind had started hurrying down the myriad, twisted alleyways of speculation, guessing and the-

orizing about a map I was not even sure existed, I might
have added, but didn't.

"I hope you won't consider me one of those mean-
minded tattlers who go about disrupting households," Leonard went on. "But you are carrying such a burden of responsibility—and all alone. Oh, I know you have guests,
but if you will pardon my saying so, they seem concerned
only with themselves. Although, to give credit where credit
is due, I must commend Miss Hempstead for her interest
in the boys."

"Miss Hempstead?"

"Yes, she came to me yesterday with a suggestion. They
hate history, as you might have guessed from the progress
report I left on the library desk." I hadn't guessed—I had
been too disturbed to read it. "It was Miss Hempstead's
idea that I use picture puzzles as an incentive to learning.
You know, they make them of famous personages, great
events of the past."

"Yes, how clever," I said in a small voice. So that was
what Leonard and Bea had been discussing. Picture
puzzles! And I, with my narrow, obsessed mind, had
thought it was the map; converting the trivial into the sinister. What a fool I felt. Relieved, but still a fool.

"To get back to the matter at hand. George. I may be
stepping out of line by presuming to give you advice, but I
feel someone should. For all your capability, Miss
Woodhill, you are still a woman. You need protection,
looking after."

My heart seemed to rise and swim, warm and fluttery
against my ribs. No man who wanted to look out for me
could possibly have feet of clay.

"Thank you. I would be most grateful for your advice."

Oh, Leonard, I longed to ask, *do you really care for
me?*

"If I were you, I'd dismiss him."

"Yes, I had thought of it. Do you think it was George
who tried to steal the portraits?" *He must care. He wanted
to protect me. Protect me, my God, how absurdly wonder-
ful!*

"Perhaps the man meant to steal them, then changed his
mind. Too big, too valuable, too easily missed and traced.
No. George is more like your petty thief, pilfering small

objects, a little cash, a few silver spoons, a small *objet d' art.*"

"And you think he's been prowling about the house?"

"I'm sure of it."

"I . . . I hadn't wanted to say anything, but last night . . ." So I told him how I had heard sounds in my mother's room and how, in going in to investigate, I had been knocked unconscious.

He was horrified. "Miss Woodhill, I'm astonished! To go into that room all alone? You ought to have roused me. Why didn't you?"

"I suppose I didn't think."

"Were you badly hurt?"

"A lump on my head," I said with a small smile, the pain receding in memory.

"Do you realize, you might have been killed?"

Would you care, Leonard, would you feel sad? "Nothing was taken that I could see. I thought I should call the constable in."

"By all means. Have Mrs. Platte go over the silver and other valuables. Perhaps your guests ought to check their belongings also."

"Yes, yes, you are right. I have reason to believe he's been searching through the library as well." I told Leonard about the cupboard and the desk drawers.

"That settles it. As soon as you have drawn up a list of missing objects, I will take it to the constable myself."

"You can't know how much I appreciate your concern," I said from the bottom of my heart.

"I'm doing only what any good and loyal servant would under the circumstances." He got to his feet.

"But you're more than a servant," I said impulsively. "You . . . you're a friend."

He smiled, the little creases crinkling at the corners of his eyes. "I was hoping you would say that." His eyes held mine for a moment longer, and then he was gone.

Mrs. Platte and I found nothing missing, though she and I counted and recounted the silver in the dining room and carefully went over the various knickknacks—some valuable, others not—in each of the rooms on the ground floor. Nor did Bea, the count, or Eric find that anything of theirs had been taken.

George denied that he had stolen a single shilling, denied that he had struck me.

It was all very puzzling.

"It's no use getting the constable," I said to Leonard later. "As far as I can tell, the only thing missing is Gordon's ten shillings. All the same, I think I shall let George go."

I gave George a month's wages in lieu of notice. He made no protest when I told him that I found his work unsatisfactory; his face betrayed no emotion, his eyes, as he took the money, remained fixed on a point above my head. It was an unpleasant experience for me, and, as I spoke to him, I felt a sudden, irrational resentment toward Mother. It wasn't right, I thought, to be saddled with unwelcome guests and unsavory servants.

I watched George drive off with Leonard in the gig from an upstairs window—George, sitting tall and thin, dressed in his good Sunday black—and felt strangely troubled. I thought suddenly of Clara Grimes. She, too, had been accused of stealing. Had I done the right thing? Had it really been George wandering the house in the dead of night; George concealed in the shadows, who had dealt me that blow? I certainly could not place the theft of the wine cellar key at his feet, since Bea had filched it.

And *there* was a riddle; why had she taken the key? Bea was a tippler; that much I knew. Had she seen the key lying about, appropriated it because she could find no wine on the sideboard and later decided to keep it? Why, then, wasn't there a single bottle missing in the cellar? Poor accounting on Mrs. Platte's part?

Questions and doubts continued to plague me, but when three days had passed, four, five, and then a week, and nothing happened—no sounds of prowling at night, no signs of surreptitious search—I began to think it had been George, after all, and breathed easier.

One night as we sat in the drawing room after dinner, Bea suddenly snuffed out a cigarette the count had just lit for her.

"It's so deadly dull," she complained. "Can't we liven it up?"

The count twitched at his moustache. "I suppose we

could roll up the carpets and dance. You do have a gramophone, don't you, Constance?"

Eric grumbled, "I can't dance. Not with this foot."

"Dance!" Bea suddenly sat up, alive, her dark eyes snapping. "Of course, a dance! A party! Champagne and music and dancing! Just the four of us.

"Four?" Eric said.

"We'll invite Mr. Seagram," Bea went on. "I'll go right up and fetch him. And Jean, get busy with the carpets. Eric can give you a hand. Never mind, you can get about with that crutch better than you let on. Constance, you see about the refreshments. Oh, what fun! Why hadn't I thought of it before?"

Somehow we all got caught up in her enthusiasm. I went out to the kitchen and told Mrs. Platte to put several bottles of champagne on ice. She grumbled something about drink and the devil, which I pretended I hadn't heard.

When I got back to the drawing room the carpets had already been rolled up and the furniture pushed against the wall. Eric, leaning on his crutches, was cranking at the gramophone, and a moment later a tune, loud and tinny, blared from the trumpet.

"Marvelous!" Bea cried, drawing the count up from his chair.

Eric, perched on top of the piano, kept time with his crutch. Leonard came in, smiling at me, at Bea and de Grasse as they swayed and dipped to a waltz.

Presently Jenny appeared with the champagne bucket, followed by Esther bearing a platter of sandwiches and another of cakes.

"Open the champagne, Eric," Bea begged. "Make yourself useful."

The cork popped like a pistol shot and we all laughed as we gathered round.

"A toast!" Bea cried, her eyes sparkling like the wine in her glass.

"To happiness!" the count cried, raising his glass.

"Here! Here!" Bea chimed in.

The champagne, acid and sweet, stung my nose and brought tears to my eyes. Of all the wines, champagne was my favorite.

"Finish the bottle," Eric said, splashing the remainder into my glass.

"Mr. Seagram," Bea cried, grasping his arm. "This dance is mine. Jean, *cheri,* put on another record.

She whisked Leonard off, laughing, nestling her head against his shoulder. I watched them, their bodies close, their feet following the music in perfect time. My face went hot. I sipped at the champagne. It had gone flat, but I drained my glass.

Suddenly there was a crash and the sound of breaking glass. "Damn!" Eric exclaimed. "Look what you've done with your galloping about. Upset my champagne."

"I didn't!" Bea protested.

"Never mind," I said, happy for the interruption, "there's plenty more."

Eric stumped over to the table where the sandwiches and champagne bucket had been left. A fresh bottle was opened, our glasses filled.

"What shall we drink to?" Bea asked, her jet eyes flecked with excitement. "Health and prosperity?"

"Money," said Eric, making a monkey face. "*That's* prosperity." He tossed off his glass and refilled it.

Bea fled to the gramophone which had run down to a baritone gargle.

Leonard turned to me. "Would you care to dance, Miss Woodhill?"

Would *I* care to dance? Would I care to float in a silken barge down the Nile, to reign over Camelot, to fly?

"Yes, thank you," I said, setting my glass on the table.

I stumbled over the edge of the rug as he guided me onto the bare floor and his hand tightened on my elbow. Well, I thought ruefully, what does it matter? He'll soon discover how clumsy I am.

But after a few awkward moments I was amazed to feel myself gliding smoothly, miraculously, effortlessly; those dreadful errant feet of mine following Leonard's with ease. He drew me closer and I felt the strength of his arm, the warmth of his body. And the world suddenly became a glorious kaleidoscope of color and light; the shabby ghost-ridden drawing room I had so disliked all my life, as if touched by a fairy wand, was transformed into an enchanted crystal ballroom, the tinny music singing like heavenly violins.

Round and round we went, alone, the two of us, faster and faster. The room reeled, candlelight and paneled walls whirling past. A dip, a swing, a pause at the table, a sip of champagne, and we were back on the golden merry-go-round again. I wanted our dance to go on forever. Did his lips touch my hair, brush my cheeks? Did he whisper *Constance, darling*? I heard myself laughing as I clung to him. Leonard was my joy, my love, my life. I was happy. I was giddy.

"You're drunk!" Bea's scornful voice announced.

When? How had the dance ended?

I was standing at the refreshment table, still swaying with the music. Gone were the colored lights, my dizzy rapture. Suddenly my stomach felt queasy, my limbs leaden.

"I don't feel very well," I said in a small voice, uncomfortably reminiscent of Alistair's.

Blurred white faces swam before my eyes.

"It's all my fault," I heard Leonard say. "Perhaps I should take Miss Woodhill up."

"No," Bea said. "I think I'd better."

I have no recollection of ascending the staircase, but I do remember Bea thrusting a nightdress over my head and saying, "I'm missing the party on account of you."

And then there was the cool pillow on my cheek and I slept.

I was sitting on the floor of the Long Gallery in my nightdress, cold and shivering. Sir Edward, bushy-browed and stern, leaned down from his portrait. "You've made an ass of yourself, Constance."

And Sir Ian smiled with lidded eyes. "Didn't think you had it in you, Constance. But as long as you are here, where is the map?"

"I don't know," I said. "I thought *you* did."

"Come now, Constance." Sir Ian descended and stood over me. "You know you are lying."

Bewildered, I said, "George took it. You see he was waltzing and he waltzed right into the library cupboard."

Sir Edward snorted. "In *my* house? What are all those strangers doing in my house?"

"You're a ghost," I said. "And I drank too much champagne. And you can have your house. I *hate* it."

Sir Ian took my hands and drew me to my feet. "Don't listen to him, Constance. You and I are friends." His hands gripped mine so tightly I could feel his nails. "Tell me where the map is hidden."

His face suddenly became the count's. "Don't touch me! Don't you ever dare touch me!"

"All right, darling Constance." And he wasn't the count anymore, but Sir Ian. "Come, sweet, show me where I can find the map."

I looked up into his eyes and he didn't seem at all like a man who had been hanged for murder. He was friendly, and, well—appealing.

"Shall we start with the attic? he said, putting his arm about my waist.

"I don't like the attic. I'm afraid of it. Trina Blake lives there."

"I won't let her harm you." He had a candle in his hand. Strange I hadn't noticed it before.

"Do you know Trina Blake?" I asked as we walked down the corridor.

"She is one of us."

"Am I dreaming, Sir Ian? Is this a dream?"

"Yes, Constance, sweet, it's a dream, but a lovely one."

"No. I want to go back to bed," I whimpered, suddenly frightened.

He drew me closer, his hand pressing into my waist. "There is nothing to be frightened of," he whispered in my ear. "Darling Constance."

Up we went, softly so as not to waken the others, up and up, the candlelight flickering along the walls.

He opened a door and we went into a room crowded with gray-sheeted furniture.

"Now," he said, turning to me. "Tell me where the map is." His eyes blazed in the flame's light like dark blue sapphires.

"I want to go back to bed," I begged tearfully.

He went to the window, unfastened the shutter and opened it. The night rushed in on the wind, dark and cold.

"Perhaps a little air will refresh your memory," he said, taking my hand and pulling me to the sill.

The wind beat against my face, billowing my nightdress, the cold washing over my body, freezing my heart.

I heard *her* then, cracking her knuckles, laughing, high, gleeful, triumphant.

And I awoke to find myself holding to the windowsill, the shadowed earth reeling far, far below my horrified eyes.

Chapter 10

"My God!"

Still clinging to the window's edge, I twisted my head. Eric, on crutches, stood in the open attic door, a lamp dangling by a ring from his fingers. "How in heaven's name did you get here?"

I was cold, trembling and horribly frightened. "I . . . I don't know," I said through chattering teeth.

"You might have fallen from that window!"

I closed my eyes and could not speak.

"I heard someone going past the door and I got up to see," Eric continued. "Thank God I did. You must have been walking in your sleep."

"A nightmare," I said. "I . . . I had a nightmare."

"If that's what champagne does to you, I don't think you ought to try it again."

"No." I opened my eyes. Eric was in his dressing gown. Even in my distress I thought to ask, "But how did you know I was *here?*"

"Just a guess. Are you all right? You're not going to faint, are you?"

I shook my head in the negative.

"Come, hold on to my belt and we'll go down. I wish I didn't have these blasted crutches."

He held out his hand, and suddenly disjointed, half-remembered phrases ran through my brain: *where there's smoke there's fire . . . I was going to help myself to a cigar . . . killed by someone looking for a map . . . strong on rumor, weak on fact. . . .*

"What is it, Constance? You'd better come along, you'll catch your death of cold."

"Yes," I said, suddenly aware of my bare feet, my nightdress.

When we reached the door to my room, Eric asked, "Have you done this sort of thing before?"

"No—never."

"Sometimes, they say, a tendency to sleepwalk runs in families. Does your mother have trouble with it?"

"No. Not that I know of. And certainly not Father."

In the morning my head seemed swollen to twice its size, tender and throbbing, while my tongue tasted of green brass. I wondered why I should feel so ill when, as I remembered, I had drunk only two glasses of champagne.

I remained in bed until late afternoon. Then, feeling considerably better, I got up, took a hot bath, and dressed. I was searching through my jewel box for a cameo brooch when I suddenly realized the piece of paper which held the combination to the library safe was missing. I had put the paper in the box for safekeeping, though the jewel box itself was never locked. Perhaps I had moved it, absentmindedly tucking it away in one of the bureau drawers? But no, I recalled seeing it only the day before when I had chosen to wear my pearls for dinner. Nevertheless, I went though my drawers one by one and then through the pockets of my skirts. The paper was nowhere to be found.

It had been stolen. When? How? During the night, most probably, when I was walking about in drunken sleep.

By now I had gone to the safe often enough to know how to open it from memory. Quickly, before the others assembled for tea in the drawing room, I went down to examine it. Again everything seemed to be in order. The money—to the last pound note—was all there. However, on going through the various documents, I discovered that the rough sheepskin plan of the house was gone.

Now why should anyone want a plan of the house?

The answer was stunningly simple. If I were searching for something—a map, for instance—wouldn't I want to know the layout of the house, whether or not there were secret rooms, hidden passageways?

George was gone now; I couldn't charge him with the theft of the safe combination and house plan. Had I mistakenly blamed him for prowling about, for trying to steal pictures, for hitting me over the head, too?

During tea I secretly observed the count, Bea and Eric. Leonard and the boys were there, too, a special treat for Gordon who had mastered his multiplication tables, and for Alistair who had written a poem which he recited to us now, his voice unnaturally high his small face flushed. I watched Leonard, his lips moving, prompting Alistair when he faltered.

My heart debated with my brain. Leonard? *No, not Leonard, never Leonard!*

But he knew there was a map, had read about in the newspapers. Yet, if he were the guilty party, would he have dared to suggest fetching the constable as he had done?

I did not think so.

There was more than enough reason to distrust the others. The count, on a previous occasion, had discouraged me from calling in the authorities. Bea had stolen the wine cellar key, and Eric wore a hidden gun, and needed money desperately.

It was terrible enough to have ghosts as enemies without feeling that flesh-and-blood people were in league against me, too. Which one? Not Leonard, I thought again, suddenly remembering that all the dreadful things which had happened began only after Bea and Eric had arrived at Rommany.

Eric? Bea? The count? Were they in collusion?

I wished with all my heart that there was a map, that I had it in my hand now. I would fling it among them—those three, sitting so nonchalantly about the room, Bea lazing on the sofa, Eric making patterns on the rug with his crutch, the count stroking his infernal moustache. Here, I would say, take it! Fight over it yourselves, but leave me in peace.

That night, feeling especially uneasy, I looked in at the boys. They were both asleep; Gordon, a frown between his eyes, Alistair, fair hair tousled, his thumb in his mouth. I kissed them lightly, my heart heavy with tenderness and concern. Should I write Mother and Father the truth? I thought for the dozenth time, closing the door behind me. What would I say?

Turning to go back to my room, the corner of my eye caught a wink of light at the far end of the corridor a second before it disappeared up the back staircase.

One of the maids on her way to bed?

It was past eleven and by now (unless there was some special occasion such as a dinner party) the servants had usually retired. Curious, I went down to the staircase. Above me I heard soft footsteps, climbing.

I set my lamp down. Then, on tiptoe, careful not to trod on a loose board, I ascended step by step until I reached the second-story landing. There, I waited in the darkness, listening. Instead of sounds of movement behind one of the doors, as I had expected, the footsteps continued upward to the attic floor.

Nothing—not my curiosity, not even a team of wild horses—could drag me up there. The maids had no reason, or little inclination to go wandering the upper reaches of the house late at night. I was pondering who it might be—the count or Bea (Eric's limp would have given him away)—when I suddenly realized that the footsteps were coming down again.

My heart fluttering, I turned and began to feel my way back along the dark stairs. I stumbled over a step, catching myself on the banister, and the footsteps behind me quickened. Clinging to the rail, afraid that I should fall in the dark, my eyes searching vainly for the lamp at the bottom, I descended as fast as I dared. When I had negotiated the last step, I did not pause to pick up the lamp (which, in fact, had gone out), but hurried to my room. Once there, I shut the door and shoved a heavy chair up under the knob.

Then I went and sat down on the bed. I was shaking from head to foot.

I knew then that I could not go on much longer fighting an unseen menace, wondering if my enemy was a phantom or real. Perhaps the whole object of these recent events was to frighten me from the house. But why not the servants? Why was I the one to be singled out?

I brooded for another half hour, then suddenly got to my feet. I had thought it through; I had to have someone to talk to. I would take Leonard into my confidence. He, unlike the others, seemed to have no connection with the unsettling occurrences at Rommany. And hadn't he offered his help, his protection?

I told him everything—how I believed someone was searching for the diamond mine map he had read about in the newspaper, how the combination to the safe had been taken, and why I suspected the count or the Hempsteads, or all three of stealing it. "So you see, it wasn't George, at all," I concluded.

"I wish you had spoken of this sooner, Constance."

"I didn't want to trouble you," I replied, conveniently forgetting that until very recently I hadn't trusted him either.

"Foolish," he chided, smiling. "As if it would be trouble. But—if we could only catch this person." He frowned, looking down at the floor. "Well—there's only one way to do it. I am going to stand guard tonight."

"But what if no one appears? What if everyone sleeps through?"

"If you are right, Constance, sooner or later someone—whoever—is going to commence prowling again. I'll simply keep watch every night until I nab him—or her."

"I can't allow you to do that."

"It's no longer a question of 'allowing' me. You don't expect me to ignore this sort of thing, do you?"

"No, I suppose not. And I *am* grateful. But you must be careful."

"Oh, I will be," he said grimly. "Never fear, I will be."

I awoke suddenly, feeling anxious, unsettled. Sitting up, tense, wide awake, my eyes probed the shadows beyond the night light.

Then I heard it. A soft groan just outside my door. I was out of bed in a flash, my hand on the knob, flinging the door open.

Leonard lay sprawled on the floor, blood flowing from a gash on his forehead.

Chapter 11

Leonard had not seen his assailant. He had been sitting on a chair outside my door and had managed to keep awake and alert a good part of the night. It must have been shortly after the clock in the great hall below chimed three that he dozed off. When he awoke, he had had just enough time to sense the presence of a dark shadow looming over him before he felt the numb impact of a crackling blow across his right temple.

I wanted to rouse the count (like all insomniacs, it never ceased to amaze me how the others could sleep through so snugly), and have him go to Tenwyck for the doctor. But Leonard persuaded me not to.

"A cold compress will do fine for the present. But I think this matter is out of my hands now. Tomorrow, early, I shall go call on the constable."

The next morning there was a nasty scene. Eric proposed the theory that the dismissed chauffeur, George, had been responsible for assaulting Leonard.

"He's angry because you gave him the sack, Constance. And he's sneaked back to take his revenge."

"Of all the ridiculous notions," I expostulated. "He'd have to be daft. No, I think it is someone here in the house."

We were at the breakfast table. No one spoke while Jenny poured the coffee. When she set the silver cream pitcher and sugar bowl on the table and left, Bea said, "I always thought the one with the squint looked suspicious."

"I hope you are not referring to Daisy," I said acidly. "She's been at Rommany ever since I was ten years old, and I'd sooner call myself a thief than accuse her of anything underhanded. No, it wasn't one of the servants."

There was a short, strained silence, while Bea glared at me. "So you suspect one of us?" she said, after a few moments.

"Yes." My face burned as I stared down at the tablecloth. But I was through extending polite hospitality to the Hempsteads and the count. Fear had purged me of conventional hypocrisy.

"I'll be damned!" Bea sprung to her feet. "I am leaving! I am getting out of this miserable house just as soon as I pack my things."

"Now, Bea," Eric placated.

"You don't expect me to stay in a house where I am suspected of petty thievery, and assault, do you?" She threw her napkin on the table.

"You can't leave," I said. "Nobody can leave until the constable has had a chance to speak to us. Mr. Seagram has gone to fetch him."

"The constable?" Bea cried. "You are out of your mind if you think I will submit to a cross-examination like a common criminal. I am *leaving!* Come along, Jean. And—Eric, I advise you not to say it."

"I shall say it, Bea!" Eric's voice shook. "When will you learn to control that vile temper of yours?"

"My vile temper, is it?" she shouted enraged, and lifting her coffee cup, hurled it at Eric. It missed him by a fraction of an inch, hitting the sideboard with the crash and tinkle of broken china. There was a moment of trembling silence. Then Eric reached across the table at her, his hand poised and unsteady.

"If you slap me," Bea warned, "I shall break every dish."

The count's face had turned very white. "Bea, darling—"

"Oh, shut up! You . . . you fop! Shut up!" And with that she stormed out of the room. The count rose to his feet reluctantly and followed her.

At ten Constable Smithers arrived, a fresh-faced young man with blue eyes and a dimpled smile.

"It was good of you to come," I said.

"Not at all. It's my duty, you know," he replied, standing very tall and looking impressive in his uniform. "No, thank you, miss," this to Jenny who had offered to take his hat.

Bea chose that moment to descend the stairs, trailed by Daisy staggering under a load of suitcases and boxes.

"Oh," I said, "this is Miss Hempstead."

"Smithers, John Smithers," he said, gazing at Bea, her face exquisite under a dashing jade-green velvet hat. "I'm sorry to hear you've had some unpleasantness at Rommany."

"Indeed," said Bea, responding to his smile as a budding flower might to the sun. "The tutor's been bashed over the head. But then, I expect he explained it all to you."

"He did, Miss Hempstead."

Leonard and I had agreed beforehand not to mention the complicated business of the map unless it seemed absolutely necessary. The important thing was that both Leonard and I had been attacked, and that whoever had been responsible was still at large.

"Perhaps," Constable Smithers said, still talking to Bea, "you would be kind enough to give me your view as to what has happened?"

"I shall be happy to," said Bea, taking his arm and leading him into the drawing room just as if calling in the constable had been her own idea.

Constable Smithers, for all his fascinated glances at Bea and his boyish smile, seemed to have a fairly competent head on his shoulders. His questions, though couched in polite, tactful terms, were penetrating and to the point.

But there was not much information he could elicit from us. No one had missed anything, jewels, clothing, or money. No one had heard any unusual noises during the night.

"Dead to the world," Eric said. "Embarrassing, but I never heard a murmur from Mr. Seagram."

"Miss Woodhill," Constable Smithers turned his direct blue eyes on me. "Does someone bear you a grudge? A resentful servant, perhaps?"

Eric, tapping his crutch on the floor for attention, said, "Yes, indeed. Now, Constance, I know you don't feel George had anything to do with last night's affair. But I disagree." Then giving me a quick, apologetic glance, he went on to tell the constable how George had been dismissed on suspicion of thievery.

"Suspicion?" the constable repeated, turning to me.

"We had no real proof," I said.

The constable consulted his knuckles. "At the risk of seeming tiresome, Miss Woodhill, can you tell me what this George was suspected of stealing?"

"A wine cellar key, for one," I said pointedly, not looking at Bea. "One of those seventeenth-century iron keys, with a large 'R'—"

"Wait!" Bea cried. "I've got that key, right here in my purse." Bea dug into her voluminous handbag, bringing out an assortment of handkerchiefs, a pocket mirror, a comb, her cigarette holder, a packet of cigarettes, a powder puff, and finally the key.

"Is this it?" she asked, holding it up triumphantly.

"Why . . . yes," I said.

"I found it on the terrace. I meant to ask you about it, Constance, but I forgot."

Was she speaking the truth? Bea was the sort who could tell a lie without batting an eyelash.

Eric said, "But there's the ten shillings taken from poor Alistair."

The constable removed a small notebook and a pencil from his inner pocket. "Ten shillings," he said, writing.

"But," I pointed out, "that hardly makes a case, does it, constable?" The interview was going off on a disappointing tangent.

"What about the paintings?" Eric demanded. "Someone tried to steal those. And I'll lay a wager it was that chauffeur. Surly fellow."

"Well, now," said Smithers, scribbling in his notebook. "What else can you tell me?"

"The combination to the safe," said Eric. "Constance claims that it was taken from her jewel box."

"*After* the chauffeur left," I said. I wondered why Eric had become so eager to pin the blame on George. "Besides, nothing was missing from the safe, except a plan of the house."

"Well, well," Smithers said, somewhat perplexed. "Why should an ordinary thief want that?"

There was a small silence. I could feel that the constable was growing a little impatient with us. Perhaps he wondered if he had been fetched all the way from Tenwyck for trivial reasons.

"The map," I said suddenly, catching and holding the constable's eye.

"What map?" chorused Bea and the count.

"Good heavens!" Eric exclaimed. "Constance, I must say. . . . Why, it's a fairy tale. A family joke."

"Oh, *that*," said Bea. "Really, Constance, you *are* losing touch."

Smithers, looking from one face to the other, said in a controlled, but polite tone, "Will someone have the kindness to explain this map to me?"

"Of course," Eric said. "Reputedly, there is a map of the site of a diamond mine to which my great-uncle and Miss Woodhill's grandfather *supposedly* each had a half interest. But the map has never been mentioned in either of their papers or wills. No one, to my knowledge, has ever seen it. We think the idea originated with Sir Duncan Blackmore. According to my mother, he was a great story-teller and loved to embellish his tales of personal adventure with all sorts of exaggerated fancies."

I stared at Eric. That was not how he had spoken when first broaching the subject of the map. "It could be worth a fortune," he had said.

Smithers drummed his fingers on his knee. "That's neither here nor there, is it? It doesn't seem that an outsider would have much knowledge of family . . . family jokes." His smile dimpled at us.

"But don't you see?" I protested. "If George had gone through the safe, he certainly would not have overlooked my mother's jewelry."

"You have a point there, young lady," the constable acceded. "But thieves sometimes shun personal jewelry, preferring to take money. There was money in the safe, I presume? And none of it gone? Well, then, perhaps our culprit didn't have the safe combination. Perhaps you have mislaid it, Miss Woodhill. Now, this George—what was his last name?"

"Perkins," I said resignedly. The constable was proving far less acute than I had first imagined him to be.

"Perkins's address?"

"I'm afraid I can't give that to you. When George left, Mr. Seagram took him to the station in Tenwyck."

"So I did," Leonard said, breaking a long silence. His face was pale, the beige plaster over his wound standing out in bold relief. "George didn't say much, only that he thought he'd go up to London and try to get employment there."

"Mmmm. Big place, London." Smithers turned to me. "His letter of reference—I assume he did have one—what name did it give as his former employer?"

"I don't know," I said, twisting the brooch at my throat. "My father hired him."

"And your father?"

"He and my mother are on holiday in Italy at present."

"I see. Perhaps you could write them? As it is, I have very little to go on." He tucked the notebook and pencil into his pocket. "Meanwhile I'll keep a sharp outlook for suspicious strangers. The fellow might still be in the neighborhood, though with the way Tenwyck's grown, it's hard to tell which is stranger or native anymore. Tenwyck isn't what it used to be." He spoke like an old codger looking back down the years.

"Come now, constable," Bea said flirtatiously, "how would you know? I daresay you aren't thirty yet."

The constable flushed and got to his feet. "You flatter me, Miss Hempstead." A small smile and an appreciative flash of the eye.

Then, turning to me, "If you should have any further problem, please let me know at once. I would suggest, however, that you change all your locks."

I saw the constable out into the hall. "Thank you for taking the trouble."

"That's my job," he said, looking around at the parqueted floor, the huge fireplace, the dark paneled walls. "Impressive place, Rommany."

"Yes," I agreed, and making one last try, added, "but you see, I don't believe it was George, nor any of the other servants. I think. . . ."

At that moment Bea came out of the drawing room.

Smithers nodded. "An outsider, a vagrant, perhaps?

You may have a point there. But stout locks will take care of him. Good morning, then."

"Good morning," Bea chimed, the smile vanishing from her face as soon as the door was closed.

She began to pull on her gloves, working the fingers in quick, capable movements.

"You're leaving, then?" I asked.

"Nothing's changed," she said. "You and I don't get along. Eric doesn't need me." And—as a last snide thrust—"Now you can have Mr. Seagram all to yourself."

"I hope," I said, my face hot with anger, though my voice was cold as ice, "you have left the wine cellar key."

"It's on the table. Are you coming, Jean?" And she swept past me, imperiously, the jade-green hat held high.

The count, who had been hovering in the background, paused at my side. "I am sorry—for everything," he said, taking my hand and pressing moist lips to it.

"Jean! Please don't dally."

Deflated and depressed, I climbed the stairs to my room. Sitting at the dressing table, I stared at the tired, despondent face in the mirror. Summoning the constable had been a pointless exercise. Bea and the count had gone, but they would have done so at any rate. And where did that leave me? Perhaps, I tried to cheer myself, Bea—and later de Grasse—had been responsible for all the frightening events of the past few weeks. Now that they had departed. . . .

But it was no use. In my heart I knew that I couldn't possibly be that lucky. Not me. Constance Woodhill. What had ever gone right for me? Those two years I had spent at the academy, my brief fling in London, had been only a respite. There was something here, in this house, which had willed my return, willed that I should remain.

God knew I did not want to believe in an omnipotent fate, some powerful, black doom. I wished I could snap my fingers at the thought and say, "Nonsense!" But I couldn't.

Leonard? He had called me Constance, had offered his protection. "It's only what a loyal servant would do," he had said. Loyal servant, I thought bitterly. Love was not for me. For others, for the slim, arrogant Beas of this world. But not for me.

Bathos. Self-pity. But I was too miserable to care. It hurt so terribly inside.

I did not hear the door open, but at the sound of a step behind me I looked up. And there in the mirror I saw Leonard.

"You're crying," he said.

I bit my lips and shook my head vigorously, unable to speak.

He brought me to my feet. "Please don't cry, Constance," he said softly.

A sob caught in my throat. I tried to swallow it.

Gently he took me into his arms and I wept, my face pressed to his heart.

"Constance," he whispered. His lips touched my hair, my cheek. He lifted my head and I thought how ugly I must look with my face all blotched with crying.

"Leonard, I'm sorry—"

But his mouth was on mine and the breath went out of me. So this is how it feels to be *really* kissed, I thought. And the next instant all thought fled as I gave myself up to the moment, buoyantly, recklessly.

He was pushing me away, his hands digging into my arms. "I'm sorry, Constance. I didn't mean to . . . I—"

"No, Leonard," I protested. "No. I *wanted* you to kiss me. For the longest time. I love you. I do. I love you!"

He drew me close again, resting my head on his shoulder, stroking my hair. Neither of us spoke.

"How strange life is," Leonard said at last. "I never planned to fall in love, but I did. I think it happened the moment I saw you sitting so primly in the library. 'And what are your qualifications, Mr. Seagram?' You said. Do you remember, darling?"

I nodded mutely. *Darling, darling, darling.* Was it all true?

"But"—he held me at arm's length again and shook his head—"it's no good, Constance. I presume too much. I'm only a tutor and I expect I shall never be more."

"I don't care!" I cried. "I don't care. It doesn't matter. Mother fell in love with a farmer's son."

"Contance, that was different. He's a famous man. He's—"

"And so you shall be. You're a superb teacher. You could easily be a headmaster."

"Ah, Constance," he chided.

"Why can't you see it, then? Does it matter if you are always a tutor? It doesn't to me."

"I have my pride."

"And I love you for it, Leonard," I exclaimed, flinging my arms about his neck, "love you."

A tap on the door sprung us apart.

"Oh! I beg your pardon." Eric's face screwed up in a wry smile. "I had no idea I was intruding."

"It's quite all right," I murmured, uncomfortable, mortified. How long had he been at the door?

Leonard, his face tense, said, "I've just asked Constance to marry me."

"Leonard ... you ..." I was astonished, deliriously happy, then curiously deflated. It was not the sort of proposal I had anticipated, and in the back of my mind I wondered if Leonard had been forced to make it because he felt I had been compromised. But wasn't that just like me—to temper happiness with some dark, suspicious thought?

I smiled at Eric. "I'm so happy."

"Congratulations," he offered dryly. "But isn't this rather sudden?"

"Not at all," Leonard replied stiffly. "We've been fond of one another for some time. And now, if you will excuse me, Constance?"

"You needn't go on my account," Eric said. "I simply wanted to inform Constance that Bea and the count have returned."

"*Returned?*"

"They have decided to stay the night. The weather's turned ugly. It looks like rain, and the count doesn't like to drive on wet roads."

"They're welcome, of course," I said. "But it will be awkward. Bea left in such a huff."

"That's Bea," Eric said. "But she gets over things quickly."

"I'm not so sure."

Leonard said, "I really must be going back to the boys."

Eric stood aside as Leonard went through the door.

"Handsome devil, or have I already said that?" Eric wrinkled his nose. "Are you in love with him?"

"Madly."

"Madly," he pondered. "Your engagement will come as a surprise to the others."

"Please, Eric. I'd rather you wouldn't tell them just yet."

"Oh?" There was a faint sarcastic nuance to his voice, and it annoyed me.

"I'd like to wait until I have written to Father and Mother. Surely they should know before I make any public announcements, don't you think?"

"Quite right. But I don't fancy they'll be overjoyed at the news."

"Why not?" I demanded acidly. "Because Leonard is a tutor?"

"No. Because you've known him only a short time."

"It isn't true!" I retorted hotly, hurling the classic cry of all lovers at him, "I feel as if I've known him all my life."

The rain came a half hour later, a dark, heavy downpour, the sort of rain that gave promise of lasting for hours and hours. I hoped not. Bea's presence at Rommany was like a thorn in my side.

I spent the rest of the afternoon in the library, making work for myself, determined to avoid Bea at all costs. But as time passed and the dinner hour approached, I began to get hungry; and with hunger came a slow, burning anger. It was galling and humiliating to feel that I had to hide from Bea in my own home. I was definitely not going to have my evening meal on a tray as planned earlier. Why should I?

So I went upstairs, changed my blouse and skirt to a dress, recombed my hair and went down to the dining room with a frozen smile on my face.

Bea ignored me completely, chattering first to the count and then to Eric. The men tried to draw me into conversation, but Bea was too quick for them and would invariably interrupt whenever they tried to speak. Her manners had always been offhand, a sophisticated glossing over of convention which would have startled Grandmama, I'm sure, but on this night her rudeness was even more pronounced than usual. My dislike of her hardened.

I ate little, pushing my food from one side of the plate

to the other, vowing that if Bea was not gone by morning, rain or no rain, I would order her to leave. At last the interminable meal drew to an end. The moment I finished my coffee I dropped my napkin and rose to my feet.

"Constance," Eric said, reaching for his crutch.

"Don't bother to get up," I said. "I'll be all right."

I went upstairs, hesitated at my door, and then moved down the corridor to the schoolroom. Leonard and the boys had just finished supper and Leonard was reading to them from *Gulliver's Travels* before putting them to bed.

"May I come in?"

"Please." Leonard smiled. "We are in Lilliput at the moment."

"Yes," Alistair said. "Do go on, Mr. Seagram."

I sat down on a chair by the window and watched them—three heads: one fair, one dark, one the color of polished mahogany—bending over the book under the lamplight. Strange, yet beautiful the way Leonard's hair changed color with the angle and quality of light: russet, gold, dark copper.

He is good with them, I thought, good with children. He will be good with ours. And my mind slipped away from the present; from Bea's rudeness, my fears and uncertainties, and drifted into the future.

We would not live at Rommany, of course. Leonard, once he was married, could get a position at a good school that much easier. Somewhere near London. A suburb, perhaps. Wimbledon? We would have a small cottage on the school grounds, and later when Leonard was promoted to assistant headmaster and then headmaster, a larger place. We would. . . .

I was so deep in my picture I hadn't noticed that the reading was over and that Gordon stood beside me until he spoke. "Mr. Seagram has promised to take us to a puppet show in Tenwyck if we get our lessons done early."

"That sounds like fun," I said.

"Well, good night, then, Constance."

"Good night," I said. He leaned up and kissed my cheek. Alistair did the same. They went out the door together, whispering to one another. Alistair laughed.

"You haven't said anything to them?" I asked anxiously.

"No," Leonard replied. "I thought you'd want to do that in your own time, my love."

My love! Would I ever get accustomed to that?

"You did mean it when you told Eric," I began nervously, rising to my feet.

"That I want to marry you? Nothing would make me happier. Your parents—"

"Oh—I *know* I can convince them." Why not? Hadn't Mother tried to pair me off with that awful Talbot fellow? And Leonard was so superior to him.

He took me in his arms and kissed me—a long, lingering kiss. "How was dinner?" he murmured in my hair.

"Terrible. Bea was impossible."

"Perhaps I ought to sit up again tonight—just in case."

"You think it might be Bea or the count who attacked us?"

"Possibly." He absentmindedly smoothed the collar of my blouse with strong, well-shaped hands. "You know, Constance, I've been going over in my mind what Constable Smithers said this morning. It *could* be George, you know."

"But George is gone."

"To all intents and purposes, yes. But do you realize what a huge house Rommany is, how many places there are to hide? Why, half of it is never used, hasn't been, from what I have noticed, for years. And there are the stables, the garage."

"Perhaps we ought to make a search," I said halfheartedly. The unknown portions of Rommany, like the attic and the Long Gallery, filled me with a sense of dread.

"That was my idea, too. Tomorrow, as soon as it is light. In the meanwhile, I'm definitely going to station myself outside your door tonight."

"But you've already missed so much sleep. And your head," I protested. His face was so very pale, and there were great dark bruises under his eyes. "I can barricade myself in my room and be perfectly safe."

"No, I shall feel uneasy unless I do. I'll have a short nap now. You can wake me up just before you go to bed. All right?" He kissed me lightly on the forehead.

"All right," I promised.

About an hour later, having finished my book, I decided

to go down to the library and fetch another one. The library door was slightly ajar, and I hesitated, for I had no wish to encounter Bea.

Peeking through the crack, I saw Eric sitting on a chair, his profile to me. There didn't seem to be anyone else in the room and as if to confirm my guess, I heard Bea's laugh a moment later coming from the drawing room.

I had my hand on the door knob when I saw Eric bend over and slip the cast from his foot as easily as a slipper.

And then, before I could turn the knob, he got to his feet and walked—*walked*—without his crutches, without the slightest sign of a limp, toward the desk.

Chapter 12

"The country air," he had said. Eric had come to Rommany to heal his foot—a foot as sound and as whole as my own.

Those rumors, the gun, the time I had caught him searching the desk, and now this.

I hadn't the courage to face him alone, not then. With a dry throat, I backed away and quietly, quickly made for the stairs. I hurried along to Leonard's room and knocked on his door. When there was no answer I opened it.

His bed was turned down, lamplight falling across the pillows. "Leonard?"

I peered round the edge of the door. The wardrobe hung open, revealing several shirts—no more. Leonard, I recalled, had only the one suit. His jacket was flung carelessly over a chair, and on the ponderous, claw-legged bureau were hairbrushes, a bottle of shaving cream, a comb. A bookshelf in one corner held a dozen books. All very spare, very neat—very masculine.

He was not in the boys' room or the schoolroom, now dark, smelling of dusty chalk and echoing to the sound of drumming rain.

Frowning, I closed the door. He was probably searching the house for George. He must have sensed my reluctance to join him and decided not to wait until morning. I returned to his room, scribbled a hurried note to warn him about Eric, and left it on the bureau, fully intending to return in an hour and explain in more detail.

But I fell asleep sitting in the chair in my room, and when I awoke a thrush was twittering on the window ledge outside, and the sky above the treetops glimmered with the first coral-tinted light of morning. My head ached and my throat burned with thirst. Puzzled, dismayed, I rose and stumbled across the room to the water pitcher. It was empty. I dimly recalled having drained it the night before. What had I eaten at dinner to give me such a raging thirst, I wondered. And how was it that I had slept through the night, something I hadn't done since I was at the academy? It was as if I had drunk too much champagne again.

Too much champagne. Exactly. The large head, the thick tongue, the awful taste in my mouth. Strange.

I sniffed at the pitcher. Was there a faint spicy smell? Turning the pitcher upside-down, I shook out a few drops on the palm of my hand. It didn't seem to have any taste other than the usual strong mineral one. Perhaps I was coming down with a chill—I felt miserable enough.

I inched the door open a crack and peeked out. The corridor was empty. I wondered if Leonard had decided not to remain awake outside my room, after all. It was still too early to tap on his door, and feeling that my note was sufficiently explicit to put him on guard against Eric, I removed my shoes and without undressing, crawled into bed. Sleep came to me at once.

When Jenny entered with the tea tray, my eyes fluttered open. I must have had some sort of conversation with her, but all my numb brain could grasp was the news that Bea and the count had left Rommany—I was too tired to care and dropped off to sleep again.

At noon I awoke to a knock on the door.

"Constance?" Leonard spoke.

"Yes." I sat up with a start, my head reeling. "Just a moment." I smoothed my rumpled skirt and tucked in my blouse as I went to the door.

"We're off to the puppet show," Leonard said, "Aren't you coming with us?"

"I'd like to, but ... but I've I've got a bad head this morning."

"Oh, I'm sorry, darling." He leaned down and kissed my forehead tenderly. "Is there something I can do?"

"No, no. I'll take a headache powder and I'll be all right. Did you find my note?"

"What note?" he asked, coming into the room.

"A note on your bureau about Eric." He shook his head. "I wrote it last night. Eric—there isn't anything wrong with his foot. I saw him *walking* on it, down in the library."

Leonard frowned. "Does he know that you know?"

"No. But don't you see? He must be the one who's been prowling around. Why else would he pretend to be lame?"

"I wonder if there could be two of them?" Leonard said, more to himself than to me.

"I don't get your meaning."

His frown deepened and he shook his head. "Puzzling, very puzzling. Last night when I made a search of the house I found a crumpled cigarette box in one of the rooms. Does your father smoke?"

"Cigars. Only cigars."

"And Mr. Hempstead? Eric?"

"He doesn't smoke. At least I've never seen him," I added, remembering that he had claimed to be searching for a match when I had come upon him in the library. "What about Bea?"

"No, she fancies a different brand. Turkish. And the count, I've noticed, abstains."

"Do you think George might be hiding here, then?"

"I don't know." He took my hand. "Look, I think I'd better not go on this outing today."

"But the boys will be so disappointed," I said, feeling noble and uncomfortable at the same time. Noble because of my insistence, uncomfortable because I honestly didn't feel like going.

"It's the maids' free day, also," Leonard pointed out. "They've asked me to drive them into Tenwyck when I take the boys, which means that, except for Mrs. Platte, you would be alone. Either I must remain or you must come with us."

"There shan't be enough room for me anyway."

"We can double up. Constance, I simply can't leave you here alone."

"I'll stay close to Mrs. Platte in the kitchen, then. She's a formidable creature."

He twisted a strand of my loosened hair around his finger and smiled. "Not half as formidable as you," he

376

teased. He kissed the tip of my nose, then frowned again. "I have an idea. Suppose I drive them all in the Daimler. I'll get Jenny to escort the boys to the puppet show—you can give her an extra day off—then I'll hurry back here. Perhaps by the time they are ready to be fetched, you will feel well enough to go into Tenwyck with me.

"All right," I said. It was good to have someone strong, someone I loved worry and fuss over me.

"But," he shook his finger, "while I'm gone I want you to give me your solemn word you will stay in this room until I return."

"I can't do that."

"Why not?" he demanded.

I blushed. "There's the water closet."

He smiled. "I can stretch a point. But take care, Constance." He kissed my cheek and held me for a moment. "I'll hurry back."

After Leonard had gone, I slipped out of my wrinkled skirt and blouse and looked in the mirror. A white face and dark circles under the eyes—but how those eyes shone! Why, I thought, you actually look pretty, Constance. Is that what loves does to a woman?

And my headache had suddenly vanished too. Perhaps I ought to go with Leonard after all.

But then I heard the boys racing down the corridor, laughing and shouting to one another and I changed my mind. Why not let things be as they were? Leonard would return within the hour. I could manage until then.

Strange when I think of it, how I felt so little fear at being left alone in the house with Eric. But love and the glow I moved in seemed—at the time—the only protection I needed.

When I had changed my clothes and completed my toilette, I sat down to write a letter to Father and Mother. Presently my stomach began to growl and grumble. I had eaten nothing since dinner the night before—and very little of that—and I suddenly realized I was famished. Leonard had made me promise I would not leave my room, but what harm would it do to steal down to the kitchen? Mrs. Platte would be there, and if I felt uneasy, I could ask her to come upstairs with me, or I could keep her company until Leonard's return.

The house was oppressively silent as I crept along the corridor. I paused for a moment at Eric's door and put my ear to the panel. Nothing. He was probably in the drawing room or the library. Or taking a stroll in the garden. Crutches, indeed!

The kitchen was empty. The scoured pots gleamed on their hooks above the iron range, the clock ticked noisily on the shelf. In the pantry I found cheese and bread and sausage. I cut generous slabs of each and ate with my fingers, staring at a row of preserved pickles and crabapples, feeling much like a child raiding the biscuit box. When I had eaten my fill, I washed it all down with a jug of milk. My stomach full, I felt infinitely better.

Walking softly I went through a baize door and down a short passage to Mrs. Platte's room. Her door was partially open and I could see her on the bed, her eyes closed, her mouth hanging loose. She was napping.

Back across the great hall I went, keeping to the scattered carpets which muffled my footsteps. I had my hand on the carved post of the staircase when the weighty silence was broken.

"Constance!"

I whirled about.

Eric, leaning on his crutches, was standing at the library door. "You can come out of hiding now," he said in a bantering tone. "Bea and the count have gone."

I looked at him, one lock of lank hair falling over his forehead, a sardonic smile on his face and I still was not afraid. I was angry.

"Why didn't you go with them?" I asked.

"What? Tired of my company, are you?" He gave me a crooked smile.

"The question is," I said acidly, "whether or not our country air has healed your foot yet."

"As a matter of fact, it's on the mend. I can feel it, bones knitting beautifully, just as they should."

"You are a fraud," I said. "There's not a thing wrong with your foot. I *hate* frauds. You came here—"

"Now, wait a minute, Constance."

"No. I shan't wait!" To think that I had gone out of my way to be polite to the Hempsteads, suffered Bea's insults, the count's lascivious glances, and now Eric, posing as an invalid, speaking calmly of bones knitting; *lying!* "You can walk as well as I. *I saw you!* So throw away those *silly* crutches, and pack your bag and leave."

He stared at me for a few moments, and then let his crutches fall to the floor.

"All right," he said in a cold voice. "But first there is something I want to say."

"Save your breath, you . . . you lout!"

He started toward me. Hampered by his cast, he kicked it off impatiently.

"Now, now," I chided sarcastically. "You must remember your poor foot. You will need it to get you back to London."

"I'm not going," he said. "Why do you think I came to Rommany in the first place, you little fool?"

"Don't call me a fool! I know why you came. You came for a map. You believe in that ridiculous legend. And you think the map is here, and you—"

"Will you hold that infernal tongue of yours?" he shouted.

He was standing over me now, barring the staircase, his face red with fury. Looking up at that enraged countenance, my own anger drained. I saw everything, then, in those incensed eyes: Eric unable to pay his debts, Eric frustrated, Eric blackmailed, Eric desperate, Eric a *murderer!*

Fear shot through me like a flame. I turned abruptly and fled across the hall toward the kitchen. As I ran I heard Eric behind me, and with a new rush of horror remembered the gun he wore. My back was a perfect target and in my terror-stricken mind it seemed I could already hear the explosion and feel hot, searing pain as the bullet slammed into my spine.

The dining room door. I flung it open and banged it shut after me. No key, no way to lock it. My breath came in moaning gasps as I dragged a heavy chair from the table and shoved it under the knob. Then I stumbled through to the kitchen, racing across it to the green baize door.

"Mrs. Platte!" I shouted. "Mrs. Platte!"

He wouldn't dare kill us both, would he?

She was still sleeping. I rushed up to the bed and took her by the shoulder, shaking her. "Mrs. Platte!"

Her head rolled limply to one side. I shrank back in dumbfounded horror.

Blood had oozed from a wound beneath her iron-gray hair, a dried, rust-colored trickle. I reached out with a trembling, tentative hand and touched her cheek. It was as cold as ice. She was dead.

"Mrs. Platte," I whispered, choking on a sob. "Oh, God!"

From the direction of the dining room I heard the sound of crashing furniture and was instantly alert.

Eric!

I dashed through the door and down the passage to the back staircase.

"Constance—wait! Damn you, wait!"

The stairs flew under my feet. As I climbed, my break-neck pace slackened. The staircase had suddenly become steep as a mountain. Staggering up to the landing, I grasped the newel post, my breath labored, my mouth dry.

Flinging a backward glance over my shoulder, I saw Eric at the bottom step, removing his other shoe.

Ought I to run to my room? No, that was the first place he would look. And a chair at the knob would be no barrier to him.

Hide! I must hide, quickly!

With cold, shaking fingers I removed my own shoes, shoved them to one side in the shadow of a door, and started up the next flight. I went more slowly, trying to muffle my footsteps, taking one step at a time. A board squeaked, sending the blood humming in my ears. There were thirty steps, each one an indelible mark on my memory. Thirty steep, impossible steps.

But I made it to the top, and there, quivering with fear and exhaustion, I paused. From below I heard the sound of fists pounding on wood.

"Constance! Open your door!" Eric shouted.

My ruse had succeeded—for a while.

God, dear God, if only I could delay him until Leonard returned.

One of the maid's rooms. Esther's, Jenny's. It didn't matter. I drew open the first door and closing it soundlessly behind me, I tiptoed to the wardrobe. It was too shallow. And there weren't enough clothes—two dresses, two uniforms and a starched petticoat on a peg—to conceal me.

My eyes darted this way and that, taking in the narrow bed, the washstand, the small three-drawer bureau, the faded curtains at the window. Not even a child could hide here.

In the corridor, again, I hesitated. Then, moving cautiously to the staircase, I peered over the banister.

"Constance! Are you up there?" And footsteps began to mount the stairs.

My heart went wild with fear. Eric had killed Mrs. Platte. There was no question in my mind that he would kill me, too. I turned blindly—reason, the need to plan, caution, everything thrown to the winds, forgotten in panic, in the terrible, all consuming urgency to flee.

I was climbing again, up and up into the shadowed reaches of the house, the dread, haunted attic. But at that moment I would have fled into the very jaws of hell.

Once more the stairs became a never-ending ladder, each step a torment, a ragged pain jabbing at my side. Shadows mocked me, tore at my hair, at my skirts. Tears blurred my eyes, and I sobbed as I panted upward.

I stumbled and a swarm of black dots whirled and danced round my head. I fought through them. Still the staircase went on. And on. And on. Would it never end?

And suddenly—so abruptly, I did not have time to realize I was falling—I was down on my knees, hands grappling at the smooth, dusty floor. I had come to the top of the stairs.

Dimness and the smell of dust washed over me. Trembling, my head hanging forward like a winded dog's, I listened to the breath whistle through my nose. Beads of sweat, mingled with silent tears, rolled down my cheeks. I was exhausted, finished.

"Constance! Are you mad?"

I was on my feet again, running into the dark shadows, fleeing down a long door-flanked tunnel into the heart of my worst, most terrifying nightmare.

A doorknob came under my hand. I twisted and tugged at it and a moment later rushed through, slamming the door behind. I pressed my back against the wood, shoulders sagging, and brushed the hair from my eyes with a gritty hand. Through a red mist I saw thin, slitted light falling over a broken chair and a trunk—the iron-hasped trunk of long ago.

And then my brain—clouded until now by blind impulse—cleared and I saw with cold brilliance how I had committed a disastrous folly. Unnerved, rash, thoughtless, I had played into the hands of fate—the fate Rommany had designed for me.

I had come to this room; the room which held the very essence of ghost-haunted Rommany, the room Rommany claimed as its own. I was trapped. There was no other place to run. Death, rot, decay, pain, unhappiness, tragedy; the aura of past centuries held me prisoner.

Behind me the door shook. "Constance!"

Feeble, spent, I turned and backed away, back and back until I felt the trunk against my legs.

The door opened. Eric, white and disheveled, breathing heavily, stared at me across the narrow space which divided us.

"Don't touch me," I whispered hoarsely.

"You fool!" he cried, coming into the room.

"Don't touch me, or . . . or I . . . I'll. . . ."

What? Beat him? Fell him with one blow of my useless, dangling hands? Call upon the ghost of Trina Blake to defend me?

Mad. Ludicrous. Terrible. I began to laugh and cry, crazy, shrill laughter mingled with wrenching sobs. Eric took hold of my shoulder and shook me. His nails dug into my arms and I laughed and sobbed all the more, my heart near to bursting with terror.

"I could kill you!" he shouted.

"Kill me, then, and be done with it!" I cried, my teeth rattling in my head.

The door slammed against the inner wall, shivering the floor boards and Eric dropped his hands.

And through my tears, I saw Leonard standing in the doorway.

"Leonard," I gasped in a croaking voice. "Leonard! Thank God you're here!"

Chapter 13

I ran to him, arms outstretched, only to be met by a face set in stone.

"So—the both of you are squabbling," Leonard said coldly, pushing me aside.

"Squabbling?" I cried in disbelief. That awful flight in fear and heart-catching breathlessness through the dining room and kitchen, and up three steep, agonizing staircases with Eric close at my heels. And Mrs. Platte, her cold, gray forehead oozing dried blood, dead. "*Squabbling?* Oh, darling, you did not think Eric and I. . . ." I could not go on.

"Fighting, then," Leonard said impatiently. "You and Eric fighting over the map."

"The map!" I exclaimed. "But, dearest, you know that I don't believe in the map."

"Come now, Constance, you know you are lying."

You know you are lying. Where had I heard those words before, exactly phrased, exactly intoned? Stupified, bewildered, I could only stare at him.

"You've had a falling out with Eric," Leonard continued relentlessly, "or he has had one with you, and you each want the whole map."

Eric took a step forward. "Look here, my good fellow—"

"I am not your good fellow," Leonard sneered. He reached in his pocket and drew out a revolver. "Shock you, does it, Constance, my love? Don't come any closer, Mr. Hempstead."

Eric stiffened and said nothing. His face had gone very white.

"Now," Leonard smiled, pointing the gun, first at me, then at Eric. "I want that map—the two halves."

"Leonard, darling," I said, bright, falsely cheerful, trying to make sense of a baffling situation, "you must be joking."

"I am not joking." His eyes were the color of cold steel. I had never seen them so blue. "And I wish you would leave off that sickening 'darling.' "

The smile froze on my face. "But you *have* to be joking," I insisted through dry lips. "You said you loved me, you wanted . . . you wanted. . . ." Dear God, make him say it's all a game. "There . . . there must be some mistake."

"No mistake," Leonard said.

"You said you loved me!" I repeated, shamed, desperate, in pain. "You said you wanted to marry me!" I could believe he was a thief, a traitor, an impostor—anything but that he did not care.

"Marry you?" he asked with a mocking twist to his lips. "You are a bit too long in the tooth for my fancy."

I wanted to die. I wished, I prayed that I could. "Then . . . everything you said . . . every word was a lie?" I pleaded, begging for one crumb, one bright morsel to salvage my pride.

"You are a nice girl—and brainy," he said, throwing me the sop I craved. "More so than your friends. It was you who had me worried the most, but—marry you? You are simply not my cup of tea."

"You are despicable!" I cried, raising a clenched fist, wanting to strike him.

Leonard twitched the gun half an inch in my direction. "Don't move," he said, narrowing his eyes. "I won't feel the slightest compunction in using this."

Eric, his face expressionless, his eyes never leaving Leonard's face, said, "Do as he says, Constance."

"Precisely," Leonard agreed. "And now. Where is the map?"

I stared at him, thinking how in a few short minutes worship can turn sour, love turn to hate. His betrayal over the map did not hurt half as much as his denigrating "too long in the tooth." For that I could have killed him.

"And so it has been you, all along." I said bitterly, "prowling about at night, going through the library desk, the safe."

"Me," said Leonard.

Eric said, "I guessed it might be you. But I couldn't be sure. And then, when you were knocked unconscious . . ."

"Clever, wasn't it?" Leonard's lip curled. "Just a scratch on the forehead—self-inflicted, of course."

"Very clever," Eric said quietly.

I turned on him. "How can you stand there and compliment that . . . that blackguard? Mrs. Platte . . . Mrs. Platte is dead, murdered in her bed—did you know that?"

A muscle moved in Eric's cheek, but he did not speak.

"And *he* did it!" I had forgotten completely for the moment that I had blamed Eric for the cook's death only a short while earlier. "What are you going to do about it?"

Eric did not turn a hair. "One does not argue with a gun, Constance."

Leonard smiled, a cruel catlike smile. "I didn't mean to kill her, but she saw me come in through the service entrance and I did not want anyone to know I was here, so I tapped her on the head with the butt—rather more vigorously than planned, I'm afraid. But that hardly matters now. What does, is that I am growing impatient. I've waited a long, long time."

"How long?" Eric asked. "How long have you known of this—this supposed map?"

"All my life," Leonard answered. "Astonishes both of you, I can see." He glanced around, at the ceiling, the walls and smiled to himself. "By right this room—all of Rommany—is mine. Yes, mine, dear cousin Constance."

"Cousin?" Was he mad?

"My grandfather was Sir Ian Blackmore. His picture is in the Long Gallery, if you remember. Don't you see the resemblance?" He paused, looking at me with contempt and amusement.

"I don't believe you," I said in a choking voice.

"Observe closely, love." And he lifted his head.

The nose, the chin, the way his hair fell over his forehead. How could I have missed it?

"So you see, I am more than your lowly tutor."

Suddenly, I found myself trembling. "And your mother?" I asked.

"The name she went by before she married my father was Trina Blake."

I closed my eyes. Somehow, someday, I had always known she would find a way to get at me. Trina Blake, cracking her knuckles in the quiet of the night, her invisible skirts rustling in the hush of a darkened room. Trina Blake, laughing in exultation as I clung drunk, stupefied with terror, to the windowsill.

"The champagne," I said, opening my eyes. "You drugged the champagne."

"I thought that by doing so I could persuade you to show me the map's hiding place."

The dream, the nightmare. Sir Ian leading me down the dark corridor and up the stairs. Not Sir Ian. Leonard.

"Is that why your mother, this—this Trina Blake, came to Rommany, also?" I asked. "To look for the map?" She is still here, I thought, still greedy for it. Even now she might be hovering in a cobwebbed corner, watching with deep-socketed ghostly eyes, watching and waiting.

"She failed, I am sorry to say. She relied too heavily on the mumbo-jumbo of sorcery. Not to mention her compelling need for vengeance."

"Against the Blackmores?"

"And the Hempsteads." Then, rather pridefully, "She arranged for Harold Hempstead to be run down by a carriage."

Eric seemed to flinch. "And my father," he asked. "Did she kill him, too?"

"Mother went to see him just before she died and begged him for the map. He laughed at her."

Pain, death, murder, tossed off in a phrase, a sentence or two. Cold people, cold hearts.

"She must have killed Clara Grimes," I said.

"Clara Grimes?"

"A servant girl who worked here when your mother came to visit one summer."

"Ah, yes, I do recall Mother speaking of a servant. Seems the girl was going to run to the bishop with a story about witches. Mother had to slip a few grains of arsenic into her tea. But what does it matter? That's all in the past. I am more single-minded. I simply want the map. And I mean to have it. Now, tell me where it is, if you please."

Color had tinged Eric's cheeks, but he spoke calmly. "People have died for that map. Can't you see that if it existed, the map would have been put to use by now?"

"I don't follow your logic, my dear Mr. Hempstead. The fact that men have been willing to die for it proves its value."

Eric, his face expressionless, said, "Your mother did not kill my father—*you* did."

"He would not give me his half of the map. A stubborn man."

"Why?" I exploded angrily, momentarily forgetting my fear. "Why did you kill Benjamin? As ... as decent, as kind a man as there could possibly be. Why? For what? A piece of paper?"

"Yes," he snarled, "a piece of paper. My ticket to respectability, to ease, to freedom. Do you think I *enjoy* the horrible, polite meanness I've lived with, the misery of penny pinching all my life? My father drank himself to death on cheap gin, and my mother died for want of proper medical care. Yes and yes and yes! I would kill many times over. Your great-grandfather cheated mine out of a bride, and your grandfather Duncan had mine hanged so that he could have this house."

"He didn't! He did no such thing. Sir Ian was executed for murder and my grandfather inherited—"

But Leonard was not listening. "The map should be mine, and it shall be."

Eric said, "There is no map."

Leonard's eyes blazed. "My patience has run out. You can't think I've gone through so much—the years of planning, waiting for my chance, riding herd on those beastly brats, injuring myself—all for *nothing*? Liars, both of you! Cheats! Doing me out of what is mine, because I didn't go to the right school, don't wear the right tie."

His hand, the one holding the gun, began to shake. I stared at it, hypnotized. One twitch of the finger. . . .

"All right," Eric said, still in the same unruffled voice. "Just point that thing somewhere else and I'll tell you."

"None of that. I don't trust you."

"But if you kill us now, you will never know."

Leonard swallowed and steadied the gun with his other hand. "The gun stays where it is. And if you do not speak, I shall shoot Constance first."

So much for kisses, for rapture, for love. This man—who I had given my heart to, who had meant everything to me—would shoot, snuff my life out as casually as he would a candle flame. It was bitter—bitter and frightening.

"Have it your way," Eric said. "You win. Both halves of the map are in this trunk."

Leonard twitched the gun. "A bald-faced lie! I have already searched the trunk."

"There is a false bottom."

Leonard sneered. "You're lying."

"No, see for yourself."

"I shan't move. *You* get the map. And if it's a trick, my dear cousin here will have to answer for it."

"Very well," Eric said. "Stand aside, Constance."

What happened next happened so quickly I could scarcely believe my eyes.

Eric half turned, grabbed the broken chair and hurled it full at Leonard's face. The gun went off, exploding, filling the room with shattering sound and the smell of death.

I couldn't look. I didn't want to. Nevertheless, my eyes flew open and I stood there, frozen, petrified. Eric had jumped at Leonard's throat, grappling with him, trying to wrest the gun from his hand. Arms and fists flew as both men fell with a loud thump to the floor, grunting and cursing, rolling over and over in the dust.

Frightened, helpless, clasping and unclasping my hands, I could only watch as Leonard, swearing and sweating, pinned Eric beneath him.

"You ... you thought you could get the best of me," Leonard panted.

The gun lay on the floor, barely out of arm's reach from Leonard. I sidled along the wall and kicked it away from his groping fingers. Before I could stoop to retrieve it, Leonard caught hold of my skirt.

"You bitch!" he muttered between gritted teeth, pulling

me, grasping my ankle with fingers of steel. "I'll break your damn leg!"

Eric, taking advantage of Leonard's momentary lapse, brought his fist up and cracked Leonard on the chin.

Again they went rolling, knocking me against the wall. My eyes darted this way and that, seeking the gun. Where was it? God, where?

Eric had Leonard by the throat, his two hands circling his windpipe, striking his head against the floor. Leonard went limp. Then Eric reached beneath his coat and brought his pistol out—the same pistol I had accidentally seen light years ago. He put the muzzle to Leonard's temple.

"Eric! Don't!" I cried. "You'll be a murderer, too."

Eric turned to stare at me. His lank hair hung over glazed eyes. "He killed my father," he said.

"That won't help you now. You mustn't shoot him. There will be a trial and you . . . it will be hard to prove."

Eric looked back at Leonard. His arm stiffened. There was a sharp click.

"Don't!" I screamed.

Slowly Eric's body relaxed; the gun trembled in his hand. "Perhaps you are right."

Leonard began to stir, to mumble.

Eric grasped him by the collar and shook him. "Get up," he said. "It's all over."

Eric and I took Leonard into Tenwyck ourselves. There was no other way to reach the constable. It was a tricky business. Eric drove with Leonard between us, while I kept both guns trained on him.

"You wouldn't use those on me, would you, Constance?" Leonard said, smiling.

In the late afternoon sunshine, his rumpled hair was a mass of burnished gold. Even in distress—even on his way to the hangman—he would be handsome. For one moment my heart ached, my will faltered. God, how I had loved him!

But as I looked into those smiling blue eyes, I saw the deceit, the cruelty, and a mirror of my own shame.

"I would use these without compunction," I said. "Or do I borrow your words too freely?"

"You're a quick one," Leonard said admiringly. "Even

in your sleep. I've never seen anyone who could come awake so fast at the slightest sound."

"You drugged me more than once," I said, recalling the empty pitcher, its aroma of spice.

"I had to, love."

Constable Smithers's fresh young face was red with embarrassment. "So you caught the culprit yourselves," he said, after he had put Leonard safely under lock and key. "I never suspected anything was really amiss. Never thought it might be that one."

"Neither did we," Eric said. "I had his background thoroughly checked some time ago—so I thought. But one never knows, does one?"

"No," said the constable.

"You must send someone out for Mrs. Platte," Eric said.

Mrs. Platte. My heart constricted in guilt and sorrow. She had died because of a nonexistent map, a woman who had harmed no one.

"I have your statements," the constable said, "and I will let you know if the magistrate will want to question you further before the inquest, and of course, you will be needed at the trial."

"We shall be happy to cooperate in whatever way is necessary," Eric said, taking my arm. "But—for now, we are a little tired."

By the time we got my brothers and the maids home, we were much more than a little tired. It had taxed all my patience and ingenuity to explain to Gordon and Alistair why Leonard would no longer be with us. I could not bring myself to tell them the horrible truth—that Leonard had come to Rommany under false pretenses, that he was a murderer. They loved him too much. Later, perhaps, but not now.

However, I had to inform the maids. Since they would be called upon to testify, I thought it best they know the truth of Mrs. Platte's brutal death from the start. Predictably, they were shocked and horrified and they wept for her—and I did, too. She had not been the warmest of persons—strict and sparing of praise—but death had cancled out the unkind aspects of her character and left only the memory of her dependable presence.

Esther and Daisy, when they had recovered, gave notice at once. It was all I could do to persuade them that they could not leave without permission from the authorities. Jenny, to my surprise, said she would stay on.

"I can't see you without help, miss," she said, throwing a look of disdain at the others.

She had prepared a light supper, serving Eric and me in the library as we sat before the fireplace. Though the night was warm, I had asked Eric to build a fire, hoping it would banish the chill from my bones. We ate in silence—cold lamb, bread and cheese, and gradually the nightmare began to leave me.

"More tea?" I asked Eric, pouring myself another cup.

"Thank you, but I still have some." He smiled at me over the rim of his cup.

"I owe you an apology," I said.

"I wondered how long it would take you to get around to it," he said, his eyes teasing. Then reaching quickly across the narrow makeshift table, he squeezed my hand. "You needn't, you know. I can see how you thought I might be up to something, pretending I was lame. But I did *try* to explain. Only you wouldn't listen."

"I wish I had," I said regretfully, remembering my terrified flight. "And I *do* apologize, Eric. But I still don't understand—why the story of a broken foot?"

"I didn't think you would take me in unless you felt sorry for me," he said sheepishly. "And I wanted to be here. After my father died in what I thought was a rather odd accident, I had a feeling someone at Rommany would be next. And then I heard your father and mother had left."

"You were that concerned about me?"

"More than concerned," he said earnestly, gazing steadily at me. How strange, I thought, I'd always believed his eyes were brown; but they were hazel, flecked with green and gray. Nice eyes. "Do you remember that time you came up to London for the coming out parties and balls?"

"I certainly do," I said with a half-smile. "It was a miserable experience. And I remember how you came to my rescue more than once. Doing your duty—dancing with me."

"It wasn't duty," he said. "I *wanted* to dance with you."

He frowned down at his cup. "You see, I've always thought a great deal of you. No," he shook his head slowly, "no, it's more than that, much more." He raised his eyes. "I was just too backward to say anything."

"To shy?" I said surprised. "Why, Eric, you were always handy with a quip, amusing, derisive, mocking. I never dreamed."

"That there was a *me* inside? A me who loved you?"

I turned away from the earnest look in his eyes and stared into the fire. Love! I thought bitterly.

"I shall never love anyone again," I said.

"Constance, you mustn't . . . you mustn't grieve."

"Grieve?" I said. "One must have a heart to grieve."

Eric took my hand. "Now, Constance, I wish you wouldn't talk like that. Of course you have a heart—a little battered, perhaps, at the moment. But I have enough heart for the two of us. Look at me, Constance. Please?"

I raised my eyes. "Am I acting the sentimental fool?"

"A little. But I forgive you." A smile. Strange how when he really smiled his face was rather pleasant, almost attractive.

"I've really turned over a new leaf, you know," Eric went on. "I plan to finish my medical studies at Edinburgh this fall. That's why I sold the firm. I've no head for business; doctoring is more in my line. In fact, I'm dead serious about it. I want to set up a practice, marry, have a family, and . . . and . . . hang it all, Constance! I'm not doing very well at this, but—but what I want to ask is, will you have me?"

"I . . . I don't know, Eric." His hair did not shine like burnished gold, but he loved me. I knew that.

"Say that you'll think about it."

"Yes . . . I . . . I'll think."

"Then we are engaged!" he whooped. He came round the table and brought me to my feet.

"Now . . . wait . . . Eric . . . I didn't—"

But he had me in his arms and his mouth was hard against mine, and I thought: Could it be? Eric?

When he finally released me I felt breathless and dizzy.

"Well?" he asked, laughing.

"Perhaps . . . perhaps," I said, laughing with him, still oddly light-headed.

"Wait a moment! Stay right here. I have something in my room I want to show you."

A few minutes later Eric returned with a rather largish jeweler's box. "Open it," he commanded.

"You came prepared?" I asked, astonished.

"Well, not exactly. It isn't a ring. Go on, open it."

There was tissue inside and when I parted the rustling paper I saw an ivory fan.

"When Grandmother Veda gave me this," Eric explained, "she said, 'It is for the girl you will someday marry.' Apparently she got it from my great-uncle, John years ago, before he was killed."

"But ... but this looks so familiar. Why—my mother has one exactly like it!" I exclaimed. "I'll fetch it."

Eric stood frowning over the two fans laid out side by side on the desk.

"Constance," he said, "they are not alike. Similar, but not alike. Come see."

The fans had ivory handles and sticks, the parchment between painted in delicate shades of blue and green with a touch of brown and rose. There was no set design that I could discern, merely a pleasing flow of pale color.

"They look pretty much the same to me," I said.

"No—no. Do you have an atlas? I want a map of Africa. South Africa."

I looked at him. "You don't mean ... ?"

"I don't know. I don't know," he said in an excited voice.

I got the atlas and Eric rifled through the pages. "Not the best atlas in the world, but it will have to do. Yes— here. The Orange Free State, and here—" He traced his finger along one fan and then up the other. "The Vaal River—and this dot must be Hopetown. Yes, of course. And this one Kimberly. And this small red 'x'. . . ." He looked up at me. "Do you see it now, Constance?"

I drew in my breath. We stared at one another in amazement.

"Then it's true," I said at length, eyeing the painted ivory fans, the cause of so much torment, bloodshed and terror for three generations, "there really is a diamond site map."

When Eric and I were married six months later, Mother gave me the Blackmore fan as a wedding gift, and the two maps were joined, symbolically and literally. Ironically, though, the map was not worth the fortune so many had dreamed of. Through the years, as the surface diamonds had played out in the Kimberly area, it became necessary to sink deeper mines, using expensive sophisticated machinery. The small sites were bought out by the larger companies, and in 1888 with the creation of the DeBeers Consolidated Mines, a monopoly, the individual digger was completely eliminated.

The Blackmore-Hempstead claim had been registered legally, but as neither John Hempstead nor Duncan Blackmore had bothered to answer letters of inquiry, the DeBeers people, assuming the owners were deceased and without heirs, had simply annexed the site. Rather than go through the courts, a long, uncertain process, Eric came to an agreement with DeBeers Consolidated, and we received a fair sum for their clear title.

The "fair" sum was enough to buy Eric a medical practice in a town on the outskirts of London. I don't think there was ever a happier day in my life than the one on which we moved into that cramped, low-ceilinged house with its funny mismatched wallpaper and odd-shaped windows. No strange noises, no phantom sighs, no ghosts. A sane, sensible, utterly delightful house.

Eric, I knew, would never have a head for business, would never make more than a fair living, but he was a good doctor—and I loved him. Oh, it wasn't the dizzying, moon-gazing, girlish enchantment I had once thought love to be, but a comfortable, steady love, a feeling of being needed and wanted, of being cherished.

One aspect concerning the map still puzzled us. Why had neither John Hempstead nor Duncan Blackmore ever talked about the maps or mentioned them in their wills? Or, for that matter, said one word about the fans?

The question, whenever we thought of it, continued to perplex us until one rainy afternoon we found the answer in the Hempstead library. Eric and I had gone over to visit his mother, living alone now since Bea's marriage. (Bea had broken with the count and married the duke of Rumford instead, a man twice her age and obscenely wealthy), and Mary, having decided to put the house up for sale, wanted Eric to assist her in cleaning out Benjamin's personal effects.

Jammed between two drawers of Benjamin's desk, Eric found an old diary belonging to John Hempstead. In it was a full account of John Hempstead's and Grandfather Duncan's South African venture.

It seems there had been a third man involved in the affair; not a partner, but a so-called friend. He had tracked John and Duncan to the site, and, in trying to force them from the mine, had been shot by John. A trial followed in which John was acquitted—justifiable homicide. But the episode had left a bad taste, and the two men made a pact never to return to the site unless either of them were in dire financial straits.

"An unlikely situation," John wrote, "since we both have mined enough diamonds to make us wealthy for a long time to come."

Eric, closing the diary, said, "I think I can understand why neither of them cared to discuss the map."

"Yes," I said and shuddered. "Even at the outset the map had blood on it. Perhaps they felt it was unlucky."

I think my parents must have come to the same conclusion about Rommany. A month later, Gordon was thrown from a horse in the stable yard and narrowly missed dying. Mother, suddenly losing her taste for Rommany, persuaded Father to accept a teaching position at London University and the family moved to the city.

Uncle Ernest, without an heir, never cared for the house, and my other Blackmore uncles apparently feel the same, for the place stands empty now. But the fans are there, suitably framed, hanging over the fireplace in the drawing room for all to see, though only beady-eyed mice are present to observe and ponder over them—the mice and the restless ghosts who still haunt Rommany.

THE SWEEPING ROMANTIC EPIC
OF A PROUD WOMAN
IN A GOLDEN AMERICAN ERA!

Beginning at the close of the Civil War, and sweeping forward to the end of the last century, CASTLES IN THE AIR tells of the relentless rise of beautiful, spirited Devon Marshall from a war-ravaged Virginia landscape to the glittering stratospheres of New York society and the upper reaches of power in Washington.

In this American epic of surging power, there unfolds a brilliant, luminous tapestry of human ambition, success, lust, and our nation's vibrant past. And in the tempestuous romance of Devon and the dynamic millionaire Keith Curtis, Patricia Gallagher creates an unforgettable love story of rare power and rich human scope.

AVON   27649 $1.95

CIA 5-76